LOVE SCENES

ADMIT ONE

18

RALPH STORER

ADMIT ONE

THE AUTHOR

Ralph Storer was born in England but has lived in Scotland since taking a degree in psychology at Dundee University. He now writes full-time, having previously worked in IT. He is best known for his books on outdoor subjects, including *100 Best Routes on Scottish Mountains* and *The Joy of Hillwalking*. *Love Scenes* is his first novel, and he is working on a sequel.

LOVE SCENES
Ralph Storer

Crescent

First published in 2004 by Crescent Books,
an imprint of Mercat Press Ltd
10 Coates Crescent, Edinburgh EH3 7AL
www.crescentfiction.com

ISBN 184183 0828

The publisher acknowledges subsidy from the Scottish Arts Council
towards the publication of this volume.

Set in Book Antiqua at Mercat Press
Printed and bound in Great Britain by
Bell & Bain Ltd., Glasgow

What is love? Your voice, your eyes, your hands, your lips. Our silences, our words. Light that goes, light that returns. A single smile between us both. To live, only advance. Aim straight for those you love.

Natasha von Braun, *Alphaville*

Prologue

Alphaville
(A film by Jean-Luc Godard)

The futuristic city of Alphaville is run on logical principles by the giant computer Alpha 60. In soulless Alphaville, art has been abolished, love is forbidden, crying is an offence. Words such as conscience and tenderness are censored. Those who cannot adapt commit suicide or are executed.

Secret agent Lemmy Caution is dispatched to Alphaville to liquidate Dr von Braun, inventor of Alpha 60. He meets von Braun's daughter, Natasha, and tries to teach her censored words, but they hold no meaning for her.

When Lemmy is captured and grilled by Alpha 60 itself, he gives answers designed to confuse it. 'Do you know what illuminates the night?' asks Alpha 60. 'Poetry,' answers Lemmy.

He escapes and manages to kill von Braun and destroy Alpha 60. The city falls apart, its citizens so disoriented that they lose equilibrium and have to cling to walls. How will they survive? Think of love, Lemmy tells Natasha.

As he drives her away from the dying city of reason, she struggles to regain her senses. Hope stirs within her. Tentatively she learns to say 'I love you.'

'Je… vous… aime.'

1.

When it comes to love, I'm a sucker.

Take Emma, for instance. Not that she's typical. If you were to make a film of my love life, the female supporting cast would be pathetically small but richly diverse. I don't have a *type*. All I ask of a partner is that she comes with the standard set of female physical attributes.

Which doesn't mean that appearance is the only thing I'm interested in... although I do believe that if a woman goes to all that trouble to look good, it would be churlish not to appreciate it. It is a truth universally acknowledged, at least among men, that the one thing a woman hates more than being treated as a sex object is *not* being treated as a sex object.

What I'm trying to say is, when it comes to love, I make no preconditions. I could be attracted to anyone. And that *doesn't* mean a pulse is my only requirement.

And when I mention the standard set of physical attributes, I don't mean to be prejudiced against disability, either. I mean, in *Boxing Helena*, Sherilyn Fenn is loveable even though she has no arms and no legs and lives in a box. I could foresee difficulties trying to synchronise our lifestyles, but I wouldn't rule her out as a prospective partner purely on the basis of the fact that she's a quadruple amputee. Okay? God, it's tough being a third millennium man.

When I think about it, I've been with some pretty incompatible women in my time. Take Eileen, who dumped me over Cheddar. The cheese, not the gorge. Even after all these years, I still don't see why I shouldn't be allowed to prefer Cheddar to Brie.

It wasn't as if I was advocating the merits of that rubbery orange material that bounces when it falls off the supermarket shelf. We were in Mellis's, which just happens to be Edinburgh's finest purveyor of dairy produce, as well as my local cheesemonger. Yet even this worked against me. With a newly arrived *Brie de Meaux* quivering on the counter, my dithering between a tangy Lincolnshire Poacher and an extra-mature farmhouse Galloway merely inflamed Eileen's frustration.

Sometimes I wonder whether that last argument was about more than cheese. I've always had trouble spotting subtext.

Then there was Heather, who was only five feet tall and barely came up to my chest. Not that I'm heightist, I hasten to add. She liked Cheddar, but it turns out you can't base a relationship solely on a shared partiality to a particular coagulated milk product.

She liked Mozart and Beethoven, my brain won't respond to any musical endeavour that pre-dates the discovery of the back beat. She loved Chekhov and Pinter, I need the visual stimulation of a cinema screen. She rose early with enough energy to undertake a paper round, my lifestyle of choice would be based on Dracula's diurnal cycle. She was teetotal, I've been known to imbibe the occasional fermented beverage. In retrospect, I'd have had a more fulfilling social life with a boxed Sherilyn Fenn under my arm.

Why did it take us six months to realise that we weren't the answer to each other's dreams? If I could answer that I'd save myself an awful lot of angst in life. I can only tell you that the *possibility* of love seemed to be there, at least to begin with, and for me possibilities don't come any more seductive than that. Show me a woman with whom love might be possible and I'll put up with any amount of incompatibility for any amount of time.

Which brings me back to Emma.

Today is the fourth anniversary of the day we met. For four years I've put up with everything she has thrown at me. Sometimes literally, including the TV remote, a copy of *Halliwell's Film Guide* and a handful of Edinburgh Rock, which I can affirm is nowhere near as soft on the cheek as it is on the palate. And I'm still waiting and hoping for us to fall in love.

As I say, don't ask me how I can still feel this way after four years. All I can say in my defence is that Emma is a complex woman. Sometimes I think she has more multiple personalities than Joanne Woodward in *The Three Faces of Eve*.

If she would let me, I would love her. Unfortunately she views love as a threat to her ongoing struggle to become her own person. Love, you see, traps both partners in a self-destructive relationship of mutual dependency. If you knew her parents, you'd understand.

Yet still I live in hope that some day we will fall in love. I fantasise about lifting her into my arms and carrying her off into the sunset, like Richard Gere does with Debra Winger at the end of *An Officer and a Gentleman*. Happily ever after doesn't just exist in films, does it?

To celebrate our anniversary, I'm cooking her a meal. I've also bought her a surprise present. It's going to be a romantic evening.

If she deigns to turn up, that is.

Ralph Storer

I'm huddled in the doorway of Frasers department store, at the junction of Princes Street and Hope Street in the city centre. According to the clock that juts out from the second storey above my head, she's fifteen minutes late already. Six-fifteen on a gale-swept January evening that would not be out of place in *Nanook of the North*.

Heat-seeking swirls of hail target me as though I were the only warm-blooded creature left on the planet. And I could be. Beyond the street lamp's orange corona, the familiar cityscape dissolves into darkness, devoid of human fellowship. Trust me to agree to meet Emma here. They don't call it Heartbreak Corner for nothing.

I don't know why she couldn't come straight to my flat. I live less than ten minutes walk away, and it's not as if she needs me to show her the route. Over the Dean Bridge, down Dean Park Crescent...

Okay, that's it. One more flurry like that last one and even Nanook would begin to feel the chill. I'm off.

Twenty minutes after I arrive home, she turns up at my door and, to pre-empt reproof, gives me her startled fawn look. I respond obediently with a reassuring smile and a hug. Her body is as tense as that scene in *Wages of Fear* where Yves Montand just manages to drive his truck full of nitro-glycerine off a shaky wooden platform before it collapses.

She may have been going to offer an explanation for her tardiness, but my invasion of her personal space instead makes it imperative for her to establish boundaries.

'I don't feel like sex,' is the first thing she says.

'Would you prefer Toad in the Hole?' I say. That's the delicacy I'm preparing. No one can wine and dine a woman like I can. 'It'll be ready soon.'

'I'm not hungry,' she says. 'I've had a bad day. Can't we just talk for a bit?'

'If you want.'

I take her by the hand, lead her through to the kitchen and sit her down at the dining table.

'It doesn't matter,' she says. 'Just fuck me if that's what you want.'

'What I want is some Toad in the Hole.'

She's not quite sure whether I'm using a euphemism, so in case I intend to take her up on her offer...

'Why can't we ever just talk?'

I feel a big sigh coming on, but I catch it just in time.

'We *can* talk. We always talk about your problems, don't we?' I'm honestly not being sarcastic, but Emma immediately picks up on that aborted sigh.

'I've not been in the door two minutes and you're picking on me already.'

'I'm not. Just tell me what's happened.'

'No, I don't want to now.'

'Then let's eat.'

'I'm not hungry.'

She's come straight from work and is still wearing her old denims and baggy sweatshirt. It's a captivating *ensemble*. No, really. Because she's tall and blessed with a waist:hip ratio her friends would die for, she could throw on a city council bin liner and look as though she's just stepped down from the catwalk.

She leans forward on her elbows, rests her chin on her hands and stares at the table top, her long golden hair cascading down to hide her face. It's the reason she wears it long.

'Maybe I should go,' she says.

'I'm not letting you go until you tell me what's wrong.'

Her hair parts to reveal the look of a rabbit trapped in headlights. From startled fawn to trapped rabbit in less than five minutes. That's a new record for me. What was I thinking? Have four years taught me nothing? For a moment I think she's going to make a bolt for the door. She relents, but it was a close-run thing.

'Kyle called me an old maid,' she says.

I should explain that Emma is a ceramic artist who rents space at a craft co-operative in order to have access to a kiln. Under no circumstances must you call her a potter. Kyle is a colleague's eight-year-old son, who was unaccountably passed over when they cast the lead in *Dennis the Menace*.

The revelation that he's called her an old maid doesn't strike me as life-threatening, but I've learned to my cost to stifle such insensitivity. In Emma's world, even slights imperceptible to the rest of human-kind scar deeply enough to require reconstructive surgery.

'I'm sure he didn't mean anything by it,' I say.

'He must have got it from his mother, and she's right. I'm nearly thirty-four and look at me.'

'I *am* thirty-four. So what?'

A tear rolls down her cheek. I've read that the average person cries – I can't remember, thirty or forty, something ridiculous any-way – bucketfuls of tears in a lifetime. Emma could manage that in a week in the conducive environment I provide.

'I knew you wouldn't understand,' she says. 'You're a man. Look at you. Apart from a few extra inches round the middle, you look the same as when I first met you.'

Involuntarily, I hold my stomach in. And by the way, I intend to lose those few extra inches.

'I *am* an old maid,' she says. 'My clothes no longer fit, my breasts are starting to sag, I'm getting wrinkles and cellulite. Everyone I know is married or in a permanent relationship. Cate and I are the only ones left, and she's getting married next month.' Catriona is her best friend.

You'd think this outpouring of self-pity about being left on the shelf would be incompatible with a commitment phobia, but Emma has never been constrained by an inability to hold two conflicting views simultaneously. Which enviable talent enables her to escape the irony of voicing her fears to the one person who itches to save her from an extended shelf-life.

'What are you talking about?' I say. 'You're as beautiful as ever. You could have any man you want.'

'Is that what you want me to do? Find another man?'

'If that's what you want.' It's not what *I* want, but we're discussing what she wants. This is familiar territory and I know the ground rules.

'What do *you* want?' she says.

That's my cue.

'I want to keep seeing you.' Hopefully that won't be too overpowering a statement of intent.

'Why? We've been seeing each other for four years, and it's not as if we're going anywhere.'

'Then stop seeing me, if that's what you want.'

'Is that all you can say? After all this time?'

Yes, I know what you're thinking, but if it confuses you, imagine what it must be like for me.

'I told you I don't want to stop seeing you. I like seeing you. We have good times together, don't we?'

'Sometimes,' she says.

At this first sign of a softening in her attitude, I try humour.

'Anyway, after me you'd be spoiled for any other man.'

She smiles, despite herself.

'And where else,' I say, encouraged, 'would I find someone as intelligent, sensitive, caring, beautiful…?'

She laughs out loud. Beautiful hardly covers it. As Clint Eastwood says about Meryl Streep in *The Bridges of Madison County*, she's make-'em-run-around-the-block-howling-in-agony stunning.

I stand up and take her hands in mine.

'You look nothing like thirty-three. Anyone would think I'm cradle-snatching. I doubt Kyle even knows what an old maid is. He probably heard it somewhere and he's showing off. Anyway, what was it you called him last week – a little brat? Is old maid any worse than that?'

'I suppose not.'

'Well, then.'

We hold hands for a few moments.

'I'm hungry,' she says.

So finally we get round to eating my Toad in the Hole. Not the world's most romantic gastronomic experience, you might think, but then you've not tasted my Toad in the Hole. Nor the *petit pois* and *mélange* of Anyas and Charlottes that I've steamed to perfection. Nor the bottle of purest Napa Valley Zinfandel that was *born* to accompany them, for under a fiver too.

After dinner we head down to Blockbuster to pick out a DVD for the evening. Emma searches the shelves for the least violent title she can find and, in the pre-owned bin, comes up with a video of *Little Women* (the Winona Ryder version). She read the book when she was a girl but she's never seen the film. I don't mind watching it again with her. I figure we can't go wrong with a romantic coming-of-age film about a family of four girls.

It's one of those brittle Edinburgh winter evenings when, after the passing of the storm, the air seems to sparkle. The stately Georgian buildings of the New Town rise around us with cut-glass clarity, their sandstone walls glistening in the moonlight. Only in a city as time-honoured as Edinburgh could the old quarter in which I live be called the New Town.

We take a roundabout route home, strolling hand in hand through a magical Inverleith Park. The path is flanked by gaunt trees that cast mysterious pale shadows at our feet, while beside us a swathe of frosted grass curves down to the frozen pond with its coating of white ice. Up above is the serrated frieze of the Old Town skyline, from the twin humps of Arthur's Seat to the sturdy rock outcrop crowned by the castle.

The city tonight has the look of a Victorian Christmas card and, with Emma beside me, I can't help but feel romantic. She can do that to me. One minute she can be so distant that it breaks my heart, the next... Maybe it's her enigmatic smile, her childlike vulnerability, the accidental brush of her body against mine, or maybe it's just the moonlight on her hair, but I take one look at her and my knees turn to grilled Cheddar. And that breaks my heart as well.

A sharp gust of wind rustles the branches above our heads. Emma shivers and her breath clouds the air. In that instant she looks so pretty that I take her face in my hands and touch my lips to hers. When she doesn't pull away, I push her gently against the nearest tree and kiss her more firmly.

I have a confession to make.

I've been wanting to make love to Emma all day. When she arrived at my flat I could have done it there and then, on the landing at the top of the tenement stairwell. My mouth-watering Toad in the Hole could have burned to a cinder for all I cared. When she said she didn't feel like sex, it was because she knew that I did. Sometimes she's *too* sensitive. Sometimes she senses things in me before I do.

So her first words to me when she arrived were more reasonable than I implied.

Soon my hand is inside her coat. For a moment her body presses against mine, then her mind cuts in and the moment is past. After years of conditioning I'm now able to recognise the signs, but it wasn't always that way. I can't tell you how many times I've been accused of insensitivity.

It's really only now that I become resigned to the fact that we won't make love tonight, on our anniversary, and I convince myself that I'm content. It is enough to be in the company of this beautiful woman as she slips her hand in mine and, without a word, leads me home through the fairy-tale landscape.

Back at my flat, we settle down on the couch to watch *Little Women*. I lie back and draw Emma down beside me. She slots perfectly into the contours of my body. Our legs intertwine of their own accord and her head nestles into the hollow of my neck.

'I still don't feel like sex,' she says.

'Are we going to watch this movie or aren't we?'

Emma watches films with a furrowed intensity that permits no distraction. She'll laugh at a comic scene or pull her hair over her eyes at the prospect of violence, but otherwise she watches in silence, giving no outward indication of her feelings. For the next 115 minutes we barely move. I can only hope…

'It just goes to show,' I say as the final credits break the spell, 'they do still make 'em like that.'

But the romantic ending hasn't done the trick for Emma.

'It would have been better if Beth hadn't died,' she says.

'But Jo found the love of her life.'

'I still don't see why Beth had to die.'

I know there's barely a film been made that can evoke in us the same critical or emotional response, but my relationship with Emma is based on eternal optimism. I had great hopes for *Little Women*.

'She dies in the book,' I say.

'Well, that doesn't mean she has to die in the film. You always say a film doesn't have to be exactly the same as a book.' This is unfair, using my own arguments against me.

'I know, but it's a classic book, and we're talking about a major plot point here. What do you want from a film? A bunch of people sitting around a table being nice to each other all the time?'

'Yes,' she says, and she means it. You can forget narrative structure, plot development, character arcs. All Emma wants to see, in a film as in life, is people being nice to each other.

'That would be boring,' I say. 'Something has to happen. You've got to have some dramatic conflict. I mean, even *The Sound of Music* has Nazis.' It's her favourite film.

'Why do you always have to be so analytical? Why can't you just enjoy something?'

'I was only trying to explain...'

'Well, I'd prefer not to have it all explained away. If you want someone who thinks like you, you should have stayed with Jennifer.'

Ouch. Jenny was my last girlfriend. Emma's mention of her name, always all three syllables of her name, is a signal to end not just the conversation but the whole evening.

A yawning chasm has suddenly opened up between us. It happens like that sometimes. One minute everything's fine, and the next, there's that old yawning chasm again.

'What time is it?' says Emma.

'Eleven o'clock.'

'It's time I was going.'

What did I tell you? Was I right or was I right? There's no point in trying to stop her. The chasm won't be bridged tonight. I accompany her to the door and give her one last hug.

'I hope you have a better day tomorrow,' I say.

'Thanks,' she says. 'I'll call you.'

She leaves.

Happy anniversary, Emma.

You know all that stuff about her enigmatic smile and childlike vulnerability? Forget it. As for the anniversary present I was going to give her, she's got as much chance of getting that now as Messala has of winning the chariot race in *Ben-Hur*.

2.

The following morning, Emma phones to say she's sorry. I tell her there's nothing to apologise for. It's a conversation we have regularly and it starts the day off in reassuring fashion. But as I make my way to work, I realise I still haven't forgiven her for that remark about Jenny. She never knew Jenny, but she can't handle the fact that I did.

I really don't want to go into work today. I don't want to go into work *any* day, but especially today. More than ever, I need the bracing twelve-minute walk up to St Andrew Square to convince my body that it can function at 8.30 a.m. Even as I reach the office, January daylight is still no more than a promise beneath impenetrable skies that echo my dark mood.

Richard, my friend and colleague, senses that something is wrong as soon as I round the acoustic partition panel that screens our two-person cubicle from the rest of the open-plan room.

'How did the anniversary dinner go?' he says in his most caring, sharing voice, issuing an open-ended invitation for me to care and share in turn. He knows all about my relationship with Emma and, as a card-carrying New Man, feels it his duty to act as counsellor.

'It went,' is all he gets back for his trouble. He may be my friend and colleague, but today he can take his caring sharingness and flush it down the pan.

He's known me long enough to take my answer in good part, which only makes me more annoyed. I console myself with the fact that I've known him long enough to know that he's dying to know the cause of my surliness, and I'm not going to tell him. Ever.

Like a spurned suitor, he spends the whole morning slumped in his hi-back chair, keyboard on lap, fixated on his computer screen, his long legs jack-knifed against the underside of the desk in a manner that has polished the knees of his trousers threadbare. With his unruly hair and day-old stubble, he looks less like the consummate professional our bosses would prefer than a *Trainspotting* extra.

Only lunch with Scott in the staff canteen makes the day bearable. Scott and I have both been at the Bank for seven years now and, although we no longer work in the same project team, we still lunch together. God, seven years already. Unlike Richard, my friend and colleague Scott is motivated solely by a desire to have a good laugh at my expense, which today happens to be exactly the therapy I need.

I'm still attempting to chew my way through a first mouthful of what purports to be *boeuf bourguignon* when he fixes me with an accusing look.

'What's wrong with you today, you sad bastard?' he says. 'Didn't you get your leg over last night?'

The length of time it takes me to swallow takes the sting out of my riposte. You'd think I'd know better by now than to opt for the chef's special.

'Life is so simple for you, isn't it?' I say.

His suspicion confirmed, he shakes his head in disbelief at my amatory incompetence and attacks his haddock and chips with infuriating smugness.

'On your fourth anniversary too.'

His unshakeable conviction renders further protestation pointless. Instead, and much to my surprise, I vent my frustration with Emma by launching into a diatribe that would have feminists manning the barricades. *Man*ning?

'Why do women make sex so complicated?' I say. 'Sometimes they want it, sometimes they don't, sometimes they don't want it and then they do, sometimes they do and then they don't, and sometimes they don't even know when they want it.'

I've never understood why Richard's cordial concern locks me tight as a clam, while Scott's calculated condescension prises me open like a fig. Is he right? Is the real reason for my sullen mood the fact that I was expecting to get my leg over last night, and I didn't? Is it that simple? Am *I* that simple?

'It's no wonder you're not getting any,' he says when he's finished laughing. 'After four years it's time you got down on one knee.'

This is a typical Scott remark, shot through with his own brand of idiosyncratic logic and calculated both to amuse and enrage. When feminism hitched up its skirts and made a bolt for freedom, Scott didn't even notice that the cell door had been forced ajar.

'Is that why you got married?' I say.

'Too right, pal,' he says. 'You never heard of conjugal rights?'

'You're a selfish bastard.'

He leans forward, knife and fork poised in mid-air, as though he's about to conduct an orchestra. Except that, in his loud check jacket, he'd look more at home on a music hall stage than a concert hall podium. He's the only man in the department who doesn't have to wear a suit. We don't know how he gets away with it. He's just one of those people who gets away with things.

'And you're not?' he says. 'Tell me, does Emma *appreciate* you only wanting to shag her for her sake?'

He knows only too well how to play me. I could concede defeat now but, as ever, he makes his outrageous claims sound so reasonable that they demand contradiction. In any case, isn't this exactly the distraction I'd been hoping for?

'I feel sorry for your wife,' I say. 'At least when I make love to Emma I want her to enjoy it too.'

'Exactly. *You* want.' He resumes eating.

'Don't you care how your wife feels?'

'Of course I do. She can be as selfish as *she* wants.'

'That's your idea of consensual sex? Mutual selfishness?'

What if your partner doesn't know or can't acknowledge what she wants, I want to say to him, or what if her sex drive is different from yours, or what if her feelings change from one moment to the next?

He should get to know Emma better. Her feelings can change as swiftly as Mel Gibson's Scottish accent in *Braveheart*.

I'm about to enlighten him when we're both brought to a halt in mid-mouthful. Owing to what can only be a unique planetary conjunction, Richard joins us. Now, Richard *never* joins us. There's less love lost between him and Scott than between Spider-Man and the Green Goblin.

If he has deigned to form this unholy trinity in the hope of piercing my veil of silence over a Bank lunch, he's in for further disappointment. His past dealings with Scott should have warned him that he'd be plunged into a discussion calculated to give him paroxysms of outrage.

'Maybe if you paid a bit more attention to what your wife wants,' I say to Scott, recovering from the shock of Richard's arrival, 'you'd have a better sex life.'

'I thought you were the one who's missing out, pal,' he says.

Richard immediately picks up on this and gives me a look that says, how come you've been confiding in this Neanderthal when you've been giving me the cold shoulder all morning. Nevertheless, his antipathy towards Scott induces him to side with me.

'I feel sorry for your wife,' he says to Scott.

None of us in the office have ever met her, but we all feel sorry for her. We presume her to be the kind of downtrodden homebody that Katherine Ross would have taken a knife to in *The Stepford Wives* (1975 vintage).

Scott forces himself to acknowledge Richard's presence.

'She has no complaints,' he says.

'She wouldn't dare,' says Richard.

'You two have a lot to learn about lassies,' Scott says with an exaggerated sigh. 'No wonder you're both still single.'

He laughs at his gibe and I laugh at his effrontery, but Richard, who lacks a humour gene, chokes on a chunk of pineapple in his cottage cheese salad and has to be administered water.

'That's got nothing to do with it,' he says when he can.

I'm ashamed to say his earnestness merely encourages me to incite Scott further.

'What about oral sex?' I say. 'That's unselfish, isn't it?'

'You English pervert!' he says, as though a Scotsman is above such depravity.

'Nothing two consenting adults do is perverted,' says Richard, still ploughing a lone furrow of reasonableness.

'Any sex act that isn't about procreation is perverted,' says Scott, dangling further bait. 'Why do you think oral sex is illegal in some countries?'

Richard fumes with such indignation that for a moment I think he's going to utter a profanity, which would really make Scott a legend in his own lunchtime.

'That is the biggest load of rubbish I have ever heard,' says Richard. 'Don't you believe in contraception?'

I'm beginning to feel sorry for him. Part of me wants to bail him out before he goes down like the Titanic (James Cameron version) but, when he rises so juicily to Scott's bait, I have to accept that a far greater part of me just wants to sit back and enjoy the special effects.

Sorry, Richard.

'You English pervert!' Scott says again, to Richard this time, then with a glance to include me adds, 'No wonder we gubbed you at Bannockburn.'

Scott's wife has dropped three daughters already, but she's only in her twenties and has plenty of eggs left in her yet. It's not that he's in thrall to Papal decree, more that he plans to start a dynasty. Its theme song will be 'Every Sperm is Sacred' from *Monty Python's The Meaning of Life*.

Richard launches into a defence of contraception that encompasses unwanted teenage pregnancies in Ireland, the prevalence of abortion in Russia and overpopulation on the Indian subcontinent. I agree with everything he says, but that still doesn't make him anything other than Scott's straight man. Scott isn't arguing rights and wrongs. He's just arguing.

I wish Richard would lighten up sometimes. He's so politically correct he makes you want to run amok with a sawn-off shotgun. He once told me that if Blockbuster rented him a pornographic film by mistake, he wouldn't even fast-forward through it. I mean, come on! And more importantly: where's this branch of Blockbuster that stocks pornographic films?

Even women don't want a New Man all the time, and don't believe them when they say they do. They want a man to have an edge. Richard has less edge than a melting Dali watch, whereas Scott has enough for a whole gallery of Cubist art.

There's a theory that you get on best with people of the opposite sex who are most like you, and people of the same sex who are most unlike you. Perhaps that explains why, although I feel more affinity to Richard, I have more fun with Scott.

Hang on a minute, though. If that's the case, Richard and Scott should be best buddies. I'll need to give this more thought.

'You know your trouble, pal,' Scott says to Richard. 'Too much theory and not enough practice. Enough practice with someone else in the same room, that is.'

'I'm not even going to dignify that with a response,' Richard says in response, then finishes his meal in silence.

It's more than I can do. The silence I can manage, but I have to yield best to the rapidly congealing glutinous brown gunk on my Bank plate. When Richard leaves, he lopes out without so much as a see-you-later. He won't be lunching with us again for a while.

'I don't know how you stand him,' Scott says after he's left.

'I don't know how I stand *you*.'

'You'll miss me when I'm gone.'

This is a standing joke between us. Scott's always talking about leaving the Bank, but we both know he's a lifer. He couldn't survive without his cheap mortgage.

After lunch, as is my custom, I spend ten minutes reading the sports pages in the office's outdoor awareness area, on an oak-effect plastic bench among the indoor plants. When I return to my desk I find Richard embedded in a computer printout.

There are only four weeks left before the new system we're developing goes live, and there's the usual panic to meet the deadline. That's the way things are at the cutting edge of technology.

Joke!

Those of us who work in Information Technology are happy to

foster an intellectual mystique for the benefit of user departments, but we all know the job is as much a nine-to-five grind as any other. Electronic-age clerks, that's all we are. Just don't tell anyone.

Technically, I'm a senior programmer and Richard works under me, but we were friends before he joined the Bank and we work as equals. He doesn't know it, but I recommended him for the job. Come to think of it, he's still wearing the same suit he wore to the interview.

Our project manager is always telling him to smarten up, but he's good at what he does and that's what should count, isn't it? Mind you, when you have to sit opposite him every day and stare at that threadbare two-piece, and at that so-called designer stubble...

Sorry, Richard.

'I don't know how you stand Scott,' he says.

'Don't take everything he says to heart.'

'He's a sexist pig.'

'He's just winding you up. Women joke about guys in the same way.'

'Not the women I know.'

'You need to get out more. You should hear some of the things Emma and her girlfriends come out with.'

'Like what? I can't imagine Emma saying anything sexist.'

It's true, it is hard to imagine, but what Richard doesn't know is that Emma can get pretty wild after a few G&Ts.

He's met her several times and thinks they get on well, but he's never seen her drunk. Nor is he ever likely to, because another thing he doesn't know is that Emma finds him intimidating. The fact that he can't see behind that benign smile she keeps plastered to her face in his company just goes to show he's not as sensitive as he likes to think he is.

Sorry, Richard.

Paradoxically, Emma gets on better with Scott, who, despite having met her only twice, has the enviable knack of knowing how to make her laugh, which in turn raises her status in his eyes.

'You've done all right for yourself there, you bastard,' he once told me. The ultimate Scott seal of approval.

'How is Emma?' says Richard, renewing his attempt to extract information from me.

'As ever,' I say, renewing my rebuff, but then decide that, to redress the balance of lunch with Scott, I owe him more. 'You know, sometimes we get on, sometimes we don't.' There, that should do it.

'Let me guess which category last night slotted into.' He's fishing, but it's a good cast.

'Last night we got on and didn't get on several times.'

'Perhaps your relationship is gathering speed,' he says enigmatically.

'How's Megan?' I say to deflect further inquiry. Megan is his latest girlfriend.

'She's fine. We should go out for a foursome some time.'

Not if Emma has anything to do with it. We tried a foursome with Richard's last girlfriend Moira, who at one point during the conversation asked Emma what kind of orgasms she had, and Emma became flustered and said the usual kind, then fled to the Ladies and hid in a cubicle for so long that we had to send out a search party.

'Good idea,' I say, 'I'll speak to Emma.'

There are days when I'm genuinely grateful for Richard's concern, but today is not one of them. I stride out of the office as though I have some important business to attend to, but I merely go to the washroom and comb my hair.

In the harsh fluorescent light reflected by the mirror above the wash basin, it seems to me that today I look all of my thirty-four years. Time has begun to etch my forehead and sneak an occasional fleck of grey into my honey-blond regulation-length Bank haircut. That's right. Honey-blond. I have Eileen (the Brie lover) to thank for that. Until then I thought my hair was brown.

Maybe I'm having what Emma calls a bad hair day. After all, she did say I still look the same as when we first met… apart from a few (temporary) extra inches round the middle. Okay, so I don't have the six-pack Brad Pitt brandishes in *Troy*, but then I never did. I can still get into my thirty-four inch jeans. They're a tad on the tight side, I admit, but nothing that a few press-ups and sit-ups won't fix.

No, now that I think about it, things could be worse. It's not as if I'm decaying at the rate of Christopher Lee in *Dracula* when the daylight hits him. I'm always reassuring Emma about her appearance. Why can't she ever do the same for me?

As the afternoon wears on I resolve to play hard to get and not see her again for a while. But then, of course, she does the unexpected.

3.

In *Lord of the Flies* a group of castaway boys degenerate into savagery and murder but, as soon as adult rescuers arrive on the scene, they revert instantly to being subservient children. Emma has that effect on me.

After work I find her waiting for me outside the building. I'm late out, so she must have been standing on the pavement for at least half an hour, in a fine drizzle that has turned her hair to rats' tails. I immediately feel guilty. On Heartbreak Corner I waited only fifteen minutes.

As soon as she sees me she waves so enthusiastically that she actually jumps up and down, and it's grilled Cheddar time again. I rush to her side, unfurl my umbrella over our heads and pull her close under its sheltering canopy. She apologises again for yesterday and asks me if I want to go for coffee. Do I? If she asked me to, I'd pick it, roast it, grind it and brew it.

With our arms around each other, we make our way along George Street and down the hill to Stockbridge village and my local Starbucks. The city is all reflected light on wet pavements, like an Impressionist painting. The same dark streets that this morning seemed dull and dour are now vibrant and sparkling. It's because Emma is at my side.

Ensconced in armchairs in the cosy upstairs lounge, we hold our mugs in cupped hands and sip our warming brews – a tall skinny mocha for Emma, a grande semi cappuccino for me.

I know why she wants to see me. Despite her apologies, she's still feeling guilty about last night and wants to make up. Like me, she finds it difficult to function until we've found a way to bridge that chasm that opens up between us.

'I'm sorry I was in a funny mood last night,' she says.

'That's okay. Don't worry about it.'

She has removed her coat to reveal a clinging red sweater that gives her an unfair advantage in the reconciliation process.

'No, it's not okay. I let silly little things affect me, and then it comes between us.'

'I just wish I could have helped.'

'It's not your fault. I should never have come round last night but, if I never saw you when I'm like that, I'd never see you.'

When self-awareness pays her one of these rare visits, it gives me hope that love is still possible for us.

'I loved seeing you last night,' I say. 'I just wish I could have made you feel better.'

'Why are you so nice to me when I'm so horrible to you?'

'You're not horrible, you're lovely.'

'No, I'm not.' Like all women, however beautiful, the most she'll accept is that parts of her body are intermittently serviceable. 'I ruined our anniversary. What use is a girlfriend who won't let you make love to her on your anniversary?'

This stops me in my tracks as effectively as French Resistance leader Burt Lancaster halts Nazi Colonel Paul Scofield's express when he dynamites the railway line in *The Train*.

It's not that her attitude comes as a revelation to me. I've spent long hours trying to help her accept that it's permissible, if not salutary, for her to have a sex drive. Long, fruitless hours. I know she still feels more comfortable with the notion that sex is an activity to be engaged in purely for my benefit. As though it's my reward for putting up with her mood swings.

No, it's not her attitude that surprises me, it's the fact that she's broached the subject at all, so audibly, in the hushed atmosphere of Starbucks. She hasn't noticed that the music has stopped and that the other couple in the room are fighting an urge to look our way. In moments of clarity, she wears blinkers.

I could respond with the usual well-rehearsed arguments, but they've never worked for me before. Instead, when a new tape begins, I do as I often do in awkward situations with Emma and opt for humour.

'You don't know what I do with those photos of you in your swimsuit,' I say.

She smiles. The situation is defused.

'I'm sorry,' she says. 'I just haven't felt like it recently. You're a man, you always want sex. I'm not like that.'

Putting to one side for a moment the gross sexism inherent in this remark, she's again not telling me breaking news. Even on those infrequent occasions when, despite herself, she's overtaken by feelings of receptivity, she first needs to talk, to establish emotional intimacy, to exchange other things before bodily fluids.

And this is even before I'm required to tackle a foreplay programme for which boot camp in *Full Metal Jacket* wouldn't provide adequate physical reserves.

Not that I'm complaining. I'll happily endure such exquisite torture as often as she wishes to inflict it upon me. My only problem with these extended preliminaries is that, until Emma is ready, I have to pretend that I'm not either. Which is not always an easy front to maintain when my blood supply is so obviously draining southwards.

Of course, I realise we're not unique in having this problem. It's surely an evolutionary flaw in the dual-sex approach to reproduction. I tell Emma that sex will bring us closer, she tells me she needs to feel closer before she can have sex. *Catch-22*, and like Alan Arkin says, 'That's some catch, that Catch-22.'

'I don't *always* want sex,' I say. 'Only when I look at you.'

'You're mad,' she says. Then she looks me straight in the eye, gives me a mischievous smile and says something that stops me in my tracks a second time, like when Paul Scofield manages to repair the line and Burt Lancaster wrecks another stretch further along. 'We could go back to your place now.'

'What?'

'You could take me home and fuck me.'

You know all that stuff about her needing time to get in the mood? Forget it. I told you she was a complex woman.

'I thought you didn't feel like sex.'

'That was before.'

Fortunately common sense prevails and I inquire no further. With Emma I have learned to seize the moment, so much so that I spill the dregs of my cappuccino over my Bank tie in my haste to expedite our departure.

Back at my flat we're all over each other even before we make it through to the bedroom. You'd think we'd have settled into a sexual routine by now, like couples are supposed to do in time, but we never have.

Maybe we've never had enough sex.

As soon as I've manoeuvred her onto the bed she starts to remove her sweater, but I take over the task myself so that I can see the material linger over the contours of her body as it peels from her. She's wearing one of her simple, white, translucent cotton bras, which perfectly captures her irresistible blend of sexuality and innocence. Her still damp hair only enhances the mix.

I pull down the shoulder straps and she lies back to give me free rein, as silently as Tom Cruise when he's lowered into that sound-sensitive vault in *Mission Impossible*. She would never allow herself to make a sound of pleasure, except involuntarily, which always embarrasses her, but I can tell she's enjoying the attention because she relaxes beneath me.

When I remove her jeans she raises her body to allow me to do so, and her complicity in the manoeuvre encourages me. She's wearing a pair of her old three-pack white cotton knickers, which have seen service beyond the call of duty. Given the choice, I'd sooner have a close encounter of the third kind with her special-occasion lingerie, but I've learned to utilise the shortcomings of her all-comers under-wear to advantage. The sagging elastic at the crotch facilitates lateral access.

Swiftly I undress, lie on top of her, take advantage of that lateral access, which always excites her, and enter her without resistance. She closes her eyes and lets me get on with it. By tacit agreement we long ago abandoned sexual equality in favour of division of labour.

I do all of it.

That's okay. If we did this more often I wouldn't need to do press-ups. And when her body is as yielding as this I know she's content.

Sometimes I wonder, as when she's watching a film, what's going through her mind. A few weeks ago she had an embarrassing dream in which she was ravaged by Arnold Schwarzenegger as *The Termi-nator*, so maybe she's fantasising about Arnie now.

I take her arms and pretend to pin them above her head, as though I intend to ravage her myself, then I withdraw momentarily and whisper 'I'll be back' in her ear, in my best Austrian accent, before executing re-entry.

'I should never have told you about that,' she says. Her eyes re-main shut, but she's grinning.

I let go of her arms to free up my hands for other matters. Scott's wrong about that. I love giving Emma pleasure.

Soon she comes, noiselessly but unmistakably, and her contrac-tions set me off as well. I pull out just in time.

We don't use condoms because they dull sensation for me. I know it's not politically correct to say that, but it's a fact. I don't expect a woman to take the pill or insert internal devices, I'm just telling you how it is.

I sometimes wonder if it's because I'm circumcised, but I have no way of knowing. Other guys seem to manage okay, or maybe they only say they do, you know what men are like.

Emma tried the pill once but went off the idea, which is fair enough, it's her body, I don't know as I'd want my hormones messed around with either. But quite how we stumbled on withdrawal, how it all started, I don't remember. It may not be one hundred percent reliable

– what is? – and I'm not advocating it for everyone, but it seems to work for us.

And yes, I know what you're thinking, but yes, I am completely trustworthy. The last thing I want to do is make Emma pregnant.

'You look lovely when you come,' I say.

'Thank you,' she says primly.

I have a theory about why Emma and I stay together. It concerns rats. They conducted an experiment in which a rat presses a lever to obtain a pellet of food. But they only give it the food sometimes and, because the rat doesn't know when, it keeps pressing the lever. Psychologists call this intermittent reinforcement of behaviour.

I don't know how I know that.

It's the same reward principle that induces addiction to gambling. If you keep betting, sometimes you'll win. If Emma and I keep seeing each other, sometimes so will we.

She can't stay for the evening, so after she's recovered she has to leave. I watch her body disappear into her clothing and wonder when, if ever, I'll have the good fortune to see it again.

In the hallway I give her the present I'd been intending to give her last night. It's a small Navajo pot that I saw in the window of an antique shop. It's barely bigger than an egg cup, but it has a Vision Quest design that I thought might interest her. Normally she's not very good at receiving, but this time she's so overwhelmed that I think she's going to jump back into bed with me.

A few minutes after she's left she phones on her mobile to thank me for a nice time, and I feel pleased with myself all evening. When I make the bed I find one of her pubic hairs. It's an impressive four inches long and the colour of burnished bronze. I curl it into my driving licence so that I can carry it around in my wallet.

I'm such a romantic.

4.

When our new system goes live Richard and I are on night duty, just in case. Just in case – that's a laugh. The first run is at 10 p.m. and, much to the amusement of Ops, it crashes ten seconds into the first program in a suite of five.

We fix the program, rerun it at 11 and watch it succumb to a second bug. On the defensive already, Richard and I break team ranks to explain to Ops that one of our junior colleagues is the author. We fix the program again.

It's 2 a.m. by the time it's working. A caffeine high gets us through the second program by 4 a.m. By 4.30 we're back to square one. The third program abends because of rogue data that wasn't trapped back in the first program.

By now Richard and I are feeling like extras in *Night of the Living Dead*. When we add the necessary validation check to the first program, our fix inadvertently screws up another piece of code that was previously working.

And so it goes on.

It's 7.32 a.m. precisely by the time the fifth and final program in the suite runs to successful completion. Ops has more ammunition with which to denigrate programming staff, Richard and I are ready to kill each other, but the users will get their output on time.

After Richard goes home I stay on to update our project manager on our night's work. It's 9.30 a.m. before I leave. On my way out Scott accosts me.

'Over there,' he says, grabbing my arm. 'Those two lassies from Accounts I was telling you about.'

'Jesus, Scott, gimme a break. I've been in all night.'

'You're a sad bastard.' And off he walks again.

For a whole week Richard and I work nights and sleep days. You know how I said my lifestyle of choice would be based on Dracula's? Forget it. I'm exhausted the whole time.

On the third evening Emma wants to see me but I don't have the energy to handle her. I turn it to my advantage by telling her: See? I don't always want sex with you.

Instead I rent a DVD from Director's Cut, an independent movie outlet that has become an Edinburgh institution. Alasdair, the truculent owner, has little time for the latest mainstream crowd-pleasers. The bulk of his shelves is given over to independents, classics and imports. He even stocks a few Godard films, for goodness sake, including a copy of *Alphaville* complete with original theatrical trailer.

Emma refuses to set foot in the place. She's scared of Alasdair's grizzled look, gruff voice and girth the equal of Jaba the Hutt's in *Star Wars Episode VI: Return of the Jedi*. I tell her he's as harmless as Shrek, but to no avail.

Tonight he has pinned up his latest Top Ten. This is not, as you might imagine, a record of his most popular rentals, but a list of his top ten films on a subject of his own choosing. This month's topic is worst sequels. The usual suspects such as *Grease 2* and *Airport 1975* figure prominently.

Few people have the temerity to question Alasdair's choices. I'm one of them.

'No *Rocky 2*?' I say.

If you search the Net diligently you'll find a chat room where those who perhaps need to get out more debate his Top Tens and compile rival lists of their own. Okay, I admit it. I've been known to make an occasional contribution myself. That doesn't make Scott right, does it? I'm not a sad bastard, am I? There are worse hobbies I could have. It's not as if I'm into DIY or line-dancing.

The odd thing about my own personal Top Tens is that, when you put them all together, they constitute a series of snapshots of the story of my life, like a set of stills that encapsulate the plot of a film.

For instance, two lists that I compiled three years apart tell you all you need to know about my relationship with Emma. The first is a Top Ten Romantic Encounters list (Jean-Louis Trintignant and Anouk Aimée in *Une Homme et Une Femme*, Kathleen Turner and Kyle J. O'Connor in *Peggy Sue Got Married*, etc.). The second is a Top Ten Arguments list (Richard Burton and Elizabeth Taylor in *Who's Afraid of Virginia Woolf*, Spencer Tracy and Katherine Hepburn in *Adam's Rib*, etc.).

Maybe I'll let you see you one of my lists some time.

In addition to his new Top Ten, and much to my surprise, Alasdair also has a new rack of martial arts films.

'Kung fu?' I say sarcastically.

'You liked *Crouching Tiger*,' he says.

'That was different. You're doing this to humour Stuart, right?'

Stuart, his moronic but cheap teenage assistant, judges films according to their body count.

'They're crap,' says Stuart, shuffling in from the back room with an armful of DVDs to shelve.

Now I'm interested, because you'd expect Stuart of all people to like films whose sole *raison d'être* is violence. I skim through the titles, few of which are familiar. Certainly not the kind of material I watch with Emma.

'No Bruce Lee?' I say.

'Try this one,' says Alasdair. 'It won the Technical Superiority Prize at Cannes.' He hands me *A Touch of Zen*.

'It's crap,' says Stuart. 'Nobody bleeds gold.' In Stuartworld blood spurts out of the human body like a crimson geyser.

Alasdair allows himself a brief smirk. He knows I'm hooked.

After I get home I spend the evening bewitched by wire-free, zero-gravity choreography and fall in love with leading lady Pai Ying. I wonder if *she* has commitment problems.

As the nights pass, Richard and I have less and less to do at work. The hours begin to drag. In *Cool Hand Luke*, in a random bid to stave off boredom, convicts on a chain gang rush to finish a road mainte-nance task in double quick time. Elevating them to role model status, I throw myself into a similarly time-defying task, although in my case it's non-essential admin. rather than road construction.

Richard, meanwhile, loiters in Ops. He's bored with my new-found enthusiasm for Taiwanese Ming Dynasty costume epics.

On the fifth evening I join him and Megan for a drink at the Standing Order, the Bank's local watering hole, before we go to work. It was supposed to be a foursome, but Emma managed to concoct a reason why she couldn't make it. She's still never met Megan.

Richard has been going out with her for four months now, which in theory means she has another two months to go. Let me explain. For some reason Scott and I have yet to fathom, all Richard's rela-tionships last six months, interspersed by six month fallow periods.

His supply source is a mystery, but he always manages to come back from the Christmas break with a new partner to see him through cold winter and spring. As the annual cycle begins anew each January, Scott has a theory that its pivotal points are triggered by solstices.

This year I believe Megan could put a dent in that theory by last-ing longer than her allotted bi-annus, and I have a one pound bet with Scott to that effect. You see, what he doesn't know is that for the first time Richard has found someone who enthusiastically echoes his views on planetary warming, globalisation and birth control.

And that's not all.

Megan is the first partner Richard has found who can match him for facial hair. I'm sorry if this sounds sexist, and I accept that I may be conditioned by traditional attitudes to beauty in western society and that, for all I know, there are tribesmen in the forests of Indonesia who place hirsuteness at the top of their wish list of desirable female attributes, but I wish Megan would do something about her moustache or else give up drinking beer with a good head on it.

Physical appeal has never seemed to rate highly on Richard's own particular wish list. Not that I'm implying you need a guide dog and a white stick to go out with Megan. She could be quite presentable if she made an effort. If she ditched the grunge clothes, for instance, or sought out a hairdresser who knew how to minimise frizz.

Sorry, Megan.

I'm not saying that an obliviousness to what others find attractive is not commendable, and I'm aware of what I said earlier about my capacity to be attracted to *anyone*, but we all have our limits, don't we? I mean, in *The Hunchback of Notre Dame*, would you expect Esmerelda to date Quasimodo?

Don't get me wrong. I like Megan. I'm not suggesting that either she or Richard would make suitable applicants for a Notre Dame bell-ringing vacancy. It's just that... Look, you know what I'm trying to say. I know even Richard has his limits because there's a large woman in Human Resources who freaks him out.

Not that you'd know from his behaviour that he views Megan any more fondly.

When I go out with Emma I can hardly keep my hands off her. I want to hold her hand as we walk down the street, put my arm around her in the cinema, play footsie with her under the table in the pub.

Richard keeps his hands and feet resolutely to himself, as though he regards public displays of affection as politically incorrect. You'd think he and Megan were Platonic. You could no more imagine them making out than you could Dick Van Dyke and Julie Andrews in *Mary Poppins*.

Of course, they do, he's told me they do, and he wouldn't lie about it. In any case, I've seen the beard rash on Megan's neck. But what he mostly looks for in a woman, following the principle that like members of the opposite sex attract, is someone who's on the same wavelength as him.

Again, I'm not knocking that. Maybe I'd have more success in my own relationships if I based them on a wavelength criterion. Unfortunately I can't. For me love has nothing to do with how much I have in common with someone. It isn't a choice I make. It's just the way it is.

Take Emma again.

Why do I stay with a woman to whom I seem so eminently un-suitable and unsuited? It can't *just* be because we're intermittently reinforced lever-pressing rats, can it? Sometimes I think the reason must be chemical. Pheromones maybe. Certainly something over which I have no control.

All I know is that something happens to me when I meet a woman like Emma, something that doesn't happen to Richard. He simply gets on better with some women than with others. With him it's rela-tive, with me it's absolute. I'm struck by a bolt of lightning. I liquefy. I dissolve into my constituent parts. I become grilled Cheddar.

Maybe that makes Richard a better man than me, but at least I've had relationships that last longer than six months, so I'm not going to look to him as a romantic role model.

'We'd better not drink too much,' he says as we start on our third pint. 'We're going to be up all night.'

'This may be the only thing that's going to keep me up all night,' I say.

'Or send you to sleep again.'

'I told you, I was resting between runs. At least I don't skive in Ops.'

The strain of new system night duty always induces niggles, but we've been here often enough not to take the bickering seriously. It's one reason we work so well together. Once the week is over we'll forget the hassles and move on.

Megan, however, is new to the game.

'I hope you're not going to argue *all* night,' she says, looking pointedly at Richard. Naturally I'm happy for him to take the blame.

'I'm not arguing,' he says curtly, thereby refuting the very claim he's making.

'What's wrong with you tonight?' says Megan.

'There's nothing wrong with me,' says Richard. 'Don't be so touchy.'

Oh dear. Night duty must be taking more out of him than I thought. Even I know never to call my girlfriend touchy. Sensitive, yes. Sensi-tive is fine. Touchy, no.

'Sorry,' he says, immediately realising his *faux pas*. 'I didn't mean to take it out on you.' It's a valiant effort to restore his New Man credentials. And totally ineffective.

Megan takes a sip of house red and stares over his shoulder into the middle distance.

'Is this why Moira left you?' she says.

Richard looks to me for support. For the sake of the brotherhood, team solidarity and a peaceful pint, I offer as much as I can. Short of doing or saying anything that would betray said support to Megan.

'There's no need to drag Moira into it,' he says to her.

'Did you know her?' she says to me.

'Not really.' In other words, include me out of this.

'Maybe you'd still rather be with her than with me,' she says to Richard.

There's obviously more going on here than I'm privy to. It would appear that Emma and I are not the only ones to experience yawning chasm problems. Nor, it would seem, is Emma the only one who summons up the spectre of a previous girlfriend to confirm the unbridgeableness of the breach. Maybe Richard can come up with something I can use.

'Now you're talking rubbish,' he says. 'I liked Moira, I'm not going to say I didn't just because it's over with her, but I'm with you now.'

Oh, Richard. Whom exactly do you think that's going to help? Does it not occur to you that you're digging a deep hole for yourself here?

'So you did prefer her to me,' says Megan.

Exactly.

'Don't ask me to compare,' says Richard. I want to advise him that when you're in a hole, the best policy is to cease excavation, but cowardice restrains me. 'Every relationship is different. We should enjoy what *we* have. It doesn't make sense to ask which is better. The best is the enemy of the good.'

Now what's he saying? That Megan *isn't* the best? Here's another pearl of fortune cookie wisdom for him: reasoned argument never won fair maid. My pound bet with Scott suddenly seems less secure.

To save Richard from further spadework, I remind him that it's his round. When he goes to the bar Megan immediately apologises for dragging me into their argument. I tell her she shouldn't let Richard's futile attempts to make sense of his life detract from the fact that she *is* the best thing that's ever happened to him.

She warms to my supposed insight as though she's never had anyone to confide in before, like Laura San Giacomo in *sex, lies and videotape*, when James Spader asks her if he can video her talking about her sex life. During Richard's brief absence I learn more about Megan than I would ever have dared to ask.

She tells me that Richard is her first serious boyfriend and that, at the grand old age of twenty-eight, she's finding it difficult to adjust to being in a relationship. Her mother was an all-men-are-rapists feminist who impregnated herself with a lover's brother's sperm and raised her daughter in a lesbian collective.

And I thought Emma had a difficult childhood.

Now that Richard isn't here, Megan is willing to accept that perhaps it isn't *always* his fault, but the everyday compromises that follow from that admission don't come easily to her. In any case, she tells me, there are more important things in life than relationships: war, famine, homelessness, crime.

She makes me feel selfish, because for me there's nothing more important than a loving relationship. In my reductionist philosophy, love conquers all. If everyone were in love there'd be no more war and crime, would there?

'What about love?' I say.

'Try feeding refugees with it,' she says.

I don't press the point because, as a teacher of modern history, she'll have more arguments at her disposal than I could counter.

When Richard returns from the bar all three of us lose the art of conversation. For the first time in my life I'm relieved when it's time to go to work.

'We must make up a foursome some time,' Richard says without a trace of irony as we leave.

He walks Megan to a taxi. I don't know what they say to each other when they part, but naturally they don't kiss goodbye.

It's another long night at the office, and what makes it worse is that I can't let go of Richard's annoying piece of fortune cookie wisdom. The best is the enemy of the good.

The thing is, Jenny is a hard act to follow. Do I expect too much of Emma?

5.

The following week I'm in L. K. Bennett's and I'm in serious trouble. Emma is choosing shoes for Cate's wedding, and not only can't she decide between suede and leather, but she's having problems with heel height. And I can't help her.

'You must have some preference,' she says.

Much to the dismay of both of us, I don't. I'm trying, I really am, but at heart I'm an ankle socks and trainers man (think Olivia Newton-John in *Grease*), and that's hardly the kind of statement a twenty-first century girl wants to make.

I've had a steep learning curve where women's shoes are concerned but, when the wind is southerly, if I may paraphrase Hamlet, I now know a slingback from a mule. Considering my lack of ovaries, I think I'm doing rather well, but when it comes to nuances of material and style, I'm still as helpless as Fay Wray in the palm of King Kong.

To expedite a decision, I offer arbitrary advice.

'Wouldn't leather go better with the dress than suede?'

With a leather on one foot and a suede on the other, Emma parades up and down in front of the mirror. The shop assistant has long ago left us to our own devices.

'No, I think I'll go for the suede.'

Result!

Next she hobbles around with a low heel on one foot and a medium on the other, as unstable as a drunken Dudley Moore in *Arthur*. I try to remain straight-faced but I can feel a bout of hysteria coming on. Again she makes the mistake of asking my opinion, and again I show my ignorance.

'They both look fine. Which one feels more comfortable?'

Comfortable? As soon as I've uttered the word I realise I've made the greatest *faux pas* since Sandra Bullock agreed to do *Speed 2*. Even Forrest Gump would know that comfort is an irrelevant criterion.

'The low heels are more comfortable, of course,' Emma says as though addressing a child, 'but I won't be wearing them for long.'

She stands upright on the medium heel to view herself in the mirror, leaving her other leg dangling at her side. It's too much for me. I burst into a fit of uncontrollable giggling. She gives me a look that Hannibal Lecter would be proud of.

'Which will go better with the length of the dress?' I say in a futile attempt to redeem myself.

She doesn't even bother to answer that one.

I've run out of ideas now and can only assume a look of attentive concern as she teeters around. Finally a decision is made. The medium heels are chosen. Apparently they give a better shape to the calf, although why this should be a purchasing parameter, when the dress she'll be wearing comes down to her ankles, is beyond the likes of someone with low oestrogen levels to comprehend.

In the evening my shame is made public when we go for a meal with Cate and her fiancé Calum. Emma relates the whole shoe shop episode in detail, and she and her best friend have a sisterly laugh at my expense.

'Never take a man shopping,' Cate says with authority. 'They don't have the genes for it.'

I can't even take refuge in solidarity with Calum. He thinks she says *jeans* and requests clarification. Shopping isn't the only gene in which Calum is deficient. If they ever remake *Dumb and Dumber*, one of your leads is sitting right here.

Mind you, I'm not far off co-star status myself. We're in La Piazza on Shandwick Place and, to compound my earlier ignorance, I embarrass Emma by asking the waiter if it's possible to have Cheddar instead of Mozzarella on my Margherita.

Emma makes allowances for Calum, so why should she get angry with me?

It's a relief when the bill comes.

'We should give the waiter a tip,' says Emma.

'Don't hang your underwear out in icy weather,' I say in an attempt to regain some street cred.

Emma and Calum give me a puzzled look, but Cate gives a quick chortle, bless her, and this makes Emma realise it's a joke, so she laughs too, which makes Calum join in so as not to feel excluded.

The slow-burning but resounding success of my little quip induces only ephemeral popularity. By the time we've made the five-minute dash to the Filmhouse bar, Emma and Cate are joined at the hip in discussion about wedding plans. They forget that Calum and I inhabit the same planet. You could light a film set with the glow that emanates from them.

Behind our table, Charlton Heston in shining *El Cid* armour glowers down at me in the certain knowledge that I'll never achieve comparable hero status, in eleventh century Spain or anywhere anytime else. The poster is part of a mural exhibition of sixties' film memorabilia. Alongside it, as Moses in *The Ten Commandments*, Chuck gives me a more forgiving look, but it's scant consolation because the film's 1959 release date invalidates it as a *bona fide* exhibition entry.

I'd talk to Calum but, without Cate to lead him, he flounders for an opinion. His sole useful function in life is to act as her sidekick. If she were the Lone Ranger, he would be her Tonto, except that even Tonto imparts the occasional nugget of native American wisdom.

It's hard to believe he has the mental capacity for it, but Calum is an accountant in one of those large insurance companies that dot Edinburgh like acne. Yes, I know my own workplace gives me no grounds for superiority, but at least I refuse to let my job define me. Unlike Calum, or Richard for that matter, I'd rather die than wear my office suit to the pub.

The only interesting fact I can tell you about him is that he's into magic. Not the card-trick and sawing-a-woman-in-half variety, but the spells-and-potions sort.

The first time I met him, Emma became angry with me for some reason or other, or maybe for no reason, and stormed off to the Ladies with Cate, and he turned to me and said, with a look as unsettling as Merlin's in *Excalibur*, 'I can put a spell on her if you want.' I did not inquire further.

'Do you think it will still be raining?' he says to me out of nowhere.

I wait. His habit of asking tiresome questions would be irritating enough, were there not worse to come.

'Or do you think it will have stopped?'

There you go: his trademark superfluous second question, posing the antithesis of the first.

What does he want me to do? Go outside and take a look?

If I were tortured by Nazi dentist Laurence Olivier in *Marathon Man*, and forced to say something positive about Calum, I suppose I'd have to admit that this ability of his to be both bland and annoying at the same time is a not inconsiderable skill.

I can't believe Cate's going to marry him. Emma thinks he's nice, but Cate doesn't need someone who's nice, she needs someone who'll challenge her. Surely she'll get bored with him. He has even less edge than Richard.

It's not as if she's short of offers. Even in Emma's company she's an obvious focal point for male attention. In addition to the contours bestowed on her by Nature, her understated make-up, artfully wayward strands of hair and deceptively casual dress sense, coupled with a wide-eyed sensibility to everything going on around her, offer an alluring promise of availability.

It's a promise she doesn't always withhold. At Heriot-Watt University, where she works as a laboratory technician, she's had affairs with several colleagues and a handful of impressionable students.

Note the *impressionable*. She likes to think she goes for the strong, silent type, the mild-mannered Clark Kent type who's just itching to change into his tights and become a superhero, whereas anyone could tell her she goes for sidekicks.

There's an element of this in her friendship with Emma, who is her confidante and sounding-board. Despite their sisterly intimacy, they sometimes seem as unlikely a couple as Arnold Schwarzenegger and Danny DeVito in *Twins*. You'd think Cate would overpower Emma, but instead she takes Emma out of herself, makes her forget her problems, frees her from her insecurities.

Once when Emma was taking refuge at Cate's flat after a problem with kiln temperatures, Cate told her to make herself at home, to treat the place as her own, to feel free to do anything she felt like doing. Cate didn't mind. Emma could sit in a corner and masturbate if that's what she wanted to do. That's the kind of freedom Cate's friendship allows Emma.

It has to be said that this particular offer was never going to elicit anything other than Emma's trapped rabbit impersonation, but it certainly moved Cate up a notch or two in my estimation. To say nothing of prompting recurrent daydreams I'd prefer not to go into.

'What's the cigarette-lighting scene?' says Cate, interrupting my reverie.

'Pardon?'

'Em says she failed the cigarette-lighting-scene test.' She always calls her Em.

'It's nothing,' I say, embarrassed.

'Tell her,' says Emma.

So I do as I'm told. The cigarette-lighting scene is a scene from *Alphaville*. In Shot 1 Natasha arrives at Lemmy's hotel room and asks for a light for her cigarette. In Shot 2 Lemmy sparks his cigarette lighter, which is perched on top of the television set, by suddenly taking out his gun and firing at it.

Now this would be a pretty startling piece of business anyway, but Godard adds further impact to the scene by editing the two shots back to front. Lemmy takes out his gun and fires at the television set for no apparent reason, then Natasha arrives and asks for a light.

I maintain I can't fall in love with anyone who doesn't think that's brilliant. Emma's puzzled reaction on viewing the scene was: 'What happened there?'

'You judge your girlfriends by how they react to films?' says Cate.

'It's just a joke,' I say. Reluctantly, I've come to accept that Jean-Luc is an acquired taste.

'Poor Em,' says Cate, and they return to discussing wedding etiquette.

Calum asks me something but I don't catch it because I'm not listening.

'I said, did you come by taxi tonight?' he says again.

I wait.

'Or did you walk?'

'U-boat,' I say.

I dissuade further inquiry by pretending to listen to the girls' conversation. I can't make much of it out. It's all guest seating, bottom drawer, borrowed-and-blue type stuff. Still, Cate is fascinating to watch. She shifts from side to side, scratches an ear, drums on the table-top, taps her glass with her nail. Five minutes in her company and you're borderline hyperactive yourself.

'Can I ask you a question?' says Calum, determined to allow me no peace.

'As long as it's not chemistry,' I say. 'I'm no good at chemistry.' This is a line from a long-forgotten American movie that I think makes me sound witty. Actually, the original line referred to *math*, but I've improved on it for a British audience.

'Or maybe I should ask Emma?'

'Ask,' I say.

'Are you and Emma going to get married one day?'

'No, she failed the cigarette-lighting-scene test.'

'Sorry?'

Where's he been for the past ten minutes? I shrug my shoulders and it works. He gives me an understanding nod to pretend he knows what I'm talking about.

'Cal,' says Cate. She always calls him Cal. She seems to have a problem with names of more than one syllable.

'Yes, dear?'

'We're empty. Get a round in, would you.' It's not a question.

Emma goes to the bar to help him, and that gives me an opportunity to talk to Cate alone for the first time since her engagement.

'You're really going to marry him?' I say, with as much disbelief as I can invest the question. You'll gather that I know her well enough not to call a spade a digging implement.

'I've been with worse.'

'That's it? That's your reason?'

'I'm thirty-three years old. It's time I settled down.'

'*Et tu, Brute?* Are you in love with him?'

She gives me a pitying look. At first I think it's for my uncharacteristic invocation of Shakespeare, but then she takes my hand.

'I worry for you,' she says. 'If you're not careful, you're going to end up alone.'

She's right, and sooner than she thinks. My plan to spend the night with Emma disintegrates as I chum her along Lothian Road to her Tollcross flat.

'It's a joke,' I say. 'You don't *have* to like *Alphaville*. I don't expect you *always* to feel the same way as I do about things.'

'I bet Jennifer liked it.'

As a matter of fact she did, but so what? I'm not looking for a replacement for Jenny. I'm *not*. I *don't* expect too much of Emma. Every relationship is different. We should enjoy what *we* have.

Wait a minute. Where have I heard…?

Help! I'm turning into Richard!

'Sorry,' says Emma, executing one of her about-turns before I can formulate a response. 'The wedding's putting me in a funny mood. It's not you. It's me.'

This is the point at which I know I shall be sleeping in my own bed.

Oh, I know what you're thinking. How magnanimous of Emma to back down so graciously. How sensitive. How charitable. How *nice* of her.

Let me put you straight about that.

In the guise of shouldering blame for our communication breakdown, she has placed me in an invidious position. To agree that it is her fault will (a) confirm that I really would still rather be with Jenny, (b) fan her feelings of inadequacy and (c) make me appear insensitive. To take issue with her will (a) cap the litany of ignorance that has characterised my day, (b) fan her feelings of inadequacy and (c) make me appear insensitive.

In such a predicament not even humour can help me, so I resort to my only remaining available tactic. Even though it means I shall be sleeping alone, I give her a silent hug.

What's wrong with that, you ask? There was a time I too would have considered such a gesture reconciliatory, but for Emma it merely induces further estrangement. With the argument unresolved, and no further contribution to it from me, her only recourse is to internalise the debate. To do this, she needs to be alone. That's the trade-off.

I want to hold her tight, as though by sheer warmth of embrace I can vanquish the demons that rage through her mind. Instead, she pulls away, apologises again and walks into the darkness. As John Wayne says to Maureen O'Hara in *McLintock*, 'Half the people in the world are women. Why does it have to be you who stirs me?'

When I go to my own bed, memories of a time I was loved crowd in on me, and with them comes the old ache that gnaws at my stomach. I've tried so hard to suppress these feelings, but tonight I'm defenceless. I let them wash over me. I lie curled up beneath the duvet and wallow in memories of Jenny once more.

6.

I'd sooner be nursed by Kathy Bates in *Misery* than go to a wedding, but when Cate gets married my attendance is compulsory. The ceremony is in her home town of Dunfermline in Fife. Emma and I book a B&B for the night so that we don't have to drive back.

Belted into the passenger seat of her hatchback, I feel like Michael Caine strapped into his interrogation chair in *The Ipcress File*. The grilling starts even before we quit the kerbside. 'Have I enough room in front?' 'Can I pull out yet?' 'Should I let the engine warm up before I put the heater on?'

Once we're moving the questions come at such a rate that even Ralph Fiennes in *Quiz Show* would be hard put to answer them all. 'Is there room to overtake?' 'Do you think we have enough petrol?' 'Is it better to go left here or at the next one?'

I answer yes or no as best I can, but I'm stumped when clairvoyance is required of me. 'Are those lights going to turn red? ' 'Is that pedestrian going to cross the road?' 'What's that cyclist going to do?'

As for the critical self-appraisal that interleaves the questions, experience tells me to refrain from comment. 'I should have changed down there.' 'I should have indicated.' 'I should have overtaken while I had the chance.'

To add to Emma's distress, we're late because I couldn't decide which tie to wear with my suit, and my offence is compounded by my refusal to panic.

'You promised you'd make an effort,' she says.

This annoys me, because I am making an effort. And not only am I annoyed, but I'm annoyed that I'm annoyed, because I was determined not to be. It's a sort of meta-annoyance.

It's only sixteen miles to Dunfermline, but it takes us nearly an hour to get there. We hit traffic on the A90, find it impossible to switch lanes, have to queue at the Forth Bridge tolls and drive straight past the A823 turn-off.

We lose further time when Emma swings around a bend and the pot on the back seat moves a fraction, causing her to scream in panic. I'm made to check and double check the binding straps before she's satisfied that it's not about to go into orbit. It's a great beast of a thing about two feet high, a terracotta jardinière with lambrequin decoration, apparently. It's a late wedding present she's made.

'If you'd been ready, we wouldn't be in such a rush,' she says.

Thanks to her insistence on leaving an hour and a half early, we arrive on time after all and have another scene in the car park when I happen to mention in passing that the collar of my new white shirt feels tight when restrained by my tie. Emma says I can't go in without a tie, and she can't go in unless I do, so I save the day by bowing to her demands and enduring the physical discomfort manfully.

It's not as if it's a grand wedding. The registry office borders on the claustrophobic with about thirty of us packed in. Cate's mother prays quietly, while the couple standing next to her merely look bewildered. Even if you'd never seen them before, you'd immediately pick them out of a police line-up as Calum's parents.

The occasion is saved from looking like an out-take from *Muriel's Wedding* only by Cate's two cute six-year-old nieces, who were born to be bridesmaids at precisely this age, and who are the reason why Emma has been relegated to the subs' bench.

When the happy couple enter, Cate looks like a resplendent Cameron Diaz in *My Best Friend's Wedding*, while Calum looks as uncomfortable in his kilt as Christopher Lambert does in his in *Highlander*.

The ceremony goes without a hitch.

And that's about it, really.

The reception is a two-part affair at a nearby hotel, with a formal meal followed by an informal dance DJ'd by a friend of Cate's. The main course is a nouvelle-cuisine-sized steak oozing blood, accompanied by green beans and sprouts undercooked to an equivalent state of rawness. Perhaps the chef has been ordered to economise on electricity.

(Gastronomic note: you can always judge a meal by the calibre of potato used. No *mélange* of Anyas and Charlottes here. These are reconstituted and shaped into croquettes from instant.)

The speeches are too dull to report. The only high point is when Calum stuns the room by summoning the spirit of the Grand Wizard to cast a spell of health and prosperity over the assembly.

Much to the consternation of the caterers, Emma's pot has found its way onto the top table, where it jockeys for attention with their meticulously sculpted wedding cake. When the concoction is cut, the pot upstages it with a teasing wobble, which so animates Emma that I have to physically restrain her from rushing to its aid.

It's a relief when the whole ritual is over and we can adjourn to the function suite, to join the company of less exalted guests who have been summoned to the evening disco.

I immediately spot Scott and, with Emma in tow, make a beeline for his friendly face. He's here because he's from Dunfermline himself and has known Cate since they attended Queen Anne High School together. There's a theory, expounded in *Six Degrees of Separation*, that any one person is connected to every other person in the world, via a chain of work colleagues, friends of friends etc., in no more than six steps. In Edinburgh it sometimes seems that two or three steps are enough.

One of the main incentives I had for coming was to meet Scott's wife, and at long last here she is, looking unexpectedly elegant in a blue evening gown with lace gloves that extend to the elbows. Nothing like the mousy housewife I'd imagined.

'You've never met my wife, have you?' Scott says by way of introduction. He omits to mention her name and, as I'm sure I should know it already, I can't ask.

While I shake her hand he turns his attention to Emma. He hardly knows her but he always treats her as an intimate and, incredibly, she laps it up.

'I like your dress,' he says to her. It's long and black and has a lattice-patterned bodice.

'Thank you,' she says, cheering up in a way she couldn't bring herself to manage when *I* complimented her on it. 'I like your tie.'

'Stop flirting with me,' he says, bright-eyed, smug.

'I'm not flirting.'

'Anyone who looks like you do in that dress is flirting.'

Emma beams and his wife chuckles. I don't know how he gets away with it.

'Stop chatting her up for a minute and get me another drink,' says his wife, and he does, just like that, as meek and cuddly as a ball of wool, exactly the way Calum behaves with Cate. It's not at all how I envisaged the dynamics of their relationship.

When Emma too is dragged away to meet old friends, I'm left alone with Scott's wife.

'I like your dress,' I say, shamelessly stealing his line.

'Thank you,' she says. I wasn't sure aquamarine would work.'

So, not blue, then.

'It works for me,' I say boldly.

'I'm glad I've finally met you,' she says. 'I've heard so much about you.'

'I've heard a lot about you too.'

'Like what?'

The things I could tell her.

'Oh, you know. You and your daughters.'

'Don't believe everything Scott says about them. He likes to make out he's one of the boys but, don't tell him, you should see him with the girls. He's a doting father.'

What's she talking about? Scott has never said a bad word about his kids in all the time I've known him. He'd have a dozen more if he could. He may act like he's the best thing to happen to women since a young Marlon Brando had them swooning in the aisles in *A Streetcar Named Desire*, but Richard is the only one who takes him seriously. I know as well as his wife does that at heart he's a committed family man and patriarch.

'I'd like to have a boy,' says his wife, treating me as an instant confidant, in the same way that Megan did, 'but you know Scott, three children is already one more than he wanted.'

Hang on a minute. It's *she* who wants to breed a supporting cast, not Scott? I take a good look at her, and I see it now for the first time. It's not she who is the Stepford Wife, it's Scott.

In a house full of females, he's the one who's under the thumb. His outrageous posturing as *Master and Commander* suddenly becomes clear. His scandalous observations on sex and marriage aren't just for effect. They're his release. No wonder no one has been allowed to meet his wife before. She's blown his cover.

When he returns from the bar I'm sporting the smuggest smile since an older and less swoon-inducing Brando earned a squillion dollars for a cameo in *Superman*. Scott's reaction when he sees it is priceless. Judging from the look of apprehension that spreads across his face, he's just realised he made a big mistake in leaving me alone with his wife. He's saved from the further discomfort I'm about to inflict on him only by the arrival of Cate and Calum on their round of the room.

Cate is in an even more hyperactive state than usual. She hops from person to person like a *Bambi* extra, until we're all itching and fidgeting along with her. You'd think we'd been attacked by the swarm of flies that engulfs Bogie and Hepburn in *The African Queen*.

'You've done all right for yourself there, you bastard,' Scott says to Calum as he shakes his hand.

Calum looks overwhelmed by the sentiment, the handshake and especially Scott's kilt, which outshines his own by an order of decibels. For once the bridegroom's baffled expression seems exactly right.

Then Emma rejoins us and we're all one big happy family for a while.

'Perhaps I should ask Emma for a dance,' Calum says to Cate. She waits. 'Or maybe I should ask you.'

'Ask her,' says Cate. I'm sure I detect signs of exasperation already.

Emma solves Calum's dilemma by taking his hand and leading him onto the dance floor. Scott plus wife join them, leaving me alone with Cate.

'So,' I say, 'you've actually gone and done it.'

'It wasn't so hard,' she says. 'It's not as if it means anything.'

As if to prove the point, she grabs my tie and kisses me full on the lips. I knew I shouldn't have worn it. The shock propels me backwards into a group of relatives like a bowling ball into ten-pin skittles. Cate finds this painfully funny but quickly abandons me when she discovers she's the only one.

I offer unaccepted apologies, make my excuses and retreat to the far corner of the room, where I chance upon Richard and Megan skulking at a corner table. Even though they're here at my invitation, following Cate's call to guests to swell numbers by inviting their own friends, it's still a surprise to see them. As a social contract devised by men to oppress women, marriage isn't high on their list of approved institutions.

Richard, of course, is wearing his omni-purpose Bank suit. Megan is wearing something I can only describe as a beige sack with neck and arm holes. Even Emma would be pushed to make that look good.

'I thought you weren't coming,' I say.

'Put it down to sociological curiosity,' says Richard.

'I wish we hadn't,' says Megan, answering both of us at the same time.

'Never knock anything that includes free drinks,' I say unhelpfully.

'I'm driving,' says Megan.

And Emma thinks *I'm* not making an effort. Richard and Megan look like they've made the biggest mistake of their lives. They'd rather be anywhere but here. A funeral, for example, or a Ken Loach film.

'I like your dress,' I say to Megan, but again I can't invest the line with the same rakish conviction that Scott does.

'I made it myself,' she says in mitigation, as if sensing my insincerity.

'It's an interesting colour.'

'Organic cotton only comes in ecru,' says Richard with even less zeal than Megan.

So, not beige, then.

'Scott's here with his wife,' I say to Richard, but even this doesn't animate him.

'Why would I want to see *him*?' he says.

I now realise that I too have made a rather sizeable mistake by joining my friend and colleague and his girlfriend. It's a relief when Cate and Calum stray within reach of my outstretched arm. The two couples have never met.

'Congratulations,' Richard says to them, at last making an attempt at enthusiasm.

'Let's see how the honeymoon works out first,' says Cate.

'Are you going to take his name?' says Megan, unable to follow Richard's precedent.

'Is that your dress?' says Calum... For once, I await his follow-up question with anticipation. Is he querying whether it belongs to someone else? Could he be implying that it's not actually a dress? This one's a real cliff-hanger. 'Or did you hire it?'

There's enough material here to keep a sitcom writer happy for weeks. Never a fan of laboured storylines, I leave the two couples to their own plot devices and back away into the shadows.

For the next oh, I don't know, fifteen minutes or so, I prop up the bar and watch. It's certainly become a lively do. The relatives have massed in the corner nearest the exit, where they keep looking at their watches in the hope that it's time for the bride and bridegroom to leave. Unfortunately for them, Cate is leading the onslaught on the gin as though she's forgotten there's a bridal suite waiting.

When Emma grabs me by the arm, I see that she too has attained a state of drunken grace since I last saw her. Her voice has risen an octave and she's discovered a sense of self-esteem worthy of Maggie Smith in *The Prime of Miss Jean Brodie*.

'Why aren't you dancing with us?' she says as she pulls me onto the dance floor.

'Us' turns out to be a group of raucous girlfriends who require me to simulate a pillar while they practise their pole-dancing technique. Only when they segue into a conga am I able to use the ensuing confusion to make my escape.

Now you can understand my earlier apprehension about the occasion. This is the way it ever was and always will be for me at social functions. In the manner of a pinball, I ricochet from one awkward situation to another.

Seeking a safe haven, I scan the assembly until my gaze alights on Scott and Richard. Free of their partners, they are engaged in animated discussion at Richard's corner table. Curious to know what wicked twist of Fate has ensnared them in each other's company, and anxious to remain outwith the clutches of the unpredictable conga line, I sidestep around the perimeter of the room and home in on them.

'That is the biggest load of rubbish I have ever heard,' are the first words I hear Richard say.

'What's wrong with the missionary position, pal?' says Scott.

Immediately I understand. In an uncharted desert, they have found a comforting oasis of familiarity.

'It was only invented by men to keep women in their place,' says Richard. 'Animals don't do it that way.'

'You want to treat women like animals?' says Scott.

'That's not what I'm saying,' says Richard.

I too feel a glow of contentment.

'See you two,' says Scott, acknowledging my arrival, 'you make me laugh. You think you can learn it all from porn sites.' And he practises a deep-throated laugh that he's cultivating.

It's a good performance. Thanks to the wifely revelations so serendipitously granted me, I can fully appreciate its majesty for the first time. He's saved from the embarrassment I'm about to heap on him only by a timely reappearance by Megan.

After I've introduced her to him, he looks her up and down and whispers in my ear.

'You English bastard,' he says. He's worried about his pound.

The reason for Megan's absence is immediately apparent. In a laudable attempt to reach the general level of female inebriation in record time, she's been making a serious dent in the vino supply. I trust she doesn't still intend to drive.

The most obvious clues to her state are the newly acquired flush and the sartorial disarray. Her dress has slipped off one shoulder, exposing an ecru bra strap.

'Are you the one with the funny ideas?' she says to Scott. It's a great opening line. I love it.

'If that's what Richard tells you, I'll take it as compliment,' he says. Touché, Scott.

'You're the one who thinks that all women should do is have babies, aren't you?' says Megan.

'It's their evolutionary destiny,' says Scott.

Megan actually staggers back, whether from intoxication or astonishment, I'm not sure.

'Richard was right about you,' she says, hinting at untold accusations. 'What if a woman doesn't want children?'

'You mean what if she's a lesbian?'

He's incorrigible, but Megan comes up with an eloquent riposte. She punches him on the chin.

The shock on his face is a joy to behold, but I have no time to savour it as Megan immediately takes me by the arm and woman-handles me away.

'Nice jab,' I say.

'Can I ask you something?' she says, having already forgotten the incident to which I refer.

'As long as it's not chemistry. I'm no good at chemistry.'

She boxes me into a corner.

'Do you think I'm attractive?'

It's one of those questions that demand an instant reply, before hesitation provides a more accurate answer.

'I think you're a *very* attractive person,' is the best I can do.

'I thought so,' she says ruefully, swaying. 'I can't help what I look like. I can't help the way my hair is.'

'What's wrong with your hair?'

'Do you know what my pupils call me behind my back? Puffball.'

What's got into her all of a sudden? And why is she picking on me? That's what Richard is for.

'They must like you, then,' I say. 'We called our teachers worse names than that.'

'See those women over there?' She points to a dubious duo that a less politically correct person than Richard or I, in the local vernacular, might call mingers. 'They were in the cloakroom admiring each other's dresses, and I saw myself in the mirror beside them, and look at me, I'm a sight, aren't I?'

In truth, she's not chosen the classiest control group for comparison purposes, but that only makes her self-disgust more poignant. As Godard says in a film he made about the history of French cinema, mirrors should reflect before sending back an image.

'You wouldn't want to look like them,' I say with commendable insight.

'All Richard and I have done since we arrived is sit in a corner,' she says. 'We don't talk to anybody, nobody talks to us, and I don't blame them.'

'You don't want to be here anyway.'

'But we *are* here, and…'

'And what?'

She lets out a sigh that could power a three-master.

'I just wish that, for once in my life, I could fit in. Is that really so much to ask?'

Calum, where's the Grand Wizard when I need him?

'I bet they couldn't make their own clothes,' I say, but complimenting

Megan on her dressmaking skills merely confirms that my well of commendable insights has run dry.

'Richard and I are leaving,' she says and stomps off.

I don't understand. Megan's not supposed to care what other people think of her. And what am I supposed to do about it? I'm sorry she's feeling this way, but she's Richard's problem, not mine. I have enough on my plate with Emma.

Women and weddings, eh?

Thinking of plates makes me feel peckish again, so I escape to the dining room in search of a snack. The room is empty and the tables bare, except for one that has been provisioned to perfection. Perhaps my initial judgement on the establishment's catering standards was hasty.

I've barely inserted a Cheddar twist into my mouth when someone wraps her arms around me from behind and grabs my crotch with both hands. I expel the pellet of food like a blow dart.

'Make love to me,' says a familiar voice.

'What?'

When I turn around I see that double-glazing has been installed in Emma's eyes.

'Don't you want me?' she says.

'Here? Now?' She latches her mouth onto mine. I struggle against the suction. 'What if someone comes in?'

'I don't care,' she says.

I have to think at fast-forward speed. This is the first time Emma has wanted me since that afternoon in Starbucks, and *that* was the first time since the end of the last Ice Age. It's something that happens about as often as Bruce Willis washes his vest in *Die Hard*. It's not an eventuality for which I can take a rain check.

'Let's leave, then.'

'We can't leave. People would think we were going to have sex.'

She's an expert on those Catch 22s.

'We can't do it here.'

'Why not?'

She adopts her jail-bait look, which consists of sticking out her lower lip, tilting her head to one side and fluttering her eyelids. She seriously needs a revision tutorial on *Lolita* (preferably the Dominique Swain version), but she's still an arresting sight. Before I can devise an effective defence strategy, she unzips my fly, pushes me backwards onto a chair, sits astride me and covers me with wet kisses.

Pretty soon I begin to think it isn't such a bad idea after all.

'Maybe we could do it on the floor behind the table,' I say, defiantly loosening my tie at last.

'I want to do it like this.'

She stands up, takes off her shoes, removes her tights and special-occasion lingerie, puts her shoes back on, reaches down inside my trousers, rummages around, retrieves what she's after and, with some deft wrist action she's been keeping to herself all these years, impales herself on it.

To get a better purchase on the parquet floor, she kicks off her shoes again (she should have bought the low heels) and proceeds to move up and down on me as though she's just discovered the sexual possibilities of the piston engine.

I must be dreaming. Emma is actually making out with me on a chair in a public dining room.

Such is her urgency that she has no need of further input from me apart from the obvious one. The force and irregular rhythm of her downstrokes preclude any attempt on my part to synchronise our move-ments. All I can do, literally, is hang in there.

After one particularly deep thrust she comes to an abrupt halt with a loud creaking noise. It takes me a second or two to realise what's happening. It's not Emma, it's the swing door. It has swung open and a couple has wandered in.

Instantaneously the localised rigidity induced by Emma's manipu-lations spreads to the rest of my body. She plays dead and buries her head in my shoulder. I rock back and forth and stroke her hair, as though she has leapt on to my lap in search of comfort. Thanks to her long dress, which billows down around our legs, we get away with it.

Involuntarily, I find myself waving to the couple in a good-natured sort of way. They wave back politely, sit at a table, snigger over some private joke and pick at sandwiches. Another couple comes in and joins them. We're becoming quite a little side party.

Emma notices her knickers and tights on the floor and leans over to grab them. I catch her just in time.

'I don't bend that way,' I say through gritted teeth.

She starts to move off me.

'For God's sake don't get up!'

I manage to hook the wayward garments with my foot and drag them under the chair. It's lucky our fellow diners didn't spot them.

By the time the two couples leave I've stroked Emma's hair enough to thin it. They haven't said a word to us, but they're so concerned for Emma's welfare that they can't take their eyes off us as they saunter out.

As soon as the door shuts behind them, she comes back to life like a desert lungfish after a freak rainstorm. The interruption only seems to have inflamed her desire. She pogoes up and down on me with a velocity approaching terminal.

When she reaches the point she's been straining for, she emits a weird screeching sound, but no, it's the chair skidding across the floor as her thighs grip me. It's all too much for me, I can feel myself reaching my own point of no return. I only just manage to prise her off in time.

She collapses on me, her head lolling over my shoulder, and starts trembling. I think it's from pleasure but, when I take her face in my hands, I see that silent tears roll down her cheeks.

'What's wrong?' I say.

'I'm a whore,' she says.

'You're not,' I say adamantly.

'I needed you inside me. I'm terrible.'

'What's so terrible about wanting to make love to me?'

She climbs off, retrieves her underwear, slips her shoes on and runs out of the room.

I can't go after her because I have some cleaning up to do. I'm still pressed against a radiator when Cate walks in.

'So this is where you're hiding,' she says, slurring her words and listing alarmingly.

'I spilt some beer on my trousers.'

She zigzags over to me and grabs my crotch with a suddenness that makes me flinch. It's never had so much attention.

'You *are* wet,' she says, and puts my hand on her crotch. 'So am I.' Then she throws her arms around me.

'Cate, what are you doing?'

'Make love to me,' she says.

I wish I could attribute the new-found demand for my sexual favours to innate animal magnetism, but the more likely cause is gin.

'It's your wedding night,' I say, in case it's slipped her mind. 'You have a husband out there.'

'If you can't fuck your friends, who can you fuck? It's been so long.'

'Come on, let's get out of here before anyone sees us.'

I take her by the hand and lead her back to the function suite.

I guess you're wondering what she means by that 'it's been so long' remark but, before I get into that, just to say, thankfully, that nothing more untoward happens for the rest of the evening. Cate and Calum make their exit soon afterwards, and Emma and I just about manage the short walk to our B&B.

Emma is morose and tearful when I put her to bed, but by the following morning she has perked up and professes not to remember much about the previous evening at all. Including our *à la carte* coupling. When I describe the incident to her she seems genuinely astounded that she could behave in such a manner. At the very least, I must be exaggerating.

It won't be the first memory that Emma suppresses and I cherish.

But about what Cate said. I have a confession to make. Our relationship isn't as Platonic as I've been making out.

7.

In order to tell you about Cate I must first tell you about Samantha. Yes, I know, but bear with me. It will soon become clear.

Sam cold-called me one evening, explaining that she'd obtained my number from a mutual friend in the Bank Film Soc. The friend had assured her I wouldn't mind. She'd heard I had a video of *Alphaville* and, as a fellow Godard fan, wondered if she could borrow it.

Could she borrow it? She could have borrowed me along with it if she'd asked. Her phone call couldn't have come at a more welcome time. Emma and I had been going out for a month, had had our first quarrel and had said goodbye for ever. As far as I knew, I was a single man again.

Sam proved to be a difficult person to meet, though. Having arranged to collect the tape one evening, she had to cancel. We re-arranged another date, but she couldn't make that either. Then she phoned to say she'd managed to obtain a copy of the film elsewhere. So that was that. I wouldn't get to meet her after all.

Or so I thought.

A couple of days later she called again to ask if I wanted to meet up. Now, I *never* get asked out. We're supposed to live in an age of sexual equality, but in my experience men are still expected to make the first move. It's not fair. We seem to have lost out somewhere along the way. I was so taken aback by Sam's proposal that I had to have her repeat it before accepting.

I was sure she'd call off again or stand me up but, come the appointed time and place, Saturday evening, eight o'clock, the Old Chain Pier Bar on the Forth waterfront, there she was. Attractive, intelligent, a Godard fan…

And you know something? Never have I had it so strikingly confirmed that Richard's common wavelength principle is irrelevant when it comes to matters of the heart. In the personal columns of the *Scotsman* newspaper, a description of Sam would have matched my identikit image of a mate, yet there was simply no spark between us. Don't ask me what *spark* is, unless it's chemistry again, but it's there with Emma and it wasn't with Sam. I don't know why. I can only tell you how it was.

It wasn't that we didn't like each other well enough. In fact we got on so well that we had one of those intimate conversations you can only have with a stranger, when you know there'll be no comeback. Our separate lives made it safe for us to share secrets we would never have dared divulge, had our social circles overlapped, or had there had been any romantic undercurrent between us.

When Sam asked about my last girlfriend, I told her I wasn't sure Emma had lasted long enough to count. Had I ever been in love? Definitely. With Emma? I hadn't been allowed close enough to find out.

Where was the most unusual place I'd had sex? At that time, before the episode with Emma at Cate's wedding, it had been in a deserted out-of-season seaside tea room. The window had been broken and Jenny and I had climbed in. But this couldn't match Sam's top of a double-decker bus.

It was that kind of conversation. The kind that gives you faith in strangers. The kind that makes you feel good about your fellow man and woman.

Sam kept her biggest surprise for closing time. As we stood outside the pub waiting for a taxi, she invited herself back to my flat for coffee. And it turned out that wasn't all she wanted.

I hadn't even put the kettle on before she was unbuttoning my shirt.

Now, I know I mentioned a lack of a certain substance called *spark*, but that doesn't mean I'd taken a vow of lifelong celibacy while I awaited ignition. The manner in which we decamped to the bedroom would have done justice to a Keystone Cops car chase.

Kissing? Foreplay? Forget it. Here was a woman who knew exactly what she wanted.

'We can do it this way if you want,' she said when I climbed on top of her, 'but you won't make me come this way.'

Gallant as always, I rolled off, lay back and put my arms behind my head.

'Do anything you want,' I said. Jenny had said that to me once. It was the biggest turn-on I'd ever heard.

It worked for Sam too.

She knelt astride me, engulfed me and started moving in ways that made my life up to that point seem shallow. Outwardly she remained as immobile as a Mike Leigh camera position. Inwardly she had command of muscles I didn't know existed.

I reached for her breasts but she pushed my hands away. All she wanted me to do, in a complete reversal of my division of labour with Emma, was to lie back.

The way she moved... how can I describe it... she had perfected an internal rippling movement about which I would later make extensive inquiries. The waves increased in frequency and amplitude until her whole body started to shake, so much so that I had to cling to her hips to prevent her vibrating off me.

It did the trick for me too.

Remember I told you how condoms dull sensation for me? Forget it. With Sam I could have worn a pair of thick woollen socks, and I don't mean on my feet, and still readily succumbed to her ministrations. Whatever it was she had learned to do, with whatever part of her body she had learned to do it, should form an integral part of every girl's education.

She left without having coffee. She said she'd phone.

She never did.

Maybe I was just a one-night stand to her. Maybe she was run over by a bus. Whatever. The *ever* that Emma and I had said goodbye for turned out to last for two weeks, and when she came back into my life I consigned Sam to history. She became just one more person whose life had touched mine for one brief moment.

Or so I thought.

One year later Emma invited me out to meet her best friend Cate, and when I walked into the pub, who should I find with her but Sam, whom she introduced to me as Cate. Sam was Cate. Do you understand?

I felt like Sam Shepard in *Voyager* when he discovers that the girl he's been having an affair with is his long-lost daughter.

Before I could blurt out my surprise, Cate, as I should now call her, silenced me by shaking my hand and saying she was pleased to meet me. When still I hesitated, she squeezed my fingers and bored her eyes into mine.

Message received and understood.

Emma never caught on that Cate and I weren't the strangers we pretended to be. It helped that, although we had previously exchanged intimacies, we knew nothing about each other's personal circumstances. That gave us plenty to talk about without having to feign ignorance.

I didn't get a chance to talk to her alone, but as we left she mouthed 'I'll call you.'

She did so the following evening.

'That time that Em stopped seeing you for a while,' she said, 'she wasn't sure whether to get back with you or not, so I thought I'd check you out for her.'

'You thought you'd check me out?'

'I know. I'm sorry.'

'Let me get this straight. Emma is your best friend, but without telling her…'

'I could hardly tell her, could I? Especially after the two of you got back together.'

'So all that stuff about borrowing *Alphaville*…'

'Em said it was your favourite film.'

'Why didn't you come round for it? Why did you keep making arrangements and cancelling them?'

'I kept chickening out.'

'But you asked me out and had sex with me.'

'I know. I didn't mean that to happen.'

'You could have fooled me. Did I pass the test?'

'I don't blame you if you're angry with me, but I did like you, you know. I would have seen you again if Em hadn't decided to get back with you. And I could have talked her out of it.'

'Gee, thanks.'

'Can we still be friends? For Em's sake at least?'

'I'll think about it,' I said.

Well, we did stay friends, of course. I couldn't *not* like Cate. She has too much spirit not to like.

So now you know more about us than Emma does, and you can better appreciate why I can't understand her marrying Calum. He'll never be able to satisfy her. I mean...

Okay, I suppose I'd better tell you everything.

That time we had sex, it wasn't the only time. We did it again last year and this time there were no excuses. Emma and I were still seeing each other, Cate had started going out with Calum, and still we did it. What can I say? It happened. I could cite drunkenness as an extenuating circumstance, but you could say we should never have gone out for a drink together in the first place.

Of course, I realise now that it was an underhand, deceitful, despicable act, but it seemed like a pretty good idea at the time. Plus…
Look, there are some things a man needs to know. Despite substantial encouragement, Emma has never mastered that rippling technique. Mastered? She doesn't even know what I'm talking about. And neither do I. So my second night with Cate should rightly be viewed as research.

I wanted to tell Emma about us. I was sure she'd understand. She's an understanding person. She has empathy to spare. Notwithstanding her behaviour at Cate's wedding, she's not even interested in sex most of the time. And it's not as if we ever made a legally binding pact to be monogamous.

But Cate did a passable impression of mild-mannered Bruce Banner metamorphosing into the incredible *Hulk* at the very idea.

If what we did was wrong, surely it merely proves that we're human. To err is human, isn't it? It's not as if we murdered anyone. Turning our indiscretion into a guilty secret assigns to it an ongoing significance it doesn't merit.

We're both Emma's friends. I'm sure she'd forgive us. In fact, I bet she'd have a good laugh about it.

8.

In the weeks following Cate's wedding, Emma becomes increasingly withdrawn. Normally, when the long hot days of summer are once more a promise rather than a memory, she emerges blinking from hibernation to embrace life anew. Usually at this time of year, like Julie Andrews atop an Austrian alp, she's to be found gambolling *Sound of Music* style across the wide-open spaces of the Meadows, with fresh grass beneath her feet, infinite skies overhead and a cleansing breeze through her hair.

But this year she's lost her best friend to marriage.

As long as Cate was playing the field, Emma had an enthusiastic role model for the single life. Now the shelf on which she has been left is bare. The fact that she is incapable of sustaining a relationship is beyond her powers of acknowledgement. The fact that she has me is no comfort. Her 'whorish behaviour' at the reception (her words, not mine – it turns out she can't suppress the memory completely) makes her retreat into sexual denial.

All of which means that, rather than propelling Emma into my arms, Cate's marriage has further distanced her from me. She restricts contact to irregular trysts at a variety of coffee houses, and there's no dragging me away for sex now. She lets me hug her on meeting and parting, but otherwise you'd think we were strangers.

More than at any time in our four years together I feel that there's no hope for us.

By a process of osmosis I become more withdrawn myself. At work Richard gives up inquiring after my welfare while Scott no longer finds me worthy of derision.

One day I have to give a presentation to users of the new system and I make a complete hash of it. For my entrance I trip over the projector cable and jar my funny bone on the corner of the desk. With dexterity temporarily impaired, I proceed to show the overhead slides in the wrong order.

My audience is tolerantly laid-back about my performance, literally so, until I discover that I'm projecting the slides onto the ceiling. As no-one has ventured to disillusion me, I conclude that they're enjoying my discomfort, which of course increases it.

I make matters worse by cracking a scatological joke about systems analysts, pronouncing the first syllable long. No-one laughs. Now I've offended them. I stumble to the end of the presentation with as much panache as injured climber Joe Simpson crawls back to base camp in *Touching the Void*.

I told you I couldn't function when Emma and I aren't getting on.

In the hope of restoring some kind of intimacy, I cajole her into taking up Richard's repeated suggestion of a foursome. I tell her that Megan, whom she managed to avoid at Cate's wedding and still hasn't met, is different from previous incumbents to have filled the Richard girlfriend slot. I figure it will do Emma good to meet a woman who thinks there's more to life than marriage.

Reluctantly, she agrees to give it a go, but on the appointed evening she has a panic attack and phones to say she doesn't feel up to it. Although I should know better, I tell her she can't back out now. In other words, she has to go through with it for my sake. I'm *making* her do it.

My assessment of the situation is confirmed by the accusing look she flashes me when I pick her up. There will be a payback time for this.

We meet Richard and Megan at the Filmhouse bar. I told Emma that Megan was different, and tonight she really is. Even her moustache is different. It's not there. And she's wearing a strappy dress with, my God, is that an uplift bra?

'Did you enjoy the wedding?' Emma says to her after I've introduced them. She's not asking out of interest. She can manufacture such inquiries on autopilot. No, she's already formulating an escape plan. I recognise the signs.

She sits to attention. She flicks her hair back from her face. She picks up her glass, puts it down again without taking a sip, picks it up again. Her cheeks are already flushed from the several previous G&Ts with which she's fortified herself before venturing out. Then there's the real give-away – that permafrost smile.

'I don't understand why any woman would want to become part of such a patriarchal institution as marriage,' says Megan.

It's exactly the attitude to which I'd been hoping to expose Emma, but unfortunately I forgot to factor into the equation the compulsory nature of her attendance. Her smile remains determinedly fixed but her eyes flick from side to side. Any minute now I'm going to have to chain her to her chair.

'I'd only get married to have children,' says Megan.

'I thought you didn't want children,' says Richard, surprised.

'Not now. But who knows how I'll feel when I'm Cate's age?'

Emma is Cate's age.

Her smile is becoming ragged at the corners. It's taking a monumental effort to sustain it.

'I didn't know you felt that way,' says Richard.

'There's a lot you don't know about me,' says Megan.

Too late, as ever, it becomes apparent to me that this evening was a major mistake. Even the sixties film posters on the walls have been replaced by a local artist's abstract daubings. Their seemingly random dots and dashes, like meaningless Morse Code, symbolise our little group's inability to communicate.

I haven't seen Megan since her outburst of self-doubt at Cate's wedding, and it's not only her appearance that has changed since then. I thought her and Richard's common outlook on life would give their relationship convergence, but now she seems more intent on stressing their differences.

Given the circumstances, Emma exceeds my expectations. It's almost an hour before she feigns stomach cramps and has to leave. Normally she'd insist that I stay, but tonight she wants me to walk her home. I find out why as soon as we leave. She's not going home. We're moving across Lothian Road to the Traverse for another drink.

From cinema to theatre. It doesn't augur well. Payback time so soon?

In a corner of the downstairs bar I brace myself for punishment.

'What's wrong?' I say.

'Cate's pregnant.'

'What?'

This is such an unexpected development that I can't wrap my mind around it. Cate and a baby? Cate pushing a pram? Cate changing nappies? Does not compute. Does not compute. It's easier to accept Arnold Schwarzenegger pregnant in *Junior*.

'How can she tell?' I say. 'She's only been married a month.'

'Are you really that stupid?'

'You mean... That's why she got married?'

Emma gives me the kind of look they give John Hurt in *The Elephant Man*. Perhaps I should be offering congratulations instead of sitting freeze-framed with mouth agape, but Emma herself seems less than enthused about the glad tidings.

'So what's the problem?' I say.

She swallows hard, tries to speak, swallows again and lowers her head to let her hair fall across her face.

'It's me. I'm never going to have a baby.' She can hardly get the words out.

I move to put my hand on her arm but she pulls away and faces me with renewed resolve.

'Why don't you want children?' she says.

I had to do it, didn't I? I had to go and ask what the problem was. I should warn you that, if the conversation now follows its usual course, I'm not going to come out of this well in your eyes. Try to be magnanimous.

Sometimes it's as though Emma and I have become trapped in *Groundhog Day* and forced to re-enact the same scene over and over again. In the original script, Bill Murray's nightmare recurrent day lasted for one thousand years, which coincidentally is the length of time that Emma and I have been discussing this issue. The issue of issue.

How could Emma and I have a child? Given the fragile nature of our relationship, how could we bring another life into the equation? Emma clings to the forlorn hope that motherhood would provide a solution to all our problems. Well, to her problems anyway. She thinks that maternal feelings might teach her how to love. This, despite the example of her own mother.

But what if it turned out that parenthood wasn't the mother of all solutions? Or what if it provided Emma with a substitute relationship that excluded me altogether? No. Emma can accuse me of denying her her female birthright, but I need to be accepted as a partner before I become a parent.

Surely that's right, isn't it?

'Let's not go into that again,' I say. 'How can we have children? We haven't even slept together since Cate's wedding.'

Okay, so I could have stated my case with a tad more subtlety.

'It's not all about sex, you know.'

'I never said it was all about sex.'

She starts crying those silent tears of hers. I don't blame you if you feel sorry for her. Emma always attracts the sympathy vote. I feel sorry for her myself. She could make sniper Edward Fox in *The Day of the Jackal* feel guilty about shooting General de Gaulle.

'There's plenty of time to think about children later,' I say. 'You're only thirty-three. How can you want children with me when you don't even love me?'

It's a question to which I think I deserve a straight answer, but it turns out I've merely handed her more ammunition to use against me.

'I don't want children when I'm forty,' she says. 'By the time they're twenty I'd be sixty.' There's certainly no faulting her maths. 'How can you be so selfish as to make me choose between you and children? I can't wait forever. I've wasted four years of my life with you already.'

'Is that what you think?'

'Maybe my mother's right. She says I should leave you.'

Of course she would. She's never liked me. I'm a competing influence on her daughter. It's her fault that Emma sees love as a trap. She has never offered Emma love without expecting something in return – approved behaviour, filial submissiveness, emotional support... As a lawyer friend of Emma's once put it to me, instead of giving unconditional love, her mother makes emotional contracts.

Emma's recourse to her support signals that we have exhausted all semblance of reasoned argument and are about to degenerate into alcohol-fuelled banality.

'Do you want to leave me?' I say.

'Maybe I should. You think I'm stupid, don't you.'

'No, I don't think you're stupid.'

'You think you can reason everything out like it's some computing problem.'

'I don't.'

'Don't patronise me.'

'Emma...'

'Emma,' she echoes, as though I now even say her name condescendingly. 'If Jennifer walked in right now, you'd go off with her, wouldn't you?'

'If Jenny walked in right now I'd have some questions to ask.'

'Why don't you just say you hate me?'

I was afraid this was where we were heading. When even mention of my former girlfriend is insufficient to feed Emma's low self-esteem, she projects her perceived inadequacies onto me. It's a gambit I've never learned how to counter.

As Emma sees it, I could never love her as much as I loved Jenny, because how could anyone love someone so unlovable? Viewed another way: if I don't hate her, there must be something wrong with me. In which case, how could *she* love *me*?

I'm sure there's a Catch 22 there somewhere. There usually is.

'I don't hate you,' I say with conviction, although I know that denial is pointless.

'You say that, but I know you're lying. I'm going home.'

She stands up, sways on her feet and pitches forward drunkenly across the table. I go to her aid. She pushes me away, levers herself upright and staggers to the foot of the staircase. I go after her and, as she hauls herself up with the aid of the handrail, follow at a discreet arm's length, braced to act as backstop.

On the street she leans against a wall to recover from the exertion. I take her arm. She shrugs me off and reels away along the pavement. I go after her again.

'I don't hate you,' I say again as I draw alongside. She tells me to fuck off, but I don't. Worried about her ability to make it back to her flat, I follow her along Lothian Road at a discreet distance. The five-way interchange at Tollcross is a particular concern, but an opportune gap in the traffic permits her to jaywalk across unimpeded.

At her tenement door she opens her handbag to look for her keys. The contents tumble out onto the pavement. I stoop to help pick them up. She pushes me in the chest and swings her handbag at me. The clasp catches my wrist and draws blood.

While I stand back and lick the wound, she grovels around on the ground collecting her belongings. She finds the keys. She unlocks the door.

'Can we talk about this?' I say, more reasonably than I feel.

She doesn't reply. She's halfway through the door. I take a step towards her. She again tells me to fuck off and slams the door in my face. I'm barely a couple of inches away from a broken nose.

'You fuck off,' I say uncreatively, but it's only to the closed door.

At the end of *Planet of the Apes* astronaut Charlton Heston discovers that the barren planet on which he has crash-landed is the future earth, destroyed by humanity. 'Damn you!' he cries angrily. 'Damn you all to hell!' I know now how he feels.

I storm off in a determined huff and am almost back at the Traverse before I'm able to think more clearly. Through a fog of emotion I'm aware that this is a pivotal moment in my relationship with Emma. I've reached *Point Break*. If I walk away now, I may never come back. That's how pivotal it seems.

Do I really want this to be the end? Do I really never want to see Emma again? I try to look at the situation from her point of view. Her best friend is married and pregnant. She's had a stressful evening. She's drunk. I should make allowances.

Okay, she can have one more chance.

I return to her door and push the button beside her name. She answers on the entry-phone.

'It's me,' I say.

'Go away.'

'If I do, I won't be back.'

'Good.'

'I won't call you this time.'

'Neither will I.'

And that's that. She ends the connection and I walk away. I'm no longer angry. I'm not even sad. I'm numb.

But the following day I have to force myself not to call her. Every time the phone rings, I hope it's her. But it isn't. Nor the next day, nor the day after that.

Can this really be the end for us?

9.

In the French film *Themroc* two sleepy factory workers are able to cycle to work each morning only by leaning against each other for support. When one day one of them doesn't turn up, the other falls off his bike. He remounts and falls off again. He can't cycle on his own any longer.

That's how I feel without Emma. For four years Emma has been there. Now she isn't. I don't sink into the black hole of depression that engulfed me after Jenny left. It's not like we were in love. Yet little things keep reminding me how integral she'd become to my life.

The toothbrush I can't find until I remember it's at her flat. The packet of Earl Grey tea she likes but which will now remain untouched. A scribbled reminder on a scrap of paper I find down the back of the couch: Buy clay.

I have no one to talk to any longer about the minutiae of my life. The scrambled egg that sticks to the pan, the electricity meter reader who doesn't turn up at the appointed hour, the sock that disappears in the wash (not an urban myth after all), the day I forget to put my bin bag out for collection, that crack in the pavement that trips me up *again*.

There's no one to moan to about work, or meet for coffee on the spur of the moment, or phone first thing in the morning just to hear another voice and have some meaningless conversation about the weather or a record on the radio.

It might help if I could get angry with Emma. Instead, I continue to make the same allowances I tried to make on the night we split up. She was drunk, or stressed over Cate's pregnancy or meeting Richard and Megan, or tormented about any number of secret pottery issues.

I even put a positive spin on *her* anger, like John Wayne as Genghis Khan in *The Conqueror*, when he's set upon by Tartar princess Lisa Hayward, and he comes out with 'You're beautiful in your wrath!'

It might help if I could phone Emma. It's not just pride that stops me. If she were having second thoughts she'd phone me, wouldn't she? She's the one who instigated the separation, so she's the only one who can revoke it. I've tried grovelling before. It never gets you anywhere.

On the many occasions when I nevertheless miss the very touch and smell of her, and find my hand hovering over the handset, a demon alights on my shoulder to restrain me from unilateral action. Emma and I couldn't go on as we were, it tells me. For both our sakes, for better or worse, our relationship had to change.

It's an annoying little demon, but it's insistent enough to turn the days without Emma into weeks. This time, like the Amish in *Witness*, it seems that I really will have to turn my back and walk away. This time, if there's to be any reconciliation, any way forward, it seems that it really will have to be Emma's turn to grovel a little.

A little?

In *Fail-Safe*, to convince the Soviets that the nuking of Moscow was caused by a computer glitch, American President Henry Fonda nukes New York. A conciliatory gesture of equivalent magnitude, so the malevolent little demon tells me, is required of Emma.

It's not going to happen, is it?

Yet it's so hard to accept that we are no more. There are so few occasions in life when you meet someone with whom all good things seem possible. Even if with Emma most of them remained tantalisingly out of reach.

It doesn't help that I'm able to recall only the good times. Why can't I remember her ruining our anniversary, or thinking she's a whore whenever we make love, or slamming her door in my face. Why instead do I have to dwell on those moments when a fleeting glimpse of her out of the corner of my eye was all it took to cause the world and all its cares to crumble around me like a redundant movie set.

I seek solace in listening to soppy love songs, wallowing in sentimental films and making a list of Top Ten Saddest Endings.

When I tell Richard and Scott that Emma and I have split up, Scott gets angry.

'You stupid bastard,' he says. 'You'd done all right for yourself there.'

Sometimes I'm a sad bastard, sometimes I'm an English bastard. Stupid bastard is a level of contempt beneath even those. As punishment for my folly Scott even stops talking to me for a few days.

Richard surprisingly offers scant commiseration. One day I find out why. He's been dumped too. Megan has left him.

'I really thought maybe she was the one,' he says.

'You sure it wasn't the commitment she couldn't handle?'

I don't mean to sound heartless, but this is hardly a novel experience for him. His and Megan's six months were up. Emma and I were together for four years. I think the trend of any sympathy that's going should be in my direction. Don't you?

Not that either of us is going to put an understanding arm around the other's shoulder. That would be an invasion of both our personal spaces. It's a guy thing.

'She's been acting really strangely lately,' he says. 'She said I was too set in my ways.' He looks at me like the wounded horse in *The Horse Whisperer* looks at Robert Redford. 'I'm not, am I?'

'Maybe the two of you just grew apart.'

'Is that what happened to you and Emma?'

'We didn't grow at all.'

Only Scott profits from our joint loss, to the tune of the brand new one pound coin he accepts from me with a relish entirely consonant with his national stereotype.

'Let this be a lesson to you, pal,' he says.

Most evenings, to escape the desolation of my flat, I seek refuge in the cinema. It has been like this for me since I was a teenager, when the local fleapit became my retreat from the treadmill of school and the claustrophobia of family life.

Some days I would skip school and sit greedily through repeat performances from early afternoon till late in the evening, finally to emerge from darkness into darkness, re-invigorated, inspired, able to face the world with renewed optimism. Cinema was my lifeline, my therapy, my sanctuary.

Still is.

I revel in the womb-like security of the auditorium. The reassuringly waiting seat. The soothing darkness. The exciting whirr of the curtains as they part to reveal the portal to another world. The comforting ritual of adverts and trailers. The magic cone of light that carries the flickering image through the void. The surround sound that envelops and cocoons. The enchanting images that liberate from reality.

All for the price of a ticket.

Kevin Costner can keep his baseball pitch. The cinema is my *Field of Dreams*.

I can watch almost any film and find something of merit in it. Even the most atrociously made, banal, low-budget dud has some piece of montage, camera angle, set design or incidental music to prick my interest. Even the most depressing film can transport me to a higher plane, my heart thumping, my senses primed, my mind afire.

Take that final scene of *Numéro Deux*. Godard is slumped over his desk in utter despair at the pain of life. Yet the genius with which he captures that moment on film transforms the very act of suffering itself into an affirmation of being alive. It makes my own heartache over Emma seem petty, while at the same time it gives it meaning.

As a teenager I became desperate to know why cinema had such an impact on me. I devoured books on the art of film, learned about camera lenses and movements, lighting, editing, use of colour and music, and all sorts of wonderful terms: tracks, tilts, pans. In the tedium of the classroom I would repeat these to myself like a consoling mantra.

Now, as lonely again as that teenager, I immerse myself in films. There's nothing else I want to do. Outside the cinema, outside my flat, days grow longer and warmer. I don't care. It might be as hot as a *Backdraft* special effect out there, but I just want to sit in the cool darkness and watch.

When I'm not at the cinema I'm in Director's Cut. I rent so many DVDs that even Alasdair, who knows nothing about my personal life, begins to worry about me.

'I'm getting worried about you,' he says. 'This is the second time you've rented *South Pacific* in as many weeks.'

'It's crap,' says Stuart, popping up from behind the counter to deliver a predictable verdict.

'I like the Todd-AO colour,' I say.

Stuart shakes his head pityingly, while Alasdair is agreeably satisfied with my response. Both reactions safeguard my secret: John Kerr singing 'Younger Than Springtime' to his Polynesian lover chokes me up.

Alasdair's current Top Ten is a list of opening scenes. The long crane shot at the beginning of Orson Welles' *A Touch of Evil* is an obvious choice at Number One, but I take him to task on *Snake Eyes*.

'A continuous ten-minute steadicam is too much for me,' I say.

'Twelve and a half minutes,' he says.

'Whatever. If you want an opening steadicam, give me *Strange Days*.'

What does this say about my life, when the only person who shows any concern for my welfare is the owner of a video store I frequent? Why do I have no support group of friends, like in *The Big Chill*? School friends, university friends, workmates... they all seem to have dropped by the wayside over the years. Now I have only Richard and Scott, and I can't talk to them, not really, not about personal matters.

One evening *Alphaville* is on FilmFour. I have my own copy, of course, which I've watched so many times that I know every scene by heart, but I watch anyway. There's an extra frisson to viewing it on the box, as though its real-time transmission to the whole world, and beyond as the signal soars into space, gives it added import.

No matter how many times I watch *Alphaville*, it remains a compelling source of comfort and inspiration. Like Welles before him, Godard reinvented the rules of cinema as he filmed, and that sense of reckless adventure pervades every shot. I wallow in the disorienting camerawork, the evocative monochrome, the staccato bursts of incongruous music, the comic-book frivolity, the mesmeric monotones of master computer Alpha 60, the throwaway action against which eureka moments of truth hit you with the force of revelation.

Like any great work of art, *Alphaville* retains an eternal ability to surprise and move. This time, for the first time, I truly understand what Alpha 60 means when it says: *We are unique, dreadfully unique.* And when Natasha learns to say *je vous aime*, there's a lump in my throat.

The only person who phones to ask how I am is Cate.

'Did Emma put you up to this?' I say with hope.

'Nobody puts me up to anything,' she says, immediately crushing said hope. 'I just wondered how you were.'

I give her some platitude about getting on with my life. I haven't seen her since her wedding. You'd think I'd ask about her pregnancy, but somehow it doesn't cross my mind.

'Are you sure you're okay?' she says.

'Well, I'm not exactly happy, but I'm learning to be content.'

'What's the difference?'

'Contentment is when you adjust to the world. Happiness is when you adjust the world to yourself.'

I forget where I got that from, but I can tell from the cry of frustration at the other end of the line that it's less philosophically appealing to Cate than it is to me.

'For Chrissake. No wonder Em couldn't take any more.'

'Is that what she told you?'

'Never mind that, but you could have been a bit more understanding with her.'

'What do you mean?'

'She's been going through a tough time recently.'

'She slammed her door in my face and told me to fuck off.'

'That's exactly the kind of thing I'm talking about. She was drunk. She didn't mean it. Stop being so selfish and try to think of other people sometimes. Make allowances.'

'I do make allowances, and she did mean it. If she didn't mean it, she'd have phoned me. She told me she'd wasted four years of her life with me. Well, maybe I was the one who was wasting my time.'

I don't mean that. I don't know what I'm saying. I'm on the defensive.

'You've only got yourself to blame,' says Cate. 'You know she wanted children. You never could commit to her, could you?'

That does it. Even though Emma has left me, she's still using Cate to denounce me by proxy. Do I respond in a like manner? No way. I'm not that devious.

I attack the messenger.

'Emma's the one you should be talking to about commitment,' I say. 'You're supposed to be her friend, but you don't know her at all, do you? To you she's just some sidekick.'

'What's that supposed to mean?'

'Don't you know you surround yourself with sidekicks? You even married one.'

For a moment I think the line has gone dead. When Cate does speak again, it's in deliberately measured tones.

'I called you because I thought you and Em could work it out. I see now why she left you. If you're not careful, you're going to have no friends left.'

Now the line goes dead, and with it goes my only remaining contact with a gender that constitutes approximately half the world's population.

Under the circumstances, is it any wonder that... Look, we all have times when we behave in a manner we wouldn't necessarily sanction in others, so cut me some slack for what I am about to tell you.

10.

I've got a great idea for a film. It's called *The Sad Bastards*. It stars Richard and myself.

At work we develop a tacit arrangement that allows us to be the butt of each other's surliness. We snap at each other like those vicious sharp-toothed dolls that attack Jane Fonda in *Barbarella*.

One day we have a terrific argument over a nomadic mug of tea that he says is mine and I say is his. Neither of us is willing to claim possession, as it would then be his job to return it to the canteen. It becomes an issue of pride. Whoever gives in first will be the sadder bastard.

Over the course of a week the tension between us escalates until the air is as thick as a Dartmoor fog in *The Hound of the Baskervilles*. I spend my lunchtimes complaining to Scott, who, being Scott, merely laughs. Meanwhile the mug of mouldy tea is auditioning for the title role as Steve McQueen's extraterrestrial nemesis in *The Blob*.

It's the phone call from Cate that ends the stand-off between Richard and myself. It temporarily elevates alcohol above film as an opiate of choice. And with whom am I going drink myself into oblivion but my fellow sad bastard?

It also helps that the mug disappears. Either the cleaner has finally removed it or it has landed the part and gone after Steve McQueen.

'Did you take it back?' I say to Richard.

'No. Didn't you?'

We exchange a furtive look.

'We'll have to get another one,' I say, which cracks us up so thoroughly that we literally have to clutch our stomachs. And this is the man I thought was born without a humour gene.

Still, what do you think the chances are of us having a fun-filled night on the town together? You're right. The usual three suspects: fat, slim and fuck all.

In the event it turns out to be about as cheery as a Larry Olivier double bill of *Hamlet* and *Othello*. The depressing undercurrent of events that has brought us to this point in our lives suffuses our entire conversation, even though we talk about everything else but. The new system (at Richard's instigation), the latest EU green directive (at Richard's instigation), Highland windfarms (at Richard's instigation), a Bruce Willis season on the television (*not* at Richard's instigation).

We're on our fourth round at the Cameo before we even mention Emma or Megan. The venue is both Edinburgh's premier independent cinema and Richard's favourite bar. I have a soft spot for the place myself. It's the only cinema I know that, in recent years, has screened *Alphaville*.

'Have you heard from Emma since…?' says Richard.

'No. Have you heard from Megan?'

'No.'

And that's the extent of it. We've brought the issue into the open and explored all its ramifications with commendable economy of debate. Everything that needs to be said on the matter has been said. To probe further would be to risk straying into the minefield of male bonding.

In any case, what more *is* there to say?

Despite a determined effort, alcoholic insensibility eludes us. It could be we're trying too hard but, if that's the case, we compound our error by prolonging the attempt at a club with a late licence.

Saturday night, and I'm clubbing with Richard. What does that tell you about my life?

The nearest venue that will satisfy our needs is the appropriately named Club Inferno, which inhabits a seventies time warp and attracts a clientele that does likewise. Following an enforced visit several years ago, I'd vowed never to return, but tonight its bar is entirely sufficient to make the establishment congenial.

While Richard queues for over-priced drinks I play voyeur. The garish scene before me is swept by shafts of light from a glitterball that's as aged as the playlist. The dance floor throbs beneath a fraught mass of I-think-I'm-still-cool over-25 drunken divas who strut their stuff to a slurry of soulless disco dirges. Their karaoke cavortings to 'I Will Survive' and similar hen-night anthems have successfully driven their male counterparts to the periphery, where they cower in the shadows clutching plastic pint glasses to their chests and feigning manly indifference.

When Richard returns from the bar we assume the same pose.

As I scan the assembly, I'm nevertheless struck by an unexpected lightning flash of hope. Perhaps there is life after Emma after all. Of the fifty percent of the world's population with whom I no longer have any contact, a subset is single, a subset of those lives in Edinburgh, and a subset of those is here tonight. The alcohol must be beginning to work at last. Perhaps first contact is possible.

Take that woman over there with the blonde hair. I could have an immediate love affair with her. No preliminaries.

'Do you fancy a dance?' I say to Richard.

I don't know which of us is more surprised to hear me say this out loud.

'With you?' he says.

'No, you idiot, with those two over there.'

The blonde is dancing with a friend and, in time-honoured tradition, I don't fancy Richard's much. Mine looks like Bridget Fonda in *Single White Female*, his looks more like Henry Fonda in *Once Upon A Time In The West*.

'Let me guess which one's mine,' says Richard.

'Don't be so sexist.'

'Me?' he says, in the tone of a kettle to a black pot. 'Yours is the blonde, right?'

'So are you up for it or not?'

He hesitates, seeking a response that won't diminish his street cred.

'I'm not into dancing.'

'Take a look out there. All you have to do is hop from foot to foot and flap your arms. You can manage that, can't you?' Then the clincher. 'Stop being so set in your ways.'

'Right,' he says with sudden determination. 'Let's do it.'

What?

Faced with the prospect of action, a wave of self-doubt breaks on the shores of my conviction. All of a sudden it's coruscatingly clear to me that there's no way Bridget and I are going to have a love affair, with or without preliminaries, immediately or at any future time in the history of the universe.

She probably won't even grant me a dance, which reminds me why I gave up clubbing long ago. A documentary of my past experiences on dance floors would amount to a master class in how to deal with rejection.

Or rather, how *not*.

'Lead the way,' says Richard.

Now it's *my* street cred that's on the line. Retreat is not an option. So be it. What have I got to lose? One more rejection can't appreciably enlarge a dent in my self-esteem that is already of bathyspheric depth.

Without warning, I slap my pint down on the nearest table and march across the dance floor with a Richard-Gere-in-*American-Gigolo* swagger. It's probably something more akin to a John-Wayne-in-every-movie-he-ever-made mosey, but right now I don't wish to admit that.

Richard dogs my heels. When I stop beside Bridget he bumps into me. I tap her on the shoulder and, to my relief and amazement, she spins around and starts to dance with me. I push Richard towards Henry and she starts to dance with him. When he attempts to follow suit, Bridget and I as one execute a side-step that takes us out of his flailing reach.

Granted I'll never star in a Hollywood musical myself but, when I mentioned hopping and flapping, I didn't mean Richard to take the suggestion literally. Imagine Spider-Man climbing a wall. Now take away the wall.

Skilfully choreographing his steps against the beat, he looks as if he's gyrating in strobe light, even though there is none. It's an engrossing spectacle, made all the more riveting by his burgeoning belief that *he* could star in a Hollywood musical. There's a look of surprised delight on his face. He's finally found his true métier in life. Forget the career in IT. He should have auditioned for John Travolta's role in *Saturday Night Fever*.

Neither Bridget nor Henry gives us more than a cursory glance, but I remember now that this is how it is on dance floors everywhere. If there were night-clubs on the Red Planet, Martian girls would behave in exactly the same way towards Martian boys. Like the speed of light, it is a universal constant.

When the record changes, our erstwhile partners turn their backs on us and resume dancing with each other. That's okay. They've done their tour of duty. I shall be ever grateful to Bridget for her brief acknowledgement of my existence. To expect anything more would be greedy.

I say thanks to their backs, but Richard doesn't realise that our audience is over. He's still strutting his stuff. I take his arm and lead him back to the bar.

'Who's set in his ways?' he says with a lopsided grin.

Worse still, I find myself envying him. A single foray onto the floor and he's achieved a state of grace that has always eluded me: To dance as though no one is watching you.

But he's not so drunk that he's lost his powers of observation.

'You know why you wanted to dance with her?' he says.

'I liked the look of her personality.'

'Rubbish. She's the spitting image of Emma.'

My God! He's right! I'm shaken. Is Emma that ingrained into my subconscious? Am I going to spend the rest of my life seeking an Emma lookalike?

I sober up as fast as the sprint final in *Chariots of Fire*. I see now that this place isn't called the Cattle Market for nothing. Unfiltered by an alcoholic hue, it's a pretty bovine scene.

Not that Richard minds. He's the new prize bull.

'There's two more over there,' he says. 'Come on.'

Before I can state the case for inaction he hits the floor apace. It's my turn to follow in his wake.

Our prospective partners this time are two office workers. You can tell that from their suits – you know, the Edinburgh uniform, those tight knee-length skirts with the short slit up the back. For once Richard's suit-for-all-occasions does indeed suit the occasion.

My *un*suitability is not my only distinguishing feature in this company. In the race to alcoholic oblivion, the girls are in the finishing straight, Richard is fast approaching on the rails, while I've been left in the stalls.

Up top, mine is wearing a white satin blouse that strains to circumnavigate an ample frontage. Through the gaps between the overworked buttons I can't help but catch a glimpse of cups that runneth over, their contents crying out for more substantial support than is their lot in life. Like the Mona Lisa's eyes, they follow me wherever I go.

I really don't want to dance with her, but I can't back out now. It's a far, far better thing… Wait a minute! Would you believe it? The girls won't dance with us. *They* turn *us* down! How can they be so ungracious?

Richard is so unfamiliar with the rules of the game that he starts to argue. Again I have to take him by the arm and lead him away.

That's it as far as I'm concerned. I tell Richard I've had enough. I'm content to prop up the bar for the rest of the night. (As opposed to happy.)

By chucking-out time I've still achieved little more than a modicum of unsteadiness, whereas Richard's legs have been replaced by stilts and he hasn't quite got the hang of them yet. I put his arm around my shoulder, manoeuvre him to the foyer and lean him against a wall while I retrieve our coats from the cloakroom. (NB: Personal space is less of an issue after a few pints.)

By the time I return he's nowhere to be seen. I don't understand. He couldn't have done a Jenny Agutter, could he? He could barely stand of his own accord, never mind go *Walkabout*. Perhaps he's been abducted by aliens.

Whatever. In keeping with my every single past experience of clubbing, I walk home alone. Carrying Richard's coat.

The next day I have a terrific hangover, and even at work on Monday I still feel queasy. But at least I put in an appearance, which is more than Richard does. He phones in sick.

If only he *had* been abducted by aliens, which would at least have made the perfect set-up for *The Sad Bastards 2: The Return.* Instead, the true explanation for his disappearance turns out to be much more alarming.

Especially for me.

11.

Scott is merciless.

'I want details,' he says.

I had to go and tell him, didn't I?

'There's nothing to tell. We went for a drink.'

'And?'

'And then we went to a club.'

A beatific look comes over his face.

'And?'

'And nothing.'

He shakes his head and practises his new deep-throated laugh. He's becoming quite adept at it.

'I can just see it,' he says. He puts down his knife and fork and does a hand jive over his shepherd's pie. 'I'd have paid good money to see that.' Then he begs. 'Please can I come along next time? Please?'

Okay, he's asking for it.

'You're sure your wife would give you permission?'

Further elaboration is unnecessary. Scott knows he shouldn't have left me alone with her at Cate's wedding. He's an imaginative fellow. He can fill in the details for himself.

As he does so, he gives me an acting master class of which Stanislavsky would have been proud.

It's all there in his expression. He looks blank, then confused, then hunted, then frightened. Storm clouds scud across his eyes. Finally his face becomes contorted, like the cartoon version of Jim Carrey's in *The Mask*. His chin hits the floor and his tongue rolls out over the linoleum.

'I hope you didn't believe everything she told you,' he says, but his heart's not in it. You can't look someone in the eye when your chin is on the floor.

With a shock, I realise I've broken an unspoken agreement between us. Scott's carefully fabricated playboy persona has been a cornerstone of our relationship as long as I've known him, and I've just shaken that foundation. Our friendship is suddenly, like Harrison Ford, in *Clear and Present Danger*.

The sticky toffee pudding, which I hold in reserve as antidote to the chef's special aubergine surprise, lies limp with custard on my plate, an accusing metaphor for my *faux pas*. Instead of basking in smugness, I have to undertake damage limitation.

It really isn't fair.

'You mean, you're *not* a doting father? You'd ditch your wife and kids on a Saturday night to go clubbing with Richard?'

Scott's chin rises a few inches off the ground. 'She said I was a doting father?'

'She'd been drinking. You're right, I shouldn't believe anything she told me.'

He visibly straightens. The clouds clear from his eyes. The sun comes out. There's even, despite the sunlight, a sickle-moon grin.

'More to the point,' I say indignantly, 'what have you told her about me?'

The grin blossoms into the arc-light beam I know so well. It has irritated me more times than I can tell you, that beam, but for once I'm pleased to see it.

'Don't panic, pal,' he says with as much relief as I too feel. 'I haven't told her what a sad bastard you are.'

In an exemplary attempt at restoring parity, he follows up with a relentlessly scathing post-modernist deconstruction of my night out with Richard. Not only is it an academically brilliant analysis but, even though he wasn't there, it's uncannily accurate.

He finds endless amusement in the notion of Richard and myself attempting to dance, and he neatly side-steps his earlier enthusiasm about accompanying us by concluding that, after all, it's not a spectacle he would wish to witness.

I absorb his invective like a sponge. Whatever it takes to reinstate the status quo. Whatever it takes…

Apparently a good deal more than masquerading as a multicellular porous marine animal…

The following day I'm in the canteen again, alone, painstakingly fighting my way through a plate of chef's special lamb ragout, which bears a suspicious resemblance, both in appearance and taste, to his *boeuf bourguignon*. I've almost won the engagement and am about to leave the field of battle when Scott sneaks up behind and leans over my shoulder.

'This is Kirsty and Lisa,' he says without preliminaries, giving me a start.

I cast a brief glance in the direction of the two women who accompany him and greet them with a disconcerted grunt. I've never felt comfortable with strange women who sneak up on me. I need time to prepare. I had a sheltered upbringing.

'They're in Accounts,' says Scott.

So this is the pair he's had his eye on for weeks.

'They were asking me about the Bank Film Society,' he says, allowing me no respite.

I force a smile of which Emma would be proud. 'We meet on the second Wednesday of each month. There'll be a notice on the canteen notice board.'

'What kind of films do you show?' says one of them, Kirsty, I think. The other one, Lisa, hangs back.

'What kind of films do you like?'

'Anything as long as it's good.'

'That's a shame. We only show bad films.' Blank looks all round indicate that I'm the only one present who has a sense of humour.

Scott continues to hover menacingly at my shoulder. I can't figure out what angle he's playing. One thing's for sure: he hasn't engineered this experiment in inter-departmental fraternisation for my benefit.

'Would you like to join us?' he says to the girls.

Flight beckons.

'I'm sorry,' I say to no one in particular, 'I have to rush. I have a meeting.'

I cram a last huge forkful of mashed potato into my mouth. It's made from Santé or Maris Peer, one of those floury varieties that have all the consistency and flavour of *papier-mâché*. I roll it around my mouth to no effect, then have to prise it off all surfaces with a thoroughness behoving cunnilingus. Only a determined gulp forces it down.

I'm sure the girls are pleasant and personable people, but I'm so focussed on escape that I couldn't even tell you what they look like. If they were in a police line-up, like the crew in *The Usual Suspects*, I doubt I'd be able to distinguish either of them from Gabriel Byrne.

It's not my finest hour.

As I scurry away I notice a glint in Scott's eye, and all at once I understand. He knows me too well. This brief one-act four-hander is a means of restoring his street cred at the same time as destroying mine.

That's not the end of his campaign, either. The following day he opens up a second front by email. Apparently his wife, hearing that I'm single, has lined up someone she wants me to meet. She's called Morwenna. I have to make up a foursome for dinner and I'm not allowed to say no.

What devious plan is Scott concocting now? He must have had some input into, or at least a veto on, this invitation from his wife, so why is he allowing me to meet her again? Especially *en famille*?

What's he up to?

12.

I truly do not want to go to Scott's for the evening and I especially do not want a blind date. I haven't finished mourning for Emma yet.

Yet?

There's not a woman I haven't loved for whom I don't still mourn.

But Scott knows I can't refuse his wife.

The day arrives. Along with a colony of other Edinburgh commuters, they live at Duloch Park on the outskirts of Dunfermline. Semi-detached. Back garden. Easy access to the M90. I've never been there before, but I'm sure you can picture the place as well as I can.

The rush-hour traffic has thinned by the time I make the journey, which means it passes all too quickly. Even though I succeed in hitting every traffic light at red, keep to the 50mph speed limit on the Forth Bridge, get lost in Duloch Park and, as if Fate is taunting me, end up in the Odeon car park, I still arrive early.

Scott's wife is genuinely pleased to see me. She takes my coat, ushers me through to the living room, offers me a glass of Bordeaux. Scott is happy to loiter in the background, a subdued shadow of his Bank self. I don't trust him for a minute.

The three daughters have been packed off to Grandma's for the night. The table is set, the food cooked. Morwenna will be here soon.

On the mantelpiece there's a postcard at which I sneak a surreptitious look. It's addressed to 'Scott and family'. I guess I'll never get to know his wife's name.

'Nice house,' I say to her. Four years of studying small talk at the feet of the master have not been in vain.

'Never mind that,' she says. 'Tell me about the club.'

I glare at Scott. He blanks me.

'There's nothing to tell,' I say.

'Come on, you're not talking to Scott now. I want the truth or there's no dinner for you.'

'That is the truth.'

'Did you get a lumber?'

'No!'

As at Cate's wedding, her presumption of intimacy takes me by surprise. Never mind her use of Scots vernacular.

I'm rescued from further interrogation by the doorbell, but the arrival of Morwenna turns out to be scant reprieve. There are some people in life you can get to know pretty quickly. Others take longer to figure out. Still others remain forever impenetrable. It's immediately apparent to which group Morwenna belongs.

Everything about her is calculated to conceal. Her polite but guarded manner, her inoffensive white top and black trousers, her sensible hair and shoes, even her soft Lewissian accent, whose modulation she uses to mask rather than enhance expression...

When I shake her hand, she actually leans back to preserve the distance between us. If she had any more reservation, the Red Indians in *Cheyenne Autumn* could build an encampment on it.

Maybe she's shy. I can understand that. I'm not the world's most outgoing person myself. Maybe she's vulnerable. Maybe, like Emma, she's had to build a protective wall around herself. I can understand that too.

Unfortunately I'm not the one to lower her drawbridge.

To make matters worse, mine hosts seem oblivious to my lack of offensive capability. When we sit down to dinner they deliberately leave me to lead the conversation. Have they no compassion?

While the scrape of cutlery on crockery grates in the silence, I trawl in vain for a satisfactory ice-breaker. Forget what I said about my facility with small talk. Four years with Emma have taught me nothing. I know topics of conversation exist, because I have conversations with other people every day, but I can find absolutely nothing to say to Morwenna.

Until...

'What do you do for a living?'

That does it. I'm going to top myself. I used to be an interesting person, I'm sure I did, you can ask anyone who knew me. It must be true what they say, that you lose brain cells as you age. My brain has atrophied.

Who cares what Morwenna does for a living? As if *I* am defined by the fact that, by pure misfortune, I happen to have ended up not only in computing but in banking as well. A double whammy of a Macjob.

But wait a minute! It turns out that I've asked the perfect question of Morwenna, because she *is* defined by her job. And guess what? She's another accountant. Calum, Scott's two 'lassies' at the Bank, now Morwenna. It's a conspiracy. They're out to get me.

'I always wanted to be an accountant,' she says. 'Even at school. I've always loved maths.'

'I've always hated maths,' I say, seeking to raise the drawbridge again. Her lilting accent is beguiling, but I'm too canny to be trapped so easily. 'If I have to add up a column of figures I do it three times and take the average.'

She gives me the kind of look Emma used to give me when I was being particularly stupid. Worse still, all I've done is encourage her to dissuade me of my ignorance. As she explains the fascination of balance sheets and audit trails, I come to the conclusion that she'd sooner fill in a tax form than have an orgasm. No wonder the population of the Western Isles is declining.

Okay, okay, I'm sorry. I'm sure she's a wonderful person, beloved of friends and family. I'm just not in the mood for an accounting seminar.

I console myself with the tureen of mashed Nicolas that Scott's wife has prepared just for me. They're perfect. Creamed to the consistency of a Hokusai wave. And her venison and vegetable casserole is an ideal accompaniment to them. I wonder if she'd consider applying for the position of chef at the Bank.

In *Masculin Féminin* Godard has one of his characters relate a story about his father eating mashed potatoes. Suddenly he stops eating and shouts *I've got it!* He's suddenly realised why the earth revolves around the sun. Of course, Galileo discovered that first, but this guy *re*-discovers it while eating mashed potatoes.

That's the kind of thing a good mash can do. Trust Jean-Luc to know that.

Scott's wife now caps her culinary excellence and puts me forever in her debt by rescuing me from accountancy hell.

'Did you enjoy the wedding?' she says to me when Morwenna takes a brief pause for breath during her presentation.

'Wedding?' I say, surfacing from coma. 'Oh, the wedding. Yes. Thank you.' Thank you, thank you.

But it turns out she's not doing this purely for my benefit. Her next pronouncement confirms that she's as eager as I am for diversion. Just when the evening seemed destined to go straight to video, she comes out with a revelation that ranks alongside the plot twist in *The Sixth Sense*.

'Scott did, didn't you, Scott?' she says. 'Gave him a chance to renew old acquaintances. You know about him and Cate, I expect.'

'What?'

'He hasn't told you?' She's as mischievous as Scott, so she is. In fact, this could be where he gets it from.

'You mean, you and Cate…' I say to Scott.

He shrugs. 'We went to school together.'

'You and Cate?'

'We were only seventeen.'

'But you and Cate?'

If I say it often enough, maybe it will stick.

Then it hits me: Scott and I have both had sex with the same woman!

'You know what boys are like at seventeen,' his wife says to Morwenna knowingly. 'They peak at seventeen.'

She looks to me for a witty rejoinder in the face of this generic attack on my gender, but I'm elsewhere, stuck in a *Star Trek* transporter beam malfunction.

'I don't recall any seventeen-year-old girls complaining,' says Scott, brightening at the recollection of past triumphs.

Morwenna shifts uneasily in her seat.

'Do you not think there's something to be said for saving yourself for marriage?' she says.

Scotty fixes the transporter and I materialise beside Scott.

'What?' we say in unison.

'Surely sex within a loving relationship is better than meaningless sex?' says Morwenna.

Scott and I are now elbowing each other out of the way in our eagerness to be first over the drawbridge.

'Just because sex is better when you're in love, doesn't mean it's not good when you're not,' I say. 'You can have love without sex, and sex without love, can't you?'

Scott puts it more succinctly: 'I've never had meaningless sex.'

'I'd sooner wait until it's special,' says Morwenna.

'So you're going to starve yourself until a gourmet meal comes along?' I say.

Scott again puts it more succinctly: 'It's always been special for me.'

'You can say what you like,' says Morwenna, 'but no man is getting his hands on me until he puts a ring on my finger.'

That successfully halts our combined assault. Even Scott's wife is stopped in her tracks by this one. Get his hands on her? Is that what sex means to Morwenna? When I said she was impenetrable, I wasn't wrong. Scott is so horrified, you'd think he'd just woken from stasis to find himself alone aboard the Nostromo with only the Alien for company.

Being more magnanimous in such matters, I reserve judgement. Morwenna is perfectly entitled to her views. She may have a lot to learn about interpersonal relationships, but then don't we all? If she wants to wait until she's married, that's her prerogative. And yet…

Help! I'm on a blind date with a virgin accountant!

Scott's wife again dons her Roy Rogers outfit, saddles up Trigger and rides to the rescue.

'You're right,' she says to Morwenna. 'We should wait till we're older then marry a seventeen-year-old toy boy.'

Crisis over, it's all platitudes and awkward silences for the remainder of the evening. I'll spare you the details. It really is an effort to restrict myself to a couple of glasses of wine, especially when I'm sure that, if the Fife Constabulary knew the whole story, they'd absolve me of any drink-driving charge.

When the time comes to leave I thank Scott's wife for her hospitality and have one last, brief, one-sided conversation with Scott.

'You and Cate?'

The bad news for both Morwenna and myself is that I have to give her a lift home. Scott's wife makes the suggestion and neither of us knows how to dismiss it. The good news is that Morwenna doesn't live far away.

She sits in the passenger seat in statuesque silence. We have so little to say to each other that we could be in a silent movie, in which the few exchanges we do make, solely concerning road directions, aren't worth captioning. When I drop her off at her mother's house we exchange a terse goodbye. There's a satisfying finality to it. It's not even a 'see you'.

On the journey back to Edinburgh I try to make sense of the evening. As I drive across the Forth Road Bridge, the three great cantilevers of the adjacent Rail Bridge soar into the night sky, taunting me with their solidity. If only life had such certainty.

It's not until I reach the outskirts of Edinburgh that I come up with a tentative theory to explain my confusion. Are you ready for this?

Life really is a battleground.

No, bear with me, there's more. You're the commander-in-chief, but not only don't you know *where* the enemy is, you don't even know *who* the enemy is. And you can't retreat, because Time pushes you inexorably forward.

So what do you do? The only thing you *can* do: give it your best shot and hope you can deal with whatever unseen forces are arraigned against you.

Take tonight's engagement. This much is clear: following my introduction to Kirsty and Lisa, it constituted the second line of a two-pronged counter-offensive on Scott's part.

His wife had blown his cover. What better way to keep me quiet than to have her blow my cover too? In her presence I'm as compliant as he is. Whether she's pumping me for information about nightclubbing, watching me flounder with Morwenna, rescuing me, even rescuing Morwenna... She controlled the whole circus like an accomplished ringmaster.

After tonight, how can I ever again have the temerity to accuse Scott of subservience? We're in it together now. We have to protect each other's backs.

That much is clear.

The rest is more complicated.

I don't know where Morwenna fits in. Did Scott know we wouldn't hit it off? Did his wife? Were they truly surprised by her attitude? As for his wife's revelation about him and Cate, it couldn't have been better placed to bolster his street cred unless he himself...

See what I mean? You have to go through life without knowing what you're up against.

Sometimes I wish I were an amoeba. I bet they don't have to contend with the same existential crises. Take their version of Hamlet's soliloquy: To divide or not to divide, that is the question. The *only* question.

Other times I think I'd be perfectly happy living alone on a desert island, like Tom Hanks in *Castaway*. Content, anyway. Shelter, food, drink... what more does a man need? Not work, not alcohol, not even films.

And not a woman, that's for sure. Definitely not a woman.

Yes, Robinson Crusoe is becoming an increasingly appealing role model. Especially after what I have to endure next. *That* has me checking the atlas for uninhabited Pacific atolls.

Have you ever had a humiliating sexual experience? You think so?

Read on only if you are of a strong disposition.

13.

When Richard resurfaces after a week's absence, it turns out the reason he abandoned me at Club Inferno was that he was picked up by one of the office women who denied us a dance. This, despite the inoperative state he was in. In his off-season, too.

'She's some woman,' he says, which is more information than I need. If he doesn't wipe that smile off his face I'll do it for him.

'She's called Barbra,' he says. 'After Streisand. Her mother liked *Funny Girl*.'

'So you weren't sick, then.'

'Yours was called Maggie.'

'Mine?'

'I've arranged a foursome.'

'What?'

'I thought you'd be pleased. It's not like you're seeing anyone else.'

'That doesn't mean I want to see *her* again.' Unbeknown to him, I'm still convalescing from Morwenna.

'What's wrong with her?'

To save itemising the complete list, I summarise.

'She's not my type.'

'I thought you didn't have a type.'

When Scott hears of our proposed double date he drools with glee. Literally. He has to wipe the corners of his mouth. He's as happy as a *Zulu* warrior on finding out that Rorke's Drift is defended only by Michael Caine and a handful of British character actors.

The three of us are seated at what has become, since Cate's wedding, our regular table in the canteen. To think that not so long ago I had to act as a demilitarised zone between my two so-called friends.

'Let me give you some advice,' Scott says to us in a voice heavy with experience. 'Girls are different than boys. Remember the Three-date Rule. Play it cool. You know what cool is, don't you?'

He gives us a despairing look, like a teacher trying to find the right words to explain the theory of relativity to a class of primary school children. My classmate and I exchange looks of ignorance. As he's too proud to ask, it's up to me.

'What's the Three-date Rule?'

'Sad English bastards. No wonder you're both still single.'

He holds out his hand, palm up, and counts on his fingers as he explains.

'Date 1: Keepen den mitts offen die goods. If you get a peck on the cheek at the end of the evening, count that as a result. Date 2: Up the ante. Test the water. Cop a feel. Slip the tongue. Date 3: If you get this far without striking out, which, let's face it, is unlikely, *now's* the time to go for a home run.'

He pauses, either to consider whether he's covered all the bases or out of concern that his mixed bag of metaphors has left us flailing in the outfield. Just in case, he picks up and expands on his peck-on-the-cheek poultry motif.

'Remember: there's no way the likes of you pair are going to get into a leg-over situation on a first date, so don't count your chickens before they're hatched.'

He doesn't know that Richard has already enjoyed a free-range roam around the hen house, and Richard struggles manfully not to be so ungallant as to tell him.

I struggle less manfully not to expose his act for what it is. Unfortunately he knows as well as I do that, following recent events, I'll never again have the temerity to unmask him. His secret will remain forever safe with me. The fact that I know, and that he knows I know, and that I know he knows I know… gives his performance a new multi-layered resonance. He plays close to the edge, does Scott, and I do believe he loves it that way.

'Remember the tortoise and the hare,' he says, as if he intends to call on all branches of the animal kingdom to support his argument.

'I haven't said I'm going,' I say.

'Why not?' he says.

'Exactly,' says Richard. 'Why not?'

The world is becoming an increasingly strange place. Scott and Richard are ganging up on me.

'You've changed,' I say to Richard.

'Rubbish.'

'You have.'

'At least I'm not set in my ways.'

'Boys, boys,' Scott says condescendingly.

'Which part of "I don't want to see her again" don't you understand?' I say to Richard.

'What would I tell her?' he says.

'You must be confusing me with someone who cares. Tell her

I'm only allowed out of Saughton jail once a month. Tell her I've emigrated.'

'Tell her he's gay,' says Scott.

'Tell her I'm not ready for another relationship at the moment. That usually works.' It's also true, so I don't know why I'm making it sound cynical.

Nevertheless, as the week wears on, Richard begins to break down my resistance. He finds a counter to every excuse I come up with. What have I got to lose, he wants to know. It's just a bit of fun, he tells me. As a final resort he uses blackmail. He says he can't go out with Barbra unless I go out with Maggie. I owe it to him to make an effort.

Finally, on Friday afternoon, I crack. I'm going out with Maggie. I'm no longer in control of my life. On the way home from work I find myself humming a Doris Day tune. It turns out to be 'Que Sera, Sera' from Hitchcock's *The Man Who Knew Too Much*.

By Saturday evening Richard is as frisky as Trigger being asked to cover Black Beauty. By contrast, I'm as frisky as if *I* were being asked to cover Black Beauty.

I dress down for the occasion but still fail to reach the general level of sartorial apathy. Like Richard, Maggie and Barbra appear to possess only one *ensemble* of outerwear. I'm the only one not wearing a suit. Unfortunately that means that Maggie is exactly as I remember her from Club Inferno. Even worse, I'm completely sober this time.

It turns out we're going to the pictures. Some comfort there, you'd think.

Wrong.

On the way to the multiplex I try to hold a conversation with my date, I really do, but my train of thought is derailed every time I glance in her direction. From the superglued solidity of her bouffant hairdo to the ladder in her tights that I'm convinced advances a millimetre each time my gaze strays towards it, her appearance is as disconcerting as Richard's dancing.

Her make-up has been applied with a palette-knife. It's as thick as the magma that spews up from beneath Los Angeles in *Volcano*. And hovering ominously in peripheral vision at all times is that Mona Lisa bosom, as capacious as an usherette's tray.

Okay, okay, I'm sorry. I'm sure Maggie is a nice person, I'll probably burn in Hell for this, but I don't want to be here. The corroded ignition system of an Edwardian horseless carriage that has been left out in the rain for a century would have more spark than we have.

I want to go home even more when the film of choice turns out to be a slasher movie. I refuse to say which. It's the fifth in the series.

You know how I said I can see something of merit in any film? Forget it. My eyes drift from the screen to the auditorium in an effort to remind myself how much I love the cinema, the darkness, the cone of light and all that crap. But soon I'm forced to don blinkers and concentrate on the screen to avoid an even more stomach-churning sight – Richard and Barbra snogging.

As if that isn't enough to keep me in nightmares for a month, they urge me to do likewise with Maggie. I now realise it wasn't just bad luck that sandwiched me in the seat between the two girls. The arrangement enables Barbra to nudge me and whisper instructions in my ear.

Even more distressingly, Richard adds nods of encouragement. I wish he'd revert to some of those ways he used to be set in. Whatever happened to meaningful relationships with the sisterhood?

Maggie must be aware of what's going on but pretends not to notice. To say I'm embarrassed would be an understatement. I feel like Ben Stiller in *Something About Mary*, when he goes to the bathroom in his girlfriend's house and gets his manhood caught in his zip.

In a rebuff to Richard and Barbra's urgings I clench my hands between my knees. I haven't felt so uncomfortable in a cinema since I was eight years old, when I went with the guys to see a Mickey Mouse film, *Fantasia*, and it turned out to be about classical music.

This movie turns out to be the longest feature film ever made. Its running time is ten years. And that's just the start of my ordeal. Three of us want to go for a drink afterwards.

So the next thing, we're squeezed into a back room at the Canny Man's. Maggie and I silently sip pints while Ken and Barbie joke and canoodle, impervious to embarrassment. Richard even tickles Barbra's chin with his stubble, causing her to cackle maniacally. It's appalling to witness. I can't even seek empathy with Maggie in the face of adversity. Beneath its cosmetic strata her face is unreadable.

'Which bit of the film did you like best, Mags?' Barbra asks her when the referee calls break.

'The bit where he attacks her with the axe,' says Maggie.

'Yeah, that was good.'

'It was like Jack Nicholson in...'

'*The Shining*,' I say helpfully.

'Yeah,' says Maggie. 'Have you seen that, Babs?'

'Yeah, that one with Melanie Griffiths. I like Melanie Griffiths.'

'Yeah. Me too.'

'You're both confusing it with *Shining Through*,' I say.

'What's *The Shining* about, then?' says Maggie.

'Tracking shots,' I say.

Richard shakes his head, Maggie looks bemused and Barbra launches into a detailed description of every gory scene in the film.

In *Annie Hall* Woody Allen dates a girl who doesn't understand him. When he tells her he hasn't been himself since he gave up smoking, and she asks him when he quit, and he says sixteen years ago, she doesn't get the joke. I now know how he feels.

I try to speak to Richard with my eyes. 'What are we doing here?' they say with unmistakable clarity, but he refuses to receive the message.

Another ten years pass before closing time, and even then I'm not saved by the bell. It turns out that the girls rent a flat together, and the same three of us as before vote to continue the night's festivities back there.

So the next thing, we're at the girls' flat, Richard and Barbra have decamped to the bedroom and Maggie and I are sitting side by side on the couch practising our awkward silence skills.

When I'm down to the last two fingers in my can of Tennent's and rehearsing my exit strategy, she pre-empts me with a surprise manoeuvre. She slides forward on the couch while simultaneously leaning back diagonally, causing her skirt to ride up her thighs and her body to press into mine.

It's not the most subtle tactic I've ever seen. Even I can't mistake its intent. Barbra clearly isn't the only one who wants to decamp to the bedroom. I respond as I did in the cinema, by clasping my hands protectively between my legs and saying nothing. I have nothing to say.

Instead, I ponder the logistics of tunnelling to freedom. Admittedly we're on the third floor, but if an international cast can dig their way out of a heavily guarded POW camp in *The Great Escape*...

With the skill of a contortionist, Maggie twists her face up to mine and says, understandably in the circumstances, 'It's more comfortable in my room.'

'Okay,' I say. Just like that. As resigned as Steve McQueen to incarceration. As meek as someone who hums Doris Day tunes to himself.

Now, you may be wondering why, after everything I've said, I so readily surrender to Maggie's implicit proposal. The answer is simple: she asked me. As long as I could bask in awkward silence, I was safe. But now that she's asked me, I can't refuse. I don't have the verbal skills.

When you have spent all your teenage years fantasising about sex, fearing that your experience of it will forever be right-hand rather than first-hand, hoping against hope that one day a girl will take pity on you and allow you access to her most treasured secret, it becomes impossible to turn down what Maggie is now suggesting. It's the most precious gift a woman can offer to a man.

It's not an offer to be refused.

Ever.

Look at it as proof of my New Man credentials. I *can* be attracted to anyone.

So the next thing, I'm sitting on Maggie's bed, still with my hands between my legs, letting Fate take its course.

I remain in that position for at least two seconds before she backheels the door shut, pushes me onto my back, jumps astride me and starts kissing me with all the ferocity of a caged lion that's just been let out into the bush after years of captivity and comes across a herd of wildebeest. I've never felt so much like a wildebeest in my life.

Her clothes come off with subliminal speed. One moment they're there, the next they're gone. I expect that's one advantage of having only the one outfit. Familiarity.

I do my best to keep up, but I'm still struggling to free my underpants from my ankles when she pushes me back and jumps astride me again. I'm pinned to the bed like a wrestler to the canvas.

Liberated from years of solitary confinement, her breasts conspire with each other, hover over me like GPS satellites conducting a geographical survey of my body, then leap at my face from all points of the compass. I seek out an air pocket in their cleavage.

Suddenly I hear a muffled shriek.

'Aaaagh!'

She pulls away from me.

'What is it?' I say, alarmed.

'You're a Roundhead!'

'What?'

'Roundheads and Cavaliers. You're circumcised.'

'So?'

'I've never seen one before.'

She flips the Civil War helmet back and forth between her fingers.

'It looks funny,' she says.

'Thanks.'

'Look at it.' She points it at my face.

'I've seen it.'

'It's got a big round head.' She prods it with her finger and gives it an experimental tweak to see how it will react, as though she's researching a thesis on *Strange Phenomena of Nature*.

It's not going to be much use to her if she carries on like this. Has she never seen *The Incredible Shrinking Man*?

'How come you're a Roundhead?' she says.

'I didn't have a lot of say in the matter at the time.'

'Can Barbra have a look?'

'No!'

She fiddles some more with the curious appendage and gives it a few peremptory tugs to convince herself it's not some alien parasite that has attached itself to my body, like that pesky little monster that bursts out of John Hurt's chest in *Alien*. Finally she looks it in the eye and, when it doesn't answer back, decides it will serve.

Intermission over, she returns to action by leaping off the bed and putting out the light. I didn't think she'd be a lights-out kind of girl, but right now the darkness is welcome. If only to distract attention from my unfortunate medical condition.

It's so dark that my eyes can't adjust to it and, when Maggie's body suddenly lands on top of mine with a thump, it winds me. As I recover my breath I hear the sound of a bedside drawer opening and closing, then a hand sheaths me in a condom. I'm about as ready for her as a used tea bag, but she expertly pilots me inside. Not that even the proverbial square peg would find it an abrasive accommodation.

Then the bouncing begins. It turns out Maggie was a rodeo rider in a previous life. In the dim light I can now make out her generous silhouette as she powers down on me at random angles. Anything more acute than that last one is going to cause me serious injury. She can't use her hands for directional control because she has them clamped to her breasts, whether for pleasure or to prevent gyroscopic rotation I'm not sure.

On every downward thrust a wayward bedspring digs into the small of my back. Repeated compression between the irresistible force above and the immovable object below induces queasiness. Luckily, before I lose my dignity (or worse), Maggie wails a banshee scream, collapses over me like blancmange and starts to snore.

It's one of those full-throttle snores, the air rasping on the way in, rattling on the way out. It's not quite the soundtrack to those teenage fantasies I mentioned.

You know how, in extreme adversity, the human body can perform incredible feats of strength outwith its normal range of capabilities? I

achieve a personal best bench-press by raising Maggie's body sufficiently to allow me to slide out onto the floor.

Leaving her comatose on the bed like a stranded starfish, I stand
up, feel for my clothes, stub my toe, curse, find the light switch, dress
in record time and run. Yes, I actually run away.

That's not the end of my embarrassment, either.

14.

Monday lunchtime.

I do believe Richard has actually been waiting for Scott to join us in the canteen, to ensure my maximum mortification.

'What happened to you Saturday night?' he says to me as soon as his new buddy has taken his seat.

'What do you mean?'

'You weren't at the girls' flat yesterday morning.'

'Yesterday morning?' says Scott excitedly.

'I went home,' I say defensively.

'Maggie wondered what had happened to you,' says Richard.

'Raise your hand,' Scott says to him. He does so. Scott gives him a high five. 'Right on, pal!'

'I had too much to drink,' I say. 'I didn't feel too good.'

'She said you were a bit subdued,' says Richard.

Subdued? That doesn't sound like a word out of Maggie's vocabulary.

'Is that what she said? That I was a bit subdued?'

'Words to that effect.'

Yes, but which words? Then it hits me. They've been discussing my performance! I can just imagine the scene:

Maggie and Barbra's flat. Sunday morning. Richard, Maggie and Barbra, hunched around the kitchen table. Barbra: 'How was last night, Mags?' That's when she holds up the judging cards. Content: 0.0. Style: 0.0.

Scott is so animated he can't eat. Macaroni cheese cools forsaken on his Bank plate.

'What happened?' he says, eyes on swivel, unsure who has the better tale.

'She wants to see you again, though,' Richard says to me. I try to ignore him, but he persists. 'What do you think?'

'If I was so *subdued*, why would she want to see me again?'

'She's never been out with a Roundhead before.'

I had to ask, didn't I? I always have to ask.

It's worse than I imagined. It's a worst-case scenario. Rewind and replay.

Maggie and Barbra's flat. Sunday morning. Richard, Maggie and Barbra, hunched around the kitchen table. Richard: 'Do you take sugar in your coffee?' Maggie: 'Pass the milk, please.' Barbra: 'Sausage and eggs, anyone?' Maggie: 'Speaking of sausages…'

Rigor mortis sets in, rendering me incapable of movement. My bowl of instant French onion soup, which is all my system can handle today, cools in sympathy with Scott's macaroni cheese. I can no longer lift my Bank spoon. Richard, meanwhile, shovels another spadeful of potato salad into his mouth as though my manhood is an entirely acceptable topic of conversation around the nation's dinner tables.

Looking around, I see that Scott has left, but no, he's doubled up on the floor clutching his stomach.

'Stop! Stop!' he moans.

I recall with nostalgia the yawning chasm that used to open up between Emma and myself. I could do with an chasm to jump into.

And what does Richard mean when he says Maggie wants to see me again *though*. What list of inadequacies does that *though* conceal?

'Watch my lips,' I say to him. 'There's no way I'm seeing her again.'

'Why not?'

'Have you seen *Fatal Attraction*? I'd sooner go out with Glenn Close.'

He shrugs with incomprehension. Not only am I a freak of nature but, for some unfathomable reason, I'm sensitive about it. Surely the only concern here is Maggie's welfare?

'She's understandably curious,' he says.

'Listen to yourself. What's happened to you?'

'How do you mean?'

'Exactly what kind of criteria do you base your relationships on these days? What would you say if I wanted to go out with a woman purely on the basis of her bra size?'

'It's the women I'm thinking of. Barbra's jealous. She's never been with a Roundhead, either.'

'So now what are you saying – that you want to share her with me?'

'You should start an escort agency,' says Scott, resurfacing but still fighting hysteria. 'Roundhead for hire. No tip required.'

Okay, that's it. I am not some scientific exhibit to be placed on display for the edification of the sisterhood. With all the gravity of the title role in *The Black Hole*, I stand up, draw myself up to my full height and fix my lunch companions with a look that can leave them in no doubt as to their misconduct. Then I stomp out of the canteen with such indignation that, much to the horror of a gauntlet of spluttering dinner ladies, I deliberately omit to return my tray to the serving hatch.

You'd think my so-called friends could muster a little sympathy. In the space of a couple of weeks, I've been dumped by Emma, endured *Long Day's Journey Into Night* with Morwenna and been subjected to more trauma in Maggie's bedroom than Russell Crowe encounters in the arena in *Gladiator*.

No matter how hard I try, I'll never see *My Night With Maggie* as either the chick flick Richard seems to view it as or the gross-out romcom of Scott's perverse imagination. Slipping on a banana skin isn't funny when you're the one who's executing the slippage. Rather than playing the lead in *Carry On Roundhead*, I feel more like a token sex object in *Mags and Babs*, the low-budget sequel to *Thelma and Louise* (director's cut, naturally).

The bedroom scene wouldn't even make a list of Top Ten Funniest Sex Scenes... although compiling the list at least helps to put my misfortune into perspective.

Things could be worse, I decide. Things could always be worse. I can handle ridicule. It's not as if I had my manhood physically assaulted...

15.

I've tried cinema. I've tried alcohol. Only one option remains.

The Marquesas are a group of islands in French Polynesia, about halfway across the Pacific Ocean from New Guinea to Peru. According to my atlas, there's an unnamed island off the coast of Hiva Oa. If it's unnamed, there's a good chance it's uninhabited. I'm sure it will make a suitable retreat.

There's certainly nothing to keep me in Edinburgh any longer. Like the plot of *Memento*, my life here is unfolding in reverse. I've regressed to a time when I frequented clubs and went on blind dates. It wasn't satisfying then and it's even less so now. I can't even turn to friends for support, because their behaviour has become as unpredictable as my own. In an increasingly unsettling world all the old certainties are gone.

Scott is either a more simple or a more complex person than I thought he was. I can't decide. I have similar problems with his wife. She treats me at the same time as both a confidant and a house pet.

Richard, meanwhile, has decided he was born to boogie. He wants us to revisit Club Inferno with the girls. I have to sit him down and tell him that if he ever mentions Maggie's name again I'll give him a closer look than he'd choose to have at what lies behind his computer screen.

As for Emma... Well, Emma always could be trusted to do the unexpected, and it's no different now. Just when I'm getting used to the fact that she's out of my life for ever, she leaves a message on my answerphone.

'Hello? Hello? Oh....' she begins. Only Emma would try to hold a conversation with an answerphone.

When I hear her voice my heart races. She hopes I'm well and wants to meet me. She even gives me a time and place. I have to phone back only if I can't make it.

As if there's any chance that I can't make it.

I spend the remainder of the evening practising systems analysis on her message. I listen to it so many times that I could plot the inflexions of her voice on a graph, write a dissertation on her choice of vocabulary, produce a philosophical treatise on the meaning of her pauses, and compile a taxonomy of possible subtexts. None of it brings me any nearer to determining her intent.

As the appointed day approaches I become increasingly nervous. I know I said I wouldn't weaken but, after my recent experiences with Morwenna and Maggie, the sound of Emma's voice has a gravitational pull that could destabilise the orbits of small planets. I have to know what she wants, don't I?

We meet outside the National Gallery at lunchtime. I arrive just as the one o'clock gun on the castle ramparts informs the city's pigeon population that it's time to panic again. Two minutes later, Emma skips down the gallery steps, trips at their foot and lands in my arms. Given time, I'm sure I could devise endless witticisms to mark the symbolism of the moment, but all I come out with is a winded hello.

While my starving eyes feast on her we exchange standard pleasantries. The portents are not good. She's wearing a new strappy top. I know it's new because it has a low neckline that draws attention to a swell of porcelain flesh that has never before been exposed to daylight. It must be part of her end-of-relationship, look-at-me-I'm-single makeover kit. It looks good on her and I hate it.

'I like your top,' I say.

'You're just saying that,' she says. 'I know it doesn't go with these jeans.'

'It does. You never could take a compliment.' I kick myself even as I say it.

'I don't want to argue,' she says.

'Neither do I.'

At the self-service restaurant in Jenners department store we find a window table overlooking the castle. I'm as nervous as I would be on a first date with a stranger. Not a stranger like Morwenna or Maggie, but a stranger with whom there's a spark.

Reassuringly, we choose the same sandwiches as ever. Tuna and cucumber for Emma, Cheddar for me. Equally reassuringly, I have to pay because Emma has forgotten to go to the cash machine. I begin to relax. Emma is not a stranger to me.

On the other hand...

'I've never known you visit the gallery,' I say.

'There's a McTaggart painting of a seaside storm I like,' she says.

Why don't I know this? And how long do I have to wait before she tells me what we're doing here?

'It was a surprise to hear from you,' I say.

'I didn't know whether to call or not. I thought you might call me.'

'There didn't seem much point after what you slammed your door in my face and told me to fuck off.'

'I was drunk.'

She sits across from me, sipping Earl Grey tea, looking as beautiful as ever. It would be so easy to say yes, you were drunk, maybe I was too, we've blown the incident out of all proportion, let's not allow pride to stand in our way, let's get back together again.

That's what I want, isn't it? Our relationship may have been less than perfect but, after recent experiences, I'm in a better position to appreciate its merits. What is perfection anyway? No matter how much you love someone, you're never going to be entirely in synch. It's the nature of the human condition. People are different. Even Jenny and I had our arguments, but they never stopped me loving her.

Perhaps Emma and I needed a break to gain perspective. That's what trial separations are for. We needed this dark night of the soul to shed new daylight on what we mean to each other.

Is that why we're here? Is Emma feeling the same way? Has she come back to me?

'I was going to call,' she says, 'but Cate said there was no point. You told her you'd been wasting your time with me.'

'I didn't mean it.'

'See? It can happen.'

'So what are you saying?'

I wait for her to say the words I long to hear, but she has difficulty getting them out.

'What is it?' I say in my most supportive voice.

'There's something I need to tell you,' she says, then lets her hair cascade down to curtain her face. 'I met someone at Cate's wedding.'

'What?' That comes out less supportively.

'A man. Someone she works with. I gave him my phone number. I'm sorry. I was angry with you because you wouldn't wear your tie.'

Why is there never a pause button around when you need one? I need time to think. What exactly is she trying to tell me here?

She was angry with me, so she gave a strange man her phone number. That's not so bad, is it? That's the kind of action she would take to even a score. Now she's feeling guilty and she needs me to forgive her. I can do that.

'But I did wear my tie!'

It's not quite the conciliatory measure I was looking for. Emma gives me one of her stop-being-stupid looks.

But wait a minute...

'Was this before or after you jumped on me in the dining room?' I say.

'I didn't jump on you. Anyway, what does it matter? Before.'

Rewind and replay. Yes, it all makes sense now. Here is yet more evidence for my theory of life as a battle against unknown forces. Emma wasn't lusting after me at all. She jumped on me out of guilt. She'd given a strange man her phone number and she needed exculpation.

'Do you hate me?' she says.

'Of course I don't hate you.' In truth, it's a relief to discover the reason why she's been behaving...

'I had sex with him.'

'What?'

'I went out with him, we got drunk and we had sex.'

Suddenly everything is clear. This is why she stopped having sex with me. This is why she finished with me.

'Do you hate me now?' she says

What do love and hate have to do with it? I'm so shocked that there's no room for any other emotion. I stare vacant-eyed out of the window. Down on Princes Street, people go about their business as though they don't care that Emma has had sex with someone else.

It doesn't help that the same pesky demon that stopped me phoning her chooses this moment to pay another visit and remind me of my own past indiscretions. It tells me that, if I can justify having had sex with Cate last year, by saying that Emma and I never made a vow of monogamy, I can hardly deny Emma the same freedom.

On the other hand, I argue, I never denied Emma her conjugal deserts in the way that she...

'We've done it a few times and I like it.'

'What?'

Now what's she trying to tell me? That she didn't like it with me? That I'm no good in bed? Was slamming her door in my face not enough?

'It's not serious,' she says.

I *am* on a first date with a stranger. I don't know this woman at all.

'You're having sex with him, and you like it, and it's not serious?'

'I know.'

'What's his name?'

'Alec.'

As if it matters. What matters, what's absolutely clear, with no room for doubt, is that this is what she's brought me here to tell me. She's clearing the decks. She's not coming back to me at all.

'I was hoping we could still be friends,' she says in confirmation.

'You want to be friends, after all the things you said to me? After you've found someone else?'

'I understand if you don't want to.'

'But why?'

'Because I've missed seeing you.'

'It sounds like it.'

'I have. I never thought I would, but I have.'

'Why?'

'Because I can be myself with you. You know me.'

Once upon a time, maybe.

'Doesn't Alec know you?'

'Not like you do.'

So finally we come to the question that has been asked a million times in a million similar situations. The question without which our little tryst would be incomplete, without which I would be a traitor to my gender. Yet still I imbue it with a freshness belying its banality, a gravitas befitting its proud history and an apprehensiveness behoving its import.

'What kind of friends?'

'I don't know.' There's exasperation in her voice. I must be being stupid again. 'I don't blame you if you never want to see me again. I don't blame you if you hate me.'

'I don't hate you. How many more times do I have to tell you? I never have hated you and I never will.'

'Then can't we just see what happens?'

Her words hit me like a slap in the face. They're the same words Jenny used on our last night together.

She looks to me for a response, but I need a time-out to consult advisers. Negotiations are moving too fast. What kind of deal am I being offered here? Some sort of Platonic relationship? Wouldn't that involve all the same problems as before but without the sex? On the other hand, it's the only deal on the table. It's this or nothing.

'Okay,' I say. 'Let's see what happens.'

To bind me to my words forever, she seals the deal she has brokered in time-honoured fashion.

'I don't deserve you.'

This is the first line a girl hears her mother say to her father, the first sentence she learns to speak, the first compliment that comes into a woman's head when the currying of favour is required. It's calculated to make the recipient feel good about himself, while at the same time make her appear to be graciously accepting any blame that needs to be apportioned.

Even more, it invites, indeed demands, magnanimity on my part. If I don't forgive Emma for her transgressions, real or imaginary, if I don't accept her proffered hand of friendship, I'm a rat. *Rattus rattus*. The plague-carrying kind.

To salvage hope from our settlement, I console myself with the platitude that sometimes it is necessary to take one step backward in order to take two forward. Call it wishful thinking, but I convince myself that Emma's confession, far from dealing a death blow to our relationship, gives us new promise for the future.

She says she's not serious about this Alec person. She says she misses seeing me. Put these two admissions together and there are grounds for hope.

In retrospect, there was always too much left unsaid between us. Her new-found honesty could truly inaugurate a new chapter for us... especially when I have an offering of my own with which to establish equality. To assuage the guilt she feels at the way she has treated me. To confirm our new, open, caring, sharing relationship.

'There's something I think you should know too,' I say. 'I also had sex with someone while we were seeing each other.'

It's Emma's turn to look shocked.

'Who?'

'Cate.'

'Cate? My Cate?'

'Yes.'

I give her the time she needs to process this information. I understand that look of astonishment on her face. I know what she's going through. I've just been there myself.

'When?' she says at length.

'Last year was the last time.'

'The last time?'

I wait for her to inquire further. Instead, she pushes my tea cup over the edge of the table. A stream of steaming hot, freshly brewed Darjeeling lands on my lap. While I yelp, she stands up and walks out.

As I was saying earlier, there's an unnamed island off the coast of Hiva Oa...

How could I have been so stupid as to imagine even for a nanosecond that Emma would come back to me? They never come back.

Too often I have pursued love like escaping POW Frank Sinatra runs after the train that will take him to freedom in *Von Ryan's Express*. He reaches and reaches for that last carriage but, no matter how many times the film airs, he never makes it. The Nazis always gun him down.

Maybe I'm meant to be alone. I've been in love once. Nothing could ever match what I had with Jenny, so what's the point in looking? My God, was that it? A mere two years of bliss out of a whole lifetime?

Was that my ration? Was that my one and only shot at happiness?

16.

I haven't told you anything about Jenny, have I? The truth is, I'm scared to. I can be flippant about Morwenna and Maggie. I can be pragmatic about Emma. Anyone else you want to know about from my less than Technicolor past, just ask. But not Jenny. I'm scared to resurrect the memories.

I'll tell you how serious it was. She was the one person in my life I would have died for. Try and be flippant about that. Two years we went out. Two whole years. That might not rate a blip on a cosmic time-scale, but it's a long time to be with someone you would die for.

Twenty-five months. One hundred and eight weeks. Seven hundred and fifty-five days. I can tell you the hours and minutes if you're interested. If you're not interested, fast forward to the next chapter. I've never been keen on flashbacks myself. But if I don't tell you about Jenny now I never will.

We met at one of those parties where, as soon you set foot inside the door, you know you've made a mistake. I was alone in the kitchen, propping up the wall, cradling a Coors, when in she walked. Of all the gin joints in all the towns in all the world…

Unexpectedly, given my problems with strange women who sneak up on me, I felt an immediate ease in her company. It's this I remember more than any physical attraction. In any case, with her boyish figure and angular features, she wasn't drop-dead gorgeous in the way that Emma is. She was more cute than beautiful.

Mind you, she became beautiful to me. I would come to cherish every expanse, every nook and cranny, every blemish of her body, and to spend hours mesmerised by the topography of her face, as though it were a Cubist masterpiece.

She took a Coors from the fridge.

'Great minds think alike,' I said. Right from the start, she could reduce me to cliché.

'So do we,' she said.

I forget how, but we quickly became immersed in effortless conversation. We discussed the relative merits of European and American beers, empathised about the cliquishness of the party and at some indefinable point crossed the invisible boundary that separates the sociable from the personal.

I was twenty-seven, she was twenty-two. Yes, I was single. No, I had no girlfriend. No, it wasn't by design. She was also single. A student. Social science, whatever that was. I never did fully understand, even after two years.

It was only after she left the kitchen that I fully appreciated what had just happened. The ease between us had blinded me to it. A spark incandescent enough to ignite a sodden rainforest after the wettest downpour since records began.

One thing was for sure. I couldn't leave the party now. I had to stand guard beside the fridge. It never occurred to me to go and look for her, or that she might leave before she needed another beer.

Fortunately, although I later learned it was intentional, she did return to the kitchen. When she saw me, still propped against the wall in exactly the same pose, she giggled. My God, her giggle! I'd forgotten her giggle.

'It must be *déjà vu*,' she said as she retrieved another Coors.

'All over again,' I said.

In that moment more than words passed between us. Perhaps, so great was the spark between us, an electrical current jumped the gap. Perhaps it was a flash of recognition. It was certainly something uncanny, unsettling. A *Damage* moment.

When Jeremy Irons and Juliette Binoche first set eyes on each other in *Damage*, they're mesmerised. They try to talk but their conversation dissolves into silence, their sentences unfinished. The world stops. They just stand and stare at each other.

'Would you like to go out some time?' I said without a trace of my normal reticence. I've never been so forward, before or since.

In reply, she took a pen from the table and wrote a phone number on the back of my hand.

'Give me a call,' she said and left. I didn't see her again that evening.

When, a few days later, I finally plucked up the courage to make that call, it was brief and to the point. The effort required to fool myself into believing that rejection was unimportant left me too anxious to hold a conversation. I must have arranged to meet her, but I don't recall how.

Then, when we did meet for coffee at Black Medicine, I was nervous because she *did* want to see me. I can never win. I could barely raise my cup to my lips. The only thing that saved me from complete disintegration was the fact that Jenny was as bad. We sat opposite each other in the far corner of the coffee bar and studied the wooden table top until we knew every knot by heart. Yet in retrospect, it was that mutual ineptitude that confirmed our feelings for each other.

This became apparent on our next date when, over bottles of Coors at Bannerman's, we rediscovered the facility of our first meeting. And much more. So much more. That night, in accordance with Scott's Three-Date Rule, she stayed with me, and after that there was no space between us for further diffidence.

We soon became everything to each other. We worked on so many levels. Emotional. Intellectual. Social. You name it. We came to crave each other's presence. We became each other's obsession.

She rented a room in a student flat in Marchmont but she spent most nights with me. Only the nights made the days apart bearable. It wasn't the sex (at least it wasn't *just* the sex), it was the togetherness. Without each other, we felt incomplete.

Mind you, the sex was a revelation. Jenny wasn't my first sexual partner, but she was the first woman I'd encountered who regarded sex as an equal opportunity.

Once she lay back with absolute trust and said, 'Do anything you want with me.'

'I am,' I said.

For once I find it difficult to tell you details. It was too…

It was too *precious*.

On another occasion we were so full of feeling for each other that we couldn't concentrate on the mechanics of sex and gave up trying. If you've ever been totally satiated simply by staring into someone else's eyes, you'll know what I'm talking about. If you haven't, nothing I can say will explain that intensity to you.

Hers were a sienna sunburst, flecked with emerald rays.

I loved everything about her. The way she curled up on my lap, the way she ritualistically plucked her eyebrows, the way she stood cross-legged while waiting in a queue, the way she listened intently with her mouth open until she became aware of it and clamped it shut, even the way she picked her ear, using her little finger to probe more deeply. There was nothing she could do, no state her body could get into, in sickness or in health, that I didn't love.

She had her faults, I suppose, but to me they were appealing idiosyncrasies. They say that's how you recognise true love, isn't it? She also knew only too well how to wind me up, but I loved her even for that. For *knowing* how to. Even our rare arguments disintegrated into laughter. We could no more sustain anger against each other than you can against yourself.

For two years we lived every cliché in the romance manual. As far as we were concerned, ours was the greatest love affair ever.

In which case, you must be thinking, why did it end? No, it didn't end. Let's say it plainly. Jenny dumped me.

For Jenny, you see, love wasn't enough. The nine-to-five office job she took after graduating frustrated her in a way that couldn't be compensated for by the feelings she had for me.

She became restless. She started to joke about quitting her job and travelling around the world. She complained that I was too settled. I didn't understand the accusation. If you have a lover, what more can you want?

But Jenny did want more. Our love didn't fulfil her. I suppose that was the big difference between us. Love fulfils me.

Her family didn't help. Her father, a no-nonsense business executive, took one look at the collar-length hair I sported in those days and took an instant dislike to me. I was too old and too bohemian for his daughter.

I cultivated his approval but it was hopeless. I think he was jealous of me for replacing him in Jenny's affections. Not that I did. She loved him in a way that brooked no argument, as daughters sometimes do. She was a daddy's girl. The whole situation put great pressure on our relationship.

Anyway, do you ever really know why a lover dumps you? Maybe even Jenny didn't know completely.

One night, it was 4 a.m. to be precise, I'm not likely to forget, we awoke and made love, languidly, effortlessly. Then:

'There's something I have to tell you,' she said. 'I'm leaving my job.'

'You are?'

'I've decided to go to Australia with Jackie.' Jackie was her best friend.

'Australia?' I was suddenly wide awake. It wasn't like her to spring such a momentous decision on me without prior consultation. 'When? How long for?'

'I don't know.'

'What about us?'

'Can't we just see what happens?'

For virtually the first (and certainly the last) time in our relationship, I was lost for words. There was no big argument, not then, because I didn't realise that this was the end of us.

I couldn't understand how she could want to go to Australia without me but, if she needed to quit her job and travel for a while, I should be the last person to stand in her way. I of all people wanted her to be happy, didn't I?

'Okay,' I said, 'if that's what you want.'

'I don't deserve you,' she said.

The big argument started the following morning, when I redis-covered the petulant child in me. I was pathetic. 'How can you do this?' 'What am I going to do?' 'Don't you love me any more?' It hurt that she couldn't say yes to that last one. She was confused, she said. She was no longer sure what she wanted.

The more I pleaded with her the worse I made the situation, but still I pleaded. She was my life and she was taking it away from me.

'Maybe a break will do us good,' she said finally and, when she left that morning, she even took her toothbrush with her.

We saw each other again after that, but she never stayed with me again, never made love with me again, never even kissed me again. Slowly but surely she eased herself out of my life.

I made things worse by pressurising her with every ploy I could devise to win her back, unaware. Maybe if I'd behaved differently... I still torture myself with that thought. Instead, I diligently worked my way through the same dog-eared five-act script used by every spurned lover in history.

Act 1: Denial. You still love me, I told her. Deep down inside, you can never stop loving me. We were made for each other.

Act 2: Anger. You're acting like an idiot. You have no feelings. You think you can go around treating people like shit.

Act 3: Aloofness. Okay, so you need a break. You'll soon realise what you're missing. You'll soon come running back.

She never did. She went to Australia. I never heard from her again.

Act 4: Worthlessness. I had given my all to another person and been found wanting. To know me was to leave me.

Losing Jenny was like a bereavement, except that she was still alive, which somehow made it worse, because she was still out there somewhere. Alive but unobtainable. Her name remained in the Edin-burgh telephone directory. I looked it up more times than I care to say.

I distinctly remember my lowest ebb. I went to a butcher's shop we liked. There was a queue and, by the time my turn came, I could barely speak. All because I wanted a pork chop. For *one*. I know it sounds pa-thetic. What can I say? It *was* pathetic.

I wallowed in memories of Jenny far longer than was good for me but there was no helping it. She was my last thought at night and my first on waking. Whenever I remembered a dream, it was about her.

You think more of what has been than what will be, Alpha 60 tells Lemmy Caution.

And then:

Act 5: Acceptance. There was no sudden realisation that life could go on, *was* going on, without Jenny. Just a gradual coming to terms with the loss. Time, the great healer. It's a cliché but, if there were no truth in it, it wouldn't be a cliché.

You can't wake up and cry every day, not indefinitely. We aren't made that way. Memories are forgotten or replaced. You meet new people, have new experiences. It's like Angela Bassett says in *Strange Days*, 'Memories were meant to fade. They're designed that way for a reason.'

I still remember the day when I felt the first faint glimmering of a possible future without Jenny. It was a day like any other – the sun rose, I went to work, I came home, the sun set – but on that day I made the momentous decision to suppress every thought of her before it was sufficiently formed to disturb me. It sounds simple. The reality was anything but.

I can't tell you how much determination it took to blank out images of her that I desperately wanted to acknowledge. I placed all the letters, the cards, the photographs, the airline tickets from our holiday in Majorca, all the evidence of our love, in a foolscap folder and hid it away in the bottom of a drawer. It still lies there. A part of my life that is filed away for ever.

After years of painstaking practice I have now become so adept at dismissing thoughts of Jenny from my mind that sometimes I can't even recall the look of her face or the sound of her voice. Yet there are still other moments when a vision of her catches me unawares, invading my mind with such clarity that I reel on my feet.

It's ridiculous. With Jenny I had the most wonderful experiences of my life and I deliberately try to forget them. It seems like a betrayal. I am a traitor to our love. But what else can I do? I have to find some way to go on.

I take ironic comfort in the dying words of the evil Messala in *Ben-Hur*, after he has been reduced to pulp beneath Judah's chariot wheels. Judah thinks his troubles will die with Messala, but Messala isn't one to go gracefully. He takes hold of Judah's tunic in a death grip to tell him that his long-lost family are still alive… but dying of the plague. With his last rasping breath he says:

'It goes on, Judah.'

17.

I'm glad I told you about Jenny. Maybe there's a place for flashbacks after all. The memories bring sadness but also a new resolve. Instead of succumbing to terminal pessimism at the impossibility of ever finding someone to replace her in my affections, I remember that I am capable of loving and, perhaps even more importantly, capable of being loved.

Maybe the ancient Romans were right. They had a proverb that I came across in a self-help book I happened to glance through (purely by chance) in the months following Jenny's departure. *Quisque Amavit Cras Amet*. Whoever Has Loved, May Love Tomorrow. Just because it didn't work out with Jenny and Emma doesn't mean I won't find love elsewhere.

Instead of emigrating to French Polynesia, I've decided to cultivate a more existential acceptance of my lot, like the hero of some 1960s French *Nouvelle Vague* movie. I could never wear a Homburg with the panache of Lemmy Caution but, if I had a beret, I bet I wouldn't look out of place in the Café de Flore in post-World War II Paris, shooting the breeze with Jean-Paul Sartre and Simone de Beauvoir.

It helps that it's August. In Edinburgh that means Festival time. There is so much going on, in theatres and bars, in back-street halls, on and off the streets, from early one morning to early the next, so many foreign tongues, so much colour and commotion. Edinburgh is the place to be at this time of year. In winter it may retreat behind a cool Calvinist veneer, but in August it's as cosmopolitan a city as any budding *philosophe* could wish to find.

It doesn't even look like a British city, with Princes Street Gardens in full bloom beneath a towering castle that wouldn't look out of place on a Rhineland hilltop. It's this combination of historic setting and cutting-edge culture that gives the place its Festival frisson.

When Godard made *Alphaville*, he found his vision of a nightmare futuristic city by filming Paris at night from unusual angles. You could never do that with Edinburgh. Edinburgh could never look like a nightmare. It has its less salubrious areas, like any other big city, but you'd have to go further than in most to find them, and who wants to look?

Many of my fellow residents shrink from the summer influx and wait for autumn to reclaim the city for themselves, but I embrace the crowds. They give me anonymity. They give me freedom. They ask nothing of me. In these crowds I can be alone yet still part of the surge of life.

Above all, August is Film Festival time. This year there's a John Ford retrospective and *The Searchers*, one of my favourite movies, is showing on a Saturday afternoon at Filmhouse Cinema One.

The auditorium is full of fans who, like me, know the film frame by frame. Even so, it's a revelation. Most of us probably haven't seen it on the big screen before. You can sense the audience anticipation as each famous scene arrives. At the climax, when John Wayne rescues kidnapped Natalie Wood from the Injuns, lifts her into his arms and says 'Let's go home,' we applaud. It's an exhilarating experience.

Afterwards, I'm standing in the foyer among the milling crowd, reluctant to leave, when I feel a tug at my sleeve. It's one of Scott's two lassies from Accounts. The quiet one. Lisa.

'Did you enjoy the film?' she says. She's wearing a fitted top whose floral motif draws my gaze to her bust before I manage to refocus.

'Hi. Yes. Thanks. It's one of my favourites. Did you see it?'

'I was sitting two rows behind you.'

'Did *you* enjoy it?'

'Yes. Thanks. I like John Wayne films.'

For an unguarded moment she forgets herself and smiles, then just as quickly retreats into her shell. She's worried a show of enthusiasm will prompt me to quiz her on the actor's filmography.

'Most women I know hate Westerns,' I say.

'I don't like *all* Westerns.'

'*I* don't like *all* Westerns.'

That successfully inhibits her from venturing any further opinions. Sometimes I think I must have been off school the day they taught conversational skills.

'What's your favourite Western?' I say.

'*The Searchers.*'

She must be wishing she'd never accosted me. It's probably as much a relief to her as it is to me when another tug at my elbow gives us distraction. This time it's Alasdair. I should have known he'd be here.

'Will you ever see a better film?' he says gruffly.

Lisa retreats a step, as visibly intimidated by his manner as Emma used to be. Can't she see he's only playing the harmless straight man? I oblige by supplying John Wayne's classic punchline.

'That'll be the day.'

Reassured, Lisa covers her mouth with her hand and giggles, whether at my perfect reproduction of Duke's trademark drawl, or the opposite, I'm not sure. Alasdair's sure. He shakes his head pityingly.

'There's something I've always wondered,' he says. 'When Wayne rides out of the desert at the start of the film, what's his back story? What's he been up to?'

'Fighting Injuns, probably.'

'I think we should be told.'

'What does it matter?'

'It's symbolic,' Lisa says bravely.

'Excuse me?' says Alasdair.

'The desert,' she says, though with less assurance now that she has to justify her assertion to a Desperate Dan lookalike. 'It's a symbol of the emptiness of his life. He's coming in from the cold.' Her voice trails away as she realises that desert temperatures don't quite support her interpretation.

Sheepishly, she draws in her lips, in the manner of Scarlett Johansson in *Girl With a Pearl Earring*, and licks them with her mouth closed. Alasdair gives me a sidelong glance.

'She works at the Bank,' I say by way of explanation. It doesn't occur to me to introduce them.

In honour of our newly formed John Wayne appreciation society, and my recognition as its social hub, I ask the other two founder members if they'd like to join me for coffee, but Alasdair has to rush off to see another film and Lisa mumbles something about having a prior engagement.

Oh, well. I like being alone in the crowd, don't I? The anonymity, the freedom… After they've gone, I sit at a corner table in the Filmhouse bar, sip cappuccino and people-watch. The trouble is, without a companion to talk to, there's nothing to do *but* drink cappuccino.

Ten minutes later I walk into the daytime heat as if into a wall. The brightness makes me squint. The castle shimmers in the haze as though it's floating in the sky. It looks like one of those pale watercolour backdrops of Edinburgh that Disney had painted for *Greyfriars Bobby*.

The heat too isn't real, I tell myself. It's a special effect. It's all in the mind. In which case… I stroll down Lothian Road with my jacket hooked over my shoulder, convinced I'm as cool as Jean-Luc makes Jean-Paul Belmondo look in *À Bout de Souffle*.

As I approach the junction with Princes Street the crowds increase in density. Two men lie on the tarmac about fifty metres apart. There must have been an accident. The traffic is backed up in both directions. Rubberneckers clog the pavements. Then I notice that the men are moving and that no one is helping them.

A flyer for a Fringe production is thrust into my hand. *The Presidential Election Viewed as an Ascent of Mount Everest*. Only now do I see that the two men are joined by a climbing rope. To drum up business, they're making a horizontal ascent of Lothian Road, using lampposts as belay points. An approaching siren heralds the imminent arrival of the local constabulary.

I detour around the onlooking crowd by cutting through the grounds of St John's Church, forgetting that it hosts an equally congested craft fair for the duration of the Festival. Painstakingly I work my way past paintings, mirrors, candles, beads, leatherwork, more mirrors, knitwear and... Behind a stall selling wooden knickknacks I spot a vaguely familiar face.

'Megan?'

'Hi!' she says when she recognises me. She's so pleased to see me that she even comes out from behind her table to give me a hug.

She's barely recognisable as the same person I last saw on the evening that Emma dumped me. She's wearing some kind of ethnic outfit, all reds and golds. The colours dazzle in the bright sunlight. When I compliment her on it, I learn that it consists of a traditionally woven *campesino* dress from the Potosí region of Bolivia, offset by a headband made from Peruvian alpaca wool.

It turns out she's given up teaching and, following a month's break in Peru, has developed a passion for all things South American, including the artefacts she's selling here. Some she acquired on her travels, others she made herself.

I pick up a wooden cube with a hole in it. It's a candle holder, she tells me. The metal poles that support the stall are hung with reproductions of Incan masks of death and rebirth. Half the table top is devoted to a selection of panpipes. Megan explains the difference between a *tarka* and a *zampoña*. In the background, music from both plays on an old tape recorder.

'The people who make these are so poor,' she says, 'but their music has so much joy. I learned a lot from them.'

It's hard to believe this is the same Megan who used to go out with Richard. The change I noticed in her after Cate's wedding was obviously only the first stage in a complete metamorphosis. In her startling dress, she looks positively radiant. She's even managed to do something with her hair, which now hangs in attractive curls about her ears. It's a transformation worthy of the shape-shifting liquid metal android in *Terminator 2*.

'How's Richard?' she says.

'He's fine.'

'I wasn't right for him,' she says judiciously. 'He needed someone more settled.'

You wouldn't think so if you saw him now, I'm tempted to say, but I restrain myself. I can hardly tell her he's become a disco stud.

'I heard about you and Emma,' she says.

'You did? What did you hear?'

'She told me what happened. I'm sorry it didn't work out.'

'Emma told you?'

'Can I ask you a favour?' she says before I can inquire further. 'Would you mind watching the stall while I nip to the loo?'

She skips away before I can object. For all I know she's done no business all day but, as soon as she leaves, an obese American couple in matching khaki shorts stop to inspect the wares. I stand behind the table and adopt a proprietary air. The woman molests the pieces with podgy fingers, holds up a wooden figurine and asks what it is.

'I'm just looking after the stall for a few minutes. The owner will be back soon.'

'It's an Incan mummy,' says a voice that gives me a start.

When I look up, Emma stands before me. Uncannily sensing my discomfort from afar, she's rushed across town to my rescue.

The woman drops the figurine in horror and waddles away with her consort, leaving me alone with my saviour.

'What are you doing here?' she says.

'I was just passing and I bumped into Megan. What are you doing here?'

'I have a stall here every year.'

Of course she does.

'So you and Megan are friends now?'

'Everybody knows everybody here.'

She makes me feel like I'm trespassing. Far from coming to save me, she's come to evict me.

'Where is she?' she says accusingly.

'She's gone to the loo. You don't have to stay. I can look after the stall until she comes back. I'll tell her you were looking for her.'

'I didn't come over here to see her.'

I become aware of a glass of water on the corner of the table. In view of our last meeting in Jenners restaurant, I move it out of Emma's reach and check for other expendable objects from which I might be in danger.

'Don't worry,' she says. 'You're safe. I came to say I'm sorry about last time. You know – the tea.'

'That's okay,' I say, although I don't mean it.

'I've had time to think about things since then. I don't blame you any longer, for what you did with Cate, I mean. You're a man. You couldn't help yourself. And it was no different to what I did with Alec. Things were never right between us, were they?'

As was ever the way of it, Emma's confusion of arguments leaves me struggling in her wake. Is she really forgiving me here? If so, is my behaviour to be excused on the grounds that I'm a helpless man or on the grounds that she behaved equally badly? And what's this about us never being right for each other? As Robert Redford says of his ex-wife in *The Horse Whisperer*, 'I didn't love her because it was right. I just loved her.'

'It's Cate I blame,' she says.

So, she hasn't talked herself round to complete forgiveness, then. Some blame still needs to be apportioned. I suppose I should be grateful it's no longer coming my way, but…

Would you believe it? Instead of accepting my acquittal with good grace, I'm actually going to risk re-opening the case against me by standing up for Cate. After the way she summarily dumped me, as well. I'm my own worst enemy.

'Why blame anyone? Can't we just forget the whole thing? Cate's your friend.'

'Not any more. Not after what she did.'

'Why is that any different to what you did?'

'Are you still seeing her?'

'No! I never was seeing her. What about this Alec guy? Are you still seeing him?'

'Sort of.'

'Sort of?'

She shrugs. It's the only answer I'm going to get.

'So where does that leave us?' I say.

'Can't we just see what happens?'

'That's what you said last time, before you poured tea over me.'

'I said I'm sorry. What more do you want?'

'Okay, okay.' As she's about to produce the deeds to our settlement, I have no choice but to retake my vows. 'Let's see what happens.'

'I'd better get back to my stall,' she says.

A strand of hair falls down over her eye, making me suddenly nostalgic. Without thinking, I brush it away with my fingers. That's the kind of thing you do for Emma. Something about her invites that level of protectiveness. I once saw a woman on a station platform, a complete stranger, take out a tissue and, without a word, wipe a dirty mark off Emma's handbag.

'Will I see you again?' I say.

'You can see me next week if you like.'

'If you like.'

'Next Saturday, here, at five o'clock. It's the last day of the fair. You can help me pack my stuff.'

Without waiting for an answer, she disappears into the crowd.

Surprisingly, the encounter leaves me feeling more positive about us than before. She doesn't want to pour hot tea over me any longer. She wants to see me again. I'm under no illusion that she's going to come back to me, but at least she's not going to disappear into the ether like Jenny did.

Even if it's only to help her pack, I finally have some useful function in her life. I haven't been irretrievably discarded. I'm not completely worthless. In keeping with my new existential approach to life, it's a lot I can accept.

Perhaps Emma and I can be friends after all.

18.

For the first time since Emma dumped me, I feel that I'm ready to move on with my life, to confront whatever or whoever next turns up on my doorstep.

It turns out to be Cate. Literally. She doesn't phone, she just turns up on my doorstep. It's as big a surprise as discovering that one of the *Sons of the Musketeers* is Maureen O'Hara. (It was on the box the other day.)

Involuntarily, I back away. Cate hasn't spoken to me since I accused her of marrying a sidekick. Now she's standing on my doorstep, tapping a sharp-pointed umbrella rhythmically against her leg, as though she's about to bayonet me. When seconds pass and she doesn't, I invite her in.

We sit side by side on the couch and make more polite conversation than we have in our entire history. Even when she was Sam, we had more to talk about. She hopes she's not disturbing me. I say it's a surprise to see her. She informs me that it's raining outside.

Only when she tells me that she was upset after our last phone call do we rediscover our former intimacy.

'*You* were upset?' I say. 'You said Emma was well rid of me. You told her not to phone me.'

'Well, you said you'd been wasting your time with her.'

'Well, she said she'd been wasting her time with me.'

'You said I treated her like a sidekick.'

'You said I was selfish.'

Then she starts crying. I've never seen her cry before. I didn't know she could.

'I'm sorry,' I say. 'I didn't mean to...'

'It's not you,' she says.

Tears roll unchecked down her cheeks. I wonder whether some kind of protective gesture is required of me. I start to put my arm around her shoulder, let it hover for a moment, then withdraw it again. She solves my dilemma by burying her head in my lap with a suddenness that makes me flinch.

'I've lost my baby,' she says between sobs, correctly assuming that I would know of her pregnancy.

'What? When? How?'

I may not be the most helpful person to turn to in such circumstances, but my incomprehension is exactly what she needs, because she can explain her miscarriage to me in graphic detail. I get the over-18 feature-length version in Sensurround with...

No, I don't mean to be flippant. I feel sorry for her. I *do*. I console her as best I can. I listen, I commiserate, I stroke her hair.

'I had to talk to someone,' she says.

'What about Calum?'

'I can't talk to him about it.'

'Why not?'

'Because it wasn't his baby.'

She can hardly get the words out for crying. There's a growing wet patch around my crotch.

'Whose was it?'

'You wouldn't know him. It was an accident.'

I keep stroking her hair. Whatever misunderstandings we've had, I now realise they meant nothing. We're friends. You don't stay angry at friends when they need you.

'I wish there was something I could do to help,' I say.

'You are helping.' She sits up and looks at me with big wet eyes that bring a lump to my throat. 'I'm sorry.'

'Don't be. I'm glad you came.'

'I didn't know who else to turn to.'

'What about Emma?'

'Em's not speaking to me. She blames me for what we did.'

'I'm sure she'd speak to you if she knew.'

'No. She says I betrayed her.'

'Let me talk to her.'

'No.'

She says it with such finality that it makes me wonder whether I'm the only person who knows of her situation.

'Calum does know, doesn't he?'

'Of course. I could hardly keep it from him. He's doing his best to be supportive. He makes me cups of tea and runs baths for me, but if he's not careful...' She pauses to consider the import of what she's about to add. 'I'm a terrible person. The harder he tries, the more irritated I get with him.'

There's a lot I could say here, but I restrain myself.

'Can I ask a favour of you?' she says, dabbing the wetness from her cheeks. 'Can I stay the night?'

That's a conversation stopper.

'I don't mean for sex,' she says when she sees the startled look on my face. 'God, that's the last thing I want just now.'

'Of course you can stay,' I say with relief. 'But what about Calum?'

'I'll phone him. I'll say I'm staying at Em's.'

'I'll make up the bed in the back room.'

'Can't I sleep with you? I just want to be close to someone.'

Someone other than her husband, obviously. I'm actually beginning to feel sorry for him. Still, I can hardly say no, can I?

After she's phoned Calum, we have mugs of hot chocolate and go to bed. I'm not quite sure what the rules are, so I follow her lead. When she strips down to her underwear, I do too. We clamber under the duvet and she snuggles up to me. I put my arm around her and pull her protectively towards me. She cries out in pain.

'What's wrong?' I say.

'My breasts,' she says. 'They're still tender. They're expecting to feed my baby.'

She starts crying again and I hold her more gently. She seems so fragile. I've never thought of Cate as fragile. My heart goes out to her. She cries herself to sleep in my arms.

By morning there are no tears left and she's keen to get home. There are explanations to give to Cal, there are family members to meet, there's a doctor's appointment, and so on. She says she can't thank me enough. I tell her to call me any time.

After she's gone, I've never felt less like going into the office. IT has never seemed such a trivial pursuit. I get through the day by throwing myself into the design of an interface for a new database query program. Its pointless intricacies prove comfortingly absorbing.

Of course, Richard would choose today to ask me out for a drink, and I can't refuse his olive branch because we've barely been on speaking terms since I threatened to bury his head in his computer screen.

After work we duly join the other suits in the Standing Order. Richard engages me in conversation so inane that it's clear we're not here merely to lubricate working relations. Like Cate last night, he's feeling his way towards telling me something.

'Have you heard from Emma?' he says when the time is right.

Immediately I'm on guard. If this is his opening gambit in a campaign to entice me back to Club Inferno, he can take his olive branch and shove it where all but systems analysts fear to go.

'She wants to be friends,' I say tentatively.

'Do you?'

'We'll see what happens.'

Then I understand. His intentions are entirely honourable, after all. I duly ask the question that *his* question was designed to elicit from me.

'How's Barbra?'

'She's good. I know you don't like her much, but...' He hesitates, starts to say something, decides against it, thinks again, wonders whether this was a good idea after all.

'I never said I didn't like her,' I say to encourage him. 'If *you* like her...'

'I do like her,' he says. 'More than I would have thought. I've never been out with anyone like her before. She has no airs and graces, no hang-ups, no baggage...'

He sounds as though he's trying to convince himself.

'So what's the problem?'

'She has nothing to say for herself. We never talk.' Then he goes for it. 'All she wants is sex.'

How am I supposed to respond to this? Apart from the fact that the image he's just implanted in my mind is going to be difficult to shift, he doesn't seem to realise that he's confiding in a born-again celibate who doesn't wish to be reminded of the fact.

'And you're complaining?' is the best I can come up with.

'I know, but sex isn't everything.'

'Sorry, I didn't realise, that night you left me at the club, that you'd gone back to her place for an intellectual discussion.'

'It's not funny.'

'Sorry again, but I thought the whole point of going out with Funny Girl *was* to have fun. What have you got to lose? Do these words sound familiar to you?'

'I know, but...' He looks at me with spaniel eyes. 'I miss Megan.'

That's another conversation stopper, equivalent to Cate's request to spend the night with me. Of all the semi-annual girlfriends he has conjured up, I've never heard him admit to missing one of them. In fact, I do believe this is the first heartfelt emotion he's ever confided in me. I'm genuinely touched. And slightly unnerved.

Perhaps I've been too quick to judge his recent behaviour. Perhaps, like me, he's had some issues to work through. Fresh from my success with Cate, I offer him advice.

'I bumped into her at the craft fair,' I say.

'Megan? How is she?'

'She's selling South American knick-knacks.'

'I don't understand.'

'She's given up teaching and started selling Incan artefacts.'

Judging from his expression, this doesn't improve his comprehension any.

'Look,' I say, 'it doesn't matter what she's doing now. What's important is that she's moved on, and so should you. If it's not working out with Barbra, move on again.' This is my life-enhancing advice for everyone at the moment, including myself.

There are only a few months to go until Christmas and Richard always finds another partner at Christmas. I almost tell him this, but worry that it will break the spell, like when an actor over-analyses his technique.

'I know you're right,' he says without conviction.

Not for the first time in recent memory, we stand at the edge of the precipice of male bonding. In joint recognition of this precarious position, we pull back as one and return to discussing more impersonal matters until it's deemed time to go home.

A few days later my counselling skills are in demand again. This time it's Calum who turns up on my doorstep. My doorbell has never seen so much action.

He hopes he's not disturbing me but he wants to ask me about Cate.

'She told me she stayed with you the other night,' he says. 'I'm worried about her. Do you think she's going to be all right?' I wait. 'Or not?'

He looks so helpless that I invite him in. He doesn't question me about Cate's sleepover. It would never occur to him that she slept in my bed, or that her child wasn't his. He looks more bemused than ever. Cate lost him along with her baby, if not long before.

'I'm worried about her,' he says again.

'She'll be okay.'

'What if the Dark Side prevails?'

Dark Side? What Dark Side? Fortunately, I don't say this out loud.

'You make sure it doesn't,' I say.

He doesn't stay for long. Re-motivated by my support, he has to go home to summon up the Forces of Light.

I feel sorry for him, especially given the way his wife is treating him, but I'm not about to cast spells with him. He must have his own friends to turn to, mustn't he? I may have become the world's agony uncle, but I can't solve everyone's problems. I'm only just beginning to address my own.

When he leaves, he thanks me.

'Any time,' I say. 'May the Force be with you.'

At the end of the week I visit Emma at the craft fair, as promised.

When I pass Megan's stall she again greets me with a hug. She tells me she's off to Patagonia to trek around the Torres del Paine, then she's going to work her way up through Argentina and Chile, and then, well, she'll *see what happens*. She's picked up Emma's mantra.

'Who knows where life will take us?' she says and presses a coloured pebble into my hand. 'It's an Aymará good luck charm, from Bolivia. It will help you find someone.'

This brief encounter with Megan turns out to be more fulfilling than the ensuing couple of hours with Emma. I've come in a positive frame of mind, but she's in work mode, totally immune to distraction. She treats me as little more than a hired hand. I wrap pots, carry crates and load her car. She thanks me for my help but checks and double checks everything I do. Nothing is to her satisfaction.

I hitch a lift back to her flat, help carry her stuff upstairs and invite her out for coffee, but she's meeting people from the craft fair later and she's beginning to feel rushed. I leave voluntarily before I'm dismissed.

Her indifference towards me is revealing. More than any amount of anger, more than a new boyfriend, more than a new low-necked top, it's final proof that she's moved on from me. A few short weeks ago, that realisation would have been hard to take, but I'm becoming accustomed to my new status.

As I leave her flat, my overriding feeling is one of relief. Relief that she hasn't hurt me. Relief that perhaps she can no longer hurt me. It persuades me that I really do have her in some kind of perspective. That I have... what's the word... closure. Yes, that's it. Closure.

It's such a comforting feeling that I make a promise to myself.

From now on, nothing and no one is going to be allowed to disturb my equanimity.

19.

Each season in Edinburgh brings something new to look forward to and autumn is no exception. With the tourist tumult of the Festival over and the excitements of Christmas and Hogmanay still to come, the city settles down to a few months of peace.

It is a time for moderation. The sky has neither the hazy languor of summer nor the crisp clarity of winter, the days are neither long nor short, the temperature fluctuates between high and low as if unable to make up its mind.

A grey mantle envelops the city, sometimes literally, as the haar creeps in off the North Sea. The Seven Hills of Edinburgh peek above it like nunataks. In harmony with the city, I too feel becalmed between what has gone and what will be.

I continue to see Emma but, now that we can no longer hurt each other, our occasional meetings over coffee are little more than opportunities to update each other on our lives. Physical contact is limited to a tentative hug when we meet and part. When she tells me about her latest pots, I listen. Sometimes I'm even interested. Mostly I'm just being polite. What I'm really doing, from the high ground of hindsight, is wondering what happened to us, where we went wrong, whether it was inevitable.

She spends most weekdays throwing vases commissioned at the craft fair, while at weekends she gets drunk with the new friends she made there. This year's fair has been quite a turning point in her life. She has left the craft co-operative and now works in a converted conservatory belonging to a new colleague who is a stained glass maker.

She's still seeing Alec, but she shows more passion for ceramics than she does for him. Perhaps it's true, what she told me when we still discussed such matters, that it really isn't serious for her.

Once the rush of pre-Christmas craft fairs is over and she sits down to take stock, that's when the true test of her feelings for him will come. When the future stretches before her unsignposted, when she starts to panic at the choices to be made... Let's see if Alec can survive that.

She sees more of Cate than she does of me. That's right, they're on speaking terms again. Cate did the same thing to Emma as she did to me. She turned up unannounced on her doorstep, full of apology and need. You could have predicted Emma would be a sucker for that. In *Alphaville,* where tears are forbidden, a dying fellow secret agent tells Lemmy Caution to *Save those who weep*. That could be Emma's motto.

Except where I'm concerned, of course. If I tried that tactic she'd hit the highway faster then Road Runner in flight from Wile E. Coyote. She can handle me as long as I make no demands on her, whereas the exact opposite is the case with Cate. Cate's need has brought a new equality to their relationship. Emma's anger at her best friend's indiscretion with me has evaporated along with her feelings for me. The two of them have never been closer.

Following my recent abortive excursions onto the social scene, I've retreated to the sanctuary of my flat. The emptiness I found so oppressive after Emma left now seems welcome. Undisturbed, I spend most evenings watching DVDs. Alasdair has moved up the pecking order of my acquaintances to become my prime social contact. Director's Cut is my social hub.

The high point of October is when his new list goes up. Top Ten Best Cuts. At Number One he has *North By Northwest*. Cary Grant pulls Eve Marie Saint from the rock face of Mount Rushmore straight into the top bunk of a sleeper compartment, after which the phallic train symbolically enters a tunnel. More for the sake of conversation than argument, I take issue with his choice. For my Number One I want the interleaved subliminal edits in *The Pawnbroker*.

Not a riveting way to spend an evening, you might think but, to maintain the equanimity I've promised myself, I'm content to remain *un*rivetted. I can do without more drunken evenings clubbing with Richard, to say nothing of blind dates with the likes of Morwenna and Maggie.

Even emigration to French Polynesia is losing its appeal. When I think of the logistics... the travel arrangements, the medical requirements, the financial considerations, the paperwork... No. For the moment, I'll stick with existential acceptance of my lot.

In any case, a desert island might not be the refuge I imagined it to be. It could be nothing more than a symbol of the emptiness of my life, like Lisa from Accounts said of John Wayne's desert in *The Searchers*. I'm reminded of this when I venture out of my flat one Sunday afternoon and bump into her again.

It must be the romantic in me but, when the city is at its most monochrome, I find myself seeking out its secret enclaves of autumn colour. One of my favourite haunts, when turning leaves carpet the riverside walkway, is the deep valley of the Water of Leith between Stockbridge and Dean Village.

Cocooned against the wind and rain inside my hooded anorak, I follow the path under Dean Bridge, through the gorge that encloses the village, past the waterfall formed by the weir, into a wild dell where tall trees thick with ivy crowd high banks. It's a stretch of temperate jungle in the heart of the city, except for a small clearing where a storm-damaged tree has been removed and replaced by a bench, and on that bench I find Lisa.

I don't mean to creep up on her, but she's so lost in thought that she jumps when I greet her.

'I thought I was the only idiot who came out in this weather,' I say, then realise I've just implied she's an idiot too.

'What's wrong with it?' she says abstractedly, looking through me rather than at me.

I've clearly disturbed some deep reverie. She's wearing nothing more substantial than jeans and an old woollen jumper, yet seems oblivious to their clinging wetness.

'There's nothing wrong with it,' I say. 'I like the rain. It makes the leaves sparkle. We could be in the rainforest here.'

She turns her attention back to the river.

'Or the desert.'

What's this obsession with deserts? She's an enigmatic one, is Lisa.

'It must be the sand and the heat that does it,' I say.

'It's the space,' she says.

That's exactly the kind of thing I'm talking about.

'There's not much space here,' I say, gesturing towards the steep valley sides.

She continues to stare at the water, mesmerised by the current. Droplets of water drip unnoticed from her short blonde hair.

'There could be,' she says. 'You can't see anything beyond the trees. You can't hear anything beyond the waterfall. There could be anything out there.'

She's like fragile thistledown waiting for the next breath of wind to carry her away. If she were wearing a thin cotton dress, you could imagine her as one of those ethereal girls who disappear mysteriously among the crags in *Picnic At Hanging Rock*.

'That's what makes it safe here,' she says.

I feel as though I've walked into a cinema halfway through the film and I can't pick up the plot.

She shivers and curls her fingers into her sleeves.

'Are you okay?'

'Yes. Don't let me keep you.'

I take that as my cue to leave. Whatever parallel world Lisa from Accounts is inhabiting today, there's patently no place in it for someone exuding autumnal equanimity. I don't wish to harp on again about my theory of life as a battleground against unknown forces, but who knows what circumstances have brought her to this bench, in this clearing, in this weather, in this impenetrable mood?

I'm happy to move on because I'm in a contemplative mood myself, because of Morwenna of all people. I never expected to give her another thought after that evening at Scott's, but now I find myself having to reconsider the whole occasion. It turns out she had an unhappy childhood. Well, if you must know, Scott tells me that she told his wife that she was sexually abused by her father.

No wonder she has problems relating to men. I could kick myself for the cavalier way I treated her. A Roundhead should know better. I've probably set her back ten years.

Okay, so I wasn't in possession of all the facts, and Scott and his wife were equally dismissive, but even so… I cringe when I think of some of the things I said to her.

I can only hope I didn't cause her further hurt. I didn't mean to, but isn't that always the way of it? People hurt each other all the time without meaning to. That's why we collect hurts as we go through life. It's not necessarily that anyone *wants* to hurt you, it's just the way it turns out.

Jenny didn't want to hurt me. Emma and I hurt each other without meaning to. Maybe I hurt Morwenna. Maybe Lisa harbours hurts I can't begin to guess at.

Cate hurts people too. She's hurt Calum. She's kicked him out. Don't ask me what's happened to him. Cate now lives in their flat on her own.

Like Emma, she's thrown herself into her work. With Emma, she gets drunk with the craft fair crowd at weekends. The two of them have had their hair cut short. Emma's now looks like Lisa's.

Richard is about to hurt someone too. He's going to dump Barbra. Being a dumper rather than a dumpee is a first for him, so he turns to his counsellor for advice on how best to proceed.

'Why are you asking me?' I say. 'You've got more experience in these matters than I have.'

'How do you figure that?'

'You've been dumped more times than I have.'

At this, his lower lip starts to protrude. It's a dangerous precedent.

'What I mean is,' I say quickly, 'you know which dumping strategies hurt more than others.'

This proves no palliative. Any further lip extension and gravity is going to cause it to tremble. It's down to me to save us both from such an embarrassment. It's a close run thing, but just in time I come up with the kind of insight that relationship counsellors spend their whole careers hoping to find.

'Try the space-time approach,' I say. 'Let her down gently. Tell her you never expected to get so involved. You need time to think. You need space to understand what's going on. If you loosen the ties gradually, it will be easier to let them go completely.'

'I hear what you're saying,' he says, 'but I think a clean break would be best.'

Glad I could be of help. Still, it worked for Bogie in *Play It Again Sam*: 'It's over.' 'What?' 'Us.' 'Over?' 'That's right, toots. Over. Kaput.'

At least I've prompted Richard into a decision. At least I've induced lower lip retraction. Even if it is at Barbra's expense.

'That will hurt,' I say, recalling the shock of Jenny telling me she was going to Australia.

'It always hurts,' says Richard. 'Time will heal the hurt.'

Not that he could be so insensitive in person. Oh no. To bolster his credentials as a man in touch with modern cultural trends, he dumps Barbra by email.

Her feelings on the matter can be inferred from the actions of her flatmate. One evening, Maggie knocks on Richard's door and, when he opens it, before he can even speak, knees him in the peripherals.

It certainly moves Maggie up a peg or two in my estimation. Although not enough to see her again, obviously.

I can't blame Richard, though. He didn't *want* to hurt Barbra. It's like I say. People get hurt. Anyway, it's Richard who is my friend, not Barbra, and you stand by your friends.

Unlike Emma and Cate, he hasn't had his hair cut shorter than Bank regulation length, but he has started shaving regularly. I seem to be the only one of my circle who doesn't feel the need to make a depilatory statement of some kind.

Mind you, a dispassionate outlook on life isn't as easy to maintain as I'd anticipated. With no one to care for, with nothing to care about, with no commitment of any kind, one day becomes much the same as any other. One Saturday morning I even go into the office before I realise I shouldn't be there. Slowly but inexorably, perhaps inevitably, my equanimity degenerates into something far less salubrious.

Apathy.

It creeps up on me so furtively that, by the time I recognise the symptoms, it's too late to remedy. Its most obvious outward manifestation is increasing slovenliness. I doubt that this is what Darwin had in mind for the future of the species, but I am evolving into a slob. Moreover, as though immediately adapting to this new state, I like it. I like being *able* to be a slob.

Without Emma to chide me, the washing-up can wait until tomorrow, the dust can accumulate undisturbed, the pattern on the carpet can be allowed to mask debris. I can slouch around the flat in sweatpants with an elasticated waistband. There's no one to make an effort for.

On one November day indistinguishable from any other, it occurs to me that I'm no longer merely *content* to be alone, I can actually see the advantages. I'm happy in my apathy. I have achieved a state of *hapathy*.

Not only don't I *need* a partner to share my life with, I no longer *want* one. It's like King Arthur says to Guinevere in *First Knight*, after he's lost her to Lancelot: 'Only fools dream of the one thing they can't have.'

I'm even beginning to see the benefits of solo sex. There's no one else to please, there are no emotional hassles, no foreplay is required. I wish I'd known that when I was a teenager.

To desire something or someone I can't have would imply that there's something lacking in my life. In *me*. Why can't I be a complete person on my own?

I draw up a list of Top Ten Male Role Models. Clark Gable in *Gone With The Wind*, Kevin Costner in *Dances With Wolves*, James Bond in every James Bond film... None of *them* let themselves be hidebound by a significant other. They follow their own truth.

What have relationships ever done for me except cause grief? Emma was right about them all along. By definition, even if compilers of dictionaries conspire to conceal the truth, they generate problems.

It's like Al Pacino says in *The Devil's Advocate*, 'Love is over-rated. Chemically it's the same as eating large quantities of chocolate.'

I'm glad I've put all that behind me. I'm glad I've finally seen the light.

And you can quote me on that.

20.

So I'm not infallible. Excuse me for not knowing everything. Yes, I know I said you could quote me. That was before.

Life would be pretty boring if we always knew what was going to happen next. I can change my mind, can't I? Is that purely a woman's prerogative?

I see now that all that guff about putting relationships behind me was a pure accommodation to circumstances. I was merely trying to make sense of my own allotted span of quiet desperation. Some of the greatest minds in history have failed in similar endeavour.

On the second Wednesday in December, at the last Bank Film Society event of the year, I find my hard-won apathy, née equanimity, peremptorily disturbed. Even more disturbingly, I welcome that disturbance as avidly as the end credits of the slasher movie that functioned as foreplay for my night with Maggie. One evening, that's all it takes, and my existential acceptance of my lot takes a convoluted route out the window, up the spout and down the drain.

The cause of this about-turn? Kirsty and Lisa from Accounts. And, of course, *Alphaville*. A potent cocktail, as it turns out.

I haven't told you anything about the Film Soc. because our monthly screenings are little more than social rituals. We watch a film in the staff canteen, we adjourn to the Standing Order for refreshment, we go home. The same crowd every time. The same kind of film every time – always English-language, usually Hollywood mainstream, never controversial. For most of our members the screening merely delays an opportunity to exchange Bank-related gossip.

The second Wednesday in December is different. For this one evening of the year we hire Filmhouse Cinema One and attract our biggest audience. Although some of the newcomers profess to attend purely for upholstered seating, I prefer to think the choice of film is the main draw.

According to tradition, our pre-Christmas offering is a musical that plays to a rowdy audience of cynics who are encouraged to hurl derision at the screen. This year we've had the brilliant idea of showing *Paint Your Wagon*. How could a comedy musical Western about a *ménage à trois* fail to titillate our audience of sophisticates?

I'm especially looking forward to the response to a young Clint Eastwood attempting 'I Talk to the Trees,' and a grizzled Lee Marvin growling his way through 'I Was Born Under a Wandering Star.' But in the event the women go all misty-eyed over Clint while the men go all misty-eyed over Lee.

The ensuing bar session is a more lively affair than usual. Again according to tradition, it's a time to ply committee members such as myself with suggestions for next year's programme. It's one of those rare occasions when I remain unfazed by strange women who sneak up on me.

Two girls from Human Resources want us to show *Muriel's Wedding* and *Priscilla, Queen of the Desert*. They're just back from a holiday in Australia. How about *Newsfront* or *Rabbit-proof Fence*, I say. They look at me blankly. A young teller tells me he's never coming again unless we hold an all-night horror event based around the *Nightmare on Elm Street* series. We'll miss you, I say.

That's when I become aware of Kirsty and Lisa. As on the occasion when our paths crossed at *The Searchers*, Lisa announces her presence with a tug at my sleeve.

'So you finally made it,' I say to them. 'What did you think of the film?'

'It's got Clint,' says Kirsty, feeling no need to elaborate.

I look to Lisa for a more enlightened review.

'It's got Clint,' she says.

'You're both obviously wasted at the Bank,' I say. 'You should be film critics.'

'Film's got nothing to do with it,' says Kirsty. 'It's sex we're talking about.'

She embellishes her point by waving around a bottle of strawberry-coloured liquid. My guess is that the solution is not entirely devoid of alcohol, and that it's not her first bottle of it this evening.

'What she's trying to say,' says Lisa, 'is that we can spot talent when we see it.'

She's cradling an identical bottle, which may explain why she's in a more expansive mood than when I last saw her staring into the Water of Leith.

'In that case,' I say, 'give me some ideas for next year's programme.'

'Oh, don't ask me,' says Kirsty, 'I don't know anything about films.'

'*The Searchers*,' says Lisa.

'It would never get past the committee,' I say.

'What's *The Searchers*?' says Kirsty.

'A Western,' says Lisa.

'Men with guns killing each other?'

'You've just watched a Western,' I say.

'That wasn't a Western. That was a musical. I thought you were supposed to know about films.'

'Do your John Wayne impression for Kirst,' Lisa says to me.

'That'll be the day,' I say as if by command.

As on my previous attempt, Lisa giggles behind her hand. Kirsty momentarily sobers. I guess the performance still needs some work.

'I suppose *Citizen Kane* is your sort of film,' says Kirsty.

'I thought you didn't know anything about films.'

'I don't. That's Lisa's favourite film.'

'Good choice,' I say.

'Don't encourage her,' says Kirsty, putting her hand on my arm and whispering in my ear. 'I brought her here tonight to educate her about what makes a good film.'

Lisa may be an enigmatic one, but anyone who likes both *The Searchers* and *Citizen Kane* deserves the benefit of the doubt. I should find out more, but Kirsty's touch distracts me.

Apart from that night with Cate, which doesn't count, and that night with Maggie, which I refuse to acknowledge, and an occasional Platonic hug from Emma and Megan, this is the first positive female contact I've had since Emma jumped on me at Cate's wedding. Kirsty's hand on my arm is hardly a tactile gesture in the same league, I grant you, but it's a shock to the system all the same.

Scott would no doubt have a few choice words to say about it if he knew, but it's only now, six or seven months after he first pointed my two companions out to me, that I take a good look at them for the first time. Both are medium height, thirty-something, I guess. Kirsty is the more immediately eye-catching, with curves of almost mathematical precision accentuated by a tight jumper and fitted trousers.

Beside her, Lisa looks neat, trim, androgynous. The impression is heightened by her cropped trousers and sheer, sleeveless white top, which hangs in an unbroken line from neck to waist.

Kirsty is obviously the prime mover in their relationship. With her outgoing manner and casual intimacy, you can't help but gravitate towards her.

'What's yours?' she says.

'I'll have another Coors,' I say from a million miles away.

'Nice try. I meant your favourite film.'

'Oh, right. *Alphaville*.'

'What's that about?'

The most difficult question of all. Even if I recounted the plot in the manner of what passes for a tabloid review, it still wouldn't explain what the film is about. Would recounting the story of my life explain what *that's* about?

'Well?' says Kirsty, elbowing me in the ribs to encourage a response.

I've no doubt the gesture is intended as amicable, but she catches me unawares. I flinch so convulsively that the beer froths out of my bottle.

'Looks like he's pleased to see us,' she says to Lisa, then turns her attention back to me. 'Well?'

'Of course I'm pleased to see you.'

'The film.'

'Oh, right.' I opt for a genre description. 'It's science fiction.' Emboldened by that success, I venture a tentative theory. 'It's about what happens when a society forbids its citizens to express any emotion.'

That's when it hits me. The whole out-the-window, up-the-spout, down-the-drain, equanimity-disturbing thing. Isn't that the state I've forced myself to live in since Emma's departure? Haven't I deliberately numbed myself into apathy in order to dull the hurt of losing her? My God! I've become one of Alpha 60's drones!

It's a eureka moment. I now see *Alphaville* in its true light as the ultimate anti-Buddhist statement. All those monks have got it wrong. Denial of feeling is counter-productive to the pursuit of happiness. Immunity to emotion is *not* a laudable goal. What is life without feeling?

'Sounds heavy,' says Kirsty.

'Just because it makes you think doesn't mean it's not fun.'

I describe the cigarette-lighting scene. The girls react to it as they did to my John Wayne impression. Lisa laughs, bless her, while Kirsty looks puzzled.

'I want to see it,' says Lisa.

'I can lend you the DVD,' I say.

I have a brief flashback of making the same offer to Cate, when she was masquerading as Sam. Lisa may be less approachable than Kirsty, but that doesn't mean she doesn't have hidden depths. I'm not that approachable myself. Maybe once you get to know her…

How sad am I? Thank goodness Scott's not here to see my performance. I spend five minutes with two women I barely know and I'm already forming a *ménage a trois* and wondering which way to turn.

The evening is certainly giving me plenty to think about. Not least of which: after Morwenna, how could I find *anyone* in Accounts interesting?

'Why *Citizen Kane*?' I say to Lisa.

'I thought you liked it.'

'I think it's brilliant.' When no answer to my question is forthcoming, I prompt her further. 'I gave you a scene from *Alphaville*, you give us one from *Citizen Kane*.'

'My favourite,' she says without having to pause for thought, 'is the one where Orson Welles says he's lonely because he knows too many people.'

She can certainly come out with them. I don't even remember the scene to which she's referring but, after a moment's reflection, it strikes me that it holds the key to the whole film. Forget Rosebud. A moment later and I'm convinced she's unearthed a profound truth about the very nature of modern society.

'That doesn't make sense,' says Kirsty.

'Have you never been alone in a crowd?' I say.

'Have you never wanted to escape to a desert island?' says Lisa.

'I know one in the Marquesas,' I say, 'just off the coast of Hiva Oa.'

Kirsty gives me another of her dubious looks, but Lisa acknowledges my support with a warm smile. In fact her smile radiates so much heat that I have to take off my jacket.

I feel so unaccountably comfortable with my two accountants that I abandon my committee duties and join them at a distant table for the remainder of the evening. Our conversation segues easily from films to books, Edinburgh, university, jobs, television...

We even talk about the Bank. I ask them about Accounts, they ask me about IT. They have as little reverence for their occupation as I have for mine, so for the first time in the history of labour, a discussion about white-collar work is interesting.

Fuelled by alcohol, Kirsty treats me as though she's known me all her life. It's a very attractive trait. Lisa is equally amiable but characteristically less forthcoming, which makes her more intriguing. I keep wanting to know what she's *really* thinking. I'd forgotten how pleasurable female company can be.

By closing time Kirsty is finding a bipedal gait insufficient to maintain lateral balance, so I offer to help Lisa see her home. It turns out they both live in New Town flats, not far from mine. The journey wouldn't be a long flight for an eagle, but it's a major overland expedition for Kirsty, even with Lisa and I upholding each unfledged wing.

Suspended between us like a dead weight, she struggles to maintain locomotion. After only two blocks she gives up the battle, succumbs to gravity and collapses against a lamppost in a giggling heap. Transportation by taxi appears to offer the only possibility of continued progress, except that, at this time of night in the city centre, the Loch Ness monster is a more likely sighting than an unoccupied taxi.

Not that I'm concerned. To my shame, I wouldn't mind if a nuclear pulse fried all vehicular electrical systems so that we had to wait here until Kirsty sobered up. I have been handed a window of opportunity to speak to Lisa free of her chaperone.

But would you credit it? The moment coincides with a cruel loss of my communication skills. Just when I most need it, my database of English vocabulary has been wiped from memory.

'I'm sorry about last time we met,' says Lisa, filling the void. 'You know, by the river.'

'Sorry for what?'

'I was in a funny mood. You must have thought I was really strange.'

'Who wants to be normal?'

Where do I get this stuff? I mean to establish empathy, instead of which, after implying then that she was an idiot for being out in the rain, I've told her now that she's abnormal. To make matters worse, I have no time to rectify the situation before, would you know it, a taxi driver with an ice cube for a heart stops to pick us up.

We prop Kirsty between us on the back seat. Her head lolls on my shoulder. Lisa says nothing, which merely verifies the fact that I've offended her. When we reach Kirsty's flat, Lisa helps her out and says she can handle things from here on.

Then the world slows down on its axis as Lisa leans back in, puts a steadying hand on my arm and kisses me on the cheek. Taken by surprise, I have no time to find any kind of response before she shuts the door and the cruel driver accelerates away. As the world speeds up again, too fast, surely too fast, I sit dazed while orange street lamps flash past in a blur.

Back home I rush to the bathroom mirror to check my cheek for evidence of Lisa's kiss. A smear of lipstick, perhaps, or a small indentation from the pressure of her lips. Nothing. But wait! What's that…? Only a speck on the mirror. I wipe it off and compare the kissed cheek to the unkissed one. Again nothing.

All that remains of Lisa's kiss is the memory.

I sit in the kitchen, drink black coffee and contemplate its meaning using all my training in structured systems analysis. It wasn't an air kiss. It wasn't even a peck. I know what a peck is. Contact time exceeded the duration required for a peck. So what kind of kiss was it? A *friendly* kiss? What kind of friends? No, don't go down that road again.

When I go to bed I replay the whole evening in search of further clues. Kirsty's mathematical curves and casual intimacy, so unnerving at the time, are now mere background to Lisa's tug at my sleeve, her laughter at my recounting of *Alphaville's* cigarette-lighting scene, the furnace of her smile...

What do these moments, so sharply etched in memory, mean? Was she simply drunk? Will she revert tomorrow to being her normal reticent self, mortified by her forwardness? Will she even remember? Or is it just remotely possible that she likes me?

And why is that so important to me? Am I so sad that to have a woman, any woman, physically acknowledge my existence on the most superficial of levels sends me into agonies of navel-gazing?

One thing's for sure. The autumn is over. Apathy is but a distant memory. In its stead has reappeared a familiar restlessness.

You know all that crap about the joys of singledom? Forget it. If I'd been truly happy, I wouldn't be feeling so disturbed now.

Here's the give-away. When I took my first good look at Kirsty and Lisa tonight, at our table in the Filmhouse bar, I noticed something I didn't tell you about.

It might not mean anything these days, but still I choose to see it as a sign: neither of them wear wedding rings.

21.

The morning after the night before, when I awake from a fitful sleep, there's only one question on my mind. How can I see Lisa again? It's the best hangover cure ever.

Over toast and black coffee I devise a plan. Scott is the key. He introduced Lisa to me. He can act as my go-between. He'll need no persuasion to take on the role. It will give him a lifetime's ammunition to use against me. I don't care. It will be worth it.

Let me explain something to you about romantics. When we see a chink of light in the darkness, be it ever so dim, be it real or imaginary, be it nothing more than a deceptive speck on the retina, we rush towards it in serried ranks with all the blind enthusiasm of *The Charge of the Light Brigade*.

I find Scott at lunch with Richard. They no longer need me to mediate.

Richard's presence inhibits me. Although we've re-established communication since he dumped Barbra, his mood remains subject to more unknown variables than my database interface program. Whereas I'm prepared for Scott's taunts, the role of fool is not one I wish to play in front of Richard.

I bide my time, listening to them bandy opinions on a television programme about the age of consent, while I cram forkfuls of chef's special vegetarian haggis and neeps into my mouth. The haggis has the consistency and, for all I know, the taste of grit. The neeps have been disgorged and recycled.

Over desert... Now there's a Freudian slip. Over *dessert*... a brief opportunity presents itself when Richard goes to fetch a glass of water.

'Have you seen anything of those two women from Accounts?' I say to Scott with impressive nonchalance.

'Okay,' he says, putting down his cutlery, 'tell me.'

'Tell you what?'

'Why have you got that stupid grin on your face?'

'I haven't.'

'Why are you going red?'

'I'm not.'

At which point Richard returns to ask a question so inopportune you'd think they'd arranged the whole scenario.

'Wasn't it the Film Society last night?'

'That's it!' says Scott, his eyes flashing like a slot machine that's just hit the jackpot. 'They were there, weren't they?'

'Who?' says Richard.

This isn't at all how I envisaged the unfolding of my plan. To give me time to regroup, I toy with a spoonful of pudding, taking pains to ensure that it has precisely the right ratio of chocolate sponge to custard.

'What if they were?' I say impotently.

'Who?' says Richard.

'Kirsty and Lisa,' says Scott.

'Who are Kirsty and Lisa?'

'I'll tell you later, pal.' Scott's eyes remain firmly fixed on mine. He can barely contain his excitement. 'Well, what happened? You know you're going to tell us sooner or later.'

Now I'm back-pedalling like a canoeist at the edge of a waterfall. No, make that back-*paddling*. Whatever. Words congeal in my brain like... like custard on my spoon. I never realised how much symbolism resides in a spoonful of custard.

'Nothing happened. We had a few drinks and got a taxi home.'

'A threesome?' says Scott, salivating.

'Do you always have to bring it down to your own level?'

He deliberately takes my protestation for confirmation and raises his hand for a high five.

'Lisa kissed me, that's all!'

I had to say it, didn't I? I had to go and tell them.

Richard's eyebrows rise of their own accord. Scott gives a perfect rendition of his new deep-throated chuckle.

'Tell me you at least launched a tongue probe.'

'It was on the cheek.'

'Sad bastard.'

'What about the Three-date Rule? You said if you get a peck on the cheek on a first date, it's a result, and this wasn't even a date.'

In retaliation at having his words quoted back at him, he repeats his accusation with even greater conviction.

'You sad bastard.'

If the charge stands, then I have nothing more to lose. This exposure of my true nature is paradoxically liberating. It frees me from any further pretence of dignity.

'Suppose, just suppose,' I say, 'that I wanted to see her again... How... I mean, how...?'

Scott's beam puts the canteen's fluorescent strip lighting to shame.

'Sometimes I wonder how you ever lost your virginity.' A look of deep concern spreads across his face. 'You have, haven't you?'

The truth is, I wouldn't have done if a predatory woman hadn't made the mistake of thinking I was experienced, but there's no way you, Scott or anyone else is ever going to hear that embarrassing little tale.

'Phone her,' says Scott.

'I don't know her number.'

'Look it up in the phone book.'

'Don't you know her number?'

'Why should I know her number?'

'Do you know her last name?'

'Phone her at work,' says Richard. 'Her office extension will be in the Bank directory. There can't be that many Lisas in Accounts.'

Brilliant! Richard! My friend! After all, he's not forgotten the debt he owes me for my advice on how to dump Barbra.

And yet… 'What would I say to her?'

I am truly the saddest of sad bastards.

'I've got a better idea,' says Scott. 'Strike while your iron is hot. Hang around Accounts at five o'clock and accidentally on purpose bump into her.'

Brilliant! Scott! My friend!

If I see Lisa today I can ask her how she's feeling after last night, then she'll ask me how I'm feeling, then the conversation will flow as it did in the Filmhouse bar and… Then we'll *see what happens*. Where interpersonal relationships with the opposite gender are concerned, a plan can take you only so far.

Accounts is on the fourth floor. I'm there at 4.55. There's a long corridor with offices off. Lisa must work in one of them. I loiter with intent, covering both the lift and the stairs. Employees eye me suspiciously as they leave. What if Lisa has left early? Or what if she had a hangover and didn't make it in today. Or…

There she is!

It's true, your heart really can skip a beat.

'Hello,' she says, looking as gorgeous as only she could in a boring dark blue suit. How come I've never noticed her gorgeousness before? How could I ever have thought she was androgynous?

'What are you doing here?' she says.

'I had to deliver something on my way out,' I say from my prepared script. Please voice, don't waver. 'How are you feeling after last night?'

'Don't ask.'

I wait expectantly, but she doesn't feed me my next line. Instead of returning the inquiry she lowers her gaze before mine. It's as I feared. She's retreated into herself again.

'I have to go,' she says when our silence crosses the threshold of awkwardness.

I dog her heels as she walks the short distance to the lift. Four other employees await the lift's arrival. Two men in pin-stripes and two women in those default office skirts with the short slit at the back. It's an audience I hadn't factored into the equation.

'How's Kirsty?' I say, pretending to care, when all I want to do is give Lisa the kiss I failed to return last night. Right now, here in this corridor, in front of all these people.

'She didn't make it in today.'

I can hear the lift rising up the shaft, or maybe it's my heart rising into my mouth. Other clichés follow. My collar feels tight. A bead of sweat appears on my forehead. Why do they keep the central heating turned up so high on the fourth floor? Maybe it's for Lisa's benefit, to remind her of the desert.

Must our Bank colleagues stand here in silence listening to our every word? Have they nothing to say to each other?

'I was wondering,' I say to Lisa through a fog of desperation, 'would you like to go and see a film some time?' I blurt it out as though I have no control over my vocal cords, at a decibel level that makes the woman nearest me skip a step backwards.

My God! I've asked Lisa out!

In an attempt at nonchalance, I put my hands in my pockets and lean against the wall. Unfortunately it's further away than I anticipated and, when my shoulder thuds against it, I'm left listing at an acute angle. I compensate by smiling Emma's fixed smile. This so unsettles the other woman that she too takes a furtive, crab-like step away from me.

'Thank you,' says Lisa, 'but I can't. Tomorrow's my last day, then I'm on holiday until after Christmas.'

Cue more silence while all six of us stare steadfastly at the closed lift doors. It can have been no more still before the birth of the universe.

The lift arrives. The doors open. Our co-workers elbow each other out of the way in their eagerness to enter. Lisa steps in with them. I push myself upright and approach the doors. It doesn't occur to me to enter. This is *their* lift. I'm an intruder from IT.

All five turn and stare back at me, willing the lift to fulfil its function. Lisa gives me that look of hers, the one that focuses on a point some distance behind me.

When the doors start to close, I unexpectedly jam my foot between them. Instead of bouncing back off the obstacle, they clamp it like a vice.

'What about after Christmas?' I say to the occupants through the small gap afforded me.

There's the longest ever pause in a conversation. It's longer even than the wedding sequence in *The Godfather*. I need an answer. Any answer. From anyone. The metatarsals of my right foot are about to be irreparably crushed.

'Okay,' says Lisa. 'I'd like that.'

Relief floods through me, but mainly because I can now retrieve my foot. Except that I can't! The doors have it firmly by the instep. I pull on my knee to no effect. One of the men pushes from the other side. One of the women presses the doors-open button. Nothing works. The fire brigade will have to be called. And the paramedics.

Finally the other man gives my foot a sharp kick and I shoot backwards like a human cannonball. The doors close and the lift takes Lisa away.

From that moment on, the evening is a blank. I guess I walk down the four flights of stairs. I suppose I walk home. Or limp. Maybe I have a meal. At some point I probably go to bed.

Unlike Lisa I have one more week to work before the Christmas break, which means that I have to file a report with Scott and Richard. To forestall further ridicule I embellish the story. I paraphrase the truth. Okay, I lie. Scott wants details. I shrug. What details? I asked her out, she said yes. What more is there to say?

My workmates remain unconvinced that I could have conducted myself with such aplomb but, with no evidence to the contrary, they both have more pressing concerns to occupy their minds. Scott has numerous Christmas errands to run for his wife. Richard is gearing up for a Christmas with his parents and another dip into his mysterious pool of untapped girlfriend material.

Which frees me up for more important matters.

'I'd like that,' Lisa said to me. What did she mean exactly? Did she mean she'd be going to see a film anyway, so she might as well go with me? Was she just being polite? Did the presence of her colleagues inhibit a refusal? Or did she mean she wants to spend time with me, whether we go to see a film or not? What is the *that* that she'd like – to see a film or to see me?

One thing's for sure. Following an October of equanimity and a November of apathy, my etymological imperative for December is something far more dangerous.

Anticipation.

22.

Christmas and Hogmanay, the twin festive highlights of the winter, pass nowhere near quickly enough.

In a break with Yuletide tradition my parents spend Christmas with my aunt in Cornwall, so I escape filial obligation. For the first time in my life I spend Christmas Day alone in my Edinburgh flat. I receive only one present. Can you guess whom it's from? No, not my parents. No, not Emma. It's from me. I give myself a movie trivia quiz book.

I simulate a Christmas dinner with chicken breast, packet sage and onion stuffing, frozen mixed veg. and Peruvian Blacks from Harvey Nichols, accompanied by a single-person-size can of supermarket wine. My day may not brim with traditional festive joy, but it's a welcome change to be allowed to do as I wish, especially when that includes control of the remote and the option of an occasional pine for Lisa.

I haven't done any pining for a while, and it feels good. It feels good to have a reason to pine. To have someone to pine for. Everyone should have someone to pine for once in a while.

She's probably gone home to her parents for Christmas. They'll be really nice people. Their house will be the kind of cosy cottage you see on Victorian Christmas cards. It will be snowing outside, but inside a roaring log fire brings a rosy glow to Lisa's cheeks. They'll all be having a lovely time singing heart-warming carols around a real Christmas tree.

All in soft focus.

In the late-afternoon I wander uptown. Maybe it's the thought of Lisa's Victorian Christmas but, with its dark, traffic-free streets illuminated by magical Christmas lights, the city today has the serenity and innocence of a more romantic age. On Princes Street I pass by the floodlit outdoor ice rink and stop at one of the picturesque wooden stalls in the German market for a glass of Glühwein.

I want to be in love in this city.

Hogmanay is an altogether different proposition. While the deserted streets of December 25th make hibernation acceptable, December 31st is the social occasion of the year. To be alone at Hogmanay, in the city that boasts 'the world's biggest party', is to be suicidal. Ask the staff at the Royal Infirmary.

Humanitarian aid arrives in the unlikely form of Richard. Luckily for me, though not for him, he returns from a Christmas down south without a new girlfriend. He must have exhausted his supply. We turn the situation to our advantage by deluding ourselves into thinking, notwithstanding recent evidence to the contrary, that Fate has given us an unparallelled opportunity to spend a spirited Hogmanay together, unencumbered by partners.

Actually, it's a moot point whether we see in the New Year together or not, because at midnight we're running. We misjudge the time, leave the pub too late and, as the first fireworks explode overhead, rush to join the crowd on the grassy knoll above the pond in Inverleith Park.

We arrive just in time to see the last great starburst over the Old Town skyline. On a cold, clear, still night such as this, there is surely no better vantage point for the spectacle. In ragged ranks we stand in communal awe as the floodlit castle and its multi-coloured pyrotechnic umbrella are mirrored in the pond's unbroken surface.

In our eagerness to secure an uninterrupted view, Richard and I become separated and I don't see him again all night. I wouldn't mind, but he's carrying the champagne. In my forlorn search for the Keeper of the Bottle, I mingle with revellers, join an arm-locked rendition of 'Auld Lang Syne' and accept several nips of whisky and one barbecued sausage.

I'm in bed barely an hour after midnight but my self-respect is intact – I wasn't alone at the Bells.

Later, Richard tells me he gave up trying to find me, polished off the champagne by himself and had a knees-up with the crowd down by the pond. To preserve my street cred, I invent a tale about gate-crashing an impromptu party. It's the kind of story you could only get away with at Hogmanay.

So pass the twin festive highlights of the winter. I'm just relieved to have come through them unscathed, prey to a rare and disturbing desire to return to work. It's not that I've discovered some new-found enthusiasm for my job. It's Lisa. Lisa is at work.

I meet her by accident on the first day back. She's standing with Scott in the morning queue at the staff cash machine. It's not as much of a coincidence as you might think. On the first day back it would be odder *not* to meet someone you know in this queue.

When Scott sees me, they give up their places to join me at the back of the queue and we all wish each other a Happy New Year. I feel as awkward as you'd expect. I was going to phone Lisa. I'm not prepared for this encounter. When she gives me a coy smile, my attempt to reciprocate shapeshifts into a leer.

I have a sudden panic attack that she'll no longer want to see a film with me, even if John Wayne were to come back from the grave, make a sequel to *The Searchers* and invite us to the premiere. A woman like Lisa could go to the cinema with any man she wanted.

I ask her if she had a good Christmas. Quiet, she says. She doesn't elaborate and doesn't return the question. She never does. It's not a habit that facilitates conversation. Apart from that one evening at the Filmhouse, we never have much to say to each other. When we reach the cash machine, she withdraws some money, gives me a look I can't interpret and says she has to get back to the office.

At least Scott has the good grace to wait until we're out of earshot of our colleagues before he gives me his predictable verdict.

'You sad bastard.'

In a way, it's reassuring to see that the Christmas break hasn't altered his opinion of me.

'What am I going to do with you?' he says.

'What do you mean?'

'Are you a man or a mouse?'

'We're going to see a film.' In other words, squeak squeak.

'When?'

An idea comes to me just in time. 'I'm going to email her.' If it's okay for Richard to dump Barbra by email, surely it's okay for me to ask Lisa out by email.

Why is Scott shaking his head like that?

'You meet her face to face, then ask her out by email?'

I don't see the problem. I don't know why I haven't thought of it before.

I find her email address in the Bank directory. Richard was right. There's only one Lisa in Accounts. Lisa Nelson. It never occurred to me that she'd have a surname, but now I realise that it's a sign. Nelson is the surname of the character that Anna Karina plays in Jean-Luc's *Made in USA*.

I email her: 'Are we still on for a film?'

A reply comes back: 'Yes, if you still want to.'

Of course I still want to. How can she doubt it? But that's a definite yes, isn't it? She may be pretty quiet sometimes, but that 'yes' shouts at me from the screen. I've never had much time for email before, but now I decide it's the most wonderful invention since the cinematograph.

When no one is looking I hunch over the printer and print out a hard copy of her reply. It's black and white confirmation that she still wants to see me.

I email back: 'Yes, I still want to. I'll find out what films are on next week.'

At lunch I'm prepared for further hassle from Scott, but in the event it's Richard who is my main tormentor.

'It's your birthday next week, isn't it?' he says to me.

'So?' I see no reason to celebrate the ageing process, even if it is preferable to the alternative.

'Thirty-five, isn't it?'

'I thought you were well past that,' says Scott.

'Are you going to do anything?' says Richard.

'Like what? Top myself? You think we're in *Logan's Run*?'

'You have to do something,' says Scott. 'You're halfway through your three score years and ten. From hereon it's all downhill.'

'You should have a party,' says Richard.

Now I understand. Having failed at Christmas to land a girlfriend to see him through the cold winter months, he needs to network. He wants me to pimp for him.

'My flat's not big enough.'

'Hire somewhere.'

'Where would he find enough people to fill the back room of a pub with?' says Scott. 'It would be about as popular as a kamikaze reunion dinner.'

'Put a notice on the canteen notice board,' says Richard.

'Sure,' I say. 'A party full of Bankers, that's all I need.'

'That's what Brian Turner did, and that was a good night. Get enough people and you get a DJ thrown in for free.'

'Anyway, it's on Friday. Three days isn't long enough to organise anything.'

'Rubbish. Pitch it as a Beat Those Back-to-Work Blues Party.'

He's wasting his time.

Not so Scott. He knows exactly how to play me.

'You could put a notice on every floor,' he says. 'All the way up to Accounts.'

I splutter and prevaricate, but later that afternoon I hire the back room at the Thistle and Sporran, pin an open invitation to the canteen notice board and email Lisa again, hoping she can come to the party. A reply comes back. She'll try to make it.

I print that out too.

For the remainder of the week time moves as sluggishly as a slo-mo stream of blood erupts from a gunshot wound in *The Wild Bunch*.

When Friday finally deigns to arrive, it begins with a surprise postal delivery. The dearth of birthday cards is to be expected; the late Christmas card isn't. It's from Patagonia. From Megan. She's completed her trek around the Torres del Paine and at the time of writing is heading up to the Argentinean Lake District.

I know nothing about these places. I'm thirty-five years old and I've never travelled outside Europe. What if Scott is right and it's all downhill from here on?

The card reminds me of the good luck charm Megan gave me at the Festival craft fair. I take it out of the drawer and put it in my pocket. Perhaps it will help me with Lisa.

By the time I arrive at the Thistle and Sporran with Richard in tow, the back room is already hoaching. There's a dance floor surrounded by tables, with a bar at one end and a DJ at the other. I'm greeted by a loud cheer and an excruciating chorus of 'Happy Birthday' from people who've never met me. Say what you like about Bankers, throw a party and they turn up like CGI Orcs to a Middle Earth battle.

Can't see Lisa anywhere, though. I hope I'm not putting myself through this for nothing.

When Richard goes to the bar I'm grabbed from behind in a bear hug. The arms belong to Scott's wife. She spins me around, takes me firmly by the ears and plants a wet kiss on my lips.

'Happy birthday,' she says. 'Let's dance.'

'Later,' I say, taking cover behind Scott. Surely she can't expect me to hit the floor sober. 'I have to circulate.'

She gives me the same look Scott does when he calls me a sad bastard, and drags him up instead. He wouldn't dare refuse.

Then it's the turn of Emma and Cate, both already well ginned up, to manhandle me. An arm each. Inebriation plus nervousness, occasioned by the presence of all these strangers, have bestowed on Emma in particular an *Annie Hall* air of dizziness.

I hadn't intended to invite them. As if I don't have enough to worry about tonight. But Emma *would* phone to wish me happy birthday and ask how I was going to celebrate it, and I *would* ask her along, and she *would* invite Cate for support. Still, it's good to see the two of them enjoying themselves, I suppose.

Emma gives me a risqué card with a sexual innuendo about keeping it up. It says 'with love.' This year she's added no kisses. It's the first year in five that she hasn't given me a present, that we haven't spent most of the day together, that I won't be getting my 'birthday treat,' as we used to call it. I almost joke about this with her, but fortunately reason prevails.

Cate gives me a card that purports to be a telegram from the Queen, then wanders off for refills, leaving me alone with Emma.

'Cate looks happy,' I say.

'She is. The divorce comes through soon.'

'Already? She doesn't hang around.'

'Why should she?'

'What about Calum?'

'What about him?'

'You're right. What about you? Are you still seeing that guy?'

'Alec? No. He was starting to expect things from me, and I was starting to feel all the things I felt with you.'

She puts her hand in mine, opening a Pandora's box of emotions, but it's soon clear that it's a gesture intended purely to maintain balance.

'It got me thinking about us,' she says. 'It wasn't you, you know, it was me. I just can't let people get close to me.'

I see that self-awareness is still mistiming its visits to her. She stands here before me, vulnerable, magnanimous, available. There was a time such a combination would have given me hope for us, but no longer. I've had too many 'if onlys' with Emma.

Yet I'm glad she's dumped this Alec person, which can only mean that I'm not completely free of my ties to her. After all, why should I be glad? If we're no longer together, I want her to find another man, don't I? I want her to be happy, don't I?

'You will,' I say to her, 'when you find the right man.' It's beginning to sound like an old conversation.

'It doesn't matter,' she says, pulling away with a dismissive hand gesture that causes precious gin to spill over the rim of her glass. 'I've always been happier on my own.'

Gee, thanks, Emma. It's reassuring to see how effortlessly she retains her uncanny ability to make me feel *this* small.

'How about you?' she says. 'Have you met anyone else?'

'No.' Which again means I still have work to do on my feelings for her.

'Cate told me about the night she spent with you,' she says.

'It wasn't what you think.'

'Don't worry. She told me how nice you were to her. Anyway, it's got nothing to do with me. If you and Cate want to get back together, good luck to you.'

'What are you talking about? Cate and I don't want to get back together. There is no *back*.'

'I'm just saying, I don't mind. I want you to be happy.'

'I want you to be happy too.'

I don't know how it happens, but suddenly we find ourselves hugging each other. There's a lot of feeling goes into this clinch.

Nostalgia for the good times, sorrow for the bad times, regret that we couldn't make it.

Holding her compliant body against mine brings back such warm memories that I have to check myself. We can't go back. Emma could never love me. We would have the same problems all over again. In any case, it's Lisa I want to be with tonight, isn't it?

If she deigns to turn up.

'Enough of that,' says Scott, interrupting.

Emma pulls away, sways on her feet and grins in a way she's never done for me.

'You can get your birthday treat later,' he says to me.

Emma gives me an accusing look. I shrug in a manner that tries to convey no, I didn't tell him, Scott's just one of those people who knows things.

'Shouldn't you be looking after your wife?' I say.

'My wife can look after herself,' he says.

Indeed she can. Chameleon-like, she's as much at home here as she was at Cate's wedding and her own dinner party. She's currently twisting the night away to Chubby Checker.

'Well, go look after Cate, then,' I say mischievously. I have my moments.

'Cate?' says Emma.

'Will you stop going on about Cate?' he says. 'We were only seventeen.'

Oops!

It's not like Scott to make such a mistake.

'You and Cate?' Emma says to him, in exactly the same tone of disbelief with which I responded to the revelation.

Scott gives me a look I would have paid money to receive.

'We were only seventeen,' he says again.

My smirk doesn't last long, though, not with the Queen of Lateral Thinking at our side.

'So Cate has slept with both of you?' she says.

Guess who's not going to come out of this well?

'Not at the same time,' I say in mitigation.

Scott recovers just in time to save both of us.

'Things would have been different if I'd met you first,' he says to Emma.

He's surely pushing his luck with this one, but no, it works. Emma grins again. Not for the first time, I wonder how he gets away with it.

When he takes her to the bar for a drink, Richard re-materialises at my side.

'Are you and Emma back together again?' he says.
'We're just friends,' I say.
He considers this news with due gravity. 'What kind of friends?'
'Don't you start!'
'So she's free, then?'
I give him an old-fashioned look.
'I was just asking,' he says.
Then I feel a familiar tug at my sleeve.

23.

Lisa is wearing a knee-length, Mondrian-patterned dress whose flimsy material, gathered beneath the bust, makes the most of what she has. Kirsty is wearing a short black cocktail dress that does likewise. They wish me happy birthday. No cards, though.

I introduce them to Richard, who is plainly astonished to discover that Scott's two lassies from Accounts are more like leading ladies than the character actresses he'd imagined.

'I like your outfits,' I say to Kirsty.

I knew it. I knew I'd talk to Kirsty instead of Lisa. I always do that. I once spent an entire evening talking to the mate of someone I fancied, and at the end of the evening they both thought it was the mate I was interested in.

'Anything else?' says Kirsty.

'Like what?'

'My hair. I had this done specially.'

'It looks great,' I say. I haven't a clue what she's had done to it.

'Lisa too,' she says.

'Yours looks great too,' I say to Lisa, equally baffled.

A character flaw I've had to come to terms with over the years is my inability to make any more sensible judgements about hairstyles than I can about shoes. For four years Emma did her utmost to teach me the trichological basics, but my brain is simply not programmed to retain such data. It's just the way it is. An Act of Nature. I don't see why I should be held any more accountable for it than I should for my race and colour.

'I've had it cut,' says Lisa, sensing my ignorance. 'A whole half-inch.'

A half-inch? How am I supposed to notice a half-inch, even a *whole* half-inch? And how can you have a whole *half*?

When Emma and Cate had their hair cut, you couldn't help but notice. They had several half-inches removed. In a harsh light they looked like *Eraserhead* twins. But the trivial truncation of which Kirsty and Lisa are so proud is surely a hairdressing con. A half-inch?

'Sorry,' I say.

'You can't help being a man,' says Kirsty with an intentional sigh.

'Nobody's perfect,' says Lisa.

I can't decide whether this is intended as chastisement or mitigation but, when she holds my gaze, I realise it's neither. She's deliberately quoting the most famous movie last line of all time. It's delivered by the suitor of a dragged-up Tony Curtis when Tony informs him that he's really a man.

'*Some Like It Hot!*' I say, bringing a smile of acknowledgement to Lisa's face.

When the girls repair to the bar to buy me a drink I do something I would have bet serious money I would never do. I ask for Richard's opinion.

'Well? What do you think?'

'Is Kirsty free?' he says.

Before they return, Scott's wife traps me in a reprise of her introductory bear hug and whisks me onto the floor for a jive. I try to explain to her that my dance style is too free-form to be constrained by such a specific musical genre, but I'm not permitted the option of a refusal this time.

The best I can come up with for 'Rock Around The Clock' is a jerky sort of morris dance, while Scott's wife, whatever her name is, swirls around me as though born to boogie to anything and everything this DJ plays.

'Great party,' she says. It turns out she's taking evening classes in Ceroc and it's at her instigation that the DJ is playing this stuff.

'Sorry about the last time we met,' she says. 'You know, Morwenna.'

'No, it's me who should apologise. Scott told me what she told you. When you see her again, tell her I'm sorry. I wasn't very nice to her.'

'None of us were. If I'd known beforehand, I wouldn't have set you up with her. You need a more…'

She executes a 360-degree turn around my body that would break the arm of a lesser man.

'More what?'

She ignores my question and nods in the direction of Lisa. 'Who's the girl?' She doesn't miss a trick.

'Another accountant,' I say. 'Can't seem to get along without them these days.'

'You've done all right for yourself there.'

When the record ends I return her to Scott and have a discreet word with the DJ. He's as keen as I am to abandon the evening's trawl through rock-and-roll history, and he soon has the floor buzzing to a medley of mainstream favourites.

As birthday boy I receive several dance offers but manage to refuse them all until a ragged line dance to 'Staying Alive' with Emma and Cate turns out to be mandatory. The way things are heading, the evening could well end up even more of a nightmare than Cate's wedding. Especially when, as the focal point of the occasion, I have nowhere to hide.

Emma is as seriously drunk as she needs to be to overcome her inhibitions, but it still feels strange to be dancing with her. Even when we were together, it was an activity she could only rarely bring herself to indulge in.

I feel even more self-conscious when I notice that Lisa is watching us from a table that she and Kirsty have commandeered. Whenever my body accidentally touches Emma's, I feel unfaithful.

When the record finishes, Scott's wife inveigles Cate into a jive to 'Hit Me Baby One More Time'. This takes some doing even if you are seriously drunk, but you have to give them points for persistence. Caught in the crossfire, Emma and I take refuge on the sidelines, until Richard's approach acts as her cue to find an alternative viewpoint.

'Is it true that Cate's getting divorced?' he says to me.

I don't know how to describe the look I give him this time, but it has the desired effect. He shifts uneasily from foot to foot. Since my full exposure as a sad bastard, he seems to have lost all qualms about disclosing his own desperation.

Scott is gobsmacked by the spectacle that Cate and his wife are making of themselves. You'd think he'd just seen Sharon Stone uncross her legs in *Basic Instinct*.

'The things they must have to say to each other,' I say to him.

He counters with some of that ammunition I've been handing him, situations such as this for the use of.

'Don't you have someone you should be talking to?'

I should have known. I'm immediately on the defensive.

'I'm going to.'

'I'm going to,' he mimics in a camp, singsong voice. 'Get over there and ask her to dance.'

I can't decide whether he's showing true concern for my welfare or using attack as the best form of defence, but it makes no difference. In a single combat situation he'll always have the drop on me.

'What if she doesn't want to dance?'

It's a forlorn tactic. Without further ado, he takes a death grip of my arm and drags me over to Lisa and Kirsty's table. We home in on them like a tracking shot. Like the shot at the end of Hitchcock's *The*

Man Who Knew Too Much, when the camera crosses the dance floor to end on a close-up of the killer's eyes. Just like I end up staring into Lisa's eyes.

'It's your lucky night, hens,' Scott says to them, keeping a tight hold of my arm in case I run away. And I might.

'You took your time,' says Kirsty, and the four of us move onto the floor to the strains of the Human League's 'Don't You Want Me'.

It's called irony.

When Scott pairs off with Kirsty, Lisa starts to dance with me. She moves as I should have known she would, gracefully, sensuously. It's such an enthralling sight that I lose all co-ordination. When even my newly acquired morris steps desert me, I have to resort to shuffling movements *à la Richard*.

Not a word passes between us, just occasional awkward glances and smiles. But my God! The way the sheer material of her top skims over her body!

When the record ends, I walk her back to her table. Scott stays up with Kirsty until Richard, still an innocent in matters of dance floor etiquette, moves in to relieve him. Scott is so surprised that he gives way with unforeseeable grace. As Cher belts out her regrets about being unable to turn back time, I notice that there has been no improvement in Richard's co-ordination since Club Inferno, but right now I envy him his facility of movement.

It never occurred to me to ask Lisa to stay up.

'Mind if I join you?' I say bravely, speaking to her for the first time. Scott slinks away. He's done as much as he can. It's up to me now. If I deliberately trap myself at Lisa's table, I'll be forced to do something. Even if it's only dribble.

She motions for me to sit down, then saves me.

'Have you seen *Before Sunrise*?' she says.

'Yes, and *Before Sunset*. I like Julie Delpy.' It's hardly an in-depth critical analysis, but I'm suddenly aware of Lisa's resemblance to the French actress.

She makes a telephone with her hand and simulates a ringing sound. It's a game that potential lovers Julie Delpy and Ethan Hawke play to get to know each other better. You pretend the person you've just met is a friend, whom you're phoning to tell about the person you've just met. Does that make sense? It does in the film. I answer Lisa with my own hand-shaped telephone.

'Hi,' she says. '*Comment ça va?*' Nice touch, that.

'Fine,' I say. 'How are you?'

'I'm at a party and I've just danced with this guy.'

'What's he like?'

'I've known worse,' she says with a giggle.

Hey! What a wonderful game! I've never seen Lisa like this. Talking at one step removed seems to have emboldened both of us.

'He sounds like a real catch,' I say.

'Who knows? You know how difficult men are.'

'In what way?'

'Oh, you know, you never quite know what to make of them. Sometimes they're really friendly, other times they don't seem to want to know.'

'Maybe he's shy.'

'You think so?'

'It might explain it. Do you like him?'

She gives me one of her long pauses. I'm dying here.

'Yeah,' she says, as though she's weighed up a whole list of pros and cons and, on balance, can just about give me the benefit of the doubt. But she says it with a grin that could melt Antarctica.

'He wants me to go to the pictures with him,' she says. 'Do you think I should?'

'I think you definitely should.'

'Oh, I'm running out of money. I'll have to go. Can you phone me back? Bye.' She puts the phone down. 'Your turn.'

'Dring, dring,' I say.

She picks up the phone.

'I've just met someone too,' I say.

'What's she like?'

'Not bad, I suppose.' I shrug non-committally.

'You don't sound too sure.'

'You know how difficult women are. You never quite know what to make of them.'

'How do you mean?'

'Oh, you know. She has moods.'

'Moods?'

'Yeah. Sometimes she's really quiet. You're never quite sure what she's thinking.'

'Maybe she has hidden depths.'

'You think so?'

'All interesting people have hidden depths. Do you like her?'

I make her wait, as she made me wait.

'Yeah.' Quick, think of something else. 'I like her hair.'

'What about it?'

'She's just had it cut.'

'How do you know, if you've just met her?'

'She's the sort of person who gets her hair cut when she reaches a crossroads in her life.' I'm on a roll.

'What makes you think she's reached a crossroads in her life?'

'She's just met me.'

She laughs out loud, without even hiding behind her hand. I wish I could be as articulate when I'm not pretending to be Ethan Hawke pretending to be a character in a film.

'What's going on?' says Kirsty, rejoining us.

Lisa and I dismantle our telephones smartly.

Cut to end of the evening. If events of world-shattering importance occur during the intervening couple of hours, they pass me by unnoticed.

At closing time the DJ plays 'Happy Birthday'. Everyone joins in and it's as embarrassing as you'd expect. When all eyes turn to me I feel like Jim Carrey in *The Truman Show*. Just to eke out my discomfort a little longer, I have to endure 'For He's A Jolly Good Fellow' as well.

The last dance is a slow one. I'd have the guts to ask Lisa up for it, I really would, but my guests start to leave and they all have to say goodbye, including Scott and his wife and people I didn't know at the start of the evening and still don't know now.

Emma and Cate have disappeared, but I keep an eye on Kirsty and Lisa to make sure they don't do likewise. Richard, meanwhile, sticks to me like superglue until Kirsty duly asks us if we want to share a taxi with them.

It's at this point that I come out with a most brazen announcement.

'Lisa and I have decided to walk,' I say.

I haven't even asked her. See? I'm not always the sad bastard that Scott makes me out to be. Something inside me isn't going to let Lisa vanish into the night like she did last time. It's a gamble, but…

Her face is turned away from me, unreadable, but she doesn't contradict. She and I are walking.

As soon as we start down the street, I know that I shall act. There comes a point when you have to act. Like when Max von Sydow steels himself to confront the Devil in *The Exorcist*. This is one of those moments. Not that I'm comparing Lisa to Beelzebub. What I mean is, it would be harder *not* to act.

'I'm glad you came tonight,' I say, heart pounding. Then the words tumble out in a torrent worthy of Geoffrey Rush in *Shine*. 'I know I hardly know you, but I really like you. That's why I never know what to say to you. It's not because I don't like you, it's because I do. I get nervous and tongue-tied.'

There. I've said it. Maybe I've said too much, but the relief at having said it is overwhelming. Whatever will happen now will happen.

'Me too,' she says.

'Really?' I look at her in amazement. 'You mean, you like me too?'

'I thought about you all Christmas, and I hardly know you either.'

'Really?'

'Every day.'

Every day? Can this be true?

Without realising it, we've stopped walking. We're standing face to face, on the corner of the High Street and George IV Bridge. It's 1.30 in the morning. Revellers brush past us as they radiate homewards from the city centre. We're oblivious to their presence. A chill wind eddies around the corner. We're immune to the cold.

On an impulse I take Lisa in my arms and kiss her so clumsily that our teeth clash. She pulls away and looks into my eyes. And takes my breath away.

'I think I love you,' she says.

For a brief moment the world grinds to a halt, causing me to lose balance. I cling to the wall like an Alphaville inhabitant faced with a new world of emotion. She thinks she loves me? How can she think she loves me? Love is a memory. It can't be here again now, like this, so suddenly, in the form of Lisa. Can it?

'How can you?' I say.

'I don't know. I didn't mean to. I'm sorry.'

I run my fingers through her hair. It feels strange because it's not mine.

'I think I love you, too,' I hear a voice say. I hear it from a long way off, as though it belongs to someone else. But it's mine. It's definitely mine. I'm not even sure I believe the words. It's as though I'm trying them out to see if they ring true.

I pull her to me. She presses her cheek against my chest. My hands explore her back. Her fingers clutch at my waist.

'This is crazy,' I say.

'I know,' she says.

'We can't love each other just like that.'

'I know.'

'We hardly know each other.'

'I know.'

But floodgates have been opened in my heart, and I want to be allowed to wallow in the emotions that pour out. It's been so long. I have someone to speak words of love to, and I want to speak them, now, before the moment passes, because surely it will, because something like this can't happen, not like this, not so suddenly. Not to me. Something like this doesn't happen to me.

But I have no more words to speak. I'm struck dumb. We're both struck dumb. We pull apart, hold each other's hands, both hands. As one, we turn and start to walk again, automatically, our arms around each other's waist, fighting to come to terms with what we have just heard ourselves say.

'Can this really be happening?' I say to myself out loud.

Lisa's hand cuts and parts the air in front of her, as though she's trying to shape it to fit some new notion of her universe.

'I knew it,' she keeps saying to herself, as though whatever it is that she knows is outwith her control.

We walk down the Mound, across Princes Street, up Hanover Street and down Dundas Street into the New Town. How long it takes us, I don't know, but now the city centre is deserted. It belongs only to us. That is our very own castle, this is our very own National Gallery, these are our very own shop window displays. We reach the corner of the street where she lives.

'Leave me here,' she says.

'Leave you? Why?'

'This…'

That's as far as she can get with an explanation. She can make no more sense of *this* than I can. She draws in her lips and runs her tongue along them, in that Scarlett-Johannson-*Girl-in-a-Pearl-Earring* manner she has.

'I have to go,' she says.

'I don't understand.'

'Neither do I. I'm scared. I need to think.'

'Then tell me again. Tell me it's not just me.'

'It's not just you.'

She pulls away and runs down the street. She runs away because she thinks she's in love with me, and I'm left standing alone on a street corner beneath a faltering street lamp. There must be some kind of sense to it.

Back at my flat I slump at the kitchen table and stare glassy-eyed at the fridge. It's a tall fridge-freezer, with the fridge at the top and the freezer at the bottom. The doors are covered with fridge magnets. An hour later, I'm still staring at those magnets.

Do you make a distinction between the mysterious principles of knowledge and those of love? asks Alpha 60.

There is no mystery to love, replies Lemmy Caution.

24.

Now, you're going to have to bear with me here, because I'm likely to behave in some strange ways. If you've ever been in love you'll know what I'm talking about. Okay, so it's all a bit sudden, but that's the way of it sometimes. It was like that with Jenny, and that lasted, at least until she dumped me.

In any case, it's not as though Lisa and I are strangers. We've known each other for months. Why shouldn't we fall in love? Be sceptical if you must, but I've got to give some name to these emotions I'm feeling.

You can call it infatuation, lust or whatever, but love is what Lisa called it on the corner of the High Street and George IV Bridge, and that will do for me for the time being. I'll give it more serious consideration later. For now, let me wallow in the emotions, okay?

If I thought I spent Christmas Day pining, I now realise that was mere preparation for the real thing. On Saturday I'm worse than John Mills in *Ice Cold In Alex*, when he's in the desert fantasising about that perfect glass of cold beer. I'm at a loss as to what to do. I can't go round to see Lisa because I don't know her address, and I can't phone her because her number isn't in the directory.

In the afternoon I watch *Ivanhoe* on the box, and I can hardly bear it when Elizabeth Taylor tells Robert Taylor: 'I love you with all the longing in the lonely world.'

And I'm sorry to say there's worse. I dig out my CD of 'Hello' and sing along with Lionel Ritchie: Is it me you're looking for?

I know. Make allowances. (It's a present from a former girlfriend, honest.)

On Sunday I panic. Maybe it isn't love after all. Maybe it *is* just infatuation. Maybe I'm on the rebound from Emma. Maybe Lisa is on the rebound. After all, I don't know anything about her. Can I trust the feelings of someone who falls in love with me so suddenly? Can I trust my own feelings? Maybe I'm just desperate to be in love. Period. With anyone.

In any case, Lisa didn't say she loved me, she only said she *thought* she loved me. Maybe she doesn't love me at all now she's sobered up. She's shown temporary interest in me before under the influence of alcohol. Maybe she's regretting the whole thing.

Or maybe we were both under a temporary spell cast by Megan's good luck charm.

Monday surprisingly arrives on time. At work I email Lisa straightaway: 'Please tell me I didn't dream it. Please tell me you still feel the same way as Friday night.'

An email comes back. I'm scared to open it. 'Yes, I still feel the same way. In fact I feel worse.'

Yes! She feels worse!

I try to print the email, but the printer's down.

I send another: 'Can I see you today? Any time. Anywhere.'

Reply: 'Meet me at five o'clock outside the main entrance.'

Five o'clock doesn't want to arrive. The minute hand on the wall clock slows almost to a stop. The hour hand is surely broken.

I avoid Richard as best I can. At lunchtime I give the canteen a body swerve in order to avoid Scott. I need to speak to Lisa first. As if I could eat anyway.

Somehow the day passes in regulation time and at five o'clock precisely I'm waiting on the front steps as Lisa comes out in her dark blue suit. I've imagined us rushing into each other's arms, like Jean-Louis Trintignant and Anouk Aimée in the train station at the end of *Une Homme et Une Femme*, but in the event such a romantic gesture, especially without a Maurice Jarre soundtrack, seems inappropriate on the front steps of the Bank.

Instead, we cross St Andrew Square to the Downtown Diner, find a secluded booth, face each other across the table and order Manhattan lattes. We don't kiss, we don't touch, we barely speak, but I swear the air between us shimmers. It's like *Brief Encounter*, but with coffee instead of tea.

When at last I reach across the table to take Lisa's hand, her touch is electric. Literally. I receive a shock. I've never seen that elusive substance I call spark so plainly manifested. It could be something to do with that shimmering air I just mentioned, or more likely it's some static my shirt has picked up. It does that sometimes.

At least the shock breaks the tension.

'Is that what they mean by court and spark?' I say.

'I hope it doesn't mean we're allergic to each other,' says Lisa.

I take her hand again and she grips mine back. Suddenly we're in deadly earnest.

'I liked your email,' I say. 'I'm glad you feel worse.'

'It's not funny,' she says, but not without a complicit smile. 'I haven't been able to eat all weekend.'

'I know. I'm the same.'

'I've never felt like this before.'

'Have you never been in love before?'

'I thought so, but now I know I wasn't.'

She makes me feel like Kate Winslet makes Leonardo Di Caprio feel on the bow of the Titanic. King of the World. How can she feel this way for me? Why me? How can she love *me*?

'Have *you* ever been in love before?' she says.

'A long time ago.'

'Did it feel like this?'

A brief pause. 'It was a long time ago.'

The waitress brings our Manhattans. We let go of each other's hand like guilty teenagers caught necking behind the bike shed.

I've never been in a situation like this before. I don't know how to act. Lisa and I are strangers in love, dropped into the middle of a love affair without preliminaries. Nothing has prepared us for the feelings we have. No shared activities, no all-night conversations, no long lingering kisses, no sex. Here we are exchanging words of love, and I feel shy even holding her hand.

'Can I kiss you?' I say when we're alone again.

'There's something I have to tell you first,' she says falteringly and plays with the handle of her coffee cup.

I wait, but she seems more interested in that handle.

'What is it?'

'I don't know how to say it.' Her hand is shaking now.

'Just say it.'

'I live with someone.'

Her voice breaks, as though it's the hardest thing she's ever said. It's even harder to hear. I feel as though I've been punched in the stomach. Suddenly there's none of that shimmering air stuff going on any longer.

'I should have told you before,' she says, 'but I didn't know how to.'

To all the other emotions coursing through me you can now add dejection, hopelessness and a whole bunch of associated synonyms from *Roget's Thesaurus*. I try to think of something useful to say, but my brain is the consistency of a bowl of mashed Maris Pipers.

'Say something,' she says.

'I don't understand. If you live with someone, what's going on here?'

'I don't know what's going on here. I still feel the same way as I did on Friday, but…' She leaves the sentence hanging. It's the most wretched unfinished sentence I've ever heard.

'Do you love him?'

'I thought I did once, but now I know I never did. It's been over between us for some time.'

'So leave him,' I say, grasping at renewed hope.

'I can't just walk out.'

'Why not?'

'I don't know what he'd do if I just walked out. We've been together for seven years. He doesn't realise it's over.'

'Tell him.'

'You don't know him. He's not like you. We don't talk. He goes out and gets drunk with his mates every night.'

'So what are you saying to me?'

She leans across the table, takes my hand again and finally looks me in the eye. 'I meant what I said on Friday. I don't understand what's happening between us, but I know I have to find out. Just give me time to sort things out with Jeff.'

I desperately want to believe her, but this isn't quite the romantic tryst I'd envisaged.

'Don't you have some things to sort out too?' she says. 'What about Emma?'

'Emma? What do you know about Emma?'

'I saw you with her at the party. The way you held her. I asked Scott about her. Have you told her about me?'

'No. No, I haven't, but it's over with Emma.'

Even as I say it, I realise what Lisa is trying to tell me. Maybe we both come with baggage.

'How much time do you need?' I say.

'Two weeks.'

'Two weeks?' I'm impressed by the precision of her answer. 'How do you know you need two weeks?'

'Because I have to go skiing with Jeff in Switzerland next week.'

'You're going on holiday with him?'

'It's been booked for ages. I can't call off now. In any case, it will give me a chance to sort things out with him.'

She makes it sound as though going away with this bozo is the best thing that could happen to us. It feels almost churlish to have reservations. I slump back on my seat, awash with conflicting emotions.

What if she has such a good time with this Jeff character that she changes her mind about us? What if he persuades her to give *them* another go? What if…? There are too many 'what if's.'

'What if you forget me while you're away?' I say pathetically.

'What if you forget me?'

She's right. I'm being ridiculous.

'Trust me,' she says.

Maybe that's the problem. Maybe, after four years with Emma, I've forgotten how to trust.

'When do you leave?'

'Saturday.'

'Can I see you again before then?'

'I don't know. It might be better if we…' Again she leaves the sentence hanging. 'Have you told anyone about us yet?'

'No.'

'Then promise you won't. Please. Jeff knows people at the Bank. I need to talk to him first. I haven't even said anything to Kirsty.'

'Of course I promise.' But I can't disguise the confusion I feel.

'Please don't be angry with me.'

'I'm not angry, I'm just…' It's my turn to find no way to finish a sentence. 'Can I kiss you now?'

We lean forward awkwardly and just about manage to touch lips across the table. I feel like Johnny Depp in *Edward Scissorhands*, when he tries to get off a waterbed without puncturing it.

I move in beside her, take her in my arms and make a second attempt. Given that I've been dying to do this ever since we parted on Friday night, it's a surprisingly chaste kiss. The simple brush of her lips against mine feels like the ultimate intimacy. She feels it too. I'm sure she does. Her body trembles.

'Are you okay?' I say.

'I don't know,' she says softly. 'I feel like I'm going to burst.'

I do sympathise but, at the same time, part of me is inordinately pleased to be the cause of her discomposure.

Allowing her no respite, I kiss her a third time, more impulsively than before, and this time her mouth opens to mine in the most intoxicating way. When we part… Well, you know that staring into each other's eyes that lovers tend to want to do indulge in, instead of doing something constructive with their lives? I'm afraid we get into that for a while.

Until the sound of her voice jolts me out of my reverie.

'I have to go now,' she says.

'You're running away again? That isn't going to solve anything.'

'No, I have to get home. I'm sorry.'

I don't press further. She may have commitments I don't wish to hear about.

'So when can I see you again?'

'I get back a week on Saturday. I'll phone you Sunday morning.'

And that's it. She gives me one last brief kiss on the cheek, I move aside to let her out and she leaves.

That's right. On the cheek.

Maybe you were right to be sceptical.

25.

It's not until the following lunchtime, when I face Richard and Scott in the canteen for the first time since Friday night, that I realise the full ramifications of my promise to Lisa to keep quiet about us. Scott could give interrogation lessons to the Spanish Inquisition.

'Well, what happened after the party?' he says, even as I sit down.

Now, you have to believe me when I say I've never been one to boast about his experiences with the opposite sex. I've never been a notch-on-the-bedpost sort of guy.

Apart from Mary, that is, but I was only ten years old then, and I didn't get more than a glimpse of her knickers, and I'd have felt slighted if I hadn't, because she showed them to all the other boys, and if I hadn't been able to describe them I'd have been the laughing stock of the playground.

But apart from Mary, I've never viewed a woman as a conquest. So why do I now feel like a primitive hunter who's captured the biggest game and wants to show off to the rest of the tribe? And why, just when I'm desperate to, am I not allowed to? Why is life like this? It would be safe to tell Scott and Richard, wouldn't it?

'I walked Lisa home,' I say. This much is already public knowledge.

'And?' says Scott.

'And nothing. I just walked her home.'

He nods sagely. 'What did I tell you?' he says to Richard.

Richard raises an eyebrow, whether out of surprise at my amatory incompetence or because I've not even divulged this much to him, I'm not sure.

'No kiss this time?' he says.

'On the cheek,' I say with a shrug, as if it's of no consequence. I have to lie. I'm under orders.

He holds out his hand to Scott.

'That doesn't count,' says Scott.

'Rubbish,' says Richard. 'One pound, please.'

The bastards! The fact that Scott and I have had similar bets about Richard in the past is no mitigating factor.

'Bastards!' I say out loud as Scott reluctantly presses a one pound coin into Richard's outstretched palm. To say nothing would confirm that I have something to hide. To say more would do likewise. 'Bastards' is about right.

'What about you?' I say to Richard, employing diversionary tactics. 'What happened to you?'

'He went off with Kirsty in a taxi,' says Scott, seeking revenge for his financial loss.

'I didn't go off with her,' says Richard. 'We shared a taxi. There's a difference.'

Hang on a minute. Richard and Kirsty? Kirsty and Richard? I've been so preoccupied with Lisa that I've been missing out on other developments. But Richard and Kirsty? I suppose I can't see any reason why not. I mean, I hardly know Kirsty, but then I hardly know Richard these days.

'For a couple of simple Sassenachs,' says Scott, 'you're both being very mysterious.'

Richard and I turn our attention to our respective plates of chef's special *spaghetti banca* (don't ask). It's clear that, like me, he's hiding something, but I can hardly interrogate him when I have secrets of my own to keep.

The following day Scott corners me in the print room and tries again.

'You know you're going to tell me sooner or later,' he says. 'I know there's something going on between you and Lisa.'

'There's nothing going on.'

He knows I'm lying. I can barely look him in the eye.

'What's this all about, then?' he says, pulling a sheet of paper from his pocket. It's the hard copy of Lisa's email that I thought I'd failed to print out. 'What does she mean, *Yes I still feel the same way. In fact I feel worse?*'

Bloody computers.

'She had too much to drink. She wasn't feeling well.'

Scott looks at the date on the email.

'Three days afterwards?'

I appeal to his baser nature.

'Women and booze, eh?'

'I guess I'll have to ask Kirsty, then.'

'Kirsty knows nothing.'

'So there is something to know?'

Jesus gets less provocation in *The Last Temptation of Christ*.

When I made a promise of secrecy to Lisa, I should have requested exemptions, but I can't renege on that promise without asking permission. I decide I'd better get to Kirsty before Scott does and find out exactly how much she does know.

Not a lot, as it happens. When I phone her, I discover she's been seconded to another office for the week and hasn't spoken to Lisa since the party.

'Did she get home okay?' she says.

'Yes. Did *you* get home okay?' I'm becoming more proficient at evasion techniques than Richard Attenborough in *The Great Escape*.

'Yes, thanks. Richard and I took a taxi.'

'Oh, so you went off with Richard.'

'I didn't go off with him. We shared a taxi.' These are exactly the same words that he used.

'And?'

'And nothing. What kind of girl do you take me for?'

In which case, what's Richard being so coy about? Does he want Scott and me to think there's something going on when there isn't? Does Kirsty want me to think there's nothing going on when there is?

'What about you and Lisa?' she says. 'What's going on there?'

'Nothing!' You can't get much more evasive than that, but what choice do I have? Loyalty to Lisa has a higher moral imperative than honesty.

Still, all this prevarication is making me even more desperate to tell the truth to someone, anyone. It's killing me to keep it to myself. This Jeff character may know people at the Bank, but surely my promise of secrecy doesn't extend to every single *non*-banker in the country.

I wouldn't be breaking my promise if I told Cate, would I? I can trust Cate to keep a secret. I can also trust her to tell me exactly what she thinks. She always does.

I meet her at the Filmhouse bar and recount my tale in satisfyingly exhaustive detail. She listens attentively, laughs at all the right moments, makes cooing sounds at all the right moments, looks suitably concerned at all the right moments. Then she gives me her verdict.

'It's infatuation,' she says authoritatively.

'No,' I say, distressed. 'It's more than that.'

'In that case, tell me what you see in her.'

'What do you want? A list?'

'Alphabetical order will do.'

'You can't itemise love.'

'Let me tell you what you see in her, then.' I wait breathlessly. 'You think you love her because she thinks she loves you.'

'Don't be stupid.'

'I know you. Of course you're going to jump at that. It's infatuation.'

'Don't say that. I don't know that.'

'You're thirty-five years old. You should know that. Plus she's already living with someone. You don't seriously expect it to last, do you?'

'She's finished with him.'

'Have any of your relationships lasted?'

'This is different.'

'Just like it's always been different before?'

This is unfair use of inside knowledge.

'Every relationship is different.'

'And most of them don't last.'

I'm beginning to think Cate's working through her own agenda here, not mine.

'Now you're just being cynical. Just because it didn't last for you and Calum.' No, that's not fair either. 'Sorry.'

She smiles and puts a protective hand on mine.

'It's okay. You're acting like a little boy. It's sweet.'

I pull my hand away sharply. 'Don't patronise me.'

'Don't be so touchy. You know what your problem is?'

'No doubt you're going to enlighten me.'

'You want love like it is in the movies. You want to meet someone, fall madly in love like this (she clicks her fingers) and live happily ever after. Real life's not like that. I'm worried for you. If you're not careful, you're going to get hurt again.'

'If I get hurt again, I get hurt again.'

'Why not cool it for a bit?'

'Because I don't know how.'

'There speaks a true romantic.'

She makes it sound like a failing, but I accept my guilt willingly, without the need to mount a defence.

'Well, I hope it works out for you,' she says in a gesture of conciliation. 'Maybe Lisa is the love of your life. What do I know? I've never been in love like that. I've always thought that if you had sex, companionship, fun, all that, well, what more could you want? Your kind of love doesn't seem like much fun to me.'

I could tell her I'd rather spend a lifetime pining for Lisa than having sex, companionship, fun and all that without her, but somehow I don't think that would further my position.

'You always did set your sights too low,' I say.

She laughs hoarsely. 'Tell me about it.'

She takes a sip of her G&T and, all of a sudden, I realise that my problems, like Bogie's in *Casablanca*, don't amount to a hill of beans compared to what she's been through recently.

'Do you still see Calum?' I say.

'No. He's out of my life.'

'And how do you feel now about…' My voice trails away. I'm not sure I should be broaching the subject.

'My baby? It's okay. I can talk about it now. I'll always wonder, but you know me, I'm not one to dwell on the past. You've got to get on with your life, haven't you?'

'That's all I'm trying to do.'

'Then let's agree on that. Here's to getting on with life.'

She clinks her glass to mine in a toast.

'Have you told Em yet?' she says.

'I told you, Lisa doesn't want me to tell anyone.'

'Tell her.'

'Don't you think I should at least wait until things are clearer?'

'She needs things to be clearer now. Tell her.'

That night I have a dream. For all I know, I dream every night, but this one I remember. I'm in a cinema with my lover. It might be Lisa, I can't tell. The cinema is empty apart from us. The film is about a man and a woman who are in love. They're up there on the big screen in two-shot close-up. The thing is, though, we're not looking at them, they're looking at us.

I'm not sure I like this dream. I *don't* expect love to be like it is in a film. I'm *not* in a movie. I'm *not* acting out a part. The ending has *not* been pre-written. Lisa and I are free agents. *That's* why we can make it work.

Two days later I do as Kate tells me and meet Emma in Jenners. It feels like old times, especially when I choose a Cheddar cheese roll and Emma gives me one of her long-suffering looks.

It turns out I'm aggravating an already bad mood. When I ask her if she enjoyed the party, she tells me she had such a good time that she's been feeling depressed ever since. It's the kind of logic that only Emma could concoct.

'It made me realise how empty my life is,' she says. 'You have so many friends. I have no one.'

This is so untrue, it's hardly worth contradicting. I told you she'd get depressed after the pre-Christmas craft fairs.

'You have lots of friends.'

'Not close friends. I even had to finish with Alec because he was getting too close.'

'He's not the only man out there.'

'I know, but I'm used to you. I've been with you so long that I only feel comfortable with you.'

My hearing must be going. I think I've just heard her say she only feels comfortable with *me*.

'The last time we met, you said you'd always been happier on your own.'

'I didn't realise.'

Timing has never been one of Emma's strong points, but she's chosen some moment to experience this revelation.

'So what are you saying?'

'I don't know.'

'You said things were never right between us.'

'I know. I'm confused.'

'Maybe when you meet the right man, you won't be.'

'What if there is no right man?'

'There is. In fact, there's more than one.'

'How can you be so certain?'

'Because there's more than one person for everyone.' Okay, here goes. 'I mean, I met someone else at the party.'

'You mean that woman you spent all night talking to?'

'I did not spend all night talking to her.'

'You did so.'

'Is that why you left without saying goodbye?'

'What's her name?'

'Lisa. She thinks she's in love with me.'

Emma sits up straight, as though affronted. 'That was quick.'

'We already knew each other. She works at the Bank.'

'How do you feel about her?'

'I don't know yet. I have to find out more.' Well, that's true, isn't it? Allow me some room for diplomacy.

'I don't know what to say,' Emma says and puts on her fixed smile. Now I know for sure that she's hurting. 'I'm happy for you.'

'I don't know what's going to happen,' I say. As if that will ease her pain. 'I hardly know Lisa. For all I know, I'm on the rebound from you.'

'You're still on the rebound from Jennifer.'

'That was years ago.'

'I bet Lisa reminds you of her, though. I never could live up to your image of her.'

'That's not true. You wouldn't let me love you, if you remember.'

Fortunately Emma has enough sense to pull us back from the brink of an old argument.

'You're right,' she says. 'Anyway, that's what I was trying to tell you, isn't it? I can't let anyone get close to me. Will you invite me to the wedding?'

'Stop it.'

'Is she better than me in bed?'

'Emma!'

'Sorry.'

'I've hardly spoken to her, never mind anything else.'

'I hate myself.'

She drops her head to hide behind a curtain of falling hair, forgetting that it's still too short to perform that function. I've never seen her look so vulnerable.

'Emma, you didn't want me. You *don't* want me. Was I supposed to hang around forever in case you changed your mind?'

'I know. I'm sorry.'

Then I remember how glad I was when she told me she'd dumped Alec.

'I'm sorry too. Anyway, it'll probably come to nothing. Relationships usually do, don't they?'

'Well, I'm sure she'll be better in bed than me.'

'Can we change the subject?'

'I haven't slept with anyone since Alec, and that was before Christmas. Not that I have a sex drive anyway.'

'You will when you meet the right man.' There I go again.

'He'd better turn up soon or I'll be past it. And you'll be married with two kids. That'd be funny, wouldn't it? Does she want children?'

'I don't know.'

'You'd better find out.'

'Give me chance. For all we know, you'll meet someone tomorrow and I'll be on my own again.'

She looks unconvinced. She needs reassurance that the only man she feels comfortable with isn't suddenly going to disappear from her life.

'Whatever happens,' I say, 'I hope you still want to stay friends.'

'What kind of friends?' she says without a trace of irony. Anyone would think it was I who had slammed the door in *her* face.

'Can't we just see what happens?'

It's a role reversal worthy of Nicholas Cage and John Travolta in *Face/Off*. It's enough to make you give up trying to make sense of life. How can you take anything seriously when even the deepest emotions and most entrenched positions turn out to be so arbitrary, so subject to the vagaries of time and circumstance? It's true what they say: what goes around comes around.

The one certainty I cling to is Lisa's return. As the day draws ever nearer I become as nervous as Gary Cooper in *High Noon*, waiting for the clock to strike twelve. On the Sunday morning, just as she promised, she phones. It's a short conversation.

'It's me,' she says. 'I'm back.'

'I've missed you.'

'Can I see you?'

'When?'

'Now?'

'Where? What do you want to do?'

'Anything you want.'

'Anything?'

'*Every*thing.'

Yes!

26.

Sunday afternoon. Three o'clock. My bedroom. Late January sun slanting through window blinds. A three-kilowatt fan heater to augment the central heating.

'Don't ask me anything yet,' says Lisa. 'Not yet. Just make love to me.'

It would be impolite to refuse.

We lie down on the bed, fully clothed, face to face, and I enfold her in my arms as I would a fragile flower. She feels soft, warm, pliant, compliant, vulnerable, yielding, alive. Her fingers clutch at my waist, as they did on the corner of the High Street and George IV Bridge. I feel as ungainly as Shrek beside her.

I run my fingers along the outline of her body, beginning at her knee, moving up her thigh, over her hip, across the indentation of her waist.

'You feel nice,' I say for want of a more eloquent exposition of my feelings, but you can't expect great oratory from me at this precise moment.

My hand comes to rest on one of her breasts. It's so… cuppable. It kind of nestles into my palm of its own accord.

'I like your breasts,' I say.

'They're too small,' she says.

'No, they're perfect.'

'You need glasses.'

She's wearing a dark red woollen dress, zipped at the back. In a style she favours, the material is gathered under her bust, from where it skims out over her hips. Quickly, before Fate realises it has made a mistake and handed me more than my usual portion of good fortune, I feel for the zip and tug it down. A moan of contentment escapes from Lisa's lips. I've never before made a woman moan just by touching her zip.

'This is like a dream.' I only mean to think it, but I say it out loud.

She puts a finger to my mouth and searches my eyes with hers.

'No,' she says, 'it's real. Nothing has ever felt so real.'

I realise this must sound like a romantic fantasy I'm spinning you here, but I can only tell it as I see it. When David Lean made *Ryan's*

Daughter, the critics slated him for the scene in which Kirsty Miles makes love with Christopher Jones in the woods. It's all sparkling sunlight, soft breezes, swaying branches and every romantic cliché you've ever seen.

What the critics didn't realise is that we're seeing it from Kirsty's point of view. That's how she experiences it. It's the most romantic thing that's ever happened to her. What I'm saying is, you can't expect me to be objective about making love to Lisa.

When the zip reaches the end of its trajectory, my hand trembles.

'I want to take my time undressing you,' I say, 'but at the same time I don't want to wait. I want you right now.'

'Then take me,' she says. Honest. That's what she says to me.

It's one of those invitations you spend your whole life having wet dreams about, but I'd trade all those times for this one precious moment, here, now, when Lisa utters these words to me. All my resolve to be a gentle, caring, responsive lover evaporates in an instant. I give in to a more primal urge to possess Lisa's body. Now. Immediately.

I want to tell you exactly how we make love. I want to savour every moment. If you find such matters indelicate, I suggest you skip a couple of pages, but I make no apologies for what I am about to tell you. On the contrary, I celebrate it.

Lisa lies on her back and raises her hips so that I can pull her dress down. When it's clear of her body, she lies before me in nothing more substantial, despite the temperature outside, than white silk lingerie and lace-topped hold-ups. For a moment I'm dazzled by her sheer femininity. You'd think I'd never seen a woman before.

'You're beautiful,' I say. She's reduced me to clichés.

She says nothing. She just lies there and waits for me to do whatever I'm going to do to her next. That's all she wants. I know it's hard to believe, even I can hardly believe it, but it's true. I can see it in her eyes. Right now, that's *everything* she wants.

I unroll her hold-ups and place them beside her dress on the bedside table, then I lie down beside her and unclasp her bra. It disengages easily from her breasts and I lay it on top of her dress. Now only her knickers remain, but I leave them be for a moment while I take in what I've unveiled so far.

She lies open to my gaze as my eyes rove greedily over the soft curves of her body – her neck, her breasts, her waist, her thighs. I feel awkward by comparison, all angles and points. One part of me especially.

How can she think her breasts are too small? They're the most perfect breasts that have ever been formed. As perfect as every other part of her body, from the smattering of freckles on her shoulders to the birthmark on her right thigh, from the red sore on her left calf, where I suspect she cut herself shaving this morning, to the small mole beside her navel.

'I was wrong,' I say. 'I don't like your breasts, I love them.'

She looks at them with curiosity, flattened against her chest.

'You're sure you don't think they're too small?'

'I told you, they're perfect. They're you.' Then I can't stop myself saying it again: 'You're beautiful.'

'I'm not, but you make me feel beautiful.'

She shows no sign of embarrassment as she lies before me, arms by her side, eyes fixed on mine, expectant. I hook my fingers in the waistband of her knickers, pull them down her legs and get my first breathless glimpse of the neatest triangle of pubic hair I've ever laid eyes on. Pale gold at the perimeter, shading to deepest bronze where it lines the secret cleft hidden between her closed thighs.

I brush it with my fingers. It feels springy beneath my touch. Surely she must trim it. No individual hair can be more than half an inch long. It's a wonder of nature.

She's totally naked now, while I'm still fully dressed. I move down the bed, take her ankles, one in each hand, and delicately, without resistance, part them. With mounting anticipation, I kneel between her legs, bend towards her, run my hands up the inside of her thighs and press my lips to that cleft I told you about.

I forget what I was going to do next because I get side-tracked down there. It could be any amount of time before Lisa suddenly gasps and puts a restraining hand on my head.

'You'd better stop,' she says.

I get to my knees and unbutton my shirt. Lisa sits up, eases it from my shoulders and, without a word, lays me on my back. I surrender to her as she did to me. She undresses me as I did her, item by item. She strokes my arms, plays with the hairs on my chest and dangles her breasts over me. Although there may not be much to dangle, what there is is beguiling. When she releases my penis it leaps into her hand as though it's found its purpose in life.

'I think it likes you,' I say thickly. She strokes it delicately with the tip of her finger. I can't adequately describe how good that feels.

'You're beautiful,' she says.

'Thank you,' I say stupidly.

She brushes it against her cheek.

'I want to feel you inside me,' she says.

I can manage that.

She lies back down beside me and opens her arms to receive me. I retrieve a condom from a long-held three-pack in the bedside cabinet and unroll it with trembling haste. Our bodies are so ready for each other that, as soon as I lie on top of her, I'm drawn straight into her. We barely need to move at all. It's enough simply to stare into each other's eyes... until all of a sudden she wraps her legs around me, changing the angle of our union.

That's all it takes. It's so effortless.

Afterwards we lie face to face, each totally absorbed in the mystery of the other.

'I can't believe how much I wanted you,' she says.

'I know.' What I mean is, I felt the same way.

'I've never felt like that before. I wanted to give myself to you. I wanted to be taken completely.'

'I know.' It seems to be the only phrase I'm capable of formulating.

'No, you don't know. You can't know.'

'Then tell me.'

'I love you.' It's the first time she has said these three words to me as simply and plainly as that, without qualification, without question or reservation.

'I love you too.'

'Even that first time Scott introduced us to each other in the canteen, I knew there was something about you. And when you gave that talk.'

'What talk?'

'The one on the new system.'

'You were there? When I tripped over the projector cable? I was terrible.'

'No, you were fine. And every time I saw you after that, at *The Searchers*, that afternoon by the Water of Leith, at the Film Society, every time, I just knew. There was something... some kind of spark... I didn't know what it was, but at your party and afterwards, everything suddenly became clear. I know it sounds crazy.'

What's crazy is not that she can feel these things, but that she can feel these things for *me*.

'I'm sorry,' she says, 'I know I'm not making much sense. I'm not used to talking about my feelings. With Jeff I've always had to bottle everything up.'

I squeeze her hand in encouragement.

'You can say anything to me.'

'I know,' she says. 'I know I can.'

She sits up beside me, rests her chin on her knees, wraps her arms around them and stares down at the duvet. It's patterned in coloured squares and can be quite mesmerising if you let your eyes glaze over, like when you look at a 3D stereogram.

'When I was growing up,' she says, then pauses, as though she hasn't yet decided what to say next, 'I always thought there were two kinds of people: those who were happy and those who were sad. And I was one of the sad ones. I thought that was the way things were. That's one reason I ended up in a backroom job in Accounts. Nobody bothers me there. Does that make sense?'

'Yes.'

'All my parents ever wanted me to be was a good little girl. I was never allowed to…' She pauses again. She has so much to say, so much she's needed to say for such a long time, that she can no longer find all the words. 'Have you seen *Splendor in the Grass*?'

'Yes.'

'You know that scene where Natalie Wood shouts at her mother because she can't stand being a good little girl any longer? That was me. Except that I kept it all inside.'

'For me it was that scene in *Rebel Without a Cause*, when James Dean shouts at his father for being such a doormat.'

'You were like me. You escaped to the pictures. I saw that in you from the start.'

'What about Jeff?' I had to ask some time.

'Films were a dream, but he was real. I thought he was my way out. It sounds stupid now.'

'What happened while you were away with him?'

She again takes a moment to search for the right words.

'I realised why I needed to be with you.'

She doesn't need to say more. I don't need to hear more.

'Did you tell him about me?'

'I told him I needed some space. He was more understanding than I expected. He must know things haven't been right between us for a long time. When we got back yesterday I moved into the spare bedroom. I haven't told him, but I'm going to start looking for somewhere else to stay and, when I move out, he'll realise it's over. He doesn't need to know about us. It would just complicate matters.'

'So there is an us?'

'I want there to be, if you want.'

'I want,' I say and squeeze her hand again to emphasise the point.

'Does it feel as scary to you as it does to me,' she says, 'falling in love with someone you know so little about?'

'We know everything we need to know. The rest is just details.'

'You know what I think?'

'What?'

'I think we were both ready for this, but we didn't realise it until your birthday.'

She's right. I, we, have both been suppressing our need for affection for a long time. Like Lemmy and Natasha, perhaps we can escape loveless Alphaville together.

There's a word that crops up in Jean-Luc's films over and over again. *Tendresse*. Tenderness. It's one of the words that are forbidden in Alphaville. In *Masculin Féminin* it's Jean-Pierre Léaud's favourite word. You can't live without it, he says, you might as well shoot yourself.

Until this afternoon with Lisa, I'd forgotten what *tendresse* was.

Yet there's one question that, no matter how hard I try, I can't stop myself from asking.

'Did you have sex with him while you were away?'

It's Lisa's turn to squeeze my hand.

'Once,' she says. 'I didn't want to, but... Don't be angry with me.'

I'm not angry. I just can't stand the thought of her with this Jeff character.

'It won't happen again,' she says. 'Not now. I know now how right it feels with you. I mean...' She lowers her eyes and licks her lips in that covert manner she has. 'I've never felt much before. In bed, I mean. But with you... I don't know, I can't explain it. It just seems right.'

'I know.' I'm reduced to that again. I can't explain it any more than she can, but it *does* seem right. Sometimes things just seem right.

Even if I tried to compile a list of what attracts me to her, that still wouldn't explain why I feel the way I do about her. It's like I said to Cate, you can't itemise love. Emma was wrong about me needing to analyse everything like it's some computing problem. Whatever's going on here between Lisa and me, I'm happy for it to remain a mystery.

'I love it when you do that,' I say.

'Do what?'

'Lick your lips like that.'

'Like what?'

I show her.

'I don't, do I?' She clamps her hand to her mouth.

'No, it's sexy.'

I wish I could find a way of telling her how I feel about her that's as articulate as the way she's voiced her feelings for me, but sometimes words are inadequate. Sometimes you have to go beyond words. The moments that matter, in film and in life, the ones you remember when everything else fades, are always silent. That's why every screenwriting manual begins with the injunction: Show, don't tell.

Lisa still sits beside me with her knees drawn up. Gently I take hold of her ankle. Immediately she sees the urgency in my eyes. Willingly she lies down beside me.

We take longer this time.

And, eventually, we're not very silent at all.

27.

The cold, dark evenings of winter. I love them. The cold encourages you to snuggle up with a loved one. The darkness reduces horizons, conceals distractions, allows you to inhabit your own cosy little universe, untainted by the harsh light of day. On a winter's evening in Edinburgh all things are possible. There is no season more romantic. You can keep your tropical desert island. Give me a windswept street corner and a woman who needs to be kept warm.

And snow. Snow is the jewel in the crown of winter, the icing on the cake, the soft cushion against the vicissitudes of life. Who could not be enchanted by snow? When I walk Lisa home after making love to her for the first time, or rather the second time, it snows. It wraps about our hair. It lies two inches on the ground and crunches beneath our feet.

In a snow-frosted Inverleith Park we stroll hand in hand through a gauntlet of trees outlined spectral white against the grey sky. A gust of wind whips up a swirl of spindrift, giving us excuse, if excuse were needed, to cling to each other ever more tightly. Lisa kisses snowflakes from my eyebrows.

Along the sheltered Water of Leith there is by contrast not a breath of breeze. The silence is fantastic. The carpet of snow dulls all sound except the ripple of running water. It's as though the city, the world, has come to a halt. The world has come to a halt in homage to our love.

In Stockbridge there's a power cut. The shops are decked in candles that throw dancing shadows onto the street. Above, candlelit living room windows turn tenement walls into an illuminated advent calendar. Passers-by converse in hushed voices. The old village has never looked, sounded, felt so magical.

The rest of the way to Lisa's street corner, we walk through a silent movie. Even parting has no need of words. A lingering kiss encapsulates everything that needs to be said. It's like Alpha 60 says, *Sometimes reality is too complex for oral communication.*

When I get home there's a message on the answer machine from Emma. She knows I'm seeing Lisa today and wants a progress report. Still flushed with feeling, I phone her back, aching to tell her, tell anyone.

'Have you seen her?' she says.

'I've just left her.'

'Is she still in love with you?'

'I think so.'

'Are you in love with her?'

Her voice cracks a little. She disguises it with practised skill, but she can't hide it from my practised ear. Just in time it tells me how selfish I would be to speak of feelings we could never share.

'I'm still trying to find out what's going on,' I say. It's a kind of truth.

'Did you fuck her?'

'Emma!'

'You did, didn't you.'

'No.'

Not much truth there, you might think, but I didn't *fuck* Lisa. We made love. No doubt Emma would find the distinction somewhat pedantic, but it enables me to tell myself I'm not telling her unmitigated lies.

'Why not?' she says.

I can imagine the state she's worked herself into over this. She doesn't want me, yet now that she has no one, she can't seem to let go of me.

'Look,' I say, 'I don't want to talk about this over the phone.'

'Then I'll come round.'

'No. I have things to do. I'll call you later.'

She doesn't seem to realise I'm not the one she needs to talk to. I should never have phoned her back. I feel guilty now. Even though we're no longer together, I'm still hurting her, which in turn hurts me. Emma! How can you dump me and *still* cause us heartache?

Later, she phones to apologise.

The following day, Monday, I abandon Richard and Scott for lunch with Lisa at the Downtown Diner. We're like giggling adolescents, beyond caring whether we're pathetic or not. We play footsie under the table. In the afternoon we swap emails that I won't sicken you with. We're worse than Tom Hanks and Meg Ryan in *You've Got Mail*.

On Tuesday we meet after work. On the way back to my flat we stop in a secluded close for a quick fumble to keep us going, and we barely make it through my front door before we're undressing each other. I'll let you imagine the details for yourself this time. I've probably already told you more about Lisa than I should have done. She'd be mortified if she knew.

This time it's my turn to send her home early, because I've promised to meet Richard at the Cameo bar. There's someone he wants me to meet. He wouldn't say who, but presumably she, I assume it's a she, in fact I assume it's Kirsty, is the reason for his recent coyness.

When I arrive I find him sitting with Emma and Cate. He must have rounded us all up for a grand unveiling, but why Emma and Cate? He hardly knows them. Why would Emma especially put herself through this? To see me?

Wait a minute. Richard doesn't know about Lisa. What if he's engineered this meeting for my benefit rather than his? What was it he said? There's someone he wants *me* to meet? Is he setting me up for a blind date? Another Maggie? Please, no.

But again, why would Emma and Cate be here?

'What's going on?' I say.

'Take a seat,' he says.

I do so. 'I didn't expect to see you and Cate here,' I say to Emma.

'I didn't expect to see you and Richard here,' she says. 'Cate said she wanted me to meet someone.'

'That's what Richard said to me.'

Wait another minute.

'You don't mean...' I say to Richard. He flashes a grin as sly as the one Orson Welles sports in that doorway in *The Third Man*.

I point rudely at Cate. Richard laughs. Cate laughs. Emma looks puzzled.

'You and Cate?' I say to him. It doesn't seem that long ago that I was asking Scott the same question in the same disbelieving tone.

'I thought you'd be surprised,' he says.

Surprised doesn't cover it. I'd be less surprised if he disappeared into a telephone booth and emerged in cape and tights as Superman.

'You mean...' says Emma, as the realisation hits her too.

They all look to me for some sort of pronouncement.

'When?' is the best I can come up with, although what I want to know is how and why.

Richard and Cate? If Richard and Kirsty made no sense to me, Richard and Cate plumbs new depths of infeasibilty. He may be, well, my best friend, I suppose, but even Megan moved to another continent to get away from him. Surely he's too set in his ways for Cate.

As for Cate, surely she's too wilful for him. There's no way this can work. It must be a relationship of convenience. Yes, that's it. Each of them in the right place at the right time. Single, lonely, desperate... And sex? No, I don't even want to think about it.

Too late! An horrendous thought elbows its way into my mind. Cate has turned Richard and me into shag-mates!

It's a turn of events that's certainly achieved something I would never have thought possible this evening – it's taken my mind off Lisa.

'It was at your party,' says Richard.

'Rich was drunk enough to ask me out,' says Cate.

'And she was drunk enough to say yes,' says Richard. Or is it *Rich* now?

'And I've been saying yes ever since,' says Cate.

They exchange a glance of mutual longing. It's sickening. I mean, Lisa and me you can appreciate, but this is truly sickening.

Emma and I exchange a glance of mutual mystification. It takes me the remainder of the evening, utilising trips to the bar and toilets, to get her and each of the two lovebirds on their own to obtain some straight answers.

Cate is first up, while Emma helps Richard fetch a round. She tells me that Rich is so different from Cal. He's intelligent, stable, reliable, good in bed. Good in bed? Please, no. He has no rhythm. Has Cate never seen him dance? If he's better than me in bed, I'll top myself.

Help! Cate must know!

She'd met him before, of course, at her wedding, but says she only began to take notice of him at my party. I have to admit he has changed since the wedding, and especially since Megan left him. He's much more willing to make an effort these days. Even a bit wilful sometimes?

He even looks more presentable without that felled forest of stubble he used to sport. And there's something else different about him this evening. I can't quite put my finger on it. Maybe I should try to see him through Cate's eyes. As he is, not as he was.

Cate has questions for me too. She wants to know if I've consummated my relationship with Lisa. I tell her the truth I wouldn't tell Emma and she congratulates me as she might one of her toy boys for passing an exam. I make her promise not to say a word to Richard because of the bozo-knows-people-at-the-Bank complication, and also not to talk to Emma until I've had a chance to. She tells me to be gentle with Emma. I promise I will.

When I get Richard on his own, he tells me that Cate is a compendium of the most desirable aspects of all the women he has ever dated. She's as intelligent as Megan, as fun to be with as Barbra... Plus she does things in bed that he didn't know women could do. Please, no, not that rippling thing.

I must try to be magnanimous. Maybe Cate is good for him. Maybe they're good for each other. Maybe there is some sort of complementary equality here. I mean, look at the way they're both fiddling with their glasses. He's mirroring her fidgetiness already.

No, what am I saying? Richard and Cate? It's about as likely as Mark Wahlberg's fourteen-incher in *Boogie Nights*.

Emma can't get her head around it either, she tells me when it's her turn for a private conference. Just when she was getting used to having her best friend back, she loses her again to my best friend. But far be it for her to pass judgement. Richard is nicer than she remembers, and he certainly looks better, especially in his new suit.

Of course! That's what's been bugging me about him. In a plot development of jaw-dropping proportions, he's wearing a new suit for the occasion. This one even fits him.

If he and Cate like each other, Emma says charitably, good luck to them.

I suppose. Good luck to them.

When they leave together at closing time, I end up on the street with Emma.

'I'm sorry about the phone call the other day,' she says before we part company. 'It's just that it feels like I've finally lost you.'

'I thought you'd finished with me anyway,' I say without rancour.

'Have you fucked her yet?'

'Emma!'

'Sorry.'

But perhaps now is as good a time to tell her as any. The gin will help dilute the pain.

'Look, I have to tell you something. I lied to you the other day. We did make love on Sunday. I was scared to tell you because I didn't want to hurt you.'

There, it's said.

Emma makes me wait for a judgement. She sways from foot to foot, keeping her eyes on mine to maintain stability, while she weighs the information in ways I can only imagine. I'm prepared for a tirade of recrimination, self-recrimination, a combination of both or any of a host of unpredictable reactions from her vast store. When she eventually delivers her verdict, it's as unexpected as I should have expected.

'I understand,' she says calmly. 'I know I'm not being sensible. I do want you to be happy. I hate myself for feeling this way. Congratulations.' She gives me that smile, the one that masks the hurt. 'Was it good? Sorry.'

If even the gin isn't working, there's not much I can do to soften the blow. I tell her that I want to stay friends, that she'll always be special to me, that I'll always be here for her. Clichéd sentiments, but I mean them. When she steps into a taxi and disappears into the night, I feel as though I'm letting her loose into a big wide unfriendly world that will find it hard to accommodate her.

I worry about her all the next day, but I can't keep it up, not when the day after that Lisa is in my bed again. Her body is hungry for mine. She wants to drain me into her. And I learn she doesn't trim her pubic hair after all. It's clever enough to know when it has attained its optimal length.

Until she moves into a place of her own we devise lies she can tell the bozo so that we can spend as much time together as possible. Over the next couple of weeks we give each other crash courses in our likes and dislikes, hopes and fears, family and friends, upbringing and education, sexual history. Not once do we hear anything that doesn't bond us closer.

One evening she props herself on her elbow and gives me a long, hard look.

'You do love me, don't you,' she says. It's a statement, not a question. It's a statement full of wonder.

Another time we drag ourselves away from the bedroom to watch *Alphaville*. She laughs at the cigarette-lighting scene, bless her, and she laughs even more loudly at the swimming-pool scene.

A man on a diving board is shot dead by a firing squad. To applause from spectators, his body is retrieved from the water by synchronised swimmers. Incorrigibly, Jean-Luc makes the incident even more startling by offering no on-screen explanation of it, so I give Lisa the benefit of my exhaustive research on the subject. This is the way citizens who succumb to emotion are executed in Alphaville.

She says she finds the film hypnotic.

Yes!

Another time I take her down to Director's Cut. Alasdair's current Top Ten features best entrances. At Number One he has the scene from *Dr No* where Ursula Andress walks out of the sea in that bikini. Number Two is the scene from *Once Upon a Time in the West*, where the baddie who kills the nice family turns out to be – shock, horror – good old Henry Fonda.

'What about John Wayne in *Stagecoach*?' says Lisa.

'You were at *The Searchers*, weren't you?' Alasdair says and looks at his list ruefully, realising it now requires amendment. I beam with pride.

When we get home I tell Lisa about my own lists and their seeming ability to reflect the story of my life. She likes the idea so much that she helps me add another to the series. Top Ten Most Erotic Moments.

Where did this woman come from? This woman who stimulates and satisfies my body and my mind. I haven't felt like this since... my God, since Jenny. Yes, this is what it used to feel like with Jenny. Now here it is again, the excitement, the adventure, the feeling that I am not alone in the world, that this is what life is meant to be about. Emma's wrong when she says Lisa reminds me of Jenny, but loving Lisa reminds me of loving Jenny.

On the day before Valentine's Day Lisa pays me the nicest compliment I've ever received.

'You've made me realise I was only half alive before I met you,' she says. 'I know now, I've found my soul mate.'

I give her a Valentine card to open the following morning. The printed message on the front says: 'I've dreamed of you all my life.' Inside I've written part of the speech that Kevin Smith wrote for Ben Affleck to say to the woman he loves in *Chasing Amy*. It's the greatest movie love speech ever written. 'You are the epitome of everything I have ever looked for in another human being.'

I've signed it, so that in years to come Lisa can read my name next to that sentiment, and remember.

I spent a whole afternoon choosing that card. I used to think Jenny was the one I'd dreamed of all my life. For a while she was. Now I'm learning that there's more than one person who can fulfil that dream.

I wish I'd known that before. I wish I'd known we're given more than one chance. I think we should be told.

The following day, Friday, she's out of the building. I won't see her again until Monday, but I pine no longer. I feel reassured of my worth. Validated as a man. Wanted, virile. Cocksure.

I'm unusually polite and helpful to everyone in the office. I say hello, I smile. I let Richard blether on about Cate. I smile good-naturedly at Scott's taunts about my newly mysterious life. I phone Kirsty to inquire after her welfare. I hold the gaze of secretaries (every one of them a woman) just a moment too long.

The world has become a wonderful place. On my way home every stranger on the street is my friend. Women especially are wonderful. I love their femininity. I love the way they move, the way they think, the way they talk, the topics they talk about, the timbre of their voices. Well, maybe not all women. Not Maggie, for instance. But in general.

It's Lisa's fault. Lisa has done this to me. It's a pretty feeble excuse, I know, but how else can I explain why I do what I do next?

28.

When I arrive back at my flat after work on Valentine's Day, I find Emma sitting on the landing. Another heavy session with her isn't high on my list of priorities, but I hold to my promise that I'll always be here for her. Maybe my positive mood will rub off on her.

We haven't spoken since I told her I'd made love to Lisa, but she continues our last conversation as though there hasn't been a two-week gap in-between. She tells me she's been doing some thinking. She sees now that I needed something she couldn't provide. She understands how difficult she is, and why I found it hard to tell her the truth.

Also, and this she *can't* understand, her sex drive has returned from wherever it went. In fact she's been so desperate for sex that she can't leave herself alone. She sits beside me on my couch and tells me this.

'It's a pity you didn't feel like that before,' I say jokingly, although on second thoughts it's not so funny.

'I know,' she says.

'You'll always be special to me, you know. I'll always be here for you.'

I've said it before, but it's a sentiment worth repeating. I put my arm around her shoulder to emphasise the point. We've been through a lot together. Why shouldn't we be good friends? Today I want everyone to be my friend, especially Emma.

Whoa! What's going on here? Her hand has fallen to my knee and is at this very moment starting to feel its way up my thigh.

'What are you doing?' I say.

'I don't know,' she says. 'I want you.'

In confirmation, she takes a lunge at me and kisses me with a passion that pins me against the back of the couch.

'Emma!' I say in admonishment when I manage to extricate myself.

'I can't help it,' she says.

I retrieve my arm from around her shoulder and remove her hand from my leg.

'I think you should stop. You don't want me. Not really. We've been through all that.'

'I do want you.'

'No. You only think you want me because you can't have me. I felt the same when you were with Alec. You *don't* want me. Not really.'

You'd think I'd be used to Emma's contrariness after all this time, but in all the years I've known her she has never confounded my expectations as deeply as she does now.

'No,' she says, 'you don't understand. It's because I've lost you that I now know I want you. It's like a weight has been lifted off me. Now you don't want anything from me, I'm free to feel what *I* want.'

It's suddenly clear to me why that McTaggart painting of a seaside storm in the National Gallery is her favourite work of art. More than anyone, she understands that chaotic sky.

'And what I seem to want right now,' she says, in case I haven't got the picture, 'is sex. Now I don't *have* to want you, I do want you. Touch me, just for a minute.'

In a movement as swift as Gene Wilder's gun draw in *Blazing Saddles*, she jumps astride me, places my hands on her breasts and latches her lips onto mine again.

It really isn't fair. I love Lisa, I want only Lisa, but I can't count the number of times I've wanted Emma to want me like this and, apart from Cate's wedding and one or two other occasions etched deep into memory, I've always had to want. Timing was never Emma's forte.

What she is offering me now is not an easy thing to resist. Let's face it, I couldn't even turn down Maggie. I see now why she's wearing an uncharacteristically short skirt. It's ridden high up her thighs. My body is starting to respond of its own accord.

'I don't think this is a good idea,' I manage to say, but there's less conviction in my voice than I intend.

'Just touch me here for a minute,' she says as she places my hand between her legs and rubs it back and forth. The hand is too limp to put up a fight. It's about the only part of me that is limp.

'I've been like this all week,' she says. 'Can I take my tights off? Just for a minute.'

She doesn't wait for an answer. She doesn't just take off her tights, either. With her skirt around her waist and her underwear on the carpet, she climbs back astride me, repositions my hand on the appropriate spot and opens up magically beneath my touch. Resistance is futile, as the Borg say in *Star Trek: First Contact*.

But when she reaches for my zip, Captain Jean-Luc Picard would be proud of me.

'No,' I say.

There was a Catholic girl I once knew. Richard, the old Richard, would not approve of me saying this, but she could enjoy making love only by saying *no* all the time, in order to assuage the guilt she felt. My body doesn't believe I mean *no* either. But I'm trying. You've got to give me marks for trying.

'You're hard,' says Emma. 'I'm going to come.'

She's correct on both counts.

It's been a close run thing but... Look, have you seen *Disclosure*? When predatory Demi Moore drapes herself all over Michael Douglas and he tries to resist the physical responses she arouses in him, I bet your sympathies lie with poor old Mikey. Gimme a break here.

I'm sure Lisa would understand. She's my soul mate.

'Are you all right?' Emma says from a crumpled heap beside me.

'I think so,' I say as I rearrange the body parts she has left in uncomfortable disarray.

Emma, where were you when I needed you? Lisa, where are you now when I need you? If you didn't still flat-share with the bozo, if you were here with me now, instead of Emma, this wouldn't be happening.

After Emma has gone, she phones with her customary apology, says she hates herself, says it won't happen again. I listen attentively and make reassuring noises, but I don't believe her. After *Diamonds Are Forever* Sean Connery said he'd never make another Bond movie, and look what happened there. *Never Say Never Again*.

The next day the postman delivers a Valentine card from Lisa. The message is a traditional 'Please be my Valentine,' but she's added: 'Forever. I love you more than anything I have loved in my whole life.' And she's signed it. It's the first positive evidence that would stand up in a court of law that she loves me. I can't tell you how many times I read that message. If Emma arrived on my doorstep now, I really would turn her away.

In the evening there's a departmental leaving do in the same back room at the Thistle and Sporran where I held my birthday party. I've arranged to meet Richard there, but he doesn't turn up. Now that he's half of Rich and Cate, he has better things to do.

There's no one else I wish to talk to but, before I leave, I sit in a corner and drink a couple of Coors. Not that I'm miserable. How can a man be miserable when he's received the Valentine card that I have? No, I'm far from miserable. So when Kirsty materialises out of the crowd and asks for a dance, I'm up for it.

Pretty soon I'm glad Richard hasn't turned up. Kirsty is one of those people who make conversation seem like the easiest thing in the world, after all. I never feel shy in Kirsty's company. She seems interested in everything I have to say. She's also much less of an embarrassment than Richard on the dance floor, even if her moves do become increasingly idiosyncratic in direct proportion to her alcohol intake.

The evening passes more quickly and pleasantly that I could ever have imagined. Kirsty even remains sober enough to walk home unaided this time, and to put me on the spot as I chum her down Dundas Street.

'You're sure there's nothing going on between you and Lisa?' she says out of nowhere.

'Don't you talk to Lisa these days?'

'She says you're just friends.'

'There you go.'

I don't understand why Lisa can't tell her about us. They're best friends, aren't they? Kirsty's not about to run and tell the bozo.

'So you don't have a girlfriend at the moment?'

'Chance would be a fine thing.'

'So you haven't had a Valentine kiss today?'

Whoa again! I'm not so drunk that I don't understand a leading question when I hear one. What's going on this weekend? First Emma, now Kirsty. There must be something new in the water – I've just had my plumbing redone. Or maybe it's Lisa's fault again, for not being here now.

I'm glad it's dark, so that Kirsty can't see my face. I don't want her to think I don't find her attractive, because I do, and if it weren't for Lisa... Okay, if she wants a kiss, she can have one. Friends are allowed to kiss.

I kiss her.

She responds with such enthusiasm that we lose balance and topple sideways into a stack of pallets that stands on the pavement beside scaffolding. The pallets keel over and take us with them.

In an attempt to hang on I cut my right hand on a sharp corner. Drops of blood drip from my fingers, like in that scene in *Stigmata* where Patricia Arquette gets nails through her wrists.

I press a tissue to the wound, then notice that Kirsty is missing. She can't have dematerialised into thin air. Or even thick air.

I hear moaning, and it's not from pleasure.

'Where are you?' I say.

'Down here.'

I dislodge some pallets to discover her in a most ungainly pose, on her back, legs in the air. In retrospect, she'll be glad she wore trousers tonight rather than a dress.

'Are you all right?'

'Do I look all right?'

It takes some minutes to retrieve her and set her upright, not only because of my own injury but also, I'm afraid to say, because I'm additionally hampered by incipient hysteria. She's injured her hip and can barely walk, but her cries of pain are intermingled with drunken giggles too. I flag down a taxi and take her home. She lives on the second floor and it's a major achievement to hoist her up there without a stair lift.

Once inside her flat she hops around with the aid of a ski pole. It's a vision I can't take seriously. Instead of offering sympathy I do Long John Silver impressions.

'It's not funny,' she says.

'Jim, lad,' I say.

She reciprocates by refusing to view the gash in my little finger as anything more than a minor graze.

'I may never walk again,' she says.

'I may never wank again,' I say.

'Pardon?'

Did I say that out loud? I must be more drunk than I thought.

She finally deigns to clean and bandage my hand, then I manage to make us some coffee left-handed, then we feel tired and she says why don't I stay the night.

Whoa, whoa and thrice whoa!

Kirsty, where were *you* when I needed you?

'I thought you weren't that sort of girl,' I say.

'I'm not suggesting what you think I'm suggesting, but you can't leave me on my own like this. What if I can't walk in the morning?'

She's right. I can't be so ungallant as to leave her alone, can I? And I must admit, the prospect of venturing out into the cold night air again doesn't appeal. It's very cosy in her living room. She has an electric fire that specialises in mesmerising flame effects. I decide I need to get one.

'Okay,' I say. 'I'll crash on the couch.'

'Don't be silly. I've got a king-size bed. Just don't go getting any ideas.'

I don't have any ideas. My mind is a blank. I may never again have any ideas.

While she hops to the bathroom, hops into her night-gown and hops into bed, I sit on the couch and stare vacant-eyed at the *faux-flame* effect.

'Are you coming?' she calls from the bedroom.

I join her.

'Well, are you going get in or stand there all night?' she says.

'Are you sure?'

'For goodness sake, we're both adults.'

That's my point. Still, I doubt I could manage any adult activity at the moment without a splint, and I don't mean on my finger. This is a purely Platonic arrangement. Kirsty needs the reassurance of my presence. As I'm partly to blame for her condition, it's the least I can do.

I strip down to my underwear and climb in beside her.

'I won't forget this in a hurry,' she says.

'We'll always have the scars to remind us,' I say in a Humphrey-Bogart-to-Ingrid-Bergman-in-*Casablanca*-we'll-always-have-Paris kind of way.

'Is being with you always this dangerous?'

'A man's got to have an edge.'

So here I am in bed with Lisa's best friend. I don't know what you think about that. I don't know what I think about it myself. I don't fully understand how it's happened. I met her, I danced with her, I walked her home... and here I am. I'm sure Emma would have the necessary logic to explain it.

In any case, it *is* a big bed. Is this any different from the night Cate spent with me after she lost her baby? If Lisa knew, I bet she'd love me all the more for being such a caring person.

In the morning I awake to find Kirsty asleep at my shoulder. When I rouse her she's in so much pain that there's nothing for it but a taxi ride to Accident and Emergency at the Royal Infirmary. I get six stitches in my finger and an impressive dressing. Kirsty has a hair-line fracture of the hip. I'm jealous. She'll get time off work. I won't.

Back at her flat I ensconce her on the couch with a mug of coffee and the Sunday papers, tell her to call me if she needs anything, and leave.

On my way home I'm accosted by a woman with a small child.

'John!' she says.

'I think you've made a mistake.'

'It *is* you.'

'You've got me confused with someone else.'

'Stop it.'

'I'm sorry.'

'Don't be like this.'

'I have to go.'

I walk away. She comes after me.

'Please, John.'

'I'm not John.'

I walk faster. So does she. I start to run. So does she. She calls John's name again and again. Only the child being dragged tearfully in her wake enables me to outpace her.

It's been that sort of weekend.

The sort of weekend you don't need the foresight of Nostradamus to predict would cause trouble.

29.

On Monday morning Lisa sends me an email asking me to meet her at lunchtime in her clearing beside the Water of Leith. It's a cold, damp February day. The bare trees shiver in the grey gloom, a sheen of frost makes the shaded path treacherous, the river is sluggish and loath to flow.

Lisa sits on her bench, wrapped in a long black woollen coat. The top button is missing so she holds the collar tight around her neck. I can tell from her casual shoes that she hasn't been into work today. She must have emailed me from home.

'Kirsty phoned me,' she says. 'She said you slept with her.'

I'm stunned into immobility. I feel like I'm in one of those silent movies, bound to a railway track while an express train speeds ever nearer.

'I was going to tell you,' I say meekly.

She gives me a disbelieving look.

'I *was*.'

'Then tell me.'

'There's nothing to tell.'

'You slept with Kirsty and there's nothing to tell?'

'I *only* slept with her.'

'What do you mean, *only*?'

She's completely baffled. How can her lover have done this to her? How can he have betrayed her so casually? I'm a bit baffled myself. We're like Inspector Lestrade in a Sherlock Holmes film.

'It just sort of happened,' I say. 'We were at that leaving do on Saturday, and she fell over and hurt herself.'

'So you slept with her?'

'She asked me to. She didn't want to be on her own.' In other words, it was a gallant gesture on my part. 'We didn't do anything. I kept my underwear on.' What else? There must be more. 'She only had the one bed.' There. Surely that's enough.

'Then why does she think she pulled you?'

'What?'

'She said she pulled you.'

'She didn't pull me.'

'So you didn't kiss her?'

'That was before. She asked me to.'

'Did you do everything she asked you to?'

'It was just a friendly kiss.'

'She said it was a Valentine kiss.'

'No, she's got it all wrong. If you'd told her about us, it wouldn't have happened.'

'So it was my fault?'

'No, but you can't blame Kirsty.'

'I'm not blaming Kirsty.'

Now I know how nuclear engineer Jack Lemmon feels in *The China Syndrome*, when he struggles to explain a reactor malfunction in plain language.

'Did you tell her about us?' I say.

'I could hardly do that after she told me she'd pulled you.'

We take a moment to gather our thoughts. Cold wind, scudding clouds, waving branches. Weather as emotion, like when Audrey Hepburn and George Peppard embrace in pouring rain in *Breakfast at Tiffany's*. Except that Lisa and I aren't embracing.

'Did you mean it when you said you loved me?' she says.

'Yes!' I say with as much conviction as I can muster.

'Then I don't understand.'

'It's like I said, we were drunk, she was hurt, it just sort of happened. It didn't mean anything.'

'It seems to have done to Kirsty.'

'Well, I'm sorry if she got the wrong impression. It won't happen again. Isn't that what you said after you had sex with Jeff on holiday?'

No, no, why did I have to go and bring that up? I only mean to remind Lisa that if I could forgive that, how can she not forgive this comparatively minor misdemeanour on my part? Instead of which, I've made my behaviour with Kirsty seem equally reprehensible. Plus Lisa now thinks I haven't forgiven her at all. I can see it in her face. She probably thinks I've slept with Kirsty to even the score.

I sit down beside her and search for a way to explain my behaviour to her, to myself.

'After being with you last Thursday, I felt so alive. It's like you said, I was only half-alive before I met you. I had so much energy. You know that crowd scene at the end of *Bob and Carol and Ted and Alice*, where everyone is strolling up and down the street feeling warm and loving towards each other, and there's that Burt Bacharach song on the soundtrack: 'What the World Needs Now is Love, Sweet Love'? That's the kind of mood you put me in.'

She gives me a look I recognise. It's the one I give Richard when he's in a hole and still digging.

'I can't share you like that,' she says.

'I'm not asking you to. I'm just trying to tell you how I felt. What I felt for you somehow spilled over into the rest of my life. I'm sorry if Kirsty thinks there's more to it than there was, and I'm sorry if you do, but we didn't do anything. I just slept over.'

'Slept over? You still sleep over at your age?'

She laughs, but not because she finds it funny. Nevertheless, it gives me something to work on. I don't know what comes over me, but I do one of those crazy things I warned you about. I get down on my knees in front of her, on the cold hard ground, and I plead and grovel.

'Please forgive me,' I say, 'I'll do anything. I'll crawl a thousand miles on hands and knees over broken glass just to fetch you a new button for your coat.'

She laughs again, more warmly this time, but leaves me in the dirt long enough for me to be in no doubt as to the seriousness of my offence.

'Okay,' she says begrudgingly, after due process, 'you can get up now.'

'Am I forgiven?'

'I'll think about it.'

I knew it! I knew she'd understand. I knew she was my soul-mate.

I leap to her side and take her in my arms. It's such a clumsy lunge that I catch my injured finger on her shoulder and cry out in pain.

'Serves you right,' she says. 'Kirsty told me about your little accident. How's the finger?'

'I feel like I'm auditioning for *The Mummy*,' I say, cradling the impressively bandaged digit.

She gives me a sly look.

'Slept over? That's a good one. I think you'd better speak to Kirsty and set her straight.'

'It was a crazy weekend,' I say. 'This woman chased me along the street with a small child shouting *John! John!*'

'I'm beginning to think you've got a secret life.'

'*And* Emma was on my doorstep when I got home from work on Friday.'

'Emma?'

What am I saying? Do I have a death wish? My eyes lower for no more than a nanosecond, but that's all it takes. Lisa is on to it like a *Jurassic Park* velociraptor.

'I didn't sleep with her,' I say in pre-emptive defence.

'I never suggested you did,' she says, now more suspicious than ever.

The unspoken question of what I did do with Emma hangs in the air between us. In the second or two I have before replying to it, I decide I don't ever want to lie to Lisa. She understands about Kirsty. She'll understand about Emma.

'She made me touch her.'

Lisa looks at me as though I'm a complete stranger.

'She *made* you?'

'Yes. That was all, though. I didn't go to bed with her or get undressed or anything.'

'You seem to think it doesn't count as long as you keep your underwear on. I don't understand. First Kirsty, then Emma.'

'No, Emma was first. Kirsty...'

'I thought you loved me.'

'I do.'

Unconvinced, unsure of anything any longer, she studies my face a moment longer then turns away.

'I'm sorry,' I say to her back. What's that line from *Love Story*? 'Love means never having to say you're sorry'?

I lay my hand, my good hand, on her shoulder. She shrugs it off and walks down to the water's edge. I follow. We stand side by side and watch the current.

'I'm embarrassed,' she says eventually, which isn't quite what I was expecting.

'Why?'

'It was special with you. I thought it was special for you too.'

'God, Lisa, it was. It is.'

I turn her around to crush her to me, but she puts a restraining hand on my chest.

'Then how could you? How would you feel if I did that with Jeff now?'

I'd be jealous. Insanely jealous. Isn't that the right term? I'm an idiot. I'm a hypocrite. I'm the biggest cad, bounder and blackguard since fortune-hunter Montgomery Clift seduced rich spinster Olivia de Havilland in *The Heiress*. I hate myself.

How can I have been so insensitive to Lisa's feelings? Look at her. Look how sad I've made her. She's finally found someone to love and given herself to him completely, only to discover he's playing around with her best friend and his ex-lover.

If only she'd ditch the bozo and get a place of her own... If we didn't have to keep meeting in secret, if we could be together when we chose to be, she'd see the truth of my feelings for her.

'If we'd been together,' I say, 'none of this would have happened.'

What's wrong with me today? In my eagerness to dig an ever deeper hole for myself I've thrown away my spade and hired earth-moving equipment. Why can't I be granted the foresight of under-standing the implications of what I'm going to say before I say it? Is that really so much to ask?

'Are you telling me you can't be trusted unless I'm with you all the time?'

'No, that's not what I mean.'

While I search for inspiration, we do more of that staring at the water.

'I need to be able to believe in you,' she says.

'You can. I am trying to disentangle myself from Emma, just like you are from Jeff.'

'You're sure you wouldn't sooner be with her?'

'No! Didn't you get your Valentine card?'

No answer.

'I meant what it said. I have dreamed of you all my life. If I lose you now...' I let the sentence hang. I can't bear to think how it might end. 'Do you still mean what you wrote on mine?'

Again she doesn't answer, doesn't even look at me. I wait for her to speak, I don't know how long, because by a quirk of relativity theory every second lasts an eternity. Now I know what I'll do if I've lost her. I'll jump in the river and let it carry me down to the Firth of Forth and out into the North Sea.

'There's something I have to tell you,' she says at length, using the same words as when she told me she lived with someone. 'When I asked to see you this morning, it wasn't because of Kirsty. She phoned later. It was because of Jeff. He found your card.'

I search her face for clues as to how I should react to this, but her expression tells me nothing.

'Good,' I say. 'Now we can get everything out in the open.'

'No. You don't know him. You don't know what he's capable of. He'd kill you if he knew.'

I take it she means this metaphorically, but then I notice some-thing. Her upper lip is cut.

'What happened to your lip?'

She turns away from me again.

'Did he hit you?'

Again, no answer.

A host of emotions crowd in on me. Suddenly a lot of things make sense.

'If he touches you again,' I say, 'I'll kill him.'

'No,' she says, rounding on me with a suddenness that makes me start, 'don't you ever be like him.' The tremor in her voice tells me more about Jeff in an instant than everything she has told me about him in all our previous conversations.

'It's not the first time, is it?'

'It was an accident. Sometimes he lashes out. He doesn't mean it. He calmed down after I told him the card was a joke from someone at work.'

'And he believed you?'

'You can believe anything if you want to.'

It sounds to me as though she's the one who's fooling herself.

'You have to leave him,' I say. 'You can't stay with someone like that.'

'I told you, I can't just walk out on him. It would destroy him. I can't do that to him. I can't build a relationship with you based on that. Do you understand?'

'I'm trying.'

We're separated by no more than a small saucer-shaped depression in the ground, but it might as well be one of those yawning chasms that used to put Emma beyond my reach.

'I can handle him,' she says, making one last attempt to convince me. 'I know you think it's crazy, but I owe him something for seven years.'

I make one last attempt to dispel her fear.

'Lisa, you don't have to be a good little girl any longer.'

'Stop it!'

She puts her hands to her face and gives a short, sharp scream that's swallowed up in the surrounding greyness.

'I've got you pulling me one way, Jeff pulling me the other. I feel like I'm being torn apart.'

'I didn't know it was a tug of war. I thought you wanted to be with me.'

When yet again she has nothing to offer me but silence, all my frustration pours out.

'What do you think it's like for me? Every night you go home to some guy you've been living with for seven years. How would you feel if I went back to Emma every night? I have all these feelings for you, and I can't act on them. I know I've done some stupid things this weekend, and I'm sorry, but I'm burning up here. I'm impatient for you. I love you. I'm sorry.'

I shout it out, at Lisa, at the trees, at the sky. I don't know if it makes any sense, but that's the way it comes out.

And finally, as I'd longed for when I arrived and saw Lisa huddled on her bench, she turns and wraps her arms around me.

'Don't apologise for loving me,' she says. 'Don't you *ever* do that. As long as we have each other, everything will be all right, you'll see.'

In the sanctuary of her arms, soothed by her words, a wave of relief washes over me, a wave that would give the tsunami in *Krakatoa East of Java* a run for its money.

30.

Why is life so complicated? Is this normal?

Lisa, the woman I love, lives with an ex she can't bring herself to leave. Emma, the woman I wanted to love and with whom I have recently been intimate, if I can put it that way, wants to go out for a drink, and I'm scared she'll jump on me again, even though she says she won't. Kirsty, Lisa's best friend and another woman to whom I have recently become closer than anticipated, and I'll put it no stronger than that, wants me to visit her during her convalescence, and Lisa still hasn't told her about us, and I can't pretend I'm busy forever.

After spending months as the only female cast member during the making of *Sphere*, Sharon Stone said she'd learned a lot about men. They're quite simple, really, she said, they always say what they mean. I'm sure I don't need to spell out the reverse implication.

Okay, so I may have been less than completely honest myself in some of my dealings, but that only goes to prove I'm in touch with my feminine side.

I'm not blaming Lisa, but the course of true love might be running a tad more smoothly if she'd let us be open about our relationship from the beginning. Is it really necessary to be so secretive? And what's Emma *really* after? And what does Kirsty *really* want from me?

I feel as though I'm in a David Mamet movie. Nothing is as it seems. I need a spreadsheet to keep track of what's going on, who wants what, who knows what about whom, and who isn't supposed to know what about whom.

I speak to Cate about it all. She has become my confidante, my only available confidante, in these matters.

At a succession of Cowgate hostelries, noisy enough to drown my embarrassment, I give her the latest instalment. She listens attentively, as fidget-free as I've ever seen her, barely raising an eyebrow, giving me little more than an occasional wry smile of encouragement, opening her mouth only for clarification. *Pallets? How many stitches?* I think she's enjoying it. I end my tale of woe with the question I keep asking myself: how did I get into this mess?

She offers me an answer culled from a lifetime's getting of wisdom.

'I'd say you've been saving up your shag points and you're blowing them all at once.'

'Cate, I'm pouring my heart out to you here.'

'What do you want me to say? I don't have any answers. Keep me in the loop, though. It's the best story I've heard in ages. You should turn it into a novel.'

She sips her G&T as though nothing more incisive is required of her, but she's not getting off that lightly.

'What am I going to do?'

'About what? Lisa's forgiven you, hasn't she?'

'I think so. Yes.'

'So what's your problem? Do what she says and give her time.'

'How much time?'

'Is she worth waiting for or not?'

'Of course she is, but that doesn't make it any easier. We never have fun any more.'

'I thought you'd sooner suffer for love than have fun.'

I hate it when people do that to me.

'It's all right for you and Richard,' I say peevishly. 'You can see each other when you want.'

'Rich and I have different problems.'

Again she turns to her G&T, as though there's no more to be said on the matter, and again I have to prompt her.

'Like what?'

'He's too serious. He wants too much commitment.'

'I thought that's what you wanted. I thought that's why you married Calum.'

'Exactly. Been there, done that. I'm not going to make that mistake again. Maybe I've learned something from you. Maybe I want what you've got.'

'For Chrissake, Cate! I'm the one who's supposed to be the romantic here!'

She's clearly incapable of offering me constructive counsel and, a couple of days later, over lunch with Richard and Scott, I find she's not the only one.

'You know Donny McDonald?' says Scott, all innocence.

We're sitting at our regular table in the canteen, shovelling chef's special stovies. What makes this particular dish special is the unknown provenance of its ingredients. Among the slurry we recognise flakes of corned beef, but the other constituents defeat our powers of recall of previous days' menus.

'Works in Accounts?' says Richard.

'He was passing the Downtown Diner the other day and happened to look through the window,' says Scott.

All of a sudden, the earth's gravitational field shifts and my forkful of stovies becomes too heavy to lift.

'Said he saw Lisa, playing footsie with some guy.'

'Which guy?' Richard says naively.

Scott gives me a pointed look. Richard gets the message and follows suit.

'I wanted to tell you,' I say, blinking sheepishly in the glare of the spotlight, 'but Lisa wouldn't let me.'

'We're waiting,' says Scott.

I give them the abbreviated version, stripped of the emotionality permissible in female company. Lisa and I are in love but there's a bozo in tow and I've been sworn to secrecy until she dumps him. I don't tell them about her cut lip, or about my escapades with Emma and Kirsty. In truth, it's a relief to tell them the truth. And apparently just as great a relief to them to be able to pronounce judgement.

As ever, Scott's first up.

'You canny bastard,' he says without need for reflection. 'I knew she was your type.'

As ever, I'm immediately on the defensive.

'What are you talking about? I don't have a type.'

'She could be Emma's sister. They even have the same haircut.'

'Don't talk crap.'

Richard gives the matter more consideration, such that I find myself awaiting his findings with unexpected anticipation. He's going to approach the problem with the methodological thoroughness befitting his occupation and offer a fittingly constructive solution.

'She's your type because she has problems,' he says.

Thanks a million, Richard. Without a positive role model since losing me to Lisa, he's clearly lost the capacity for rational thought.

'You always go for women with problems,' he says. 'You think you can help them. They satisfy some protective urge you have.'

Why is it that everyone needs a theory about why I love Lisa? Emma thinks it's because she reminds me of Jenny, Scott thinks it's because she reminds me of Emma, Cate thinks it's because she loves me, now Richard thinks it's because she has problems. Why can't people accept the mystery of love without having to explain it away?

'Maybe you've got something there, pal,' Scott says to his accomplice. 'If a woman is needy, perhaps she'll need him.'

That can't be right. I'm not *that* sad. In any case, all women have problems, don't they?

'You're both talking crap,' I say.

'You're lucky,' says Richard.

'How do you figure that?'

'It's a test. All love affairs are put to the test at some stage. Some couples have to wait years to be tested. You're going to find out now. If Lisa loves you enough, she'll leave the ex. If she doesn't, she won't.'

Thanks again, Richard, Rich or whoever you are these days. I don't want to be tested now, not while Lisa continues to cohabit. As Matthew Broderick says in *The Night We Never Met*, 'Sex is a little like politics. The incumbent always has the advantage.'

And what's all this about an affair? *Affair* seems so temporary. So *Brief Encounter*.

'You're lucky,' Richard says again.

'Stop telling me I'm lucky! You and Cate are lucky.'

'What's this?' says Scott.

'Richard and Cate,' I say. 'You knew about them, didn't you?'

Scott's face disappears behind his smile.

'You haven't told him?' I say to Richard.

'Anyway,' he says, making a brave attempt to turn the spotlight back onto me, 'what choice do you have? If she's worth waiting for, she's worth waiting for.'

'That's what Cate said.'

'Cate knows about this?'

I feel a sudden pang of guilt, as though I've been seeing his girl-friend behind his back, which I have, but not in *that* way.

'Cate and I are friends. You know that. I've known her a long time.'

'She told me she can't be friends with anyone she hasn't had sex with.'

I'm sure this is intended as a passing remark rather than an in-sinuation, but it catches me unawares. I hesitate. Of all the reactions I could have had, it had to be hesitation. I look away but, in peripheral vision, I see realisation take hold of Richard's face.

It's Scott's turn to get the message.

'You don't mean...' he says. He laughs the deep laugh at which he's become so accomplished that, for special occasions such as this, he's experimenting with the addition of a bass vibrato. He's having the kind of lunchtime he'll be able to tell his grandchildren about.

'Okay,' I say, quickly accepting that denial is no longer an option, 'but it was a long time ago, just like with you and Cate.'

'What?' says Richard.

If he found it hard to accept the news of Cate and myself, you can imagine the horror with which he receives this follow-up bulletin concerning Cate and Scott. He's just discovered that both of his colleagues have had carnal knowledge of his girlfriend.

He looks at us like Glenn Close looks at Jeff Bridges in *Jagged Edge* after she discovers that he is the killer after all.

There's more exchanging of meaningful glances among the three of us than in an afternoon soap. The spotlight can no longer keep up with the action. If this were a trendy romantic comedy, along the lines of like *Martha, Meet Frank, Daniel and Laurence*, we'd settle back for an adult, intelligent and witty discussion about life's little ironies. Instead, I feel guilty, Richard looks mortified and Scott does some calculations.

'Edinburgh's a small place,' I say to Richard by way of explanation. Well, compared to somewhere like Mexico City, it is. With someone like Cate working her way through the male population, it would be more statistically significant if the three of us gathered here at this table *weren't* shag-mates.

Sadly, Richard is no longer New Man enough to accept the voice of reason.

'I'm going,' he says and, true to his word, stands up and lopes out.

Unwisely, I look to Scott for support. He's finished his calculations.

'I'm glad I saw her first,' he says.

For several days afterwards Richard avoids the canteen and, in our cramped working quarters, cold-shoulders me more effectively than you'd think possible. But Scott and I have done nothing wrong, have we? How were we to know that Richard was going to plough the same furrow?

Meanwhile Emma continues to phone with such convincing apologies that I actually begin to believe them. Not enough to see her again, though, just in case. And, as if that isn't enough to deal with, Kirsty continues to phone with complaints that I haven't been round to see her yet.

Oh well, at least I have Lisa. Some of the time, anyway. How much longer do we have to go on like this? Is she ever going to find a place of her own? Is the flat rental market that depressed?

The most profound insights, whether in art, science or life, are often the simplest. Alain Robbe-Grillet, a fellow director of Jean-Luc's, once observed that a film always takes place in the present tense.

I keep telling myself that life should be the same. I should enjoy the present, give Lisa the time she needs, take of her what she can give me now. If I live for the future, I shall destroy what we have now.

I must heed the words of Alpha 60: *No one has lived in the past and no one will live in the future. The present is the form of all life.*

31.

Three a.m. on a Monday morning in early spring. The bozo has had to go away for a few days, so Lisa and I are at last spending our first whole night together. I can't sleep because her unfamiliar presence in my bed disturbs me, but I'm happy to lie awake and be disturbed.

Sunday has been a special day. In the morning I met her at her flat, my first time there. We made love in her bedroom, with the window wide open and spring sunlight streaming in. At lunchtime we drove to Cramond foreshore, sat arm in arm on the sea wall beside the Forth and had tea and scones at the tea-room.

In the afternoon we strolled hand in hand on dappled paths through Inverleith Park. Swans congregated at one end of the pond like billowing cumulus. The trees were heavy with cherry blossom. Pink snowflakes cascaded around us. Some landed in Lisa's hair.

'I love you,' I say softly in her ear as she lies beside me.

She turns towards me, only half-awake, and nestles into my shoulder. I tell her again. She nestles closer still.

'Tell me you love me,' I say, wanting once more to hear the words on her lips, as if I still can't believe that we have found each other.

She turns away.

'I can't go through with it,' she says.

The words hit me like a sledgehammer. I know immediately that I have lost her. I know it in an instant.

'You're going to stay with Jeff?' It sounds incredible.

Three a.m. on a Monday morning in early spring. It's happening again. My lover is leaving me. Just like Jenny left me. She too left me in darkness, when everything seemed so good between us.

In some sort of cruel joke, history is repeating itself. I've been given a second chance at love, and it's been snatched away from me again, in exactly the same way as before. All the hopes. All the dreams.

'This can't be happening,' I say.

I sit up in bed, stunned. Lisa says nothing. She's said it all. If I stopped to think, I would know that now is not a time to argue. But I don't think. I fight. God, do I fight.

'I thought you were happy with me. I *know* you're happy with me. You don't love him.'

No reply.

'Talk to me. I don't understand.'

'I can't leave him,' she says.

'Why not?'

'I just can't. We've been through too much. I have to give him another chance.'

'And throw away what we have?'

'I don't know what else to do.'

'Leave him.'

'I can't.'

'He hits you!'

'He says he won't do it again. The counsellor thinks we have a chance.'

'Counsellor? What counsellor?'

'Jeff thought we should see a counsellor. I went along with it because I thought it would make him realise there was no hope for us.'

'And?'

'She told me I should put my relationship with you on hold until I've sorted out my relationship with Jeff.'

'What's to sort out? You'll never feel for Jeff what you feel for me. You told me that. You love me. Tell me you don't.'

'I can't.' She prolongs the word, straining against the truth of it.

'So how can you leave me?'

'I have to make a decision. It's tearing me apart. The counsellor says I can't keep living two lives like this.'

'You don't have to live two lives. Leave him.'

'I can't give up someone I've been with for seven years for someone I've been with for two months. Not without giving him another chance.'

'God, I could. I'd give up anything for you.'

'What if it doesn't last between us? What if it's just infatuation?'

'Infatuation? Is that what the counsellor says?'

'It might be, mightn't it? Sometimes I think I'm living a dream.'

'You said nothing had ever felt so real.'

She has no answer to that.

'You said you were going to leave him.'

'I meant it when I said it.'

'Trust me, you said.'

'I know.'

'I owe it to myself, you said.'

'I know. But I owe something to Jeff too.'

'To hell with him. You made a mistake with him. You said so yourself. You owe him nothing.'

'I can't be that selfish.'

'It would be selfish to stay with him out of guilt. You can't build a relationship on that. You'd never be happy. He'd never be happy.'

'I have to try.'

She still lies with her back to me. My senses are heightened by the thought of losing her. Her hair has never looked softer. Her skin has never felt smoother.

I have to keep trying too. I can't give up. You don't give up on something like this until every possibility, and every variation on every possibility, has been exhausted. Then you try again.

I take hold of her shoulder and turn her to face me.

'What about me? What about us? Don't you owe anything to us?'

She looks into my eyes, and I see that hers brim with unshed tears.

'I can't bear the thought of hurting you,' she says, 'but I can't have a relationship with you based on hurting him.'

'You can have a relationship with him based on hurting me.'

Words, words. What use are words? No matter how much sense they make to me, they're not going to change her mind.

'I wish I'd met you all those years ago,' she says, 'but I didn't.'

'You mean, you base your relationships on first come, first served?'

This is hopeless. Sophistry will only entrench her in her position. It's space she needs. Somehow I must find the strength to give it to her. It's my only hope.

I take her in my arms and press her naked body to mine. She offers no resistance.

'Why didn't you tell me before?' I say. 'We had such a great day together. How could you only tell me now?'

'Because I didn't know how to.'

'Then why now, when you're lying in my bed? Are you telling me you don't want this?'

'I do want this.'

'Yet you're going to leave me?'

'I have to.'

'This is crazy!'

I roll away from her. When she puts a consoling hand on my shoulder, it burns my skin.

'If I don't do this, I'll go crazy,' she says. 'Can't you understand that?'

'No! Don't ask me to understand how you can give up on us. It doesn't make sense.'

Think, brain, for God's sake, think. Think like you've never thought before.

'What if you do what your counsellor suggests?' I say. 'Stop seeing me for a while. Put us on hold while you sort things out with Jeff. That doesn't mean you have to finish with me, not forever. Then if it doesn't work out with him, I'll still be here.'

This sounds reasonable, surely. I'll do anything to hold on to Lisa. Even not see her.

'I can't do that,' she says. 'Don't you see? If I know you're waiting for me, nothing's going to change. Like you say, you'll still be here. I have to cut you out of my life completely, for your sake as well as mine. I don't want you thinking there's still a chance for us.'

Despite herself, she nestles closer, spooning her body around mine. It's exquisite torture. The thought that this will be the last time we'll lie together like this is unbearable.

'You'll be all right,' she says. 'You don't need me. You have Emma. And Kirsty. You could go out with Kirsty now.'

'How can you say that? Of course I need you. I thought you understood about Emma and Kirsty. Are you my soul mate or aren't you?'

I feel so desperately sorry for myself, and the only person who can comfort me can do nothing to help. She presses her body against mine and puts her hand on my arm. I feel her breath on my neck, but she has nothing more to say. She's exhausted. We're both exhausted. So much so that at some point, although it seems impossible, we fall asleep.

When the alarm goes off, *Reality Bites*. It's Monday morning. We have to go to work. At least Lisa does. There's no way I'm going in today.

Without a word, she gets up and puts on the office clothes she has brought with her. Skirt, blouse, jacket. I have to look away. I can't bear the thought of never again seeing her without them.

We barely say a word to each other. She's reverted to being reserved and distant, with that air of sadness that characterised her before we became lovers. Mechanically, I make her toast and coffee. And renew my efforts.

'We can't stop seeing each other completely,' I say, 'because we work in the same place.'

'In different departments,' she says.

'We can still be friends, though, can't we?'

I have to maintain some form of contact. Without contact, I have no chance to change her mind. With contact, given time…

'I hope so,' she says. 'Eventually. But not now. I have to stop seeing you altogether for a while.'

She couldn't even say: What kind of friends?

So I'm not to see her at all, never mind talk to her, never mind make love to her. How can she eat toast at a time like this? These are our last few moments together, of our first and last night together. I'll never eat again.

She finishes her coffee, brushes her teeth, puts on her shoes and coat, the one with the missing button, gathers her stuff. I stand helpless, watching. I open the door for her. This is it. She's about to go. This is my last chance.

'Look, this is a big thing you're doing here. Please call me and let me know you're okay.'

'It's difficult calling you from the flat.'

She walks out onto the stairwell.

'Then email me. Don't leave me in the dark. Don't end it like this.'

'If you want.'

One final appeal.

'Tell me you don't love me.'

She draws in her lips and runs her tongue along them one last time, as unaware as ever of the gesture I've come to love.

'I can't.'

'Then tell me you do.'

I hold her with my gaze, hoping that, like some kind of tractor beam, it will prevent her from leaving. Instead, it gives her strength. She puts a finger to my lips, one last touch of skin to skin, and burns into me Natasha's final words from *Alphaville*.

'Je… vous… aime.'

Then she turns and walks out of my life.

32.

After Lisa has gone to work I'm at a complete loss as to what to do. It's not yet nine o'clock. The whole day stretches ahead of me. My whole life stretches ahead of me. I can't go to work. I can't go back to sleep. I can't eat breakfast. There's nothing I want to do. There's nothing *worth* doing.

You'd think, maybe, after my experience of being dumped by Jenny, second time around wouldn't be so bad. Instead, it re-ignites the still glowing ember. The one feeds off the other. Maybe it will always be like this. Maybe it's my fate always to be abandoned in Alphaville, the city of nightmares, *La Capitale de la Douleur*, where love is forbidden.

On an impulse I clear away all evidence of Lisa's presence in my flat. You'd think I'd be more likely to preserve every last trace of her, but instead I figure that a clean sweep will somehow erase the hurt.

I wash the plate and mug she used for breakfast. I put away the food. I wash the T-shirt of mine that she wore in bed last night and which is still creased by the contours of her body. I change the sheets, which still retain her warmth, and the pillow cases, which are still scented with her shampoo. I raise the toilet seat. I change the towel.

In a foolscap folder I place, among other memorabilia, a hair clasp, her Valentine card, hard copies of her emails, a back cover of a *List* magazine on which she doodled a heart, the receipt for the petrol I bought on the way to Cramond, a petal of cherry blossom she found in her shoe, a button I bought for her coat but didn't give her. I file the folder away in a drawer, next to my Jenny folder.

Then I phone Emma. It's automatic. Despite everything we've gone through in the past few months, she's still the first person I turn to. She immediately invites me round, greets me with a prolonged hug, takes me through to her bedroom and lies me down on her bed. I crawl into her arms and cry all the tears I held back from Lisa.

'You can make love to me if you want,' she says.

This time it's an offer, not a plea. This time it's for my benefit. In some instinctive way she knows that what I most need in the world right now is to be wanted as a man. It's an animal need. I'm not even aware of it myself until she offers herself to me. It's as if the sheer physical act of making love to another woman will prove to me that I'm not worthless, that I'll not be alone for evermore, that there is hope.

So Emma and I have sex. It's mechanical, perfunctory. It's what Al Pacino in *Frankie and Johnny* calls a Band-Aid on loneliness. It provides only momentary relief, but its importance goes beyond the moment.

'Why are you being so nice to me?' I say afterwards.

'I know I've been acting strangely lately,' she says, 'but I'll always be here for you.'

Oh, Emma, why couldn't you have fallen in love with me?

I spend the remainder of the morning lying in her arms, talking, falling silent, talking, telling her details she probably doesn't want to hear, trying to make sense of it all, until she decides she should take me out to face the world.

In a Tollcross eatery I avoid looking at anyone but Emma in case I see a romantic couple and fall apart again. She tries to make me eat a Cheddar cheese roll, but the bread's dry and the cheese musty, and I'm not hungry anyway, and it seems like the end of the world. We leave before I break down in public, over stale bread and cheese.

With her arm in mine she walks me around town. It's another bright spring day, just like yesterday when I lay with Lisa in her flat, a lifetime ago. In Princes Street Gardens we sit on a bench beneath the trees and watch the squirrels with a fascination deserving of an endangered species. Along George Street she distracts me by looking in clothes shop windows and asking my opinion. At L. K. Bennett's she reminds me of my incompetence at helping her choose shoes for Cate's wedding.

When we pass the Downtown Diner I have to look away. I'll never enter the place again. It shouldn't even be called the Downtown Diner. For city northsiders like myself, who live down the slope towards the Forth, it lies *uptown*. I decide to write the manager a letter of complaint.

Eventually Emma walks me home, past the scaffolding where Kirsty and I had our accident when life was worth living. At the door to my tenement she leaves me. She's devoted her day to me and has other things to do. There's an important commission she'll now have to spend the evening catching up on. But if I really need her, she'll stay.

I let her go. She's done more than I could rightly have hoped for. She's got me through the day. I'll never forget that.

Alone in my flat again, I have time to think. Time to care. Too much time. I can't stand it. I have to get out again.

Without prior warning, I turn up on Cate's doorstep, as she once turned up unannounced on mine. On her couch I tell my story all over again, as though the telling will somehow ease the pain of loss.

'You can say it if you want,' I say.

'Say what?' she says.

'I told you so.'

'Is that what you think of me? Just don't expect me to give you a mercy fuck, like Em.'

A mercy fuck. That's exactly what it was. Emma gave me a mercy fuck. Trust Cate to tell it like it is.

'I've become a charity case,' I say.

'It will get better. Just like it did after Jenny.'

She means well, but there's a time to invoke such memories and now isn't it. As fresh tears well in my eyes, I lay my head on her lap to hide them.

'It's not fair. How can this happen to me twice?'

'Some of us have never been in love once.'

She's doing the best she can. I can't expect her to have the same degree of expertise as Emma in these matters.

'Don't tell me, it's better to have loved and lost than never to have loved at all.'

'Just because it's a cliché doesn't mean it's not true.'

'Next you'll tell me how lucky I am.'

'You *are* lucky.'

'There you go.'

'I'm sorry, but if you're looking for sympathy you've come to the wrong place. You'd only been seeing Lisa for two months. All this proves is that she wasn't the right woman for you. You'll find someone else.'

Again, I'm sure she means well but, if she's going to resort to reason, there's no point in discussing the matter.

'No I won't.'

'Yes you will.'

'You once told me I'd end up on my own, and you were right.'

'No, I wasn't. You'll always have someone. If I'm not careful, I'm the one who'll end up alone.'

'Now I know you're talking crap. How many men have you had in the past year alone? You've even got married and divorced, and started seeing Richard.'

'And stopped.'

'What?'

I sit up, unexpectedly distracted from my self-pity.

'Do you know what he said to me?' she says. '"Is there anyone I know who you *haven't* had sex with?"'

'Shit! That was my fault. I didn't mean to tell him. I *didn't* tell him exactly. We were having lunch...'

'Don't panic. He told me what happened. I'm not blaming you.'

'He dumped you because of that? That's not like him.'

'No, I dumped him.'

'I don't understand.'

'It wasn't working anyway. It seemed a good time to end it.'

The way she tells it, she might be describing scrapping an old car that's failed its MOT. A car that's outlived its usefulness. I envy her ability to treat relationships like old bangers.

'I'm sorry,' I say, although it's Richard I should really be commiserating with. He's the one who's been scrapped. He and I are both in the knacker's yard now. Again.

'Life goes on,' says Cate with characteristic pragmatism. 'I know it's not much comfort right now, but it does.'

She takes my hand and we drift into silent reverie. The only sound is the ticking of the clock on the mantelpiece. I've not visited Cate's flat often, but every time that clock has annoyed me.

'It's funny,' I say with a mirthless grin, 'Lisa also thinks I've had sex with everyone I know.'

'They don't understand us, do they?'

'No.'

'We're better off without them.'

'Yes.'

It's nearly midnight by the time I leave, but still I can't face the prospect of going home to an empty flat. I feel like paraplegic Wesley Snipes in *The Waterdance*, who dreams he's dancing on the surface of a lake. He can stay afloat only if he keeps dancing, dancing, no matter how exhausted he becomes. I need to keep dancing too.

On the street outside Cate's flat I phone Kirsty on my mobile. I tell her I need to see her. Now. She asks me if I know what time it is. I tell her I do. She asks why it can't wait. I say I'll tell her when I see her. I'm insistent.

In her cosy living room, in front of the electric fire with the seductive flames, she sits in her armchair, her hands resting on the sides, a white dressing gown drawn tightly around her, and listens to me tell my story for the third time today. Her expression gives nothing away, but the important thing is not how she's taking it, the important thing is to tell her the whole truth, finally.

When I've finished, her response is not long in coming.

'The bitch!' she says. Not quite the verdict I was anticipating from Lisa's best friend, but one with which I'm happy to concur. 'She lied to Jeff, she lied to you and she lied to me. She never said a word to me. Even when I told her you'd spent the night with me, she never said a word. The bitch!'

But I'm not entirely to escape censure for my part in the deception.

'So you lied to me on Valentine's Day when I asked you if there was anything going on between the two of you?'

'I'm sorry. Lisa wouldn't let me tell you. I didn't mean to lead you on.'

'You spent the night with me.'

'You asked me to.'

'You were seeing Lisa but you slept with me because I asked you to?'

She's not the first person to ask this question, and I still have no answer to it.

'God, is it that easy?' she says. 'Is that where I've been going wrong all these years?'

'It wasn't just that. I do like you. I didn't want to leave you on your own. Maybe I wasn't thinking too clearly.'

'Thanks.'

'No, I don't mean it like that. I just didn't think it through, what it meant.'

'It obviously didn't mean much. What am I talking about? It meant *nothing*.' She bangs her fist on the arm-rest in self-recrimination. 'I'm an idiot.'

'You're not an idiot.'

'I'm always seeing things that aren't there.'

'Don't say that. I wouldn't have stayed if I didn't care. I didn't mean to hurt you.'

'Nobody ever does.'

She's clearly tapping into a history I know nothing about, and that context has given my behaviour towards her a meaning I never intended. I'm reminded of my theory of life as a battleground against unknown forces. Is it any wonder that lasting relationships are impossible?

'Can we still be friends?' I say.

She gives the matter consideration worthy of a life-or-death choice, then decides that further clarification is necessary.

'What kind of friends?'

Afraid of saying the wrong thing, and God knows I'm more than capable of doing that, I parry the question.

'That's up to you.'

'Really? You're saying that whatever kind of relationship I want with you, you're okay with that?'

Now I'm even more afraid to say the wrong thing, so I'm grateful when Kirsty answers her own question.

'It seems to me you don't know what you want. If it's all the same to you, I'll take a rain check. You know where the door is.'

Oh well, at least *Kirsty* knows what she wants.

It's 2 a.m. by the time I arrive home. Twenty-three hours since. Less than a single turn of the earth on its axis, yet already I've exhausted the complete cocktail of remedial treatments. Emma gave me a mercy fuck (a consolation prize in the true meaning of the word), Cate reasoned with me, Kirsty turfed me out into the cold night air. None of these palliatives provided more than temporary relief.

I never believed that they would.

When I first told Cate about Lisa, she told me I wanted love like it is in the movies. But why *can't* love be like that? Why do the movies hog all the happy endings? If it's a man's world, as every woman tells me it is, why do I feel like a redundant extra in a chick flick, forever doomed to be discarded on the cutting-room floor?

I go to bed drained, echoing Jean-Luc's plea from *Masculin Feminin*: Sleep, which sometimes shuts the eyes of pain, free me for a time from myself.

33.

I invent a mystery viral illness and manage to get signed off work for a week. I fill the days as best I can, incapable of concentrating on anything, unable to see the point of anything. I spend mornings in bed, waiting to get up. I spend afternoons on the couch, waiting for the evening. I spend evenings staring at the television screen, waiting for the night. The nights never end.

Images of Lisa haunt me. Flashbacks of our parting taunt me. Whenever the phone rings my heart leaps, but it's never Lisa. Usually it's Emma. Sometimes it's Cate. Once it's Kirsty, who's decided she was too hard on me and wants to know if I'm surviving. It's never Richard or Scott. They never call me at home. I wouldn't know what to say to them if they did. I couldn't tell them how I really feel. It's that guy thing again.

Although Emma continues to offer the most sympathy, it's Cate's pragmatism that increasingly gives me more solace. I was with Lisa for two months – one year and ten months less than I was with Jenny. Surely it won't take as long to recover this time. One twelfth as long? I'm like Bruce Willis in *The Last Boy Scout*, who believes in love like he believes in cancer.

One thing I do know. I'm not going to repeat the mistakes I made with Jenny. I shall make no phone calls and write no letters. I shall not seek Lisa out to remind her of how good it was, or harangue her for her stupidity. I shall not ask her why, why, why.

How do you survive Alphaville? Here's the advice given to Lemmy Caution when he arrives in town: *Don't ask why, say because.*

This is how I rationalise it. Lisa left me because she's a coward. I can't believe she'll not come to regret what she's done. I can't believe that the life to which she's reverted is going to make her happy. Well, if our love wasn't enough to give her the strength to leave the bozo, Cate's right, she was never the woman for me. She deserves no more of my tears. In Alphaville it is forbidden to cry.

I wish I could go and sit in a dark cinema and let shining images transport me to another place, but the cinema reminds me of Lisa. This, despite the fact that, in another of life's little ironies, we never made it to the pictures together.

Even Alasdair's latest Top Ten elicits only passing interest. Ten Best Titles.

'*Spot Marks the X?*' I say.

'It's about a dog that uncovers buried treasure,' he says.

Who cares?

I watch only one film. *El Cid*. The restored uncut version is on the box one afternoon. I don't intend to sit through the whole 182 minutes, but it holds me spellbound. The screenplay speaks directly to me. I can hardly bear to watch the scene where, after Rodrigo has been forced to kill his lover's father in a duel, and she has sworn revenge on him, he visits her and tries to win back her love.

'Why did you come?' she says.

'I tried not to,' he says, 'but my love will not die.'

'Kill it.'

'You kill it. Tell me you don't love me.'

'I can't,' she says, 'not yet. But I will learn to hate you.'

Will Lisa learn to hate me in the same way? Can I learn to hate her? For leading me on, for lying to me, for ruining movies for me? No, I could never do that. Even if I wanted to, I could never do that. As with Jenny, I can never not love Lisa. That would be a denial of everything I felt for her.

On the other hand, I can't allow myself to continue to feel love for her, either. Not at the moment, anyway. It's too painful. Until time brings perspective, as surely it must, as hopefully it will, what I must feel is precisely nothing. Does that make sense? It's the same process I had to go through after Jenny left. I must banish all thoughts of Lisa from my mind.

On Friday Emma invites me to lunch at Jenners. After so many hours closeted behind closed curtains, the daylight makes me squint. We find a window table overlooking Princes Street and, for a while, it's almost like old times. A tuna and cucumber sandwich for Emma, Cheddar for me. It's the first intimation that, as Cate keeps telling me, life *will* go on.

But I soon discover we're not here solely for my convalescence.

'Can I say something?' says Emma, by way of introducing a sensitive subject.

I give her the go-ahead.

'Don't be angry with me, but I'm starting to feel pressurised again.'

'By me?'

'I'm scared that now you don't have anyone, you'll expect things from me again.'

'I won't.'

For once I welcome her misgivings. I know I've leaned on her heavily this week, but I'm under no illusions that, especially after the depth of feeling Lisa exhumed in me, we're ever going to ride off happily into the sunset together. In the light of recent intimacies, it's a relief to hear she feels the same way... although, when I think about it, she was due for another about-turn.

'Stop worrying,' I say. 'I just want to be as good a friend to you as you are to me.'

She gives me the most genuine smile I've ever seen her manage. Who would ever have thought we'd both be so pleased, simultaneously, not to be desired by the other?

'In that case,' she says, emboldened, 'there's something else I've been wanting to tell you.'

Again I give her the go-ahead, but first she waits while a waitress cleans away our empty plates. Whatever she has to say is for my ears only.

'I've met someone else.'

What? She's met someone else? Emma has someone and I don't?

'He's called Duncan,' she says. 'He's a biscuit designer.'

'A biscuit designer?'

'Someone has to do it. Who do you think decides whether they're round or square, or what patterns to put on them, or what fillings to put in them, or what flavour to make them, or whether to put icing on them, or what combination of ingredients to use?'

'I guess I never thought about it.'

'He's designing a biscuit for me. It's a salted cashew nut biscuit sandwich, with brie and gruyère flavoured cream filling.'

It wasn't so long ago that I was consoling Emma with the thought that she might meet someone tomorrow while I'd be on my own again. I didn't expect this latest role reversal to occur so soon.

There are so many questions I want to ask. Where did she meet him? What's he like? What's his story?

'Have you had sex with him?'

'Yes.'

'And?'

'It was nice.'

Nice? Here are some of the things that Emma finds nice: tuna and cucumber sandwiches, warm summer breezes, *How To Make An American Quilt*, the scent of mimosa, Scholl foot balm. I've never heard her describe sex as nice. Maybe that says it all about our relationship.

'Better than with me?' I say.

'Stop it. You're as bad as I was when you met Lisa.'

She's right. Just as she had to come to terms with losing me to Lisa, I now have to come to terms with losing her to someone else. Alec didn't count. This Duncan character obviously does.

Her taking me to bed on Monday morning now seems an even more generous act.

'Does he know about Monday morning?' I say.

'No, and don't you ever tell him.'

So she's going to lie to him? The way Lisa lied to me?

'Do you love him?'

'Give me a chance. I hardly know him.'

'Lisa and I hardly knew each other.'

'Well, I'm not like you. Maybe that was our problem all along.'

'What about all that stuff about never being able to get close to someone?'

'Well, maybe I can. You always said I would if I met the right person.'

'So he's the right person?'

'I don't know yet, but he's special.'

Ouch. Emma has dumped me to have nice sex with someone special. A vision of the future opens up before me and, shorn of the sheen of Lisa's love, I see, perhaps for the first time, that Emma isn't in it. I can't expect her always to be there for me now. I want to be happy for her, but part of me wants her to remain free and available to me forever.

I wish I were a better person.

'What do you think?' she says.

'I don't know what I think, but I know how I feel.'

'How?'

'Crummy.' My God, I've cracked a joke. Even bigger surprise, I smile at it. My facial muscles still work. Emma looks puzzled. She never did understand jokes.

'Biscuits?' I say. 'Crumbs?'

'Oh,' she says. 'He's working on a new formula to minimise crumbs.'

'I'm sorry,' I say. 'I'm a bit confused, just like you were when I met Lisa. But I do know I want you to be happy.'

'Thank you,' she says. 'You'll find someone as well.'

It's the same platitude that Cate gave me. It means nothing.

'Would I like him?'

'I think so. I've made him a plate.'

It sounds like the perfect match, for afternoon tea at least. A plate of biscuits. Probably a firmer basis for a lasting relationship than she and I ever had. Or Lisa and I, for that matter.

So, as if Lisa dumping me wasn't enough, Emma is to follow suit. Again. Less dramatically this time, less traumatically than Lisa, but with equal effect. And not to be outdone, Cate follows close on their heels with her own brand of executive action. I accept that, technically, this one's more of a defection than a dumping, but I'm learning to view anything short of total commitment to my cause as the gravest of slights.

Equally abandoned by Emma for someone more 'special', Cate takes me out that same evening for a reprise of our previous trawl through the Cowgate bars. You'd think that, now we're both single again, we'd find common cause against the world but, like Emma, Cate too has moved on, both from Richard and from me. I discover she's already receiving all the consolation she needs from a fresh-faced computer science student.

'You're not ready for sex yet,' she says out of nowhere.

'Thanks,' I say. 'Did I ask?'

'No, but I know what you're thinking. We're both single again. You're a man. I just don't see you in that way any longer.' She pats me on the knee. 'You're more like one of my girlfriends now.'

As if being condemned to a life of chastity isn't sufficient punishment for my failings, I'm now to be emasculated as well.

'I don't want to be a girlfriend,' I say, ever capable of being pathetic when the need arises, 'I want to be a boyfriend. I want to be Lisa's boyfriend.'

'Stop it,' she says. 'That's over.'

'I can't just turn off what I feel.'

'You can turn it on quick enough. That's your problem. You feel things too deeply.'

'How *can* you feel things too deeply?'

'It blinds you to reality. Let me ask you a question. What was her underwear like?'

'What?'

'It's a simple enough question.' She speaks as one sister to another. 'Did you ever see her in her old knickers?'

'How do I know? Her underwear was always immaculate.'

'I thought so. Take it from me, you never really knew her.'

For the life of me, I can't decide whether this observation is the shallowest or most profound litmus test of a relationship I have ever heard. But it opens me up to the possibility that I never really did know Lisa.

Maybe when she told me she loved me, I saw only what I wanted to see. Maybe she did too. Wasn't it she herself who said, when the bozo found the Valentine card I sent, that you can believe anything if you want to? Cate and centuries of folklore are right: love *is* blind.

At the end of the evening she gives me a sisterly hug and sends me on my way. As I cross the Dean Bridge, I pause to peer over the retaining wall at the Water of Leith, invisible but audible in the darkness far below. After the bridge was built in 1832, it became a popular suicide spot until the local council chanced upon an ironic preventative measure. They studded the top of the wall with small iron spikes. After all, no one wants to hurt himself or herself while committing suicide.

It gives me an idea.

Back home I make a list. Top Ten Extravagant Ways To End It All. Butch Cassidy and the Sundance Kid, Arnold Schwarzenegger in *Terminator 2*, Jean Reno in *Leon*... Dean Bridge leapers...

Contrary to what you might expect, the list gives me hope. It puts my own petty problems in context. Given such an insignificant motive as rejection, I could never compete with such grand gestures.

The following evening, Saturday, another night, another bar. Tonight's venue is the Filmhouse and tonight's companion is Kirsty. Her suggestion. She's still feeling guilty about the way she treated me. Well, what she actually said on the phone was, 'Screw Lisa. Let's go out and have some fun.'

Surprisingly, by avoiding all mention of recent events, we actually succeed in the endeavour. We argue animatedly about pop music and reality television, we gossip about the Bank, we discuss the relative merits of various chef's specials, we swap stories about embarrassing moments. It brings back memories of how much we enjoyed each other's company here at the pre-Christmas Film Soc.

'Does this mean we can still be friends?' I say on the pavement outside her flat.

'I asked you out, didn't I?' she says. For a moment I wonder if she's going to invite me in, and if I should accept, and what that would mean, and what it might lead to, and...

'Just don't expect me to visit any more building sites with you at the moment,' she says as she walks to the tenement door, still with a slight limp.

'What about Lisa?'

'What about Lisa?'

'Can you be friends with both of us?'

She searches for her key. 'I'm not sure I want to be her friend any longer.'

Mention of Lisa's name makes me suddenly hungry for any information Kirsty can give me about her.

'How is she?'

'I have no idea. We've been avoiding each other all week.'

'But you work with her.'

She unlocks the door and turns to see the desperate look on my face.

'I'll tell you this,' she says. 'I don't know what you did to her, but she looks hellish.'

I ache to know more, but Kirsty needs the loo and has to go.

When I go to bed, I put so much effort into analysing Lisa's hellish look that my head aches. I'm annoyed at myself. She doesn't deserve to cause me sleepless nights. I'm better off without her. I'm better off with friends like Kirsty, and Emma and Cate. Even if they now see me as an honorary girlfriend. When you think about it, that's quite a compliment.

Who needs the hassle and heartbreak of love when you have friends? Remember what James Stewart's guardian angel inscribes in the book he gives him in *It's a Wonderful Life*? 'Remember: no man is a failure who has friends.'

Cate's right. I do fall in love too quickly. I do feel things too deeply. Why is that? Why am I different? What's wrong with me?

Can I change?

34.

One week after Lisa dumps me, I return to work. I log on to the computer with trepidation, but there is no email from her. Another promise broken. The last one.

Richard inquires after my health, which puzzles me until I remember that I've been ill with a virus. I tell him I'm feeling better.

'Have you heard that Cate left me?' he says.

His confession puts me to shame. While I lie to him about my own misfortune, he shares his with me as though he's been waiting the whole week for the opportunity.

'Yes. I'm sorry,' I say. Then I remember that, before my absence, he wasn't speaking to me. 'I hope it didn't have anything to do with me and Scott.'

'No. It was a shock finding out about that, but it was my problem. Cate and I weren't right for each other, that's all.'

He shrugs his shoulders in a manner intended to represent the sum total of the emotional impact her leaving has had on him.

'You're taking it well,' I say, offering him a chance to disagree.

'Life goes on,' he says with a smile that doesn't even appear to be rueful. In the few weeks he went out with Cate, he clearly learned a lot from her.

'Are you doing anything tomorrow night?' he says. 'There's someone I'd like you to meet.'

'You've got someone else lined up already?'

He's learned so much from Cate that he could now give *her* lessons. Rather than being upset by her dumping him, it's the best thing that's ever happened to him.

'Come along and find out,' he says. 'Same place, same time as before. Bring Lisa.'

'I can't. She dumped me.'

It just comes out.

'Oh, no,' he says with genuine concern. 'I'm so sorry.'

He puts his hand on my shoulder. It's the first deliberate sober physical contact we've ever had, and the gesture makes the ache well up inside me once more. Richard is my friend. Maybe I've not always appreciated how good a friend.

'What happened?' he says.

I have to swallow before I can speak.

'I don't really want to talk about it.'

'Old boyfriend trouble?'

That does it. I can't hold out against that. It brings down an emotional barrier that Richard and I have maintained as long as we've known each other.

'She won't leave him,' I say in a small voice.

Richard takes a moment. He doesn't want to say the wrong thing.

'Maybe she just needs more time.'

'No, it'll never happen now.'

'You don't know that for sure.'

'I do.'

'Rubbish. From what you've told me before...'

'No. Don't give me hope. I couldn't stand to hope.' For the first time in my life, I'm defenceless in front of another man.

'Sorry,' he says again. 'I didn't mean to... I take it you weren't ill, then.'

'Don't tell anyone, will you?'

'Of course not.'

At lunchtime he leaves me alone to put a different spin on the situation for Scott. I tell Scott that Lisa has decided to put our relationship on hold while she sorts out her life. He sympathises in his own way. His suggested course of action is to eliminate the bozo, which enables us to polish off even the chef's special crunchy cranachan while we devise elaborate and satisfying murder strategies.

The following evening I arrive at the Cameo five minutes late. Richard is already there with the new woman in his life. She sits with her back to me, but I can tell from her neat hairstyle and smart blue suit that, to use Scott's expression, he's done all right for himself this time. As I approach, she turns, and I can hardly believe my eyes.

'Megan?'

'Surprise!' she says and jumps up to embrace me.

'What are you doing here?

'Miss me?'

It turns out she's spent the whole winter in South America. Following her trek around the Torres del Paine in Patagonia, she bummed around Chile and Argentina then lived for two months in a small village on the Bolivian Altiplano. She peppers her tale with exotic place-names. Now she's back in Edinburgh as, of all things, a businesswoman. She's started a craft co-operative in Bolivia and is importing goods to Britain.

'It's a proper business,' she says. 'The villagers get a liveable wage, we get some beautiful craftwork, I make some money and get to travel, everyone's happy. Feel this jacket. Pure baby alpaca wool.'

I'm impressed. There's no comparison between the dishevelled, insecure girl I first met and the attractive, self-confident woman I see before me now. I can hardly wait for Richard to go to the bar.

'Back in Edinburgh *and* back with Richard?' I say, when he does.

'I know,' she says, 'but I'd forgotten how much we have in common. I guess we both had a lot of growing to do. I know I did. I have a photograph someone took of us at Cate's wedding. I've framed it as a reminder of what I used to be like. Richard's changed a lot as well, don't you think?'

'I guess.'

When he returns from the bar, she takes his arm.

'Anyway,' she says, 'we're going to give it another try.'

'Good luck to you both,' I say and raise my glass.

'And you. Richard told me about Lisa.'

'I hope you don't mind,' says Richard.

'I'm just glad you're back with Megan,' I say. 'Maybe it will stop you dragging me out clubbing this time.'

Megan gives us a puzzled look.

'Thanks, pal,' says Richard.

So this is how it is. Emma is with Duncan the biscuit designer. Richard is back with Megan. Scott, as ever, is with his wife, whatever her name is. Cate is with a selection box of toy boys. Lisa is with the bozo. I'm with no one. This is how it is.

And this is the way I intend to look at it. I used to think you could fall in love only once in your life, but now I know it can happen twice, and that's not counting Emma, who wouldn't let me love her, and if you can fall in love twice, you can fall in love three times. It must be true, what everyone keeps telling me. Somewhere out there, there's someone else for me to love. It's simply a matter of finding her. This is the way I intend to look at it.

In accordance with this m.o., I've made a decision to become a 'yes' man. I shall say yes to all invitations. I shall socialise, network, meet new people. The more people you meet, the more people you meet, and one day I shall meet someone else with whom I want to share my life.

Not that I'm thinking that far ahead.

One day at a time. One step at a time. One rung at a time. Rung? I have a new theory of life. You ready for this?

Life is a ladder that needs to be climbed one rung at a time. If I run out of rungs before I meet someone 'special,' to use Emma's term, I shall merely do as fire chief Steve McQueen does in *Towering Inferno*, when confronted with a fire in the world's tallest building.

He requests a longer ladder.

The actuality isn't as straightforward as that, of course, not when I have to work in the same building as Lisa. As Julie Delpy says in *Before Sunset*, 'Memory's a wonderful thing as long as you don't have to deal with the past.'

During my first few days back in the office I expect to bump into Lisa at every turn. When I think I see her, in a corridor or in the canteen, my heart beats faster, just like when the phone rings. But it never is her on the phone, and it never is her in the corridor or the canteen.

There's one moment in particular that almost topples me off my ladder.

For a capital city, Edinburgh has such a compact centre that, if you wander up and down the main drag x number of times, you'll bump into everyone you know. Someone should conduct an experiment to find the value of x. I bet it's lower than for any city of comparable size.

I'm strolling along Princes Street after work when Calum materialises in front of me.

'Cate told me you'd been dumped,' he says, undeterred by considerations of pleasantry or tact. 'Are you all right?'

Although I haven't seen him for a while, some memories never die, so I wait.

'Or aren't you?'

'You've seen Cate?'

'We had some divorce papers to sort out. She says if I'm not careful I'll always be on my own. Do you think I will? Or do you…'

'Are you all right?' I interrupt.

'Life goes on,' he says, echoing Cate's platitude.

'That's true,' I say, responding in kind.

'But are you happy?' He gives me an earnest look. He really needs to know. He wonders if my experience can inform his. 'Or aren't you?'

'I'm learning to be content. Contentment is when you adjust to the world, happiness is when you adjust the world to yourself.'

'That's not right.'

'Pardon?'

'True contentment lies in knowing that there are only fleeting moments of happiness.'

The bastard! Are there no universal constants in life any longer? Now I'll have to go away and rethink even this basic principle of existence.

'I knew I'd bump into you,' he says, 'because I cast a spell.'

'You did?'

'I summoned the spirit of the Grand Wizard to marshall the Forces of Light to guide her back to you.'

I'm unconvinced. The Grand Wizard hasn't won any prizes for marshalling the Forces of Light to guide Cate back to him.

'I couldn't practise on Cate,' he says, sensing my scepticism. 'Selfish abuse of the Knowledge has grave consequences.'

Now I'm convinced. His conviction convinces me. It's at this moment that the ladder wobbles.

'You think it'll work?' I say feebly.

He gives me a condescending smile. In the post-Lisa world I now inhabit, even Calum treats me with condescension. Without another word, he walks away.

It's an unsettling encounter.

In an effort to regain some semblance of control over my life, I try replacement memory therapy. I go for a drink at the Thistle and Sporran, to banish memories of the night that Lisa told me she loved me. I watch *The Searchers* again, alone. I wander through Inverleith Park and along the Water of Leith. The cherry blossom has faded as quickly as our romance. Even more symbolically, the bench in Lisa's riverside clearing beyond the Dean Village has been vandalised.

As the weeks go by I become accustomed, if not inured, to the fact that she is out of my life completely. Gradually, falteringly, apprehensively, I become able to think of her again with a warmth in my heart rather than an ache in my stomach.

In *City of Angels* Nicholas Cage falls in love with Meg Ryan but, because he's an angel, he has no sense of touch. He becomes mortal to be with her, but she dies in an accident. How does he handle it? 'I would rather have had one breath of her hair, one kiss of her mouth, one touch of her hand, than an eternity without it.' That's how I feel about Lisa. I can't regret having known her.

In one sense the way she treated me is irrelevant. What matters is what *I* felt. Nicholas Cage gets some great lines. Here's another he gets to speak in *Adaptation*: 'You are what you love, not what loves you.'

As a mark of my tentative emotional growth, I even allow Emma to introduce me to Duncan. The three of us meet for coffee one Saturday afternoon and it turns out he's... well, I can only use Emma's word of the month... he's a *nice* guy. Gentle, genuine, sincere.

There's a defining moment in my relationship with him, when Emma goes to the toilet and leaves us on our own for a moment, perhaps deliberately.

'Can I say something?' he says to me. 'I know you've known Emma a long time. I want you to know she'll be safe with me. It doesn't mean you can't still be friends with her. I hope we can be friends as well.'

It's still hard for me to come to terms with the fact that he has more priority in Emma's life than I do, but I can't not like him.

At the beginning of April, about four weeks after Lisa's departure, Kirsty phones to suggest meeting up again.

'We could go for a cup of coffee on Sunday afternoon,' she says.

Not quite the evening of alcohol abuse I'd been hoping for, but all invitations are acceptable. If I may borrow a word from Emma, it's *nice* to be wanted, whatever form it takes.

'I'd like that,' I say.

'Would you mind if I brought along a friend?'

'A friend?'

'Yes, a friend.'

It's heart-warming that my friends want to introduce me to their new partners. I'm so lucky.

'Who?'

'Don't worry, you'll like her.'

Her? *Her?* I'll *like* her? Wait a minute. Is Kirsty fixing me up with a blind date?

'Her?'

'Don't worry,' she says again, sensing my disquiet.

'Okay,' I say resignedly. 'If you want, bring her along.'

Kirsty's right. Why worry? Not all blind dates have to turn out like the one I had at Scott's. What was her name again? Morwenna. Yes, that's it. Anyway, I need to meet people. This will be a good test of my new approach to life. Am I a yes man or not?

'We'll meet you outside Frasers at three o'clock on Sunday,' says Kirsty.

So be it. If Natasha can leave Alphaville for an uncertain future, I can certainly forsake another empty Sunday afternoon in front of the television to embrace whatever life has in store for me next.

35.

Heartbreak Corner. The junction of Princes Street and Hope Street. Beneath the clock that juts out from the second floor of Frasers department store.

Again.

Three o'clock on a breezy Sunday afternoon in April, the air fresh after rain, the city centre abuzz with shoppers and sightseers, pavement cafés humming with trade, the castle resplendent beneath a patchwork sky, new growth in the gardens below.

Spring has come to Edinburgh. Snowdrops carpet the greens of Swanston Village, crocuses line the Meadows, an aroma of wild garlic hangs over Colinton Dell, new season Jersey Royals add a touch of class to my local greengrocer's shelves.

It's a good day to start a new chapter in my life, even if Heartbreak Corner is a rather inauspicious location for the occasion. Generations of expectant lovers have stood where I now stand and worn the pavement smooth while waiting for one who would never come.

Today there are three other supplicants besides myself. We align ourselves at discrete intervals along Frasers' store front. As the last to arrive, I'm displaced to the Hope Street end of the window displays, where I play escort to a mannequin that sports a lime green skirt and jacket from the new spring collection.

To my left, a businessman in a belted mackintosh checks his watch as he paces his allotted space like a sentry. Beyond him, a sturdy middle-aged matron, dressed in stirrup-slacks and anorak, stands at the store's corner entrance and cranes her neck to search the Shandwick Place crowds.

The fourth member of our company is a smart young man who couldn't have taken more trouble over his appearance if he'd been invited to the Film Festival Opening Gala as principal guest. He waits around the corner on Princes Street, but every so often he wanders into view, checking for stray hair and brushing imagined specks from the lapel of his jacket.

On one such appearance our eyes lock in mutual recognition. We know it at once. We're both here on the same quest.

I wonder if he was lured here with the same false promises that Kirsty made to me. She pulled out of our meeting this morning with the pathetic excuse that she has a hairdresser's appointment she'd forgotten about. On a Sunday? Not only that, but as it was too late to get in touch with her friend to cancel, would I mind meeting her alone?

At 3.05 precisely, according to the clock, the beslacked matron is greeted by her well-worn husband, and the two waddle into Frasers. Now we are three.

I don't know the first thing about Kirsty's friend. I don't know what she looks like, I don't even know her name. All I know is, I'm to wait here until accosted.

You have to laugh, don't you? I mean, I've been standing on this corner, on and off, for over a decade. I've stood here for Jenny and Emma, among others, and once for a woman who never turned up. I waited half an hour for her, and that's all I'm waiting this time.

Yes, there's a distinct feeling of déjà vu about this. How come, after all these years, I'm here again, waiting to meet a complete stranger? I thought life was supposed to be like a novel, with one scene leading causally to the next. My life is more like a series of short stories in which I repeat the same theme with different variations. The same theme and the same mistakes. Am I the only one who never learns from experience? Are there others who remain impervious to life's lessons?

3.10. A high-heeled woman wearing a matching blue skirt and jacket totters up to the raincoated businessman, and the pair of them head off along Shandwick Place in heated argument. My hidden brother-in-arms peers around the corner once more. Yes, I say silently, I'm still here too. Maybe I'll always be here.

If my life is nothing like a novel, it's even less like a Hollywood movie. Reel life always has a happy ending, whereas real life always ends in sadness. You're born, you live, you die. In that order. In fact, when you think about it, it's the order that makes it sad.

I don't mean to sound morbid, I mean to be philosophical. *C'est la vie* and all that. I intend to view my life as a work in progress. If you were to draw a graph of its emotional ups and downs, it would resemble a roller-coaster ride. Whether times are good or bad simply depends on which point of the graph you study.

If I'd stopped telling you my story three months ago, it would have ended on the euphoria of Lisa falling in love with me on my birthday. If I'd stopped one month ago, it would have ended in despair, with Lisa dumping me and the future stretching out before me like the expanding blackness of space. If I'd told you the story of my life seven years ago, Lisa wouldn't even have appeared in it. It would have been about Jenny.

What point of the graph are we on now? On an upward curve, I hope. When you hit bottom, what other way is there to go? One thing's for sure, the roller-coaster won't stop here. If you want to know where I'll be in five or ten years time, come back and ask me then.

3.15. My comrade gives up and hurries off with bowed head, as though he has some important business to attend to. He doesn't fool me.

A teenager, all sweatshirt and baggy jeans, commandeers the corner position.

As I was about to say, concerning this new improved post-existential approach to life that I'm cultivating, I can't pick and choose when to practise it. I must apply it to every situation, because it's the difficult cases that will determine its efficacy.

Take Emma and Duncan. I would never have believed it, but I can now bear to see them together without feeling a sense of loss. When Duncan holds Emma's hand now, I'm actually happy that she has someone. I like Duncan. She's in good hands. They're a couple in a way that she and I never were. I've even given her the good luck charm that Megan gave me at the craft fair.

The second time around, Richard and Megan look good together too. Megan is busy with her new business. Next week she jets off to the wilds of Bolivia again. The dual lifestyle suits her – third-world saviour and first-world businesswoman.

Richard is left behind to languish at the Bank with increasing restlessness. Like Scott, he now insists he's going to get out. He's talking about computerising Megan's business, and living and working with her. They've both come a long way in the past year. I hope it works out for them.

Scott will never get out. His wife is pregnant again. Whatever he thinks about that, or says to the contrary, it means there'll be another mouth to feed. He doesn't seriously want to leave the Bank anyway. Despite his ritual protestations, he's as happy there as he would be anywhere. Or should that be *content*?

Not me, though. After the trauma of the past few months, I'm as unsettled as Richard. I don't want to work in the Bank for the rest of my life. I could probably obtain a similar position elsewhere, but what would be the point? One computing job is much the same as another. Maybe I'm having an (early) mid-life crisis, but I want to do something different. Maybe I should go into business with Richard, or…

Promise you won't steal this idea, but my current ambition is to open an upmarket potato outlet. I'm going to call it *Pomme de Terre*. I'm convinced there's a gap in the market for such an enterprise.

Whenever Scott broaches the subject of his imminent departure, both Richard and I, in unison, tell him it's the biggest load of rubbish we have ever heard. For his part, he treats our own threat to quit with equal condescension, but at heart he's worried we'll go through with it. He's worried he'll end up the saddest bastard of all three of us.

Cate says I should try contracting, or work from home. Sometimes she jokes that the two of us should make the most of our single status, pack it all in and take a round-the-world trip together. If she were only half-serious, I swear I'd take her up on it. I want to go to the desert, to Monument Valley, where John Wayne made *The Searchers*.

If Lisa had stayed with me, we could have gone together. If she can imagine the desert in a rain-drenched clearing by the Water of Leith, God knows what she'd make of the real thing. I bet she'd actually see Duke riding across the horizon.

My life would be so different if she'd stayed with me.

The other day Cate asked me what I'd do if she came back. It'll never happen, I said. But what if, she said. I don't want to think about it, I said. But of course I do think about it, just like, over the years, I've wondered what would have happened if Jenny had come back.

Would I embrace Lisa with open arms, or would her betrayal of our love prevent me from ever giving myself completely to her again?

Suppose she comes back and tells me she had to go back to the bozo because it was the only way to be sure there was nothing still there for her. Now she knows there's nothing there, she can come to me with a clear conscience. If she hadn't tried, she says, our relationship would always have been plagued by guilt.

But can I overcome the doubt that comes to me in the middle of the night? I want to believe absolutely, without reservation, that Lisa will never leave me again, but I need constant reassurance. Will I ever be able to trust her again?

One thing I do know: if Lisa did come back to me, it would be one thing that Jenny never did. Perhaps it would be the difference that makes all the difference.

Whatever.

Lisa is gone. They never come back. I have to come to terms with the fact that my life must begin over again. Alpha 60 says: *Once we know one, we believe we know two, because one plus one equals two, but we forget that first we must know the meaning of* plus. Certainly nothing adds up to anything meaningful in my life at the moment. It's sometimes quite astute for a computer, that Alpha 60.

3.20. The teenager's mate turns up and they wander off along Princes Street. I'm on my own now. Hundreds of people pass me by, but I'm on my own. Ten more minutes and I'm off.

To be honest, I don't care whether Kirsty's friend turns up or not. If you put yourself in the firing line, you're going to get shot occasionally. I can take the odd flesh wound. It's all part of my new open-armed approach to life.

Life is not a novel or a movie. It's not even a roller-coaster. Well, not only a roller-coaster. Are you ready for this? Come on, sit up and pay attention now. I'm about to tell you my latest, state-of-the-art model of existence.

Life is a spinning plate.

No, don't laugh.

Sometimes it's a roller-coaster and sometimes it's a spinning plate. Nothing confusing about that. It can also be a battle against unknown forces, a ladder with rungs to be climbed and goodness knows what else. All at the same time. It's probably something to do with quantum physics.

Today it's a spinning plate. You know, like those that jugglers keep aloft on the end of long sticks. The spinning plate hypothesis gives life two important properties. Firstly, the spin causes it to keep repeating itself, which immediately explains more about everyday experience than most rival philosophical theories. Secondly, the edge rotates faster than the centre.

Some people prefer to live a sedate life at the centre, but I've come to the conclusion that I'm one of those who likes to sit at the edge with his legs dangling over the abyss. That's where you find laughter and tears, joy and sorrow. That's where you get hurt, and where you hurt others. That's where you feel. Cate is wrong after all. It *is* impossible to feel too deeply.

The edge is not a place for those of a nervous disposition, but those of us who choose to live there would have it no other way. It may be a giddy and sometimes scary place to reside but, my God, it's exciting.

So, as I stand here at Heartbreak Corner, at 3.25 on a breezy Sunday afternoon in April, I *welcome* the unknowability of the future. As I'm whirled around on the spinning plate that is my life, I don't care where it will take me. It's the journey that counts. Who was it who said that, although every journey has an end, the true end is the journey itself?

Maybe Kirsty's friend will turn out to be the next love of my life. And if she doesn't turn up at all, well, there'll always be a next time. Cate's right about that one. I will always find someone. I choose to believe her.

Wait a minute…

Something peculiar is happening. I feel giddy. My legs feel weak. I'm just going to lean against this window for support. Sorry about this.

The street scene before me has become an image on a cinema screen. The action has slowed down to such an extent that, like in *Matrix* bullet-time mode, I can track every movement.

I scan the image frame by frame until… What's this?

Zoom in. Enlarge. Enhance.

A face has appeared out of the crowd. A face I recognise.

Lisa!

She's walking towards me from the direction of Shandwick Place, carrying a Habitat shopping bag, wearing a tailored black jacket I haven't seen her in before.

Suddenly everything makes sense. Kirsty has organised the whole scenario. A friend, she said. You'll like her, she said. Megan's good luck charm has worked. Calum's spell has worked. Reason has prevailed.

Lisa is coming back to me after all!

Because she's moving in slow motion, it takes an age for her to reach me. She doesn't even bother to look up, because she has no need to, because she knows I will be here, that I will wait forever if need be.

She passes the zebra crossing, the post box, the machine that dispenses tourist maps of Edinburgh. Now we are separated only by the benches where shoppers stop to rest. Yes, I can forgive her everything, there will be no doubts.

The crowds are so dense that they force her out towards the edge of the pavement. She has to take to the road, beside the Hope Street taxi rank, in an effort to outflank them.

She's nearly upon me now. Another moment or two and she'll be safe in my arms.

But… now what's happening? A taxi door is opening. Lisa is getting in. The driver is pulling away.

Hasn't she seen me after all? Does she think I've stood her up? Is she just out shopping? Is it pure coincidence that she's here at all?

I'm about to run after her when a restraining hand latches on to my arm. It distracts me long enough for the taxi to accelerate out of reach. As Lisa rides away from me, I spin around to confront my assailant.

Before me stands a complete stranger. I've never seen her before in my life, I'm sure of it, and yet... There's something disconcertingly familiar about her...

The same, long, straight, jet-black hair, framing a coquettish face with perfect cheekbones and pale, flawless complexion... The same sweet smile... The same trim figure asserted by a short A-line dress...

I step back in renewed shock.

She's the spitting image of Anna Karina as Natasha in *Alphaville*.

She fixes her wide kohl-framed eyes on mine and says:

'Excuse me, are you Michael?'

Bonus Material

TOP TEN SADDEST ENDINGS
(Warning: may contain spoilers!)

The Age of Innocence

On the Atlantic seaboard Daniel Day-Lewis watches Michelle Pfeiffer, the love of his life, gaze out to sea. If she turns to face him before a boat passes a nearby lighthouse, he will leave his fiancée and go to her. She doesn't turn. Decades later, with his wife now dead, he is taken to Paris by their son to see Michelle, but baulks at meeting her after all this time. He sits on a bench outside her apartment and stares at her balcony. A figure comes to the window, the light glints and dazzles. He remembers the boat and the lighthouse, and imagines Michelle turning to face him. If this is she at the window now, he will go to her. But it's only a servant. Daniel stands up and walks away, leaving his unrequited love to memory.

The Bridges of Madison County

Clint Eastwood is a footloose photographer. Meryl Streep is a bored housewife. Over four days they meet and fall passionately in love, but she can't bring herself to leave her family for him. After they part for the last time, she catches one last glimpse of him while driving through town with her husband. Clint is standing bedraggled in the rain, staring at her. They exchange a forlorn smile. He gets in his pickup and drives away. Meryl and her husband pull up behind him at traffic lights. She sees him take a pendant she gave him and hang it from his mirror. The lights turn to green. He doesn't pull away. Her hand is on the door handle, turning it. Her husband toots his horn. Still Clint doesn't move. Meryl is ready to run to him. Her husband toots again. Clint pulls away, out of Meryl's life forever. She breaks down, remembering his last words of love to her: 'This kind of certainty comes but once in a lifetime.'

Brief Encounter

In an age of gentility and steam trains, Trevor Howard and Celia Johnson meet in a railway station refreshment room. They're both married with children, but they can't help falling in love, and the station becomes a refuge for their clandestine meetings. Despite their passion, they realise they can have no future together and must part. They spend their last moments over cups of tea in the refreshment room. 'I love you with all my heart and soul,' says Trevor. 'I want to die,' says Celia. His train arrives. He gets up to go. He puts his hand on her shoulder one last time, then he's gone. The camera tracks and angles in on Celia's anguished face as the piercing whistle of an approaching express train grows louder and louder.

Cleopatra

In the Burton/Taylor version, when Mark Antony thinks his beloved Cleopatra is dead, he falls on his sword, only to find out in his dying moments that she's not dead after all. Servants carry his failing body to her for a touching final scene in which he breathes his last and she commits suicide by clutching an asp to her bosom. It's the same misunderstanding/double suicide ending as in *Romeo and Juliet*, which is no surprise because both films are based on the plays of Shakespeare, who liked the idea so much that he used it twice. Notwithstanding, Mark Antony's last words in the film get me every time, as he looks at Cleopatra and says: 'Kiss me and take my breath away.'

Shadowlands

Ten years after dying of cancer in *Terms of Endearment*, Debra Winger is at it again, this time with husband Anthony Hopkins at her bedside. 'Don't leave me,' he says. 'You have to let me go,' she says. But he can't, and the final scenes of the film, in which he struggles to come to terms with her death, are unbearably moving. In a last voice-over he asks: 'Why love, if losing hurts so much?' And he answers: 'The pain now is part of the happiness then. That's the deal.'

Sommersby

After the American Civil War, Richard Gere turns up on Jodie Foster's doorstep posing as her long-lost husband, and she believes him. She comes to realise he's an impostor, but she stands by him because he's nicer than her husband was, he's better in bed, and basically she's never had it so good. They fall in love. When he's condemned to death for a murder committed by her real husband, he goes to the scaffold rather than admit his true identity and thereby lose his new name and marriage. But he can die peacefully only if she is there with him, and in his last moments on the scaffold he can't see her. He starts to panic, he calls her name. And here she comes, pushing her way to the front of the crowd, calling his name. He sees her. Now he can die in peace.

Starman

(Artistic licence requested. This isn't the end of the film, but it is the end of a relationship.)

With tears in her eyes, widow Karen Allen watches home movie footage of her deceased husband Jeff Bridges, when who should peek through the window but an extraterrestrial who, to make himself less conspicuous, adopts Jeff's form. From then on the movie goes downhill all the way, but you'd have to be made of stone not to be affected by those touching opening scenes, as Karen faces the pain of those flickering images and the shock of her husband's seeming re-appearance.

Titanic

No movie has such a double whammy of a sad ending. First there's a young Kate Winslet losing her lover Leonardo DiCaprio to the icy waters of the Atlantic as he slips away from her outstretched arms. Then there's the old woman Kate has become in the present day, imagining the *Titanic* still afloat with laughter, and Leo waiting for her younger self as she runs up the Grand Staircase into his waiting embrace. It's a cry from the heart for lost loves everywhere.

The Way We Were

A chance meeting between former lovers Robert Redford and Barbra Streisand shimmers with the poignancy of lost love remembered. She's married, he has a girlfriend. She asks him back for drink. 'I can't come,' he says. 'I know,' she says. They embrace one last time. And it's all there in their eyes. And that irresistible, Oscar-winning Marvin Hamlisch score.

Acts of Love (in development)

Romeo and Juliet meets *Bonfire of the Vanities*

Our hero is the son of a Democratic candidate running for Senate. Our heroine is the daughter of his Republican opponent. They meet at an all-party conference and fall madly in love. Like a modern-day Romeo and Juliet, their relationship is doomed from the start because of their families' antagonism, but they can't help themselves. When their parents threaten to ostracise them, they run away together. Only when the ensuing scandal causes the girl's father to have a heart attack does she finally submit to family pressure and return to the fold. When we last see our heartbroken lovers, months after the agony and remorse of their final parting, they are made to shake hands at a political rally and, in that lingering touch of skin on skin, we sense a million lost dreams.

TOP TEN FUNNIEST SEX SCENES

Bananas

Woody Allen stages his wedding night as a live television sports broadcast. His bride awaits him in bed surrounded by sports fans. Woody jogs in like a boxer, with a towel around his neck and a trainer in tow. He dives under the covers and consummates the marriage to great cheers, with every move described by real-life sports commentator Howard Cosell. Woody announces that their next bout will probably be in the late spring.

Don Juan de Marco

Johnny Depp masquerades as legendary lover Don Juan. He wears the mask and cape, and speaks with a Spanish accent. 'No woman has ever left my arms unsatisfied,' he claims. He approaches a woman in a restaurant and informs her that he can give her the greatest pleasure she has ever experienced. She melts as he kisses his way along her fingers, comparing their parts to her feet, her knees, her thighs. 'And finally…' he says, planting a kiss at the junction where her fingers meet… What woman is going to resist that kind of patter from Johnny?

Everything You Always Wanted To Know About Sex (But Were Afraid To Ask)

Courtesy of Woody Allen's imagination, ejaculation is enacted as a World War II bomb launch. The operation is orchestrated by a NASA-type mission control inside the man's head. His eyes are used as cameras to monitor outside events. Down in the engine room, erection is achieved with the aid of a winch. Sperm, including Woody dressed from head to foot in white, sit around like nervous paratroopers waiting to be dropped into enemy territory.

Forrest Gump

Simple-minded Tom Hanks has never been with a girl. When he and his best friend Jenny get soaked in the rain and have to change in her room, he can't take his eyes off her chest. Dressed in her room-mate's bathrobe, he watches while she removes her bra. When she places his hand on her breast, he has an orgasm there and then. 'I think I've ruined your room-mate's bathrobe,' he says. Cue a change of camera angle to reveal the room-mate lying quiet as a mouse on an adjacent bed, a look of horror on her face.

The Graduate

There are worse fates for a young man to suffer than seduction by Anne Bancroft as the worldly-wise Mrs Robinson, but virgin Dustin Hoffman is so nervous he can barely function. When he clumsily kisses her, she nearly chokes because she's just taken a drag on her cigarette. When she takes off her top, he lamely cups her breast in his hand. He walks away and bangs his head against the wall. He can't bear his awkwardness. Until she calls him inadequate. What more encouragement does a young man need?

The Man With Two Brains

Steve Martin is kept at arm's length by his teasing new bride Kathleen Turner. As he sits with his hat on his lap, she torments him with her body, so much so that when he stands up he needs no hands to keep his hat in place. He walks to the window and presses his face against it. There's the sound of breaking glass from below.

Shampoo

A blow job from Julie Christie isn't an offer Warren Beatty would normally turn down, but they happen to be in a restaurant at the time. 'I'd like to suck his cock,' an inebriated Julie announces to their dining companions, and in a trice she's under the table indulging her whim. It takes some effort on Warren's part to prise her off and escort her away.

10

Dudley Moore can't believe his luck when Bo Derek wants to make love with him to Ravel's *Bolero*. Alas, once in bed a catalogue of mishaps befalls him. In the heat of passion Bo nearly tears his hair out. Her hair beads dangle in his mouth and nearly choke him. Worst of all, her husband phones and she makes Dudley speak to him. Emancipated Bo takes it all in her stride, but poor Dud is put right off his stroke.

When Harry Met Sally...

In a Manhattan diner Billy Crystal challenges Platonic friend Meg Ryan to fake an orgasm. And she does, at a decibel level that has every man and woman in the audience wondering if they're missing out on something in their lives. Billy and the audience aren't the only ones who are impressed. A woman at a nearby table, when asked by the waiter for her order, replies 'I'll have what she's having.' It may be some consolation to know that it took Meg dozens of takes to achieve the desired climax, after which the crew saluted her efforts by presenting her with a large salami.

The Sad Bastards (in development)

Cyrano de Bergerac meets *American Pie*

When our humble hero's girlfriend suggests they consummate their relationship, he's worried he won't match up to expectations, so he persuades his well-endowed friend to stand in for him. Somewhat self-defeating, you might think, but we all do dumb things when we're in love. Of course, it all goes horribly wrong. In the most hilarious sex scene ever devised, our hero is in the bedroom with his girlfriend, his friend is under the bed waiting, he switches off the light, he and his friend try to swap places, there's a tangle of bodies, he's kissing his girlfriend while his friend is seeing to matters down below, but the friend can't perform, so the girlfriend provides manual assistance while our hero mouths responses. It all gets very confusing. What do you mean, it's too OTT? You're obviously out of touch with current cinematic trends.

TOP TEN MALE ROLE MODELS

Casablanca

In World War II Casablanca American ex-pat Humphrey Bogart remains his own man. Any intrigue worth its salt takes place in his gin joint of a café. It helps that he always has at his disposal the perfect one-liner to defuse any potentially threatening situation. Naturally all the dames love him. He offers the perfect combination of danger and protection, barely concealing beneath a world-weary exterior the heart of a true romantic. Play it, Sam.

Dances With Wolves

Abandoning the horrors of the American Civil War, soldier Kevin Costner decamps to the Wild West to live alone, explore the wide open spaces of the prairies and become one with nature. Sioux medicine man Graham Greene tells him that he is on the most important of life's many trails – the trail of a true human being. He learns to overcome his prejudice towards the Indians and live in harmony with both them and the land. He's a man who learns to get his priorities right.

El Cid

Misunderstood, defamed for sparing the lives of enemies and exiled from the kingdom of Castile for daring to challenge a weak king, eleventh century royal champion Charlton Heston is down on his luck. Even fiancée Sophia Loren has dumped him. How could she? Fortunately she comes to her senses in time to offer wifely support when his army is confronted by invading African hordes. An inspirational leader, his influence remains undiminished even by death. When he is killed in battle he is mounted on his horse so that he can continue to lead his army to victory. Now that takes class.

Gone with the Wind

If a man must have an edge, man-of-the-world Clark Gable has it in spades. He always tells it like it is. He informs wilful Vivienne Leigh that she needs kissing badly, and by somebody who knows how. When he later comes to realise she's no good for him, he brushes off her entreaties with one of cinema's classic parting shots: 'Frankly, my dear, I don't give a damn.' He may be a rogue, but he's a man's man in a crisis and has a forceful charm that retains an enduring appeal to women everywhere.

The Great Escape

Steve McQueen smiles through every adversity in a way that is an inspiration to us all. After failed escape attempts from the World War II German POW camp where he's being held, he spends most of his time in the cooler, but he never loses that trademark cheeky smile. He's such a hero that even when he does escape, he returns to give his fellow prisoners vital logistical information. On the climactic great escape he's caught entangled in barbed wire as he tries to leap his motorcycle over a fence into neutral Switzerland, but he's still got that smile on his face. And when he's put back in the cooler, he's still got that smile on his face.

High Noon

Gary Cooper's gotta do what a man's gotta do, in this case fight four desperados without help. Okay, so he's the town marshal, but it's his retirement day *and* his wedding day, so you'd think he'd get a bit of help from the good townsfolk. No way. They're too scared, too uncaring, too drunk or too whatever. John Wayne hated this film because of its lowly view of human nature, but it certainly makes for a gripping climax as Gary faces the baddies and makes them bite the dust. A paean to doing the right thing, standing up and being counted, and much more besides.

In the Heat of the Night

The prize for keeping a cool head when all around are losing theirs, for dignity in the face of intense provocation, for unflagging determination, and for being the only one in town with any fashion sense, goes to Sidney Poitier. He's a black Philadelphia homicide detective stranded in white sheriff Rod Steiger's hick racist town. Not only does he solve a murder case against the odds but he also earns Rod's grudging respect. To solve the crime *and* the race problem in a few days, now that's no mean feat.

James Bond films

What man wouldn't want to be James Bond? You get to save the world on a regular basis, bump off baddies in spectacular ways, spend time in lots of exotic locations, play with Q's armoury of toys, always have a witty remark to hand and always survive unscathed to return another day. Oh yes, and bed the most beautiful women on the planet. In *Goldeneye* a female M calls Jimbo a 'sexist, misogynist dinosaur', but the perks of the job surely outweigh the odd bit of carping. Maybe the guns, gals and close calls would pall after a while, but what man wouldn't swap his day job to find out?

The Man Who Shot Liberty Valence

John Wayne is the archetypal man's man, good and dependable, brave and strong, never lacking in humour, sensitive when required. The kind of man you'd like beside you in bar-room brawl. Everybody knows him, everybody likes him, no one messes with him. His response to girlfriend Vera Miles getting angry at him? 'Ya know, ya look mighty pretty when ya get mad.' Even when tenderfoot James Stewart steals Vera from him, he still saves Jimmy's life. He just can't help doing the right thing.

Some Kind of Man (in development)

I can see the billboards now. 'This film must be seen.' 'This film changes lives.' Our hero is an everyman for the new millennium. He's virile, caring, sensitive, sexy. He's good in a crisis and good in bed. He's every man's best buddy and every woman's dream date. I don't have a plot yet, but if you have any ideas, let me know.

TOP TEN MOST EROTIC MOMENTS
The Age of Innocence

Although he's engaged to be married to someone else, Daniel Day-Lewis is smitten by Michelle Pfeiffer. Consummation of their growing relationship is inconceivable in straight-laced 1870s New York society, but that merely intensifies the erotic charge of a scene in which Daniel removes Michelle's glove in the back of a horse-drawn carriage. Director Martin Scorsese lingers over the de-gloving in a sequence of overlapping close-ups that stretches the sexual tension to breaking point. Daniel takes Michelle's gloved hand, undoes the wrist clasps, eases the leather apart and kisses the bare flesh of the inside of her wrist. And when he finally turns to kiss her lips, the breathless force of their suppressed desire scorches the screen.

Another Time, Another Place

In northern Scotland during World War II, farmer's wife Phyllis Logan stoically endures her husband's dour lovemaking. No wonder she becomes attracted to one of the charismatic Italian prisoners of war who work in the fields. When he pins her against a wall and displays an estimable prowess in manual stimulation, we're rooting for her as she reaches one of the most convincing and intense orgasms ever seen on film. Go for it, Phyllis!

Barbarella

You don't have to wait long here to see Jane Fonda in her prime disrobing for the camera as the eponymous 41st-century space adventuress. The whole title sequence, during which she divests herself of her metallic spacesuit, is a zero-gravity strip-tease. It ends with her floating naked around her space capsule while teasing titles play hide and seek with her pubic hair, and two breasts at the height of their perkiness hove into view before our grateful eyes. Let's also give thanks for Jane's wondrous battle with the lethal orgasmatron, which blows a fuse in its efforts to satisfy her.

Cat People

Sex with Nastassia Kinski is an activity that requires more than the normal precautions, because orgasm turns her into a menacing black leopard. Is zoo curator John Heard going to let such unladylike behaviour put him off his stroke? No way. He ties Nastassia to the bed. He ties her left wrist, then her right, then he eases her legs apart and secures her ankles. As he mounts her the camera swirls over them to the insistent beat of a Giorgio Moroder soundtrack. Nastassia strains against her bonds and, when she lets out an animal cry, you know Johnny's hit the spot.

Don't Look Now

Lovers Donald Sutherland and Julie Christie display admirable positional inventiveness in a Venice hotel room, but what gives their coupling its erotic power is their obvious desire to please each other. To emphasise that their lovemaking is about more than sexual gratification, the scene is played silently to a soundtrack of romantic music, intercut with everyday shots of the couple dressing afterwards. The whole adds up to an erotic eavesdrop on a loving relationship that leaves us feeling both warm and envious.

L'Eté Meurtrier (One Deadly Summer)

Pick a scene. Any scene. Isabelle Adjani strides through the film with a naked, sultry, teasing abandon that leaves you goggle-eyed with astonishment and gratitude. Check out the scene where she inflames our hero with a sneak preview of her underwear. Or the one where she walks proudly naked across the farmyard. Or suckles at her mother's breast. Or bathes naked in the kitchen. Or... Thank you, Isabelle. While we're talking about her, let's also give thanks for that wet-dream scene in *Ishtar* where, swathed in sexless Arabian clothes and head-dress, she lifts her top to expose a breast to Warren Beatty. 'Hey,' Warren shouts to Dustin Hoffman, 'It's a girl.' Yes, Warren, it's a girl alright.

Inserts

Pornographic film director Richard Dreyfuss can't get it up any longer, until producer's totty Jessica Harper agrees to do the inserts for his latest epic. Inserts being close-up action shots. Camera in hand, Richard kneels astride Jessica and encourages her with vocabulary you won't find in a family newspaper. She responds with a few choice words of her own, which provide not only some sensational footage for his film but also a swift cure for his condition.

No Way Out

Naval officer Kevin Costner and high-class hooker Sean Young fall in lust at a Washington political function and leave early to satisfy their desires in the back seat of a limo. The car cruises around the Washington monuments at night to a lush Maurice Jarre soundtrack, city lights reflect romantically on wet tarmac and everything's nice and easy, just the way it should be. Afterwards Kevin and Sean lie back on the vast limo seat and find the perfect way to end the perfect one-night stand. They exchange names.

Strange Days

As Juliette Lewis cavorts in front of Ralph Fiennes in a skimpy crop top and micro bikini pants, we see her through his eyes as he films her. She teases her top off, douses herself with water to cool down, removes her pants, lies down on the bed... all the while staring coquettishly at Ralph, the camera, us. Then we're making love to her, and she's so obviously enjoying it that it's the viewer who now needs dousing with water. So as not to show favouritism to Isabelle (see above), let us also give thanks for that eye-catching scene in *Kalifornia* where Juliette lifts her T-shirt and exposes a breast to Brad Pitt.

The Tightrope Walker (in development)

Se7en meets *Emmanuelle*

This tough thriller pitches a charismatic male cop and an equally charismatic female crime reporter against an ice-cold but surprisingly charismatic killer. Absolutely essential to the story is a cracking sex scene between our hero and heroine. Extract from screenplay:

His fingers flit across her bare flesh with almost unbearable slowness. His touch is electric to her. She feels as though she is going to faint. He pulls down her panties and casts them aside with a gesture that says she will have no further need of them. He takes hold of her ankles firmly, parts her legs, kneels between them and gently lowers himself onto her. He moves his body against hers, gently at first, then more insistently...

TOP TEN MOST EXTRAVAGANT WAYS TO END IT ALL
(Warning: may contain spoilers!)
The Big Blue

Jean-Marc Barr is obsessed with the sea. His one aim in life is to stay underwater without oxygen for as long as he can. Finally he leaves his lover Rosanna Arquette to dive beneath the waves one last time. 'I've gotta go and see,' he tells her. She realises she has to let him go and, with breaking voice, says: 'Go and see, my love.' He disappears forever beneath the ocean's steely surface.

Butch Cassidy and the Sundance Kid

Taking refuge in a building, outlaws Paul Newman and Robert Redford seem oblivious to the fact that they're outnumbered, even though the whole Bolivian army appears to be out there gunning for them. They also don't seem to realise that in their current state, holed by bullets and leaking badly, they're going to be slowed down somewhat. Instead, they joke and make getaway plans, before running out into an elegiac sepia freeze-frame of terminal gunfire.

Deep Impact

If you decide to commit suicide by standing in front of a tidal wave over one thousand feet high, you'll probably die of old age waiting for the right environmental conditions. Unless, that is, a comet is about to hit earth and displace the ocean. Téa Leoni gives up her chance of escape to be reunited with her estranged father on the beach and face the raging onslaught by his side. 'Daddy!' she cries in poignant confirmation of their reconciliation, as the wave hits.

Dr Strangelove

Old cowboy Slim Pickens is captain of a B52 that has been mistakenly ordered to drop an atomic bomb on Moscow at the height of the Cold War. While sorting out a technical problem, he finds himself sitting astride the bomb when the bomb-bay doors open and release it. Swiftly coming to terms with the situation, he rides the bomb earthwards like a bucking bronco, whooping and hollering and holding his stetson high in one last crazy gesture of defiance.

Last of the Mohicans

In a film that challenges many of the clichés of the cinema epic, the most telling moment is given over not to the love affair between leads Daniel Day-Lewis and Madeleine Stowe, but to the barely-stated romance between supports Eric Schweig and Jodhi May.

Arch-villain Wes Studi disembowels Eric in a cliff-top fight and lets his body slide lifelessly over the edge into the void, then advances menacingly on a terrified Jodhi. She backs to the cliff edge, looks down, looks at her enemy, looks down again and, in a heart-stopping moment, chooses to fall backwards into space, her skirts billowing around her as she finally becomes united with Eric in death.

Leon

If you've gotta go, you might as well take the chief baddie with you. So decides hitman-with-a-heart Jean Reno when shot by corrupt cop Gary Oldman. As he lies dying, he places something in Gary's hand. It's a pin from a whole arsenal of grenades strapped inside his jacket. As the explosion engulfs them, Gary mouths a fitting epitaph: 'Shit.'

Pierrot le Fou

The suicide method chosen by Jean-Paul Belmondo demands a fair bit of preparation, requiring as it does a tin of paint and sticks of high explosive. Betrayed by his lover, he performs an act of ritual self-destruction, replete with as much symbolism as in any other Godard film. He paints his face blue, wraps belts of high explosive around his head and lights the fuse. At the last moment he has second thoughts. Too late.

Runaway Train

Jon Voight at his baddest is an escaped convict on a runaway train plunging through the wintry Alaskan wilderness. Rather than shut the train down and give himself up to the cops, he opts to let it hurtle to its destruction. In a chilling ending to this existential thriller, he climbs onto the roof of the engine, hauls himself to his feet, braces himself against the wind and snow and, grimacing maniacally, rides to oblivion. We last see him atop the train as, still gathering speed, it disappears into the blizzard.

Terminator 2

There's not normally a vat of molten metal around when you need one, but one turns up at just the right moment for Arnold Schwarzenegger. He's a metal cyborg from the future who must commit suicide in order to destroy all evidence of his existence in the present. What better way to go than immersion in the serendipitous vat, especially if you have no pain receptors? Hanging from a chain, he's lowered feet first into the vat. The last we see of him is a raised hand disappearing beneath the surface, giving us one last defiant thumbs-up.

New Town Boy (in development)

Amélie meets *Local Hero*

Our hero lives in the New Town area of Edinburgh. He's in love with the city. It's the most beautiful and inhabitable city in Britain. It has hills, castles, parks, rivers and wonderful buildings. It's a capital city that's neither too big nor too small. It has culture, grace and a cosmopolitan atmosphere. Then films like *Trainspotting* spread lies about the city, suggesting that some of its inhabitants take drugs and even swear. It's too much for our hero. He climbs the 287 steps of the Scott Monument, throws himself off the top and is impaled on one of its exquisitely-fashioned Gothic pinnacles.